Traces

A KATE ROARTY, P.I. NOVEL

PATRICIA FILTEAU

Traces
Copyright © 2017 by Patricia Filteau

This book is a work of fiction set in the future. Any reference to historical events, real people, or real places are used fictitiously. Other names, characters, places and events are products of the author's imagination, and any resemblance to actual events or places or persons, living or dead is entirely coincidental.

All rights reserved.
No part of this book may be used or reproduced in any matter without prior written consent from the author.

Cover design: Laura Boyle
Cover image: 123rf.com/ farang

ISBN: 978-1-54390-277-8

"To swim, as to write, is to choose an intense state of socially acceptable aloneness."
—Hanya Yanagihara

To Lee Close.
Thank you for being there and taking Jack dog on many, many early morning walks.

1

Cape Town, South Africa

The Zodiac could not land due to rough waters and sharp rocks. Kate slipped out of the boat while it remained in deeper water. She swam through the thigh-thick kelp to reach solid ground on the shoreline of Robben Island, where she stood up to register the beginning of the swim. It put her in the frigid waters fifteen minutes before the official timing started and at risk of experiencing a bloodletting injury that could attract sharks. The winds were picking up and blowing the sea into high swells. Kate launched into the swim, ploughing through the waves, fighting off the cold and pushing into the crosswinds.

Kate had travelled to Cape Town, South Africa, to attend an international mining conference where she was presenting a paper on Intellectual Property Rights. Attendees had come from all over the mining and investing world. Before going there, she had qualified to do a solo swim from Robben

Island to the mainland. Her business was investigating and restoring stolen intellectual property to its rightful innovators. Her pleasure was open-water swimming. She could fuel both preoccupations in South Africa.

South Africa had a long history of gold mining that paralleled the Canadian experience. The South Africans were proud of their long-distance, open-water swimming achievements carried out in the coastal waters along white sand beaches and sun-filled shorelines. The summer season south of the equator on the African continent offered Kate an open-water swimming opportunity that would have to wait another six months in her Canadian homeland, where lakes, rivers, and coastal waterways were shackled by freezing winter temperatures, ice, and snow.

Kate was swimming hard and fast through waters rendered frigid by coastal currents. She was also being battered by fierce cross-waves. Despite the conditions, she swam on, confident that she would make the designated landfall, 7.8 kilometres from where she had entered the water. The Zodiac kept weaving in precariously close to her. The motors on the back of the boat appeared large and menacing from her position in the water. Kate yelled at the operator to back away. He seemed unable to hear her above the noise of the wind, the waves, and the motors. He manoeuvred the boat in closer then shouted, "Kate, the water temperature is dropping and the winds are picking up. We may have to abort."

Kate glanced up at the Zodiac just long enough to lose her rhythm. She was slammed by a two-metre-high wave that destabilized her stroke. Undeterred, she regained her positioning and ploughed on with a strong breaststroke. Her mind slipped into a visualization of bathing in a hot pool: enticing, silky, soothing, and warm. Taking a breath as she stroked on, she saw what appeared to be a small, high-powered craft skimming across the waves at top speed, heading right toward them. From beneath the water, she did not detect the telltale ping of an engine approaching rapidly. She glanced back at her Zodiac. Rapidly it did a tight sweep, placing it between Kate and the fast-approaching craft. Kate plunged deep, feet first, as the muffled sound of an explosion rocked the surface of the water and debris shot down around her.

Breathless, she surfaced — nothing. Both vessels were gone. Her mind raced. The swim was registered, and the South Africans were impeccable at managing open-water solo swimming. They had never lost a swimmer on an officially registered solo swim. She dodged a floating object — the lid off an outboard motor — as she treaded water. She was very cold and probably experiencing shock — a deadly combination. She searched the waters for some sign of her boat operator and the spotter, but there was nothing.

2

Ottawa, Canada

Most gold mining and exploration companies were staffed with experts from Canada, Australia, South Africa, and Ghana. When the price of gold shot over one thousand USD per ounce, it became lucrative to reprocess mine tailings.

Private investigator Kate Roarty, a tall middle-aged woman of medium weight who projected a fit and confident image with her brown-black eyes that engaged and held a conversant in a sincere but don't-mess-with-me attitude, was about to become involved with the technological innovation and its developers. Her ancestral Haudenosaunee origins gave her skin a slightly tanned-looking hue that blended well with her defined facial features, long, dark hair, and the demeanour of her immediate Irish-French Canadian origins. Her appearance was memorable and attractive to many and off-putting to some, those easily threatened by a person with a self-possessed presence.

Kate Roarty was working on an investigation contract with a consortium of small environmental companies tied to the gold mining sector. Several of their scientists had banded together to develop a mine tailings extraction technology. They devised a simple and effective process that was highly sophisticated in its application. Among the researchers was a Canadian-educated young scientist of Ghanaian origin named Daniel Yaw Osu. He sought out Kate by phone when she was home in Ottawa between investigation jobs and occupied with writing a paper on intellectual property rights. He asked if they could meet; he did not want to communicate digitally or electronically. Kate thought his voice sounded nervous. He would only allow that the subject matter was what she was well known for — intellectual property rights — and that she had been recommended by colleagues in academia. Kate proposed they meet for lunch at the Foolish Chicken, a restaurant in the emerging trendy area of Ottawa known as Hintonburg. The independent dining establishment was well known for chicken delights, including rotisserie chicken, similar to a preparation loved by Ghanaians everywhere.

Kate arrived early to secure a seat by the window and facing the door. She could study the character and carriage of the young man as he approached before they actually greeted one another. She had found some basic information on him through various social media sources. He was a newly minted PhD in chemical engineering, studies adapted from an undergraduate degree in geology — not an easy cross-filtration — suggesting he possessed a capable mind, focus, and sense of direction. He had picked up his undergraduate degree in geology from a Canadian university then returned to the U.K. for advanced studies in chemistry. He obtained his Canadian landed immigrant status shortly after receiving admission to graduate school at the University of Ottawa. He managed to pass the French proficiency test for admittance to this bilingual university and then slid sideways out of the science program into chemical engineering graduate studies. He was now a Canadian citizen with a newly established environmental science company and lecturing at Ottawa U. These credentials suggested she would encounter an individual with lots of reason to sport a confident swagger. However, to the contrary, she watched a young man walk through the narrow entranceway into the restaurant exhibiting outward hesitancy and apprehension. He looked about cautiously then made his way toward her. Discreetly, Kate shifted the chairs so Daniel would not have to sit with his back to the door. He greeted her tentatively, accepting her invitation to take a seat. They exchanged business cards with the grace of ice sliding across a wet surface.

"I am glad you chose this place. I love roast chicken and hear it is excellent at this restaurant."

"It is a new experience for me as well," said Kate. "I understand their rotisserie chicken appeals to the Ghanaian palate. I hope it lives up to its reputation, the name notwithstanding."

Daniel smiled, warming a little, and said, "You know Ghana?"

"I lived and worked there for a few years."

Daniel seemed to relax a bit as he picked up the menu and without hesitation made his selection. Kate chuckled inwardly. *Another hungry young scientist.*

She ordered mineral water while he ordered a large Coke. She let him take a few gulps of Coke to feel the caffeine kick, then said, "Lunch is on me. I will hold everything you tell me in strict confidence. Can you tell me what led you to contacting me for assistance? I would like to hear your story in as much detail as you can give me."

Daniel took another gulp of his drink, followed by a deep breath, then began to speak. Kate listened, giving him her undivided attention. When he stopped, she did not immediately jump in, in case he had more to add. His body seemed to slump in relief. He said no more.

Kate said, "You and your colleagues developed, rather, invented a process and designed the accompanying technology to extract trace gold from tailings. Kinkirk stole it, threatened the three of you when you confronted their top brass about it, then tried to buy you off for a pittance. You refused and have remained under threat from Kinkirk and their compatriots ever since. The companies in your consortium have been shut out of contracts with major mines, only picking up small assessment and mitigation work with the juniors. Even papers you submit to present at the big mining conventions get turned down, and investors won't give you the time of day."

Daniel said, "That about sums it up. Members of my family have been laid off from their jobs at a Kinkirk mine in Ghana, and likewise my colleague's father was laid off from a Kinkirk mine in northern Ontario just months before his retirement."

Kate said, "These guys are nasty and dangerous, and they have succeeded in terrifying you."

Daniel nodded.

Kate let a brief silence punctuate their discussion.

"While I have not taken on the mining industry before, I have run into some pretty heavy hitters during other forensic investigations to restore intellectual property to the rightful innovators. Daniel, if I take on a contract with you and your business partners, I hope it will take the heat off you and shift it to me. I enjoy a high enough profile and connections with people who can protect me that I can try to retrieve your intellectual property and keep us all alive. That is not to say there won't be some tense moments. If I succeed, it will cost you. If I fail, it will cost me. If you pull out after you sign the contract, it will cost you. A contract will require the full commitment of all three of you — no games. Do you understand?"

Daniel nodded and said, "Mrs. Roarty, your integrity is considered above repute and you have a very good reputation for success. We know there is a risk, but it can't be any higher than what we are already experiencing."

Kate smiled. "Don't be too sure about that. Now, I am anxious to know if the Foolish Chicken lives up to its reputation." Daniel made short shrift of his meal and confirmed it was almost as good as his mother's chicken.

"I'll get the other scientists in our group together. Perhaps you could meet us at the university to sign the contract." She agreed and they parted.

As Kate walked back to her car, which she had stashed on a residential side street some distance from the restaurant, she contemplated engaging the mining industry. Surely it couldn't be any worse than the pharmaceutical industry that dealt similarly in big money and levels of corruption. The mining industry struck a nerve centre with Kate, like a tunnel burrowing back through her life growing up in a gold-mining town. Her father worked in the mines, eventually succumbing to emphysema and silicosis, which compromised his lungs, inflicted by the dust he inhaled while working in the underground stopes. He had also been a chain smoker for thirty years, undoubtedly contributing to his condition. Neither the tobacco trade nor the mining business acknowledged any role that the toxins of their industries played to shorten the lives of so many people.

She pressed the fob to open her car doors and got in then sat quietly thinking, asking herself, *Is this a road I want to go down?* She backed up and pulled out onto Goldburn Drive, noticing the signpost as she turned onto a main thoroughfare. *Now isn't that auspicious.* She decided to let her young scientists make the decision. If they signed her contract, they were good to go. If she rattled skeletons in her own closet, then so be it — they needed shaking up.

3

Cape Town, South Africa

Kate struggled to figure out where she was in respect to Robben Island and the mainland. The amount of time that had passed since she entered the water suggested she might be about equidistant. She resumed swimming toward the mainland, occasionally glimpsing a thin line of shore above the pounding waves. She heard the ping of a motor from beneath the water — *rescue or another attack?* She swam on, trying hard to visualize the warmth and comfort of a hot pool. She heard a barely audible siren above the roar of the wind and crash of the waves and swam in the direction of the sound, then saw a white Zodiac heading toward her. Within another few moments, a red search-and-rescue helicopter appeared overhead. She waved frantically in hopes that one or the other or both would spot her. A voice from a loudspeaker erupted above the noise as two wetsuit-clad and helmeted divers dropped down from the helicopter. As soon as they hit the water, a cable descended from a winch and the divers swam toward her. The first diver to reach her said only two words: "Fast shark." He slipped the winch lift around her, buckled them together, and they were lifted out of the water just as the shark swam past, directly beneath them in the water where they had been moments before. The second diver shot a dart at the shark, temporarily stunning it and buying enough time to get another winch cable around him as the helicopter rose up, clearing him from the water.

She could see the SAR Zodiac in the water slowing as she ascended to the helicopter. It was bobbing on the thrashing waves, perhaps searching for more survivors from the explosion.

Once in the helicopter and wrapped in warm blankets, Kate was able to converse with her rescuers. She directed her appreciation at the man bearing the name badge displaying "Ensign Joubert." He was young, sincere, and officious and asked a battery of questions to establish her identity then softened a bit and said, "Can you tell us what happened?"

Kate replied, "I was doing an officially sanctioned open-water swim organized with the Cape Long Distance Swimming Association. I had a boat escort — a Zodiac with an operator and a spotter. Partway through the swim from Robben Island to Blouberg on the mainland, a vessel came out of nowhere at full speed, heading directly toward us. It slammed into the Zodiac without slowing at all. I dove fast and as deep as possible. When I surfaced, I could only see a bit of debris — nothing else. I continued swimming toward the mainland until I saw the white rescue Zodiac and your helicopter. You know the rest."

The pilot barked back above the noise of the helicopter. "There is no sign of any other life, no debris, nothing — both craft have vanished with their crew. The explosion probably attracted that Great White to flesh debris from the explosion, and then he found you. Lucky we got to you in time or you may have satisfied his search." The pilot radioed down to the SAR Zodiac that they were heading back to base with the swimmer. "They couldn't see anything else in the water." He added, "The escort Zodiac occupants are presumed drowned — with that Great White still swimming around, there will not likely be any bodies or even parts left to identify."

Kate said, "Do you know anything about the second craft that slammed into the escort Zodiac?"

The captain said, "Only that there is no record of it whatsoever. Nobody seems to know anything about another vessel out there at that time. The Coast Guard, the Navy, the SAR, The Cape Swimming Association, and the dockside launch — none have recorded the presence of another watercraft of any kind in the area immediately prior to the explosion."

The helicopter swung up toward West Beach then descended down to the Blouberg Hospital helipad. Ensign Joubert advised Kate that while she would probably be fine, she should be checked out in the trauma unit before returning to her lodging. A police officer would meet her there to take a complete statement.

The medics treated Kate for mild hypothermia and dehydration, as well as a few cuts that she had not felt at all but the shark probably detected as he approached the area. English Channel Rules or not, Kate determined this was the last swim she would do in frigid waters without a wetsuit. She agreed to drop around to the Coast Guard base to review the aerial scans they would have of the incident. Ensign Joubert accompanied Kate into the hospital and stayed nearby until she was ready to head back to her lodging. He offered her a lift that she gladly accepted, still feeling a bit weak and disoriented. After confirming there was no concussion and no other head injury of any kind, the attending physician recommended a good rest and sleep if possible.

The warmth of the sunshine spilling down along the narrow street in front of the inn and across the café terrasse where Kate was staying felt inviting. Rather than rest alone in her room, she decided to take a hot shower, change, and descend to the warmth and comfort of the terrace.

Kate entered her trendy two-storey loft upgrade to the flashing lights on the phones indicating waiting messages. The first one, and several more, was from Giorgio Beretta. "Kate, please ring me back and tell me you are all right. I was waiting for you at the landing when all hell broke loose — was that you the SAR chopper picked up? Call me as soon as you get this message. I need to know that you are okay."

Kate needed to collect herself before speaking to Giorgio. She threw off the woollen blanket, turned the shower dial to maximum heat, and stepped in. The heat from the water drew out the remaining shivers and washed away the salt. The feel of water cascading over her body encouraged her to slip into a meditative frame of mind, gradually restoring equilibrium, a sense of composure and perspective until the pealing sounds of three phones ringing lurched her back to the moment. Kate stepped out of the shower and picked up a phone while shrugging into a bathrobe. Before she could speak, the anxious voice of Giorgio said, "Kate!"

"'Tis I."

"Are you okay?"

"I think so."

"What happened? No, don't tell me over the phone — I have to see you."

"How does half an hour sound on the Boutique Hotel terrace? I need hot sunshine, and lots of it."

"See you there, then," and Giorgio rang off.

Kate collapsed on the bed and closed her eyes, sinking into a deep, dreamless sleep that was interrupted by the ringing of the phone. It was Giorgio, once again sounding frantic. "Giorgio, I am so sorry. I must have fallen asleep —

I'll be right down. I am starving. Can you order a Phad Thai dish for me?"

Kate emerged onto the terrace ten minutes later, fresh and clean in a white delicately embroidered linen blouse and black shorts with black Birkenstock sandals. Before she could sit down, the waiter asked about her swim; the hotel and restaurant staff had come to know that was the reason for her visit. Stuck for words, she replied with a single word: "Eventful."

Kate allowed a sheepish smile to respond to Giorgio's silent, enquiring look, then said, "It did not exactly go as expected — it seems my swimming activity is making me more and more vulnerable to the vagaries of my profession."

Kate sipped on the gin and tonic that Giorgio had ordered for her. She could feel her body relaxing more; the long, hot shower, the deep sleep, and now this companionable comfort from Giorgio, all in the heat of the sunshine, were conspiring to work their magic. The waiter placed the plate of Phad Thai on the table in front of her. A sumptuous aroma rose to her nostrils. She slipped a fork through the fine rice noodles, releasing the flavours of cilantro and coriander. The lightly garliced tiny shrimp, finely chopped chicken, and green onions teased her palate and restored energy and vitality to a body spent from being in freezing waters and a psyche challenged by shock. Giorgio sat patiently sipping on his glass of chilled red wine and munching on a plate of mixed fresh fruit, Brie cheese, and baked crackers.

Kate finally said, "Giorgio, it is so good to have a friend at hand right now, one to whom I do not have to explain very much."

Kate reflected back to when they had worked together on a big takedown of corrupt scientists attempting to gain worldwide control of the thoughts and perceptions of leaders through the sinister application of a neural, bioengineered microchip implant. Kate and Giorgio nearly succumbed to the hooliganism practiced by those who stole the biotechnology. In banding together, they solved the crime, prevented any further deaths, restored the intellectual property to the rightful innovators, and helped put 122 corrupt scientists behind bars. Afterward, Giorgio returned to his neuroscience research in Milan, and Kate resumed her private investigation work, taking on contracts to restore intellectual property rights. This latest contract was once again large, complex, and dangerous.

Kate recounted Daniel Yaw Osu's story.

"Jesus, Kate, this sounds as dangerous as the case we worked on together. I doubt the South African police and intelligence service will play the congenial role we experienced from the Canadians, Americans, and Brits."

Kate said, "I've become accustomed to doubting the authorities — police, intelligence services, and the surrounds of private security services — assuming they may be totally implicated in the deception. I'm unacquainted with the South Africans, but I owe my life to the rescue team on the SAR helicopter. I survived the explosion and the icy waters then almost became lunch for a Great White."

Giorgio blanched. "A shark?"

"They pulled the divers and me up and out of harm's way without a moment to spare. I am afraid that the guide boat operator and the spotter both perished in the explosion; when I surfaced there was no sign of them or the boat, save the lid off one of the motors."

"Kate, are you assuming that this is indeed associated with the latest contract you have entered into?"

"Yes, the patterns of behaviour are becoming all too familiar. The theft of intellectual property starts out as white-collar crime. The kernels of dissension take seed when splashed with dollops of envy and jealousy. It escalates with an increasing number of players that grow greedy and combative. The stakes increase to sizeable sums of money, the profile begins to look like organized crime, then elements of thuggery colour the criminal terrain. When it remains at an intellectual level, I can usually navigate the shifting landscape, restore the IP to the rightful innovators, and get out. When violence takes hold, it becomes very dangerous, opening cavernous fissures that only the most wary escape from toppling into. My open-water swimming makes me vulnerable to the thuggery that sometimes accompanies the treachery practiced by those I investigate to locate and restore IP rights. As you know, the thugs go after me even when I'm swimming in pools. I'm loath to take on a bodyguard, but I'd be lying to tell you that I'm not giving the option serious consideration. In fact, while my fees were low on the Taylor case, you may recall that I did have an entire police force at my back with a number of security services as well, although there were times when we didn't know who was friend or foe, particularly with the Brits."

"And me," said Giorgio.

Kate smiled, reached for his hand, and said, "Yes, and you, my friend, but I like to think that on some level I always knew you were a good guy. Giorgio, I'm so pleased that you happen to be in South Africa at this time."

Giorgio returned her smile and said, "It was Kiran who enticed me out here again. He is working with the University of Witwatersrand in Jo-burg and the University of Cape Town in a partnership with Christ College and some biotech research firms in Bangalore, India. I was able to bring the San Raffaele Institute into the mix, so we will be spending a lot of time here over the next year and perhaps longer. Actually, some of the politics notwithstanding, I quite like South Africa. Kiran has a pile of relatives here who established the Patel lineage generations ago. While the family did disperse to Europe and North America during the ravages of the apartheid era, enough remained here to sink down enduring roots in many aspects of modern South African society. Kiran's a good connection to have here, Kate. The family is integrated into the political, academic, and business structure of this society. The Patel name carries some clout and stature and respect."

"Speak of the devil." Kate looked up to see Kiran approaching from behind Giorgio. He placed a finger over his lips then playfully bopped Giorgio on both shoulders. Giorgio jumped then feigned a stomach punch before greeting Kiran with a big bear hug. Kiran reached over to greet Kate in the Quebecois style with a peck to both cheeks then pulled over a third chair. Both men were grinning freely. The attraction between them was readily perceptible. Kate revelled in the warmth radiating from their mutual appeal.

Kiran said, "How's Jack?"

"Very well. He is off training to become a CIA operative." Both men looked at her quizzically. She smiled playfully and said, "He's on a course in California being given by a French Canadian lured out there a decade ago with the promise of big bucks and sunshine. It worked. It's a cyber security course targeted at online predatory crime."

"Converting him, are you?"

"No — not likely. He figures he doesn't need to develop any expertise in intellectual property rights when he can just hire me at minimum-wage rates."

"Ah, smart man," Kiran quipped.

"And Big Ben?" asked Giorgio about the legendary dog.

"Spoiled rotten. He has an extended family vying for care and feeding rights when I am away. Mostly, Clare takes him. They have a mutual admiration society in that relationship. Big Ben is really good company for Clare during the winter months when Meech Lake is a bit deserted, and he loves it in the summer when he can swim as much as he wants to."

"So do you, Kate."

"True, I must admit that Clare's dock is my common entry spot these days. I've grown to really enjoy her quiet, unobtrusive demeanour and sweet tea. Guy drops in on her regularly and takes his family up for Sunday afternoon swims and barbeques during the summer. She's having a wheelchair ramp put in and widening the doorways after the snow and ice goes. We only know that because a cousin of D'Angelo's is going to do the work," said Kate.

"Now, that wouldn't have anything to do with a visit from Michael Pepper, would it? I've heard they have been in frequent contact since her son's funeral and our gathering in Boston for Claude's graduation."

Kate put her hands up with a smile. "It hasn't been confirmed, so we can only speculate at this point, but we were thinking of putting Claude on to it." She laughed.

"Okay, all's well on the Canadian side," said Kiran.

"That's because Kate Roarty is out of Canada," quipped Giorgio with a smile. "How do we manage to restore safety to the favourite gal in our lives while she is here in South Africa?"

Kiran looked around and was greeted by a woman Kate recognized as one of the owners of the Boutique Hotel and Restaurant. They smiled warmly and embraced one another.

"Let me introduce my friend, Kate Roarty from Canada. This is Rajani Patel."

The woman took Kate's hand then said, "You are staying with us in the Hippo suite?"

Kate smiled and said, "Yes, I'm enjoying your establishment very much. To think I didn't have to take

TripAdvisor's recommendation — I could have just asked Kiran."

Rajani turned to Giorgio and said, "And Teddy Bear is here too." She hugged him, and Giorgio lifted her off her feet.

Kate looked at Kiran and Rajani and said, "You two could be twins."

Kiran laughed. "Yes, that weekend interloper might have struck twice on two continents. Alas, there is a decade and a half between us. Rajani is the daughter of my fourth cousin. Our connections are distant but driven closer by being part of the Indian community in South Africa."

"I think of him as Uncle Kiran," Rajani said teasingly.

"Rajani," said Kiran, "can we talk to you about a serious matter for a moment?"

"Of course, Kiran, you know seriousness and silliness are equally well accommodated in our circles."

"Kate is in need of some sophisticated security protection while she is in South Africa. Do you think Uncle Anjay's company could take this on?"

"Absolutely."

Rajani pulled out her mobile phone and hit the speed dial. She spoke briefly with her uncle and signed off. "He'll be over in a few minutes to meet you. He's thinking Jeevan may be a good candidate for the job."

Kate looked enquiringly at the three of them; they responded simultaneously, "The waiter."

Rajani laughed. "Don't worry, security is his full-time work. He just does a few shifts for me when he is between jobs. It keeps the hotel on the straight and narrow, and he makes good tips as a waiter. He is an acutely keen observer of people. He can turn on the charm or be the tough guy with equal effectiveness. Jeevan often looks out for Robbie Williams the Second when he is on the move around the country."

Kate glanced over to see Jeevan heading in their direction with a tray of drinks. She observed a compact young man cast from the same genetic stock as Kiran and Rajani. His handsome features, well-groomed hair, and dark, dancing eyes made for an exquisite presentation. He was dressed in a white shirt and black pants that were superbly tailored to fit his sinewy body. Kate could feel her confidence level rising. Kiran chimed in, "And he does not fraternize with his clients."

Kate flushed. "Jesus, don't read my thoughts, Kiran."

"We do specialize in the brain, Kate, but your gaze told everything — stop blushing."

Rajani said, "He is gorgeous and smart too. He has a masters in biotechnology but doesn't like the sedentary lifestyle that accompanies lab work."

Jeevan placed exotic-looking drinks all around. Rajani had ordered them. He looked at her and said, "My ears are burning."

"And so they should. Uncle Anjay is popping over in a few minutes."

Jeevan studied Kate for a short, intent moment then moved off. "See you in a bit then."

An older man strode up the walkway toward them. He appeared to be sixty-something, healthy, and fit, in a substantial frame that enjoyed good food and life's pleasures. His whitening hair gave an authority to distinguish his years. Rajani and Kiran rose to greet him. He looked at Giorgio and said, "The family refers to you as the teddy bear, but I imagine there is a real name to go with the doctor title."

Giorgio rose and offered his hand and his full name in deference to the respect that Anjay's age commanded. "It is Dr. Giorgio Beretta. Please call me Giorgio."

"Ah yes, the Italian Kiran met at Cambridge." Giorgio nodded.

"It is good to finally make your acquaintance. I seemed to have missed the family gatherings where Kiran brought you along — probably some celebrity or other in town who needed protection. Then he turned to Kate. "And you are the swimmer." Kate blushed again. These Indian South Africans were certainly keeping her blood close to the surface. Kiran introduced Uncle Anjay to Kate.

"Tell me what brings you here, and what protection do you think you may require? Besides from sharks."

Kate gave him the details, with a few interjections from Giorgio when she tended to understate the significance of some aspects of her experience since arriving in Cape Town and her investigative work on intellectual property rights. Anjay listened attentively without interruption until Kate finished her account. He sat in silent contemplation — a seemingly comfortable state for the Indians but less so for Kate. Giorgio had clearly adapted to the Patel cultural behaviours, and although not his own, he appeared at ease. Kate inwardly counselled, *Patience.*

After several minutes, Anjay spoke softly and clearly. "The objective is to keep you alive, preferably uninjured, to make it possible for you to present your paper on intellectual property rights at the mining conference and enable you to circulate among the delegates and financiers to gather information on the theft of the IP rights to the trace minerals extraction process."

Kate nodded. "That about sums it up."

Anjay replied, "You cannot afford my company."

Kate nodded once again. She felt her enthusiasm deflate.

"That is why these boys" — he pointed at Giorgio and Kiran — "are going to cover your costs."

Giorgio said, "Of course."

Anjay continued, "My company is handling some of the security for the conference, so we will get Jeevan set up as a delegate. Mrs. Roarty, my company is well connected with the policing and intelligence services in this country. Yes, there is a lot of corruption throughout all of the services, but there is abundant integrity as well. I know where they both circulate. If we have to bring in the Elite Forces, we will. They are highly trained, capable, and exacting. In fact, they had a small role in your Operation Chipdown."

Kate looked up in surprise. Anjay was referring to her last big IP rights contract that involved murder, violence, and far-reaching corruption — the latter on several continents. Giorgio had worked with Kate on the final takedown.

"I followed that case very closely. It was a brilliant piece of work. You saved Dr. Beretta's bacon, the iBrain company, and the future of both" — he gestured toward Giorgio — "and this guy by association." He indicated Kiran. "So, of course, Mrs. Kate Roarty, P.I., we are going to extend to you our full capability of protection while you are here in South Africa. I have only one condition."

Kate waited.

"Can you please refrain from swimming with the sharks? My company has tended to leave that aspect of security to the marine mammals and aquatics experts."

Kate smiled and said, "Mr. Anjay, I did not seek out the shark — rather, he or she came looking for me after the guide boat blew up."

"Indeed, Mrs. Roarty. What is this fascination you have with swimming out to sea?"

"I love it. It centres me; it re-establishes my equilibrium; it is adventurous; it exposes me to the mystery that lies beneath the surface of the water. It connects me to the natural environment and purges the vagaries of humanity — temporarily, at least."

Anjay listened quietly, almost meditatively, to her detailed response. When Kate finished, he sat without speaking, seeming to allow the remarks to enter his psyche and take root.

"Jeevan will begin with you later today. I wish you well, Mrs. Roarty. I pray my company will be worthy of your care." He bowed slightly to Kate and the others, strode off up the narrow, steep walkway, and was gone. The table remained silent for a few moments. Kate examined the business card that Uncle Anjay had given her. It read, *Dr. Anjay Mohandas Gandhi, President,* and *SSA – Security South Africa.*

4

Jeevan tapped lightly on Kate's door. She glanced out the window to see the shafts of sunlight retreating up the narrow street. It would be dark soon. She opened the door to let Jeevan enter her suite. He nodded, looked around, and said only, "Shall we?" as he motioned toward the door. They exited and walked down the two flights of stairs to the lobby, where she spotted Giorgio and Kiran waiting for her. Jeevan was unobtrusively attentive as they made their way to a small café several blocks from the hotel.

They descended through the narrow streets beneath Table Mountain that looms like a protective fortress over the city of Cape Town. Inertia virtually propelled them on an easy walk along the narrow Loop Street down through the city bowl sprawling like an amphitheatre reaching toward the ocean. Just as Kate was getting into the rhythm of the walk, Kiran stopped abruptly, exclaiming, "Here we are." They were standing in front of the Savoy Cabbage Restaurant, an eighteenth-century historic building rescued from demolition in 1996 when the owners had a vision to blend modernity, light, and glass with antiquity from the Cape Dutch, Georgian, and Victorian architecture and building materials. Kiran held the door open for Kate and Giorgio then followed in behind.

"Giorgio approves of the wine list, and I love the food. I hope you will enjoy both, Kate."

They were shown to their reserved table on the second level, where they could look down on an expansive wine rack reaching up toward the second floor, the glass and marble contours with exposed brick walls of the interior, and see clearly to the entranceway. The location of their table also gave them privacy and intimacy, in an art décor sort of way. Kiran said, "I think we will be safe and comfortable here."

Kate replied, "I don't want you to get all wound up about my safety."

"This is the woman who only today was attacked by a mysterious exploding vessel while swimming in frigid, turbulent waters, then was pursued by a Great White shark and airlifted to safety before being transported to hospital, where you were treated for hypothermia, cuts, and scrapes — not to mention the two men who went out with you on your swim this morning and have not even pitched up dead, just gone — blown up — probably into tiny bits. Of course, your safety is paramount during your stay in South Africa, Kate Roarty."

Giorgio chimed in, "Fine wine and good food are rather important as well. May I take the liberty of ordering us a bottle?" Kiran and Kate nodded in acquiescence as Giorgio perused the wine list.

Kiran added in mock jest, "Indeed, should Giorgio ever wish to take up a second career, he would move to the head of the pack as a sommelier."

Giorgio laughed. "The entire population of Italy could carry that title. It is our way of life. We are tutored in the craft from infancy, learning viticulture methods and the nuances of oenology by sheer osmosis. My great-grandfather was illiterate, but by modern achievement standards, he could have carried both titles with proud accomplishment.

Alas, today even grape growers and wine producers suffer the scourges of deceit and corruption — another job for you, Kate, once you have reunited the intellectual property rights with the young mineral extraction experts.

"Now, to our dining splendour — my preference is always red wine, but knowing you prefer white and Kiran will likely order fish, I think the Newton Johnson Family Chardonnay 2027 will tantalize our palates. It is an oaked, one hundred percent variety from the Hemel-en-Aarde Valley. The slight spiciness should go equally well with robust fish-based salads, entrées, and to sip on while we chat."

Kate and Kiran readily acquiesced to Giorgio's superior expertise. The waiter took Giorgio's order, and they settled back to enjoy the evening. Kate was comfortable in the company of Giorgio and Kiran. They radiated warmth between them and toward her. When she first learned about the "lads" when investigating the Taylor case, she understood that Kiran had been involved with Matti Toivenen from Finland. There seemed to have been a shift in attractions, the complexities she would undoubtedly come to appreciate in the fullness of time.

When the wine arrived, they ordered their meal selections. Kate ordered a carrot and butternut soup with chives and cream. Soups ranked high in her repertoire of comfort food, and she continued to feel a need for comfort. Kiran chose a salad of spiced roasted nuts, red wine poached pears, and feta, while Giorgio selected the beef tartare with celery, truffle oil, a quail's egg, and a parmesan crisp. For the entrées, Kiran decided upon the grilled yellowtail and asparagus risotto, leeks, and beurre blanc, while Giorgio continued with his red meat theme and ordered the grilled pork cutlet stuffed with celery, gruyère, and cumin, with an apple puree and cider jus. Kate was taken with Kiran's selection and ordered the same.

Their jovial banter gave way to Kiran's account of his extended family life in South Africa when he visited with his sisters while growing up.

Kate said, "Kiran, tell me about the transition years."

Kiran's face grew reflective. "I was captivated by the experience of real and rapid change, so much so — particularly after the apartheid era ended and Nelson Mandela became president — that I continued to return here frequently on my own. I felt a sense of belonging here, not more so than India, but in addition to my homeland — a second home, so to speak."

Kate and Giorgio listened to Kiran as he expressed quiet pride in his family connection to Mahatma Gandhi and the years Gandhi spent in South Africa as a young lawyer.

Just as they were about to consider the dessert menu and coffee, the street exploded in a volley of gunfire, screeching tires, and sirens. Jeevan appeared out of the brickwork, saying only, "Follow me." They descended quickly to the ground floor and out the back door, where an imposing black SUV with tinted windows was waiting with the engine running. The driver navigated the vehicle out of the narrow streets and onto the M62 then ascended up the mountain road until it reached Quarry Hill Road, where it swerved onto De Hoop then slowed as a black iron gate slid sideways and they entered the driveway of a small estate.

Uncle Anjay emerged from the doorway, saying, "Welcome, Mrs. Roarty. Perhaps you would like to take your coffee and dessert in the safety of my drawing room." He showed all three of them in then spoke quietly to Jeevan, who left immediately. Uncle Anjay said, "You will be safe here. Jeevan is returning to Hout Street — near the restaurant — to find out what the commotion was about. We do not know if it had anything to do with your presence at the Savoy Cabbage or whether some other personality attracted the attention of rapid-fire assault-rifle-toting thugs. It is best to remain here until he can give us an assessment of what happened and who was targeted."

A young woman appeared with a tray carrying a coffee pot, cups, milk, sugar, and Canadian maple syrup. Kate smiled, observing that the maple syrup seemed to be in the catalogue of her small desires that preceded her. She wondered if it had been referenced in some online biography she had yet to stumble across. The young woman returned a few moments later carrying another tray displaying an abundant selection of fruit, cheese, biscuits, and small cakes. Uncle Anjay thanked her and told her that would be all for the evening.

Uncle Anjay's phone rang. He excused himself, left the drawing room, and Kate could hear quiet conversation in the hallway. The exchange was brief. When he returned he said, "Mrs. Roarty, some thugs showed up at the hotel demanding to see you. When the night clerk advised them that you were out, they demanded the key to your room at gunpoint. Jeevan is over there now sorting them out. He got there before they could do too much damage."

Kate nodded and said, "Thank you, Mr. Gandhi."

"Please, Mrs. Roarty, address me as Anjay or Uncle Anjay, the way this lot does. I will always find the Gandhi name rather ominous."

"Only if you'll call me Kate, Uncle Anjay."

"Agreed. Now, there's less than an hour left in this day. Let's see if we can get you through it without threat of theft, injury, or worse."

Giorgio, Kate, and Kiran settled back with their coffee and desserts.

Giorgio said, "I think if we remain here as we are until the clock strikes midnight, heralding in a new day, Kate's fortunes will turn."

"Lovely," Kate and Kiran responded simultaneously.

5

Kate awoke at first light, confused, disoriented, and stiff. Someone had placed a cover over her and dimmed the lights. She rested her head back, gradually piecing together where she was, the events of the previous day, and what she needed to do next. Her first requirement was a pee and a glass of water.

She located a small washroom, where there was also a pure water spigot with a glass beneath it. Refreshed by the outlet and intake of water, she glanced at her watch and figured that it was midevening in Los Angeles. She hit Jack's cell number on her speed dial that went directly to voicemail. It was comforting to at least hear his voice. She left a short message for him to call her back to her personal cell number.

Kate spotted a double set of securely locked patio doors. She quietly drew back the thick drapes that blocked out the light, released the lock bars, opened one door, and slipped out onto a generous-sized terrace providing a sweeping view southwest to the ocean and northwest up to Table Mountain. Sunrise had not yet begun, but the traces of first dawn infiltrated the nighttime darkness, yielding silhouettes to distinguish the land and water masses. Kate could discern the ocean stretching out below, beyond the city and the mesa looming above. Table Mountain was outlined against the black-blue sky of retreating darkness.

"It's my favourite time of the day," said a soft, unobtrusive male voice behind her. It was so soothing that she wasn't even startled by the invasion of her solitude.

"I think if I just remain here watching, the sunrise will take over from dawn and I will get to see the city, in all its cradled beauty, come to life."

"Indeed you will," said Uncle Anjay as he handed her a cup of coffee. She sipped it and delighted in the telltale trace of maple syrup sweetening and smoothing the coarseness of South African coffee beans.

"You keep maple syrup on hand, do you?"

"Ah, yes, in anticipation of our Canadian visitors."

"You receive many Canadians, do you?"

"Once every thirty or forty years."

Kate turned to smile at him.

"I must confess, my niece sent it up with Jeevan. She keeps it on hand for her many Canadian guests at the hotel. The repeat clientele bring it to her as gifts. I dream of one day visiting one of your winter sugar bushes when the sap starts running."

During the brief exchange between Kate and Uncle Anjay, the morning light transformed from the soft, creeping dawn to a magnificent bright orange sunrise.

"When I acquired and renovated this place, I had to decide between sunrise and sunset. This side of the house offers a 270 panorama, revealing the sun lifting across the water, the city, and glancing against the mountains above. I spent mornings and evenings in all seasons for a year before I made the decision to open this side of the house with windows, doors, and a terrace. Although my wife loves everything about the entire house, I would be happy to live most of the time in this very spot. It made our move from Durban complete, and we finally stopped yearning to return to the cradle of the Indian population of South Africa."

"It would be wonderful for morning meditation," said Kate.

Uncle Anjay smiled again. "Please, be my guest. There are yoga mats and a collection of freshly washed loose clothing in that wooden cupboard under the canopy. You will not be disturbed before the sun is high in the sky."

"I accept your offer. Thank you," Kate replied.

She found a mat, quickly changed into some comfortable clothing she saw hanging inside the cupboard, and decided to let the rising sun and the din of the awakening city be her music. Kate emerged from her meditation session, refreshed, restored, and centred.

A gracious, quietly elegant, radiant woman traversed the terrace toward her. Kate was entranced by the vision of this woman, who broke into a wide inviting smile.

"I am Teja, Uncle Anjay's wife — yes, even I refer to him as Uncle Anjay, although we are the same age." She took Kate's hand in both of hers. "Now let me give you a proper welcome. We are so pleased to have you here — the woman who saved cousin Kiran's teddy bear and his strange company." Kate laughed at the appellation for Giorgio.

"I am so delighted to meet you Mrs. ... Teja..." She couldn't quite come to say Mrs. Gandhi.

"Auntie Teja will be fine."

Kate smiled inwardly, remembering the generous use of the term *Auntie* that implies respect, endearment, and connection in so many parts of the world outside of North America. She was comfortable with the term.

"Come, let me show you to a shower room, then you can join us for breakfast. Jeevan brought your things here last night. He thought it was easier to bring everything rather than try to figure out what you might wish to have with you. While you are welcome to stay here for the remainder of your visit to Cape Town, Rajani is anxious to demonstrate that you can remain safely at her hotel — with the help of Jeevan and Uncle Anjay's security company, of course," said Auntie Teja. "Jeevan dispatched some nasty brutes at the hotel last night."

Kate wondered what she meant by *dispatched* but thought it better to listen and figure it out, or failing that, question Jeevan when she saw him.

Auntie Teja showed her into a lovely bright bedroom with an adjoining shower room. Her belongings were carefully laid out on the bed, and she was relieved to see her laptop and the other hand-held cyber devices she hadn't carried with her, although she had learned to bring along crucial backup documents on several devices stashed in different places. She quickly showered, changed, coiffed her hair, and descended to the terrace, where breakfast was laid out under the umbrella. It was a very healthy-looking breakfast of fruits, chutneys, a generous platter of mini masala dosa — a crispy rice and lentil pancake served with potato curry, typical to South Indian cuisine — while a side of crispy Biltong ensured a South African context. Uncle Anjay was working on his tablet, and Auntie Teja was browsing the *Daily Sun*. Both set their preoccupations aside and rose to greet Kate.

"I hope you do not mind the intrusion of our Indian food," said Auntie Teja.

"I'm thrilled — I love Indian cuisine but rarely have the opportunity to enjoy it for breakfast."

Auntie Teja continued, "In our country you can sample such a variety of food preparations that arrived with settlers then blended with indigenous and European fare to develop a unique although not yet truly applauded South African cuisine. We tend to mix it all together, although rarely do we sit down to breakfast without some variety of dosas."

The coffee, freshly blended juices, and dosas were an additional balm to mitigate the various traumas of the previous day. Kate dug in and savoured the homemade chutney that Jeevan dolloped on the crispy dosas.

She remarked to the Gandhis, "Since arriving in Cape Town a couple of days ago my experience has swung from grace to friendship, kindness to murder, and mayhem to moral turpitude."

"Welcome to South Africa, Kate. I doubt you will have a dull moment during your stay in our fair city. We hope that we can envelop you in the former and protect you from the latter, but this contract does not come with a guarantee."

Jeevan joined them at the end of their breakfast, grabbed a coffee and the remaining dosas, then suggested it was time to return to the hotel — if that was her wish.

As they walked out to the waiting black SUV, Teja reinforced her invitation. "Kate, please return anytime — for a visit, to stay, to feel safe."

Uncle Anjay added, "We are completely sincere — it is a standing offer, Kate."

Jeevan introduced the driver. "Kate, this is Courage. He will be our driver for the duration of your stay. He drove us up here last night. Courage is fully briefed on what we are dealing with in keeping you safe and secure." Kate said hello to the handsome, black, middle-aged, muscular man sitting in the driver's seat. She observed that he appeared to be fully self-contained. Courage nodded to Kate, hit the lock mechanism for the doors, and pulled out of the driveway. The iron gate slid aside as the car approached it. It was controlled by a sensor mechanism within the SUV, much like Kate's garage door opener at home, albeit undoubtedly more sophisticated in its security features.

"Kate, this is one of three SUVs that has sensor access to Uncle Anjay's estate. Courage has direct iris and hand touch recognition as well. This vehicle will be ready and close by wherever you go. The only other driver you can trust behind this wheel is me. We will program in your iris and hand recognition as well, in case something happens and you need to drive the vehicle. The hand recognition is through the steering wheel and column, while the iris recognition is built into a sensor panel along the inside top of the windscreen."

Kate nodded.

6

Her phone vibrated, displaying the number for her daughter, Danielle. She answered. The usual upbeat "Hi Mom" was not there. The tone of Danielle's voice revealed a level of distress that Kate knew would require time and careful attention. She listened for a few moments before the SUV pulled onto the street where her hotel was located.

"Danielle, can I call you back shortly? I want to speak with you where there is privacy without distractions. I am just about to get out of a vehicle. It won't be too long — I promise."

Danielle reluctantly agreed then Kate signed off as the SUV drew up alongside the front entrance to the boutique hotel. Jeevan jumped out, opened the door for her, and as quickly removed her bag from the back. Rajani came out to greet them and accompanied them both up to her suite, where they found that all was in order. Rajani said, "I know you will be comfortable here. I hope you will also be safe."

While the mining conference would officially get underway the next day, Kate had a number of preconference meetings set up with investors, senior mine personnel, and suppliers — anyone she could connect with who might be involved in the application of the developed tailings processing technology. The conference online meeting scheduler was quite efficient. She logged on to reconfirm meeting times, dates, and locations then bring them forward to her iPhone scheduler. She was pleasantly surprised to find that none of the previously scheduled meetings had been cancelled — rather, several more had been added, awaiting her confirmation. She did not recognize the person's name or the name of the company for two of the meeting requests. She also could not confirm these two as delegates to the conference or retrieve any information on the listed company name.

While the conference scheduling software was sophisticated, with well-integrated multiple capabilities, Kate imagined it could be easily hacked. She had options. She could decline but then not know what these requests were about, or she could accept and go prepared for possible problematic encounters. She decided on the latter course of action — better to know where she was meeting the devil rather than have the menace stalking her about Cape Town. Of course, neither precluded the other, but she needed to take action.

She accepted the meeting requests and sought clarification on the contents, expecting that responses would not be forthcoming. Next, she needed to speak to Danielle, then Jack. She called Danielle back, but her call went directly to voicemail. She was likely pouring her heart out to a close female friend. That was okay as long as it was indeed the case. It could lessen the intensity of Danielle's emotions when Kate finally reached her. She made another call that went straight to Jack's voicemail — that was disappointing. Kate really wanted to speak with him about the past thirty-six hours. In addition to swimming and meditation, Jack was the other important element of her life that grounded her. His reactions and responses could still be unpredictable —

she liked that. His perceptions and sentiments made her feel alive, interacting, and connected the way nothing else in her life did. She left him a message saying only:

Hey, Jack, I'm sorry to have missed you again. Hope you're enjoying LA, the course and the change of pace. It's been a crazy thirty-six hours in Cape Town, the details of which I'll share when we speak. Suffice to say, plus ça change, plus c'est la même chose and the shark went hungry. Appelle-moi. Oh, and Giorgio sends his best.

She tried Danielle again but did not leave another message when the call went straight to voicemail.

Kate reviewed her digital messages, answered a few routine ones, then closed the secure laptop and slipped it out of sight. She plopped her tablet in her satchel and slung it over her shoulder then quietly exited the room, descending to the lobby via the stairwell. Jeevan fell in beside her, matching her pace with unobtrusive stealth. She acknowledged him. He returned the gesture with a barely perceptible nod and then proceeded in harmony with her stride out through the lobby and onto the street.

The black SUV with tinted windows drew up alongside the curb to let her in. She was desperate to walk and waved it on. Jeevan remained just far enough away to give her breathing room but close enough that he could be at her side within a moment.

7

Kate was anxious to check out a nearby public swimming pool where she could take her daily swims. The Long Street Baths, built in 1908, had been an attraction for local residents and visitors alike since the day the facility opened. Kate loved discovering these old pools, appreciating their architecture, and learning their history. She located it quickly by exiting from narrow Park Street onto Kloof Street and heading south until the fine old structure presented itself at a busy crossroads, equidistant between Cape Town's mountains and the seaside. Kate entered the attractive, recently restored, and renovated building to find a heated twenty-five-metre pool and Turkish-style baths exhibiting all the charm of a nineteenth century structure with the modern efficiency of an upgraded, well-run facility. She obtained a pool schedule and determined to return there for some swims while she remained in Cape Town. She could swim laps daily at 7:00 a.m., probably the only time she could fit it in — she would be there the next morning. As she turned to leave, she spotted Jeevan on the far side of the pool chatting with a lifeguard, a young woman about his age. She made a mental note to tell him of her swimming plans.

Kate headed down Long Street toward the Convention Centre at the waterfront, where she could pick up her delegate's kit, reconfirm the details for her speaking engagement, and head to her first investor appointment. After walking several blocks, enjoying the street-side architecture dominated by colourful wooden buildings with second-floor balconies, Kate realized that it was a one-way street heading in the opposite direction. This made it impossible for Courage to follow in the SUV. She stopped to view a window display; by discreetly turning sideways she could locate Jeevan about a block and half away.

The next thing she knew, strong arms were grabbing her as a vehicle pulled up alongside. She was thrown into the back seat, but before a door closed she heard a crunch of bone followed by a volley of gunfire and the car speeding away with the back door ajar and a man dragging along, half in and half out. Kate was trapped, unable to exit over or around this man, but traffic was heavy, preventing the driver from picking up speed. Two hands grabbed the collar of the motionless man, pulling him out of the back seat and clearing the way for Kate to exit. The driver slammed the vehicle against another vehicle parked on the street, blocking the open door and a way out for Kate. Smashing glass liberated the opposite back door. Jeevan pulled Kate out and kept her moving along a laneway connecting Long Street to the adjacent Loop Street, where Courage was waiting in the SUV. Kate had no idea how Courage knew exactly where they would come out on Loop Street. Regardless, she was grateful to see him there and even more relieved to see Jeevan slip in beside her. Courage sped off down Loop Street, continuing toward the waterfront. They pulled into the main entrance turnaround at the Cape Town International Convention Centre and got out. Words were not spoken among the three of them, but Kate sensed they were all on the same wavelength. Courage pulled away from the no-stopping zone. Kate imagined that he would not be too far away.

She fell in beside Jeevan and said, "Given we are supposed to be colleagues, it would be alright to speak and walk together in this context, don't you think?"

Jeevan nodded and replied, "Are we visiting any more swimming pools, taking any more spontaneous long walks where Courage cannot easily follow in the SUV, or disappearing into dark alleys, unannounced and alone?"

Kate slowed her pace, looked at him, struggled to contain a smile, and replied, "I can guarantee that I will not slip into any dark alleys, unannounced and alone. I'll be going swimming at the Long Street Pool tomorrow morning at 7:00 a.m. then catch a lift back to the hotel with Courage after the program is finished this evening."

"Thank you for the advance notice," said Jeevan.

Kate said, "The rest of the afternoon and evening will have a high degree of unpredictability as I begin the rounds of meetings to investigate the IP theft that I came here to try to track down. My first appointment is with an investor — a company that stands to benefit substantially by being able to rework tailings to recover trace gold from properties where their licenses will be running out shortly." The first meeting was originally scheduled in the matchmaker's forum just off the main lobby. It was relocated to a room number at the swank One&Only waterfront hotel.

Before Kate could advise him of her intention to walk over, Jeevan said, "We'll drive you there — it will take about five minutes."

Kate nodded in quiet acquiescence. It would give her some time to look around a property that was reputed to be filled with extraordinary artwork and boasted a 350-square-metre outdoor pool. The South African investment tycoon,

Sol Herzner, established the One&Only resort group, and the Victoria and Alfred waterfront property was the first in the chain.

Kate walked into the lobby and was immediately captivated by a stunning view of Table Mountain through the huge and abundant lobby windows. She walked to reception and asked for Room 507, a Mr. Beltman. Before the young man at reception could respond, a dark-suited man with a cyber communicator in his ear was at her side. "Mrs. Roarty?" he said quietly.

Kate turned to look at him. The suited man said, "Can you please follow me."

Without indicating any compliance, she responded, "And who might you be and where are you proposing we go?"

He reached into his pocket and produced a business card that he handed to her and said, "My name is Charlie Kagiso, head of security for Mr. Beltman."

She looked at the card then into the face of this small, very fit-looking man, thinking, *Not unlike Jeevan.* "You are from Botswana," she said.

"Ah yes, well, my parents. I was born in South Africa."

Good, he is destabilized. "Your name means 'peace.'"

"My last name, yes," then he quickly regained his sense of purpose and authority. "Mr. Beltman told me to bring you up to Room 507 for your meeting."

"My colleague will be accompanying me." She turned and nodded to Jeevan, who approached.

"Ah, your security, of course," said Charlie Kagiso.

Kate sighed inwardly while maintaining an outward composure. *So much for that ruse. Nevertheless, it has established some ground rules.*

She looked at Jeevan then turned and said to Charlie Kagiso, "Let's go."

In the elevator Kate drew the young man out further by saying, "I don't know South African names as well, but in Ghana, where I spent a lot of time, Charlie means 'the friendly one.'"

Charlie replied, "Few people can pronounce my real name. I picked up Charlie in middle school, and it stuck." When they reached the room 507, Charlie knocked twice then tapped a key against the sensor. They entered and were immediately greeted by an impeccably turned out, suave, middle-aged man who spoke with an accent that Kate would have to place later. The coif of his hair; trim of a slight beard; the line of his fine dark suit; his fine Italian shoes and delicate onyx cufflinks all projected care, taste, and confidence. He identified himself as Robert Beltman. She took his handshake and introduced Jeevan. "Yes, of course, Anjay Gandhi's nephew."

Charlie retreated to the kitchen. Jeevan remained in the living room, where Robert Beltman invited Kate to take in the spectacular view of Table Mountain.

"I took this suite for the view, although it is often shrouded in cloud cover that burns off by this time of the day."

"It is magnificent," Kate said.

"I am planning to attend your presentation on Intellectual Property Rights in the Mining Business. I gather by your extract published in the conference program that you think many rights are being violated."

"Yes, you are correct, Mr. Beltman. My business is restoring intellectual property to the rightful innovators. I also seek out financing for young scientists developing promising technologies."

"It appears you are rather successful at both."

"It supports my little company adequately well," said Kate.

"I'd like to buy your little company, as you characterize it, Mrs. Roarty."

"I'm flattered, Mr. Beltman, but it's not for sale. I do not plan to work for anyone but myself."

"Mrs. Roarty, what I am prepared to offer you will generously secure you for the rest of your life. You should never have to work again."

"I only work now when I wish to and for people who inspire me. I can't imagine your interest in my company. It's small, narrowly focused and of little consequence to most of the business world."

"It's the only company that I am aware of established in this line of work and networked with most of the intelligence services of the Western world," said Beltman.

"Mr. Beltman, it could never work in your corporate structure. *I* could never work in your corporate structure. Your companies are publicly traded, so it's easy to learn a fair bit about how they operate, the revenue flow, etc. My company is private and in the good graces of CRA — the Canada Revenue Agency — and will remain as such."

"What happens to your company if something happens to you?" Beltman asked a little too aggressively for Kate's liking.

She smiled. "I appreciate your interest in my company, Mr. Beltman. Now tell me about your investments in mineral recovery from tailings."

Beltman reset his polished demeanour and said, "In the right hands, the right location, and at the right pricing, it can be lucrative. We are looking at our operations in key gold mining areas in Canada, Ghana, Australia, and here in South Africa. North Central Asia could be attractive as well."

"And what will encourage you to move ahead?"

"The price of gold, of course," Beltman said then paused.

Kate waited for him to continue, and when he didn't she added, "And the availability of an inexpensive and very efficient extraction process."

"Precisely."

"A process that could have application to rare earth minerals as well?"

Beltman looked at her then silently nodded.

Kate left the conversation space between them empty. She could wait as long as it took. She did not need to say anything.

He walked over to the bar, poured three glasses of mineral water, plopped several lime slices in each, then handed one to Kate and one to Jeevan, who set his glass down immediately, keeping his hands free. Kate took her offering and nodded acceptance but still did not speak.

"How much do you want, Kate Roarty?"

"Want for what?"

"Whatever aspect of this endeavour you are willing to sell on — your company, your services, your clients, your contacts, your knowledge — some or all. We are flexible."

"Flexible enough to kill for it, Mr. Beltman?"

"No, even I draw a line at that approach to doing business, Mrs. Roarty."

"Who is the 'we,' Mr. Beltman?"

He smiled and said, "The royal we."

"The *royal we* is out of luck. Good day, sir."

"Will we see you at our reception this evening?" Beltman said as she made for the door. "The entertainment is promising to be superb. We are holding it by the pool, on the island, here at the hotel."

"Perhaps."

As she left the suite she felt Beltman watching after her, still holding his untouched glass of mineral water.

8

They descended in the elevator to the lobby in silence. Her phone vibrated just as they walked into the main lobby. It was flashing her daughter's name.

"Jeevan, can you give me a few minutes? This is my daughter calling. I need to take the call." He nodded.

Kate made her way over to a quiet sitting area in the lobby as she answered the phone. Danielle sounded more composed but still distressed.

"Mom, we lost it."

"Danielle, lost what?"

"The…" She stopped. "Hazel, our new puppy, Mom."

Kate took in a breath and let it out as though a sail fully billowed had suddenly entered the doldrums and collapsed. She said only, "Tell me, Danielle." She sat and listened until Danielle was fully spent.

"Danielle, Hazel hasn't been gone very long. It is early days. Dogs range long distances in a short time. She's microchipped and no doubt wearing a collar with tags, right?"

"She slid out of her collar and bolted after a squirrel. The shelter microchipped her, but they don't yet belong to the worldwide tracking network. It's only helpful if she remains local. The shelter hasn't picked up her signal."

Kate inwardly cursed squirrels, having experienced many squirrel incidents with her dogs over the years. She also suspected Danielle was reading too much into the disappearance of the puppy, as she was wont to do. She could feel Danielle's pain in her voice across their conversation.

They talked more, with a promise from Kate to talk again very soon and keep in close contact during this difficult time for Danielle, and she tapped the "end call" button wishing that continents and oceans didn't separate them.

Kate looked at her watch and calculated that it was 10:30 p.m. in Los Angeles. Maybe she could reach Jack before he fell asleep but after he returned to his hotel room. As she looked at the screen, it lit up with an incoming call from him. She was thrilled even just to see his name displayed on her phone. She answered, "Well, hello, stranger from across the seas."

"Kate, it's so good to finally be speaking to you — live. Thanks for your messages. Sorry I missed your calls. How are you?"

"Just a little bit better, now that I can hear your voice. Tell me about Los Angeles and the course."

"My introduction to this massive city is through the lens of law enforcement, so my perceptions don't make for positive communications about Los Angeles. Having said that, Luc's a fabulous instructor, and he's really put himself out to introduce the softer, gentler, and exciting aspects of the city. When he moved down here, the city helped him out with an interest-free mortgage, so he bought a house that had languished under power of sale. The place was a dump but located in a great neighbourhood, five minutes from the beach. Luc took it back to the studs and completely renovated it — actually rebuilt it. It took him two years to get it to where the family could move in, and he just keeps working on it. This is how he copes with the work he does; his wife says it's a godsend. Hardly a day goes by that he isn't doing something on the house. His kids speak fluent Spanish now, and they've been able to keep up their French. It's their spoken language at home, and their mom home schools them *en françaises*: grammar, writing, and literature. She eventually got a green card, so she works here now as well."

"Sounds like you're ready to move there, Jack."

Jack laughed. "It's a great place to visit, especially in February. This city puts new meaning to the term high-risk job. More than three hundred LAPD officers have been killed in the line of duty. The work Luc does would burn out most of us pretty fast. Anyway, enough about me and my activities, what about you and what about the shark reference — that's a joke, right?"

Kate loved to listen to Jack's beautiful rich baritone, softly laced with his Quebecois accent, not strong but sufficient to reinforce his French Canadian identity. They had met more than two years before during a case they both worked on. The relationship got off to an antagonistic start, and they both resisted the attraction. As the riddle of the case unravelled, the relationship strengthened, but not before Jack was shot and his car was blown up during a private visit with Kate when she was in Boston researching the IP trail linked to a murder. Jack recovered, the murder was solved, and the IP was restored to its rightful innovators. Other friendships emerged from that case, including those with Giorgio and Kiran. The pay-out fees from many different sources gave Kate a level of financial security she hadn't previously known. As a single parent, she limped from paycheque to paycheque raising two kids. When she decided to strike out on her own, the early years were lean.

Now her reputation preceded her and remunerations were large. She considered it high-risk pay. While she did not have employees per se, she had a network of highly competent cyber technology geeks that she called on to assist her in gathering data on the IP trails. She paid them well, and they performed to an exactingly high standard.

Kate finished recounting the entire tale to Jack. Sometime during her monologue, Jeevan came over with a menu and placed it in front of her. She selected a small mixed curry and chutney platter that a waiter brought over a little while later. It was delicious.

"Jesus, Kate, this is sounding a lot like the Taylor case."

"Yes, there are similar elements to the patterns of behaviour, the high stakes affecting an industry, and its key players, and of course I have already encountered the thugs."

"Thank god for Kiran's family network. Uncle Anjay's company sounds like a real find. You are too far away for me to fly in for the weekend."

"And that's just as well, Jack. I would much rather have your arms to fall into when I get home than dally with the prospect of carrying me home in pieces."

Jack laughed then got serious. "Kate, I need you to come home in one piece."

"I think Jeevan will ensure that happens," said Kate. "Jack, I've got a number of meetings to get to this afternoon and tomorrow morning. As well, I think I'll go to Beltman's reception this evening. It could be a good opportunity to see who's connected with whom. Let's try to talk again in the next day or two. I'm looking forward to more installments of life in lotus land."

They signed off after warm exchanges, and then Kate was on her feet and moving. Although desperate to walk and think, for security reasons she took the SUV back to the convention centre, where she had two more back-to-back meetings with mining industry investors. While neither bore the fruit that the discussion with Robert Beltman yielded, both reinforced the significance of the technology development to the extraction process, not only in gold mining but also in the rare minerals sector. Kate was increasingly wondering if it were not the rare minerals sector where she should be focusing her investigation. If this application were where the greatest efficacy lay, then undoubtedly the Chinese would be lurking in the shadows ready to snatch it up. She made a mental note to give Daniel Osu a call to discuss the applicability of his innovation to rare earth minerals extraction from tailings.

Kate was happy to have Courage drive her back up to her little boutique hotel. She learned from him that his middle name was Xola, pronounced "Hola," meaning "saviour" in his native Ghanaian culture. He came to South Africa many years before, enticed by an employer he had worked for in Accra. He and his family settled into a higher standard of living, including access to education and healthcare, and remained, albeit not without annual pilgrimages back to their beloved home country. Courage was delighted to learn that Kate had spent some years in Ghana and was familiar with the country, the people, and the differences. While she did not divulge that her client was a Ghanaian-Canadian, she inwardly remarked on the connections. She let both Jeevan and Courage know that she would be in her room until it was time to head out to the Beltman reception at 7:00 p.m.

9

Kate collapsed on her bed in her suite and fell into a very deep power nap, waking an hour later refreshed and with just enough time to shower and dress for the evening. She had a lovely dress she wished to wear. It accentuated her dark complexion, dark eyes, and long, dark brown hair, while accommodating her broad swimmer's shoulders and tall, lean stature. As she stood holding her selection, she realized that if there were any unexpected challenges at this event, she might not be able to move in it with the swift confidence required to either give chase or stay safe. She wished to feel feminine this evening — perhaps because she was missing Jack big-time. She suddenly remembered the little boutique dress shop around the corner from her hotel in a small mall where there was a casual, dressy feminine outfit in the window. She was out and over there in a flash. The outfit was already gone from the window, but she entered the shop anyway. The space, no more than twelve by ten, was jammed packed with women's fashions. A lone salesperson with a name badge that read "Lesedi" smiled at Kate and said, "You need something for this evening."

"You are absolutely right," said Kate. "There was an outfit in the window — beige and white, lacy, delicate yet comfortable-looking ... and quite feminine without looking like a Barbie Doll."

The young woman laughed. "No Barbie Dolls in here, ma'am, but what about this?" She pulled down a blouse and capris combination with an attached fine crocheted shawl. She showed Kate to a minuscule change room and hung the outfit on the inside door.

Kate easily slipped into it then emerged, looking for a mirror. She was stunned at how attractive the outfit looked on her, and it fit perfectly. Further, she felt feminine in it, and it was comfortable. "I'll take it," she said. She made a mental note to return to the shop to browse some more if ever she found a bit of time again.

As though Lesedi was reading her thoughts, she said, "If you're staying nearby and will be around for a bit, I'd be happy to select a few outfits and get them over to you hotel to try on at your leisure. You could just ring me with your choices, requests for different sizes, colours, and accessories."

Kate cautiously said, "Okay," and told her she was at the boutique hotel around the corner.

Lesedi laughed and asked, "The Hippo?" Kate nodded. "A cousin of mine is one of the owners."

Kate said, "I have met Rajani Patel."

Lesedi laughed again and said, "She is the Indian. My cousin is the African, Yonela Khanya. There is a third owner, Riana, the Afrikaans girl. That is our South Africa today. A business partnership like that could not have happened in my mother's time — now it is common."

Kate felt more at ease and agreed to Lesedi's suggestion. She bought and paid for the outfit then quickly exited the little shop, barely avoiding running smack into a man.

"Sorry," she said to the stranger, who she suddenly realized was Jeevan. She glanced back at the shop and said, "Sorry," again. Although fully entitled to do so, Jeevan did not display a single trace of annoyance. She hurried back to the hotel clutching her package.

Courage dropped her at the main entrance of the One&Only Hotel, from where she made her way through the lobby and out to the island where the MFinance reception was being held. Her timing was good. The crowd was gathering but not yet too numerous or noisy to inhibit easy networking. She loved the early evening February climate in Cape Town. The edge was off the heat of the day, with a slightly cooling breeze that made her shawl a perfect addition to her chosen attire.

As expected, the gathering was mostly made up of men. The smattering of women was clearly wives, staffers, and a few sophisticated call girls. Kate recognized a few female financial managers and government types, where the ranks were usually more generously populated with female professionals. Otherwise, she looked on a sea of men's suits, eclectic in their variety of design and fashion, garbed on a cosmopolitan collection of men heralding from all continents, cultures, and speaking English with many melodious accents.

A waiter approached her with a tray of drinks. She selected a bubbly mineral water as a starter to the evening. A contemporary jazz quartet with a very pleasing sound played in the background. Intrigued by the funky percussion, she made her way over to give a closer listen. She laughed to herself — *Only in Cape Town*. The superb bass player had an Arab/Indian look to him, the piano player was probably a Xhosa, the saxophonist an Afrikaans, and the percussionist looked somewhat Rastafarian. He was surrounded by a combination of traditional and ethnic drums complemented by an array of various other sound makers. On stands strewn about the small stage were a trombone, tenor sax, and an acoustic guitar with no apparent owner.

"They are known as the Cape5," said a familiar voice beside her. Kate turned to see Uncle Anjay, who was likewise enjoying the sounds.

"And where is the fifth, or is it in name only?"

"Both. The fifth was a man named Ibrahim Musunga. He was gunned down in a drive-by shooting as the band was leaving a club where they were playing one night several years ago. They never replaced him but always put his guitar out during gigs to honour his memory."

"I enjoyed a bit of jazz around town since arriving. It has all been very good," said Kate.

Anjay elaborated. "Jazz has a long history in South Africa. It parallels that of the southern US but has developed in its own way as well. You are hearing a bit of what is known as Cape jazz in this group, although Cape jazz doesn't usually include the piano, because what typifies the sound is the mobility of the instruments that make it. It is nevertheless a pleasant fusion — so to speak — of the Cape jazz sound and contemporary jazz." They paused to listen to the music, a number played almost entirely by the bassist.

"You are looking quite lovely this evening, Mrs. Roarty. I see you have discovered our local fashion industry."

Kate flushed slightly then said, "Indeed, it's difficult to find anything suitable for this climate in Canada at this time of year. Are you here as a guest of Mr. Beltman, for security, or both?" she asked.

"I have an invitation, as does Jeevan, but our Mr. Beltman knows that many attendees at this function are wearing more than one hat."

"Do you know him?" Kate said.

"Well enough — professionally. He would not be a guest at my dinner table."

"Ah — he wouldn't pass the Teja test then?"

Anjay smiled broadly as he turned toward Kate then simply nodded in response.

Kate mused to herself, *Anjay runs a security company that keeps his clients safe, and Teja's exacting judgement of character keeps Anjay safe.*

Something caught Anjay's attention, and he abruptly but ever so smoothly strode off.

Kate circulated more, picking up bits and pieces of information and strands of intelligence that suggested she was on the right track to explore the application of Daniel's process for trace gold extraction to rare mineral tailings as well. One inebriated Russian mining executive talked about spending a lot of time in Kazakhstan. He blabbed about money to be had in reworking the uranium tailings that would yield the rare earth chemicals present in abundance in that country and the neighbouring countries.

The evening wore on and the island filled, seemingly to capacity. Although Kate had considered attending this event a necessary method of intelligence gathering, she nevertheless detested receptions. She had done it for twenty years as a diplomat and hated it then — and her attitude hadn't changed despite the different context in her new line of work.

Suddenly, a blood-curdling scream shrilled above the din of the gathering. Jeevan was instantly at her side and showing her the way out. People began to press toward the far end of the large pool that defined the boundaries of the island to get a view of what was causing the disturbance. Kate and Jeevan spotted Anjay standing at the edge, looking in the water. She followed his line of vision and spotted a body floating face down. Two young men plunged in and grabbed it. Jeevan ushered Kate away and out of the hotel complex as quickly as possible. Courage was waiting right at the entrance. They climbed in the SUV and headed up the mountain.

Jeevan said, "We'll go back to Uncle Anjay's until we can find out what happened." Kate nodded.

As Courage pulled up to the electronic iron gate at the Gandhi residence, Jeevan's mobile sounded. The exchange was brief.

Jeevan turned back to look at Kate and said, "The body is that of Robert Beltman. He is dead. He was shot in the head."

10

Kate said, "I must return to my hotel now."

Jeevan nodded and leaned forward to advise Courage, who wheeled the SUV around with the skill of Mario Andretti.

A chill crept over Kate as they drove back down the mountain. She was not enamoured with Robert Beltman when she met him earlier in the day, but to learn that he was killed just hours after their meeting was unsettling. Questions rushed through her mind. *Was this in any way related to the subject matter of our discussion? Who killed him? Why?* Kate pondered the content of their discussion. *Could this have anything to do with applying the extraction process to rare earth minerals left behind in uranium tailings?* These minerals — actually seventeen chemicals — were in critically short supply and essential to the manufacture of electronic screen devices: mobile phones, laptops, televisions, tablets, rechargeable batteries, not to mention wind turbines, solar panels, and hybrid vehicles, and critical to various craft and devices used in space exploration. Kate could imagine that Daniel's newly developed, low-cost, highly efficient extraction process could be valuable enough to kill for. Neither Daniel nor his partners had spoken about the application of their process to the extraction of rare earth minerals from tailings. Another source of uneasiness was creeping over her — how much had Daniel and his compatriots really told her?

Kate would have to bring in her techno geek network and have them track where the IP was migrating to, who was involved, what its applicability was to other extraction processes such as rare earth minerals, who was buying and selling the IP rights, and what it was worth.

She was anxious to get back to her hotel and her computer equipment in order to get an encrypted message out to *trainonthetrack2030*. This was a job for Bryant. She would get him to scope out MFinance to see if they had a record of illicitly absconding with IP rights and making money on it. She also thought this could be an opportune time to take advantage of an offer from MI6 Director Karen Palmer. Many international intelligence services had made job offers to her during the aftermath of the international takedown and arrest of 122 scientists in the neuro-microchip case that resulted in the death of Vincent Bernard Taylor. She turned them all down. They went on to express a willingness to assist Kate on future cases with international magnitude.

Karen Palmer was one that Kate decided she might trust and would at some point call in an installment of the IOU. Robert Beltman was a British citizen. His firm, MFinance, was headquartered in the prestigious financial district of London known as The City. It boasted an address on Threadneedle Street, easy walking distance from the Bank of London and Lloyd's of London, two of the oldest financial institutions in the modern world. MI6 was undoubtedly well acquainted with MFinance and the late Robert Beltman.

The SUV pulled up in front of her hotel and parked. Both Jeevan and Courage got out. Jeevan told the uniformed night security serviceman to position himself by the vehicle until his return then accompanied her and Jeevan to her room. They thoroughly checked the lobby, corridors, and her room then nodded and left.

Kate was pleased to be on her own. She dug out her laptop and logged into the site where she could contact *trainonthetrack2030*. Bryant came back immediately.

What's up?

Kate dialled a number for him. It was cropped from the revolving selection offered up on his key.

"Bryant, can you track where the gold tailings processing IP has been going since it got away from the Ottawa team who developed it?"

"I've already been dabbling with it since you told me about the case. It has big money behind it — London mining investors. I'll map it out with a legend — company names, investors, applications, money, etc., and send it to you, okay? I'll convert it to an active file so I will receive ongoing updates on its status," said Bryant.

"If a guy named Robert Beltman and his firm MFinance comes into your scan, pay close attention. He was just killed this evening here in Cape Town. I met with him earlier in the day before his untimely demise."

"Be careful, Kate, this is beginning to have the look and feel of the neuro-microchip case."

"You aren't the first one to make that observation," said Kate. "I do have a few friends here who actually came out of that case. Check out Dr. Anjay Mohandas Gandhi, president of SSA — Security South Africa. They have my back — admittedly, I have needed it."

"I'll get back to you as soon as I have assembled the whole picture — one that is likely evolving as we speak." Bryant rang off.

Kate called Karen Palmer's direct line. It was the middle of the night in London, but she left a message that she could pick up in the morning.

"Hello Mrs. Palmer, this is Kate Roarty, the private investigator that you may recall from the neuro-microchip case a couple of years back. I hope the offering of working together still stands. This afternoon I met with a man named Robert Beltman who has a publicly traded company called MFinance with a London address on Threadneedle Street. He put on a lavish reception this evening at the One&Only Hotel in Cape Town. The who's who of the mining, exploration, and financing world turned up to witness him being hauled out of the pond with a hole in his head. He is dead. You can reach me on my personal mobile."

Kate looked at the time on her mobile — it was very late. If she wished to start the day with an early swim at the Long Street Baths, she had better get some sleep. She collapsed into bed and started to nod off. It lasted a matter of seconds before her racing thoughts revived a mind on overdrive. She leapt up, found some soothing, tranquil music on her mobile, and settled into a session of mindful meditation. Forty-five minutes later, she slid back into bed and into a deep sleep.

The morning light awakened Kate in time to brew coffee and throw on her gym pants and shirt. She dumped the contents of the little pot into a portable cup with a cover provided in the hotel room then headed over to Long Street for the 7:00 a.m. swim. She recognized the female lifeguard at the far end of the pool from her visit to the baths the previous day.

Kate went into the change room, slipped on her bathing suit, cap, and goggles and emerged — the first swimmer of the day. Just as she was about to plunge into the water, her eye caught Jeevan sitting in the second row of the bleachers browsing the morning paper with a large coffee in hand. He was wearing a tracksuit; she wondered if he had swimming togs underneath just in case she met a similar fate as Robert Beltman. The hour passed quickly as she churned through the water, pleased to have the exhilaration of the swim to prepare her for what the day might bring.

Jeevan was waiting for her as she exited the change room, showered, well-dressed, hair coiffed, and ready to take on the day. He fell in beside her for the short walk back to the hotel.

"Is the lifeguard on the payroll?" Kate asked.

"Something like that," Jeevan replied.

"I have a few calls to make before breakfast, so please feel free to take the time to shower and dress. I won't be going anywhere before taking breakfast on the terrace."

Jeevan nodded, accompanied her to her room, went in ahead of her to check, then exited with another nod. Just as she pulled out her wet bathing suit and towel, the phone rang.

It displayed a private number, so she answered only with, "Hello."

"Kate, this is Karen Palmer."

"Thank you for ringing back so quickly," said Kate.

"I hoped to hear from you one day. Please, let's meet for lunch the next time you're through London. The best flight connections to South Africa are still through Heathrow."

"It is a date," said Kate.

"Robert Beltman — we've had an eye on him for years. He is, or I guess it is was, very skilful. Although he skirted along the edge of international financial wrongdoing, our surveillance never caught him stepping over the line. He portrayed a perception of blue-chip. He frequently turned up at Davos, hobnobbing with the celebrated economic and financial thinkers of the moment, for their annual gatherings in Switzerland. He was very much present at the Cape Town convention held a couple of years ago. As you likely well know, since MFinance is publicly traded, it is relatively easy to monitor its activities. We suspect that it serves as a legitimate front for a backroom filled with nefarious activities that traverse the continents. Beltman's death may expose some weak underpinnings in a structure that he carefully built up. In fact, his death may be a crack that ultimately undermines the whole foundation. MI6 would be pleased to work with you on this one."

Kate thought, *Wow, slow down, gal.*

"Mrs. Palmer—" while Kate was comfortable with being addressed by her first name, she was not so comfortable in extending the same level of familiarity to a director of MI6, "—I continue to focus my work on the intellectual property rights of my clients' innovations. They come to me when their innovations are compromised or completely lost. In this particular case, my client is a small Canadian consortium of scientific companies that developed a rather brilliant and very efficient process to extract trace gold from tailings. The process may have an even more efficacious application to the extraction of rare earth minerals from uranium tailings.

"The stakes are high. I am here in Cape Town to network with the movers and shakers in the mining business. I think Beltman was involved, but I cannot yet confirm it. Key players stand to benefit handsomely, particularly in the rare earth minerals application of the innovation. In less than two days time, I'll give a presentation on intellectual property rights in the mining sector. It's slotted into the keynote addresses of the conference program, so I am expecting that it will be well attended. I'm anticipating that what I have to say will stir up the hornet's nest a little more and perhaps flush out a few of the would-be culprits. I suspect that when you get off this call you will be dispatching a couple of agents to Cape Town or activating sleepers already here. Regardless of how we may be working together, can you have your people look at the registered attendees for the conference and give me a heads-up on anyone I should be watching out for — particularly those who may wish to kill me? That lot I find most distracting. Ultimately, I hope to restore the IP to the rightful innovators — my clients — and get out. However, I fully appreciate that narrow objective may be a pipe dream."

"Kate, in spite of what you may think of MI6, we've got your back. We owe you big time from the neuro-microchip case, so if this is a chance to help you out, we're in."

Kate ended the call wondering if it had been a wise move to bring in MI6. She trusted Palmer but had reservations about the level of integrity throughout her organization. She'd tell Anjay about the call. If MI6 had agents in Cape Town, he'd likely know about them.

11

Kate was famished. The sun was high enough to cast its rays over the hotel terrace where breakfast was being served. She bounded down the stairs, out through the lobby, and onto the terrace. The waiter placed a coffee and the chip holder for morning papers in front of her before she was fully seated. She sipped her coffee and opened the *Daily Sun*. The headline read *Investment Magnate Murdered on Eve of Opening Mining Conference*. A large colour photo showing Robert Beltman floating in the water at the One&Only Hotel pond was placed directly below the headlines. There were accompanying articles describing the murder scene, the man, and his investments. A head-and-shoulder photo of a younger and very much alive Robert Beltman was placed beside a piece on MFinance and his investments in South Africa. An inside full page was given to a spread of photos, together with a series of short articles on Beltman in and around Cape Town over the past decade or so. It seems he was first attracted to South Africa by the investment conference known as Mining Indaba. Bateman was immediately taken with the environment and soon after began making some real estate investments there, then went on to spend part of every year in and around Cape Town.

Kate heard a quiet male voice saying, "Good morning, Mrs. Roarty." She looked up distractedly from a short article about a recent investment by Beltman in a drone manufacturing company. Uncle Anjay was standing at her table, smiling broadly. "I see that the efficient scribing of our Cape Town journalists has produced coverage to capture your attention."

She smiled back, offered a seat to Anjay, and beckoned a waiter over then asked for a pot of tea for Mr. Gandhi. "Have you learned anything more about the slaying?" asked Kate.

"Only that they cannot even locate where the shooter was when the shot was taken and why nobody saw or heard anything suspicious before it happened. The police have reached out to the special investigations unit to assist them. They have more sophisticated procedures and equipment to gather evidence and assess a crime scene."

Kate said, "Can I weigh in with a theory that also implicates my experience while swimming from Robben Island?"

Anjay looked at her quizzically and replied, "Of course."

"I think our guide boat was hit by an armed drone, not another watercraft. When my guide boat saw the vessel approaching, it positioned itself between what we all thought was a fast-moving watercraft and me. I suspect that the sensors on the drone remained locked on me and did not adjust when the craft moved between it and me. Its guidance system sent it right through the guide boat, the impact of which blew them both up. I was just far enough away to escape the worst of the explosion that was likely absorbed by the guide boat and the water. It destroyed the drone."

Kate allowed a bit of time for Anjay to consider this explanation then continued. "I thought the investigation of Robert Beltman's death would not reveal anything about the whereabouts or identity of a shooter, because I think a drone was used to fire on him. The drone operator probably hacked into the security grid over the island reception area. The very surveillance system set up by the hotel to protect its clientele may have been used to infiltrate the gathering without detection. I suspect that the perpetrators integrated their predatory software into the hotel's surveillance software." Kate paused to give Anjay time to mull over what she was saying.

He nodded slightly and said, "Please continue, Mrs. Roarty."

"A drone was controlled remotely within the parameters of the security grid. It was Beltman's party. The hotel security needed to know where he was at all times. Once inside, the drone locked on to Beltman's co-ordinates and hung in there like a dog with a bone. When the opportunity was ideal, such as during the distraction created by the performances, zap, he was eliminated without anyone noticing — the body was spotted floating in the water perhaps as long as several minutes after he was hit. The action was silent, almost invisible and deadly. The perpetrators could have been sitting in front of a computer network anywhere in the world." Kate paused again and took a sip of her coffee. Anjay followed suit with his tea.

"Uncle Anjay, you need to find someone that you trust with a high-level expertise who can have a look at the hotel software during that period of time."

Anjay sighed and said, "The capabilities of my company to protect its clients are as good as it gets, but we do not have adequate wherewithal to tackle UAV surveillance."

"You will acquire it." Kate smiled and said, "It will be your next business development, Mr. Gandhi."

Anjay looked thoughtful but did not reply, so Kate felt at liberty to continue.

"Robert Beltman had just made a sizable investment in an unmanned aviation vehicle company that established a manufacturing facility here in South Africa, where the test conditions are as good as the location of the parent company in the southwest of the US. This South African company got the green light from the regulatory authorities because its stated objective was to distribute vaccines to remote sub-Saharan African villages. As well, the technology could be used to provide surveillance in national parks to protect large mammals from poachers. It may very well do that, along with designing and manufacturing UAVs for many purposes, including covert and criminal activity. The company financed a pilot project in rhino protection. It was very successful in identifying where the poachers were entering Kruger National Park. The UAV operated undetected by the poachers. Abundant visual data was collected to enable arrests and obtain convictions. Word travelled fast and shut down the entire rhino-poaching network. Another pilot project successfully delivered vaccines to a remote village in Lesotho that experienced an outbreak of the plague. The kits that were dispatched by several UAVs provided diagnostics, treatment, and vaccines. The village population was successfully treated and vaccinated. The deaths were few after the arrival of the supplies delivered by these drones."

Kate passed her tablet to Anjay, displaying the article on Robert Beltman's recent sizable investment in a drone manufacturer. While Anjay read the article, she brought up the company website on her laptop and pulled over beside him to browse through the site together.

"This is what SWSAdrone is willing to tell the world. In the US, the company is known as SWdrone. It seems the local identity was reflected in the company name by simply inserting SA."

A troubled expression crept across Anjay's face. "Mrs. Roarty, the implications of the use of this technology in this relatively young post-apartheid country, struggling to assert itself on the world stage, is worrisome."

"Indeed it is, Anjay. However, this technology is rapidly becoming a pervasive phenomenon with applications in all manner of life — good, bad, and indifferent. The best we can do is accept its presence, understand its applications, and remain undisturbed by it. After all, the two pilot projects SWSAdrone undertook here had very positive outcomes. The death of Robert Beltman is another story."

He nodded in thought.

"Anjay, my job is to try to retrieve the IP rights that some players in the mining sector stole from my client. Your job is to protect me while I am trying to do this in South Africa. We have both been understandably distracted by the death of Robert Beltman. I think we both think it is somehow related — that is why we are not pulling back from the distraction. Perhaps you also see some other implications in the scope of your work and your consideration of certain agendas in this country."

Anjay nodded. "Mrs. Roarty, I have been humbled by this development, and I am very grateful to make your acquaintance. I am coming to understand more and more why Kiran and Giorgio think so highly of you."

Kate laughed. "Don't be so fast with your admiration. I'm sure Jeevan has a very different opinion. I may be driving him crazy."

"He loves this assignment with you. It's dramatically different from protecting celebrities, politicians, and businessman. Not only does he have to remain razor-sharp to ensure the best possible protection for you, but also it has reawakened his interest in science. Perhaps an opportunity may present itself for you to explore doctoral studies options with him."

Kate replied, "Gladly, of course, any time, though he does have far superior resources available at hand in Kiran and Giorgio."

"Indeed, but I think he is rather shy to approach either of them on the subject."

"We'll have to do something about that — in the case of Giorgio, he didn't acquire the nickname 'Teddy Bear' because he is intimidating. Be that as it may, I have a few connections that I have acquired through this IP work who could be valuable contacts for Jeevan."

Anjay said, "Let's get through the next couple of days. If we all manage to survive, we can revisit Jeevan's academic options."

"My ears are burning. Is there a reason for it? Ah, it is coming from co-conspirators on the terrace in the sunshine," said a gently smiling Jeevan, standing before them with a coffee and plate of food in his hands.

Kate reached over and pulled out the third chair for him to join them at their little table. She paused, excused herself for a moment, and sent a two-word text to Danielle. **Puppy search?** An immediate response came back. **Nothing.** Kate replied, **Send Hazel's adoption details, microchip ID & photo.**

As though Danielle had anticipated her mother's request, she sent the info on the pup immediately.

"We are less than a day and half away from my address on IP rights at the conference. I spoke with a reliable contact at MI6 to look at the registered attendees for the conference and provide a heads-up on anyone we should be wary about. She agreed to do it and get back to me as soon as possible. She is aware of where I am slotted in the speakers' program."

Anjay revealed a tinge of uneasiness as he took in this information. Jeevan remained completely focused on what she was saying.

Kate continued, "I rather suspect MI6 has agents in South Africa and/or some are on the way."

"Or both," said Anjay. "Like any other intelligence services, MI6 is not immune to corruption."

"I agree," said Kate. "I trust Karen Palmer, the director. As for the rest of the organization, let's remain vigilant when dealing with any of their agents."

12

Kate and Jeevan entered the Cape Town Convention Centre and took in the sprawling expanse of glass and concrete that streamed in natural light from all angles on the above-ground floors. They walked through arboretums of green space dedicated to native species of South Africa and along the water-filled canal connecting the adjacent hotels to the convention centre. The architecture effectively captured an outdoor environment flowing fluidly indoors. The fifteen-acre convention centre was designed to move thousands of people at a time with ease. It also presented a security nightmare.

Kate and Jeevan went to check out the room where Kate would do her presentation. They observed a six-hundred-seat auditorium sloping down toward the stage. She made a decision without delay that she would not remain stationary at a podium; rather, she would move about the stage to add a degree of unpredictability to her presentation style. The back screen was large and wide to readily display the presentation, notes, and photos. Kate had worked hard to incorporate humour into the early part of the program in the hope of putting her audience at ease as she moved into presenting a very serious subject. She wanted the industry and financiers to sit up and take notice of intellectual property rights — legal protection measures that were real and necessary to stimulate innovation in an industry desperately in need of modernization. Her presentation would target and illustrate transgressions by major companies. She was going to throw it into the public domain and let the chips fall where they would. Kate suspected that if she survived the presentation, the degree of personal risk would diminish. Once it was out there, there was no longer a reason to try to hide it.

Kate's cellphone vibrated as she surveyed the auditorium. It displayed "private" on the screen. She answered to hear Karen Palmer's voice: "You move with an eclectic bunch of rogues, Kate Roarty."

"That bad, is it?"

"You need an army to protect you from the number of nasty blokes who could potentially be gunning for you at that conference."

"Lovely. Tell me," said Kate.

"Kate, most of us avoid conferences like the plague, and if we go, we are generally bored out of our mind — not this one. This lot is Baader Meinhof in business suits. We consulted with Interpol to learn that it was already monitoring activity and traffic surrounding this conference. Their agents told us that each year the stakes grow bigger as the backroom wheeling and dealing intensifies. Black market intellectual property first appeared in bidding forums several years ago. We think your clients' IP is there, with the bidding starting at US 120 million."

Kate mused aloud, "Enough to kill for."

"Kate, local confectionary robbers kill for £20. Surely you have not already forgotten the 122 PhD-clad scientists we put behind bars on the Taylor case."

Kate sighed. "Of course not."

"Your man Anjay Gandhi is as good as it gets in private-sector security. He will have backup that he is both aware and not aware of — go ahead and give your presentation. Make sure it is launched all over the Internet while you are presenting it, in so many places that the most skilled hackers cannot shut it down, and get the hell out of there."

They rang off, not wanting to divulge any details of the developing plan over the phone. Kate took in the time displayed on her phone — less than twenty-four hours before she would be back in that conference room.

Much to the dismay of Jeevan, Kate slipped in a late morning swim. His lifeguard was not on duty, and the Long Street Baths were busier than usual with many visitors to the Turkish baths as well as the pool for lap swimming. Kate managed to get in, swim vigorously for an hour, shower and change, and get out without incident. She wondered if this was the storm before the calm. She was also concerned that the bait she hoped to set in doing the intellectual property rights presentation might very well succeed in ensnarling the culprits, but she might not be able to hang around long enough to expose them as well.

She would have to rely on her compatriots to reel them in. She called Giorgio.

"Can we meet?"

"Of course, my beautiful lady, where and when?"

Kate's mind raced; there could be no risk of this conversation being eavesdropped on. She said, "Uncle Anjay's garden in an hour."

"Okay, shall I bring Kiran?"

"Absolutely."

Kate called Anjay to let him know. He agreed. She had just enough time to send an encrypted message to *trainonthetrack2030*. It included the instructions about uploading her IP rights paper and queried the connection between the tailings, IP rights transgressions, and Robert Beltman.

Bryant acknowledged her request immediately regarding the rapid-fire digital distribution of her paper. He allowed that he had already skimmed it off her home and laptop hard drives, along with the presentation version that she was going to give at the mining conference. She mused to herself, *Never make an enemy of trainonthetrack2030*. Bryant was the only member of her trusted network that consistently ran two paces ahead of her, anticipating her moves before she even thought about them. She paused then hit the "send" button with the details about the puppy. **Major family distress, can you help find my daughter's pup Hazel? Here's everything I have on her. So sorry to ask but the search has gone cold.**

Bryant replied, **Good task to break in a potential new subcontractor.**

Kate's plan was coming together. She had to book a flight out of Cape Town that departed as soon as possible after she gave her paper — within minutes, or at least hours, she needed to get up and away while the international fury among mining financiers unfolded. She would like to head to London on a direct flight from Johannesburg, but London was also a mecca for these financiers and their networks. The MI6 intelligence from Interpol indicated more than fifty percent of the attendees originated or routed through London, while most of the rest of the delegates routed via Frankfurt and New York — both major centres of concentration for these guys, where they were likely to have hit men they could readily call upon. Kate selected a lower-profile routing to Seoul, Korea, then on to Vancouver and hopscotching across Canada to avoid Toronto — not easy to do, since almost all Canadian airways led to and from that airport. Fortunately, WestJet offered a direct connection from Calgary to Ottawa.

13

Kate was waiting with an iced tea in hand in Uncle Anjay's garden when the others began to arrive, gathering on the terrace, each fetching an iced tea from a tray that Teja had placed out there for them. Giorgio and Kiran came in, greeted Kate in the double-cheek-kiss French style and took a seat on the bar stools. Uncle Anjay strolled in, quietly greeting them all, then turned to introduce Charlie Kagiso, who passed through the patio doorway, tentativeness emanating from his body. Kate rose uneasily, looking enquiringly at Uncle Anjay and Jeevan.

Anjay said, "Before we begin to discuss the issue at hand, let me explain the presence of Charlie Kagiso. As you all know, Charlie's boss, Robert Beltman, was murdered last night. Charlie was in charge of his security. It was his responsibility to keep him out of harm's way — and he failed." Charlie looked completely downtrodden as Anjay spoke. "I am not sure any of the best security services could have prevented Robert Beltman's death last night. Charlie's life is now in grave danger. He came to me for help. Kate, it is of course your choice. If you do not want Charlie here, he is gone. Before you make that decision, will you hear him out?"

Kate looked over to Giorgio, who held her gaze but did not interfere with either words or facial expression. Kiran responded likewise. Jeevan maintained an unyielding stone face in response, while Anjay displayed his usual outward calm and quiet confidence.

Kate looked at Charlie, sighed slightly, and said only, "Speak."

Charlie moved over toward the bar in a solitary position, where he had them all in view. Kate was front and centre, where she could carefully study his every word and how they were delivered.

"Mrs. Roarty, I can tell you what I know and what I wish to do. I'll be frank, my actions are self-serving, preservationist, designed to protect my family and me. I expect Mr. Beltman's handlers will kill me, given the opportunity."

Kate nodded. "You have my full attention, Mr. Kagiso, please continue."

"We took every measure possible to ensure the security of not only Mr. Beltman but also all of the guests that attended his reception last night. They were pre-vetted, scanned upon arrival, and continually scanned throughout the festivities. We worked with the hotel that placed an invisible security grid over the entire area. The grid was designed to detect weapons, explosives, and digital devices that could be used in a harmful way. We continually ran facial scans, iris scans, and fingerprint scans. The food and beverage handlers were in fact all part of the security detail. The security was more intense and exacting than would have been provided for the president himself. We even anticipated the possible use of drones and ensured the grid was equipped with sensors to detect, deflect, and destroy them. Ultimately, we believe an offshore software program, integrated with the hotel surveillance grid, actually used its features to guide a miniature drone to Mr. Beltman and launched a single deadly projectile. The only way we can prove this theory is to trace the IP signature of the software that integrated with the surveillance software already in place at the hotel. It could have been manipulated from anywhere in the world."

Kate studied Charlie carefully. Everything he said was so familiar to her that he couldn't have made it up. All eyes were on Kate to take the decision about including or excluding Charlie Kagiso.

She exhaled quietly then said to Charlie, "Perhaps we need you as much as you need us. Uncle Anjay, can he work with your company?"

"Yes."

"Okay, let's do it then. I am out of here immediately following my presentation at the conference," said Kate.

Uncle Anjay said, "Kate, I would like to get you up to Jo-burg on a private aircraft booked in a different name so your departure cannot be easily tracked. There is a Gulfstream G450 sitting in a private airstrip hangar that could become available. It would simply involve calling in a favour."

All heads nodded and Kate agreed, then said, "I am going to take a slightly unorthodox routing out of South Africa via Seoul to Vancouver. I will manage those details so as few people as possible know my whereabouts while in transit. Once my presentation goes viral, I will become less concerned about staying alive. Getting it into the public domain as quickly as possible will be my safety net. Uncle Anjay, your responsibility ends when I board a commercial flight in Jo-burg." Anjay neither agreed nor disagreed.

They took a little more time to work out the details of getting Kate into the convention centre, to the auditorium for the presentation, then out immediately after she finished the Q&A. Charlie would tandem with Jeevan as Kate's bodyguards. Giorgio would remain with Kate on the stage during the Q&A session to elaborate the science dimensions of Kate's discussion for the audience. Giorgio hoped that this would keep the audience in their seats a bit longer, provide a distraction, and allow sufficient time for Kate to slip away.

Kate's mobile rang. It was Rajani. "Kate, I think you should remain at Uncle Anjay's. I do not like the look of some of the guys on the terrace. Also, I feel uneasy about a couple that just checked in without a reservation. The room was available, so before I could veto it, my desk clerk gave them the room. I can get your belongings out of your suite and up to you without attracting any attention."

Kate agreed then handed her mobile to Anjay. He and Rajani spoke briefly then ended the call.

"Kate, Rajani is going to take measures to make it appear that you are still staying there. We cannot go near the place, because I think your adversaries have identified your protectors. Let's focus on keeping you safe here. We will be in plain view tomorrow at the convention centre, because that is what will be expected. Our numbers will be augmented with others from our security team whom nobody will recognize. There will be backup as well."

Kate wanted to spend time reviewing her presentation with Giorgio and Kiran. Uncle Anjay showed her into his entertainment centre with seating for twelve and a very large screen. By the time he finished going over the equipment with Kate, her belongings arrived from the hotel. Teja placed a refreshment tray at the back of the room then left Kate, Giorgio, and Kiran to their work.

Kate said, "Let's do a run-through of the entire presentation without comment — that will only take five to ten minutes. There are several key slides we can go back to then figure out when we can subtly interject you, Giorgio."

Kiran said, "Kate, you amaze me. It is a tough job to engage an audience on a subject as dry as intellectual property. You not only bring it to life, you throw it at them, like a billion dollar sci-fi thriller filled with altruism, intrigue, corruption, theft, murder, and mayhem. You identify the cast of conspirators that prey upon scientists and the thieving thugs that abscond with the innovations and apply them to mineral extractions, making millions for a mining industry that is out of control."

"I learned well from Claude. His thesis on detecting corruption in neuroscience research was brilliant."

"Claude's thesis was dazzling because your investigations into stolen intellectual property identified murderers and thieves and exposed immoral scientists in vast numbers. If Operation Chipdown had not succeeded in stopping the development of that neuro-microchip, its capability could have destroyed humanity, as we know it. Who but you would have ever thought to get at the underbelly of a single murder by following the IP trail that connected all of the elements of the vast crime, reaching out to many continents. Now you're doing it again in the mining sector. Operation Chipdown was about power and money. This is about pure money."

Kate replied, "I think both power and money apply here as well. While this process was originally developed to extract trace minerals from gold mine tailings, its application to rare earth minerals takes it into the high-tech realm. Just think about the vast array of screens — sensors, computers, laptops, tablets, mobile phones, GPS, space technology, drone guidance systems. Kiran, that is about money and power."

Kate went silent for a few moments then said, "As I am speaking to you, I am wondering about my clients on this project. Perhaps they already knew … figured out the efficacy of the application to rare earth mineral extraction, but they didn't tell me. It wouldn't be the first time a client failed to tell me the entire story. It is time for me to go home — for more reasons than one."

"When is Jack getting back to Gatineau?" Giorgio asked.

She looked up in surprise. "Today. We haven't connected by phone because he is travelling." She felt a rush passing through her, driving her, to manage the next twenty hours and start her journey home.

Kate and Giorgio carefully crafted the presentation plan to have Kate dominating the first portion, gradually introducing Giorgio as Kate seamlessly phased out, shifting the focus to him. Giorgio would try to hold the attention of the audience by elaborating on the science of intellectual property rights while the impact of the slide listing the firms identified in the IP theft began to sink in. This key slide in Kate's presentation listed a dozen major mining companies and consortiums as well as a number of mining investment firms. Kate also listed the CEO (Chief Executive Officer), the COO (Chief Operations Officer), and the CFO (Chief Financial Officer) beside each company name, thus implicating the senior management of every business entity she named. Most of these men were attending the conference, and many would be sitting in the audience when Kate spoke, in mere hours.

It was not lost on Kate and Giorgio that once again they were teaming up to expose corruption in science and technology.

"Kate, does a second go-around mean we are beginning to make a habit of this?"

Kate laughed. "Only the big jobs. I can handle the small ones on my own."

Kiran chimed in, "To see you two in action together helps me understand how you so masterfully carried out Operation Chipdown."

Kate replied, "Oh, Kiran, there were many, many players that came together to execute that one. My cyber geeks, who always remain under the radar, were brilliant, not to mention Dr. Bosum, Jack, Claude, Lech Bogdan, you, and the other lads. The takedown couldn't have happened without a collection of intelligence services on two continents and in at least six nations. You are right, this one might be nearly as big when it all unfolds."

Uncle Anjay and Charlie Kagiso entered the room. Anjay said, "Sorry to interrupt, Kate, we need to discuss an aspect of your security tomorrow."

Charlie followed, "Mrs. Roarty, I am concerned that drones may play a role in pursuing you at the conference centre. There is a deflection technology that will divert miniature drones away from you and Dr. Beretta. I am not sure if it is perfect, but it should be good enough to buy us time to get you out of there. If you agree, we will do the work up at the auditorium where you are speaking and on your person tomorrow before you go on."

Kate nodded in agreement then said, "It's late. I think we have done as much as we can tonight. We all need some sleep so we can be alert and on our best form tomorrow. Let's meet at the conference centre shortly before the presentation time."

Then she turned to Giorgio and said, "My teddy bear, CEO of iBrain and my friend, you realize that going on stage with me tomorrow will expose you in a way that might make you a hunted man."

"Kate, I'm alive because of your quick action in Boston. I have an intact research firm, doing brilliant neurological work with utmost integrity, because you took a risk with me. Sure, I'll be exposed to danger tomorrow, but I'll also play a role in restoring IP rights to their rightful innovators and taking out the thieves who stole them. That works for me."

Kate looked at him with deep affection, smiled, then said, "Off with you and get some sleep." She retrieved her flash drive and handed the backup to Giorgio then saw him and Kiran off at the door.

Kate collapsed in bed, drained from the day's activity and pumped for what the next day would bring. She was experienced enough to know that the best-laid plans can run amok. The entire team was well prepared, but they had little idea about their adversaries' plans. She slept deeply, rose early, spent an hour on mindful meditation while the sun rose over the terrace, showered, dressed, packed, then reviewed her presentation one more time. Just as she finished, she heard a gentle tap on the door.

She opened it to Teja's radiant smile. "I hope you can join us for breakfast on the terrace."

Kate responded, "Nothing would please me more." She felt sadness wash over her as she emerged onto the terrace and said to Anjay and Teja, "My visit to Cape Town is ending too quickly. Despite the nastiness of the business that brought me here, I'm acquiring a deep affection for this country, this city, and you and your extended family."

Anjay smiled. "Kate Roarty, P.I., you will simply have to come again and tarry awhile to enjoy all that we have to offer. In the meantime, we will fantasize about seeing your polar bears, the midnight sun, and blooming tundra flowers. Now, a hearty, nutritious breakfast is in order."

14

Courage pulled up to the main entrance of the convention centre and discharged his only passenger. Kate strode into the expansive foyer and proceeded to the speakers' hall, where a middle-aged man greeted her. He addressed her by name and welcomed her into the seating area.

"Mrs. Roarty, can we take a few moments to review your requirements?" he said.

Kate replied, "Of course."

"First, the sign-up for your session exceeded our capacity to accommodate such large numbers in the original auditorium. We have made some logistical changes to move your presentation into the main auditorium. I hope this arrangement meets with your satisfaction."

Glitch number one.

"We have already posted it online and on our monitors positioned throughout the convention centre, so your audience should be able to find you easily enough."

Kate nodded, hoping that the team was already aware of the change. She said, "A colleague will be joining me for the presentation. Can you set him up with a mobile microphone and hand control?"

"Of course."

"We do not want a podium on the stage, but can you put it there then remove it at the last moment?"

Without a trace of a question on his face, the speakers' coordinator said, "Consider it done. We will put a small table with two glasses of water at the back of the stage, otherwise, it is you, your colleague, and mobile microphones."

He rose and escorted Kate backstage to the venue, where a presentation was just finishing up. "There will be a few moments for you to familiarize yourself with the setting, make sure your presentation comes up on the floor monitors and the screen, and to set up the microphones. Is your colleague here?"

Almost on cue, Giorgio strolled across the stage, greeted Kate, and introduced himself the speakers' coordinator. Beyond his shoulder, Kate saw Jeevan and Charlie adjusting the screen then walking toward her with a small case that Jeevan opened. In one smooth motion by each of them, they affixed the tiny mobile mikes to both Kate and Giorgio's neckline clothing. They backed off and said only, "Let's do a quick test."

All was in order. They were ready to go.

Kate solicited a calm to wash over her. The auditorium was filling. She glanced at Giorgio, struck by his playful flop of black curly hair, the twinkle in his eyes visible from across the stage, and so handsomely turned out in a sleek light grey suit, open-collared blue shirt, and of course, exquisite Italian light tan leather shoes. In anticipation of sharing the stage with him, Kate had dressed to balance his appearance. She wore a rich deep blue-magenta suit with a mango-hot-pink blouse that drew out her complexion and stature. Comfort and ease of movement was critical. Her life might depend on it. Lesedi at the little boutique shop around the corner from her hotel had selected the ensemble after listening to Kate's description of what she would be doing when she wore it. The suit arrived via her cousin in the Gandhi network just after dawn that very morning. A small box with an exquisite thin gold chain came along as well. It was not itemized on the bill — a small note inside said only, *Looking forward to your return.* Kate laughed aloud when she opened another box sent from Lesedi. It contained a pair of perfectly fitting multicoloured trainers that drew on the colours of the blouse and suit then added many more. Lesedi even included colour-coordinated socks and underwear. Another small note from her read, *This look will stir up the sea of dark suits and white shirts.*

Giorgio must have heard Kate's thoughts. He strode across the stage, took both of her hands, and said, "You look gorgeous, Kate. You will dazzle this audience and the mining world today."

"*We* will dazzle them, Giorgio. I could not have got this far without Kiran's family and your connections. Let's go do it."

With that, Kate stepped back as the conference chair introduced her with some biographical descriptions — apart from the expression "unusual credentials," she heard little of what was said. It was followed by a brief intro for Dr. Beretta, and they were underway.

The auditorium was comfortably full. Kate spotted Uncle Anjay at the back, close to an exit. Jeevan and Charlie remained out of sight of the audience stage right and stage left. Kiran was positioned mid wall, close to another exit. Kate paused, looked at Giorgio, focused, and started the presentation. The audience was quiet and attentive as she spoke. The gradual interjections by Giorgio to elaborate the science was working effectively. The attention was shifting from Kate to him.

Slide twenty-eight went up, listing the companies, consortiums, and investment firms, along with the respective names of CEOs, the COOs, and the CFOs. Kate spoke to it, paused, then replaced it with slide twenty-nine, and Giorgio proceeded to speak to the science application of the process to rare earth minerals. The quiet in the audience was replaced by a gathering murmur.

Giorgio continued to speak as Kate faded off the stage. She felt a firm hand on her arm, looked at Jeevan, and they were running. Kate could see the black SUV through the glass of the side exit. The rear door was open, and Jeevan leapt in, pulling Kate behind him. Charlie brought up the rear, taking the seat beside her and closing the door in one smooth motion. Courage was driving as the snap of seat belts sounded above the screech of tires. Uncle Anjay was sitting in the front seat beside Courage.

Suddenly, another SUV crossed their path, seemingly intent on stopping them. Courage reversed, taking a laneway in the wrong direction, navigating through pedestrians and sloppily parked service vehicles and emerging out onto a dual carriageway. They sped along the N2 — a route Kate recognized — then Courage exited at the last minute onto the M10, effectively losing the tail, at least for a bit. To reduce their exposure, he exited into a network of small roads at Jonkershoek Way, where he abruptly stopped beside a white SUV. They switched vehicles in a heartbeat and continued across to Steve Biko Street then regained the route to the airport via Settler's Way. They proceed for another ten minutes or so, dropping back to normal traffic speed. No more tails appeared to pick them up. They turned onto Borcherds Quarry Road then threaded through airport buildings, coming to halt in front of a hangar where a Gulfstream G450 was revving up.

Jeevan led Kate onto the aircraft. Charlie brought up the rear. As Kate took a seat, she looked out the window to see Courage and Uncle Anjay speaking, then Courage returned to the white SUV and drove off. Uncle Anjay boarded the plane. The door was pulled shut and the aircraft taxied to position at the end of a strip. Within moments, they were lifting off bound for Johannesburg. Once they levelled off, seat belts clipped open and they gathered in a conversation area while a flight attendant served mineral water.

Uncle Anjay said, "We are not out of the woods yet. A drone took out the black SUV shortly after we left it. Fortunately, the drone detector alerted the driver, and he leapt free before it blew up." He answered Kate's look of concern with, "Apart from some scratches and a fractured arm from the roll when he jumped, he will be fine. Not much worse than you were, Kate, after the helicopter rescue from your swim."

He was about to continue when the flight attendant spoke quietly into his ear. Anjay excused himself and went forward into the cockpit. He returned a short time later and related to Kate, Jeevan, and Charlie what had transpired in the air traffic control tower in Cape Town.

15

A band of heavily armed men burst into the traffic control tower at Cape Town International Airport. They positioned themselves around the perimeter of the tower, pointing automatic weapons at the heads of each air traffic controller in the tower.

One commando barked, "Who instructed the Gulfstream G450 on take-off."

Silence.

"Okay, I'll begin to shoot one of you at a time until I get my answer."

He spun around to hear a soft voice say, "It was me, sir."

"And who is me, sir?" he commanded in a surly, mocking voice.

"ATC Préfontaine, sir."

"And where is that aircraft headed?" he continued.

"Luanda, sir."

He spun around again. "Luanda, Angola."

"Yes, sir."

"Why are they going there?"

"I don't know, sir. We are rarely privy to that information."

"Is there a scheduled flight to Europe they could connect to from there?"

"Yes, sir, several."

"What is the flying time to get there?"

"Approximately 3.5 hours, sir."

"Get a list of the airlines and departure times closest to the Gulfstream arrival in Luanda."

The air traffic controller took his seat, brought up the information on his screen, then showed the commando in charge. He photographed the screen from his mobile phone and sent it onward. That action enabled the SA special services that had surrounded the base of the tower to get a digital fix on who and what they were dealing with. The SASS electronically disabled the commandos' high-powered weaponry and took them into custody with only a minor skirmish as they exited the building. When they discovered that their weaponry, save a few manual handguns, were disabled, they surrendered after a few injuries were inflicted by the special services troops who wished to drive home the message that it was over.

Kate said, "Since they think we are headed to Luanda, which is about an hour and a half further by air than Jo-burg, that should buy us some time to make our connection to the scheduled flight in Johannesburg and hopefully get airborne before they figure out the ruse."

Anjay added, "They may not have adequate connections in Luanda to do anything anyway. Since the communications from the commando unit that stormed the tower in Cape Town have been shut down, it may be a moot point.

Charlie was listening with his laptop open, browsing the net. "Mrs. Roarty, your paper has gone viral on the net."

Kate smiled to herself. *Yes, Bryant, you did it.*

"That means there is no longer any reason to keep you quiet. It is out there for the entire world to read," said Anjay.

Kate sank back into her seat, releasing the tension from her taut body that had been coiled for action since she arrived at the Cape Town Convention Centre just two hours before.

Anjay handed Kate a glass, saying only, "Drink?"

"Thanks, Uncle Anjay. We aren't out of the woods yet. I need to remain sharp."

"It isn't alcohol. The ingredients in this drink will intensive your sharpness and clarity. It is a herbal-fresh fruit concoction conjured up by Teja."

"Ah, in that case, thank you. Anything from Aunt Teja can only be fortifying." Real or imagined — actual or placebo — it did the trick. Kate was ready for the next challenge. She noticed Anjay pass the same drink to Jeevan and Charlie, then he took one himself.

She pulled out her laptop to view the reach of her paper then sent a message to *trainonthetrack2030* that said simply, **We did it.**

She leaned back and fell into a deep power nap, awakening as the pilot announced the beginning of the descent into Jo-burg.

16

En Route, South Africa to Canada

"Kate, when we land, a van will meet the aircraft and take us to the terminal door located directly beneath the boarding ramp. Several officials will be there to check your passport and give you your ticket. Once we see you board, I will leave and Charlie will stay with you."

Kate began to protest, but Anjay gently raised his hand. "It will all become apparent in due course. You have trusted me this far. Please trust me for the rest of the journey. There will be no opportunities for awkward goodbyes when we land, so let me say this now — it has been a pleasure. Please come again to enjoy our fine country.

"Finally, Jeevan should go on in school. While I would love to have him remain with me and eventually take over the business, his heart is in science and his mind is well attuned to it. Can you connect him with the right people?"

Kate smiled and said, "Yes, of course, Uncle Anjay. I'll ensure that he gets connected with the right people."

The Gulfstream landed, and true to Anjay's plan, a van picked them up straight off from the aircraft. Kate watched her bags getting loaded into the van. She had not expected to see her belongings again. She was thrilled each time everything materialized under Uncle Anjay's careful attention to detail. She was also sad to see an end to her visit to South Africa. It was so abrupt. She still had much work to do to restore the IP rights of the trace elements recovery process to the rightful innovators.

The small airport van sped toward the South African Airways Gate 43, where an Airbus 380-800 called the *Spirit of the Future* was sitting at the gate. Kate looked at its title and remembered that Airbus had fitted the 350-1200 series with drone deflection shields after one had been shot down over the Indian Ocean. The sensor system operated in a continual adaptation mode. The 1200 series aircraft was also fitted with a suite of miniature drones installed in tiny compartments in the nose and tail. These drones could be activated manually by the pilot or by air traffic controllers when they detected an inflight emergency or serious issue. The drones could also self activate when an unscheduled rapid descent, smoke, fire, or loss of power occurred. They were designed to access the landing gear to address descending and retraction issues, seal breaches to the hull, repressurize the aircraft, and neutralize approaching hostile drones and missiles. Additional capabilities were being added regularly to this suite of miniature drones. Once on board, she hoped she could relax for the thirteen-hour journey to Hong Kong, where the flight was scheduled to make a short stop before continuing on to Seoul.

Kate took her assigned seat, 47J, which was an aisle seat in a section near the back of the aircraft. As she was settling in, she glanced around to inform herself of her surroundings and other passengers. Kate was surprised to see Charlie Kagiso taking a seat opposite her own and one back in the centre aisle. A woman and two young children were already occupying the other three seats in his row. He nodded to

Kate then reached over to check the seat belts of the children. Before Kate could digest that information, a familiar voice giving routine flight and take-off info came over the address system. When the aircraft reached cruising altitude, the purser made the rounds of the cabin. The name badge on his uniform read "Jeevan Gandhi." He gave Kate a brief nod as he passed by then paused to speak quietly to Charlie. Kate could not hear their exchange. She thought she could genuinely relax — at least as far as Hong Kong. At cruising altitude, she turned on her iPhone and laptop. There were numerous messages from colleagues and contacts advising her of the media coverage of the exposure of wealthy mining magnets at the Cape Town mining investment conference. There were a few surprising messages like the one from the General Council of the World Trade Organization, known as the WTO — it said only, **You got pluck lady. Can we talk after the heat cools a bit?**

There was also a one-word note from Karen Palmer: **Gutsy.**

Kate opened an unfamiliar address. It was from a Denis Colbert, Director, Echelon Liaison. The message read, **Mrs. Roarty, would you come to my office upon your return to Ottawa?**

A voice came over the aircraft speaker system. "This is your captain speaking. We must return to Johannesburg to discharge a passenger. We will attempt to make up the time to ensure that all of you will make your connecting flights and reach your destinations close to the original times. We apologize for any inconvenience. Please avail yourself of our entertainment system, food, and beverage provisions."

Kate glanced back and saw Charlie's seat was empty. She became uneasy. Within moments, a flight attendant approached her and said quietly, "Mrs. Roarty, will you please come with me? Our purser would like a word."

She followed the attendant up into first class, where she saw Charlie and Jeevan standing at a private cubicle.

"Ah, Mrs. Roarty, this is the reason we are turning around." He indicated the motionless passenger slumped in the first class seat. "We were suspicious about him as he boarded, but his ID checked out and he cleared security without issue. After take-off, our sensors detected him activating a miniature drone. We intercepted him, destroyed the drone, and sedated him. When we searched him we found his mobile. The last text message read, **Seat 47J, do it**. We think he is the only threat that boarded. We will let Special Services take care of him when we land then take off as quickly as possible."

The removal of the sedated passenger went quickly and smoothly. He was placed on a stretched with a paramedics' escort, so the passengers probably thought it was a health issue.

Kate pondered, *Surely, I will no longer be pursued by the idea of annihilating me now that the treachery has been exposed and this threat has been removed from the aircraft.* She must have felt some confidence in her assessment, because she slipped into a deep sleep that lasted for hours. She awoke to a child's voice saying, "Daddy, it's your turn." She glanced back to see Charlie with a big, playful smile on his face, totally engaged in a computer game with his oldest child. The younger one was asleep, straddling his mother's lap.

She looked up to see the purser holding a drink. "Auntie Teja's special." Jeevan handed it to Kate as he said, "There is an empty seat in first class if you wish to move up."

Kate smiled and accepted the drink. "Thanks, I am fine here, especially with Auntie Teja's fortification."

The passenger beside her said to the purser, "Can I have one of those too?"

Jeevan said, "It is a one-of-a-kind special order, but I can bring you a tropical juice mix that has a similar taste." The passenger accepted.

The flight landed in Seoul with a shorter layover to make up the rest of the time. They had about fifteen minutes to speak in a private lounge at Seoul's Incheon International Airport. The Korean officials there were gracious, accommodating, and unobtrusive. Jeevan advised Kate that Charlie would continue with her to Vancouver while he would return to South Africa.

Charlie Kagiso said, "Mrs. Roarty, my services with Anjay Gandhi's company will continue for you until we land on Vancouver. My wife and family will carry on to Baker Lake in Nunavut, where we'll live. I'll go to a job as head of security services for a gold mine a little further northeast from that little community. My wife and children should be safe there, and it is a good job for me." Kate smiled to herself, recalling Anjay's remark about polar bears, the midnight sun, and tundra flowers.

The ten-hour flight was indeed uneventful, except for the opportunity to meet and enjoy Charlie's family. She had forgotten how lovely it was to hold a sleeping baby and answer the questioning curiosity of a four-year-old. Charlie and his wife were grateful for the help from Kate, but in fact the pleasure was all Kate's. When they landed in Vancouver, Kate would've loved to head north to the village where her daughter was currently residing and spontaneously drop in for a short visit, but she needed to get home, and she wanted to see Jack. She sent him a text that said only, **Arriving tonight WJ841 9:40 p.m. connecting through Calgary. Miss you.**

Jack Johnson replied immediately. **I am on it. Giorgio sent your flight details. Be safe. LV Jack.**

17

Ottawa, Canada

Kate descended the elevator alongside the waterfall wall to the baggage area at Ottawa International Airport. Jack was waiting just back of the bottom of the landing. His tight grip on Big Ben could barely contain the wiggling enthusiasm of the Golden Retriever. In a moment she drew Jack into her arms; his grin was only temporarily interrupted by a warm and welcoming kiss. Then Kate was down to Big Ben's level, hugging him and ruffling the fur around his neck.

Jack said, "I am glad you are a dog, or I might be just a wee bit jealous."

Kate bounced up and grabbed the first bag off the carousel — hers — then a quick, "Let's go."

She wanted to just listen to Jack's voice. His beautiful manner of speaking English, enlivened with an enchanting, ever so slight Quebecois accent that charmed her whenever they were reunited after a long absence. Kate asked, "How is Madame Clare?"

"Ah, doing very well, but I nearly had to wrestle Big Ben away from her. He is such good company for her, particularly in the winter when the lake is quiet and neighbours can only be seen at a distance as their cars pass by, heading between fireplace and ski hill or trails. I think Madame Clare also feels Big Ben gives her a small sense of her son."

Kate's thoughts drifted back to the interment in the little cemetery near Meech Lake for Dr. Vincent Taylor, Clare's son, on a sunny autumn day a year and a half before. Kate had come across his body during an evening swim on the lake. So much had happened since then.

Within moments, they turned into the driveway of Kate's suburban home. Big Ben bounded out of the car and into the house almost before Kate could open the door.

A small tray of pâté, cheese, sliced baguette, and grapes sat out under a glass cover on the kitchen island.

"I didn't know if you would be hungry or not, so I thought just a little something, in case…" He trailed off. Kate encircled his tall, lean muscular body with her arms and reached up to give him a long, deep kiss that lingered until she needed to take a breath.

Jack pulled away and looked down at her with a playful smile. "Let's take Ben out for a run to dissipate some of his energy before we slip into activity that does not include him."

Kate laughed, and they threw on coats, pulled on boots, hats, and gloves then headed outside. The air was crisp and cold for a February evening. A lot of new snow had fallen while Kate was away, rendering the surroundings white, pristine, and inviting. The dog loped playfully through the snow, chasing invisible mice, voles, and squirrels.

Jack said, "Kate, it is the last night of Winterlude. Would you be feeling up to heading out for a skate? The temperature is forecasted to turn warm, and we may lose the ice shortly." Jack knew how much Kate loved skating on the Rideau Skateway, an exotic feature of Ottawa, the nation's capital, and the largest ice surface in the world that wound its way through the centre of the city on the canal built in the 1800s in preparation to ward off an American invasion. That battle was quickly dispatched, never having reached the capital.

The canal legacy had provided more than a century and a half of boating along a lush, green, and well-treed waterway that celebrated the downtown older central core of the city. Skating was introduced in the 1970s, bringing life to the winter corridor with an even greater vigour than could be found in the summer season. A sunny, cold day in February attracted several hundred thousand skaters onto the canal.

Kate was game, and off they headed. The long round trip provided an opportunity for them to catch up on one another's lives as they skated along. The little kiosks selling Beaver Tails, a deep-fried dough lathered with different fruity tastes and smothered in brown sugar, were all closed, but soft moonlight through the cloud cover gave them a muffled quiet surrounding to skate along. Their solitude was interrupted only by the sounds from crews out removing the snow and brushing the ice clean. A giant Zamboni spread a thin application of water that quickly froze. Their skate blades sliced into the fresh ice, leaving thin, curving lines on the smooth new surface. The return trip, a distance of 15.8 kilometres, took them well over an hour. As they retrieved their boots from under a bench on the side of the canal, Kate said, "Now I am starving."

"How about the Elgin Diner? We can walk over," said Jack.

The Elgin Diner served old-fashioned fare, including breakfast 24/7. They both ordered platters of steak, eggs, beans, home fries, toast, coffee, and a slice of orange. Before digging in, Kate remarked, "This must be ten thousand calories sitting in front of me."

"We'll burn it off," said Jack as he sliced into his poached eggs on toast. Hungry as bears, they both launched into the platters of food in front of them. Just as they came up for air, Jack's cellphone vibrated in his pocket. He retrieved it for a quick look. In one swift motion he wiped his mouth, leaned over to kiss Kate, and said, "I gotta go." And he was gone.

Kate sat digesting her food and Jack's quick departure.

In a moment, her own cellphone vibrated. The screen displayed a text message: **Take taxi home. Lv Jack.**

She called for a Blue Line taxi, noting it was nearly 2:00 a.m., then paid the restaurant bill while she waited for the car to arrive. It was a short drive home. She collapsed into bed with Big Ben at her side. She would have rather it was Jack but knew he must be called to a serious situation. She had glimpsed the message on his cell screen: *agent à terre* — officer down.

18

She awoke early with the strengthening winter sun streaming into her window-filled house. She rolled over to switch on her antique radio to catch the 7:00 a.m. news report and heard the newsreader saying, "The Sûreté du Québec are investigating a shooting in Gatineau where an officer was wounded and remains in critical condition. A raid on a bungalow on a quiet residential street near the edge of the Gatineau Park uncovered not only a basement full of illegal marijuana with a street value of around $850,000 but also a large weapons cache and a cocaine stash with an estimated street value exceeding $2 million. The owners of the property were working abroad and had rented the place out. They became suspicious about the tenants when neighbours that they knew well called them to express their concerns about activity at the house. The owners contacted the SQ, who investigated and quickly mounted a search of the house. The shooting of the officer occurred when two occupants of the house attempted to flee by firing their way out. Two armed suspects were taken into custody. It is believed that another accomplice remains at large."

Kate's heart skipped a beat. She staggered out of bed. *Jack?* Others she knew on the SQ?

She grabbed her cellphone to send a text to Jack, only to find that he had already sent her a message. **Daggy hurt bad. Marny advised — contact her when you get this Lv Jack.**

A chill passed through Kate. Her mind lurched back to a week in Boston a couple of years ago. She was there investigating the neuro-microchip case that killed Dr. Taylor. Jack had driven down to spend a weekend with her. Their relationship was new and tentative. Before the week was out, Jack had been shot, his truck had been blown up, and Giorgio had been attacked. Daggy was the go-to officer with the Boston police on the case who saw them through every turn of the way that week. They developed not only a close professional relationship but became good and lasting friends. Daggy secured a secondment to the Sûreté du Québec to spend a year with the Gatineau detachment. He brought his whole family. His daughters and wife, Marny, were having the time of their lives. Daggy had just applied to stay on another year. Kate texted Marny: **How's Daggy? Call me if you can? I am back.**

A call came in on her cell from Marny before she could get the coffee perking.

"Kate, thank God you are home. Daggy is in surgery. It's bad. I left the girls sleeping. Can you go over, get them up, and bring them to the hospital? They took Daggy to the Gatineau hospital then immediately transferred him to the Ottawa Heart Institute at the Civic Campus. Make sure the girls eat something and drink something before they get here. This is going to be hard for them. Kate, a bullet is lodged against Daggy's heart. There are two other bullets in his chest and shoulder — serious but not life-threatening. The flak jacket failed."

"Christ," was all Kate could say. "I'll get over to the house to pick up the girls as soon as I can." She glanced at her clock. Seven fifteen. Roxanne would be at the 3Sisters

Coffee Shop setting up for the day. She rang the number and quickly explained her urgency. Roxanne promised to have coffee, juice, and her famous breakfast sandwiches ready for four in ten minutes. She told Kate she could settle the bill later.

Kate threw Big Ben out the back door for a pee, flew upstairs for a two-minute shower, dressed, got the dog in, filled his dish with food, and said, "I gotta go boy, be good." A few minutes later she was in the car pulling out of her driveway. Rush hour was already underway. She gunned it, and within two minutes she was pulled over by the Ottawa police. When she explained the situation, the officer believed her and radioed for backup to set up a relay escort. She made it to the Daigle house in Gatineau in record time. The SQ took over the escort once she crossed the river. They knew exactly where they were going. There was already a cruiser in front of the house to keep the media at bay. The identity of the downed officer was not yet known. The duty officer opened the door, and Kate called the girls, who staggered out of their rooms saying, "What's going on?" When Kate told them what had happened to their dad, she watched two teenage girls grow up before her eyes. They dressed in a flash and were ready to go. Guy Archambault entered the foyer just as Kate and the girls were about to leave.

Guy was Jack Johnson's 2ic and a friend and a colleague of Officer Daigle. There were quick embraces all around then Guy said, "Kate, I can drive you three in your car to the hospital. It will be faster."

Kate said, "Okay," and tossed him the key fob.

The girls jumped in the back seat and buckled up. "Your mom says you have to eat before you get to the hospital." When it came to food, Marny's words prevailed.

The girls looked in the bags from 3Sisters and said, "Yum."

The younger of the two, Rosetta, said, "This is my first cup of coffee." Kate looked back and thought, *Ah, a good distraction — something new. Rosetta will always remember the day she had her first cup of coffee. Let's hope it will be a day she recalls with amusement about the coffee, not sadness about her dad.*

Then came, "Ew, you guys like this stuff?" Guy, although looking straight ahead and concentrating on his driving, was smiling.

Kate said, "It's an acquired taste. There is juice in the bag." Rosetta opened a bottle of blueberry juice and gulped it down.

Vitalia said, "My dad is going to be okay, right?"

Kate replied, "We hope so."

"Is my mom with him, I mean right with him?" said Vitalia.

"Your dad is in surgery. Your mom said three bullets hit him, but the one that is of greatest concern is one that is lodged against his heart."

Rosetta said, "I thought the flak jacket was supposed to protect his heart."

Guy replied, "We don't yet know why it didn't do the job, but we will find out."

The escort took them across the revitalized Chaudière Bridge. Two cruisers stopped the traffic to let them through. Kate's SUV sped ahead at smooth breakneck speed with Guy at the wheel winding through the trendy Riverside zone, cloaked in winter white and signs of the Winterlude festivities. They passed the waterfalls that tumbled through the ice on the Ottawa River, leaving Gatineau, Quebec behind and entering the nation's capital. The Ottawa police escort was already waiting at the War Museum, ready to take over to get them the final short distance to the hospital. Guy dropped them at the emergency entrance to the Ottawa Heart Institute.

"Kate, I will park your SUV in the garage and leave your key fobs at reception."

Kate nodded as she jumped out of her car — unaccustomed to sitting on the passenger's side, she was momentarily disoriented — then quickly cleared her confusion and led the girls to their mother's waiting arms.

Marny's first question was, "Did they eat?"

"Mom! Yes! How's Dad?"

Marny looked at Kate. "We don't know yet. He's still in surgery."

Kate handed Marny the one remaining breakfast bag from 3Sisters. "Ah, decent coffee, breakfast fixings, and a warm, buttered scone — you are after my heart, Kate."

"When Daggy is out of surgery and out of danger, I will show you the food and coffee concessions in the concourse that connect the wings of this hospital complex. None of the food fare is up to Marny Daigle's standard, but it will get you by. Oh Marny, I recall with so much appreciation the delicious meal you brought over to Jack and me the night before we left Boston after Jack had been shot. We enjoyed a wonderful evening together."

Marny managed a tired smile. "It was the beginning of our friendship, and now you brought my girls to me."

"Marny, have you spoken to Daggy's parents?"

"Not yet. I wanted to have the girls with me and Daggy out of surgery so I might have some definite information to give them. It was also the middle of the night. I feared a call in the middle of the night would have alarmed them even more."

"May I suggest that you don't wait any longer? The media goes into a frenzy when a cop is shot. Jack will have already called his Boston police counterpart. Protocol may require it."

"You're right, let me down this coffee and eat a bit. I need fortification to make this call. I think I'll call Daggy's middle brother. He's a real rock and will know how to speak to their parents and the rest of the family."

Kate looked at Marny with quiet admiration. Her life partner, her soul mate, the father of her children, was fighting for his life. Her inner emotions must have been in turmoil, yet she was able to consider the feelings of the girls and their extended family.

Kate was not a religious person, but this was one of the few occasions when she felt compelled to reach out to a spiritual concept, to draw on a force stronger than her own to help get Daggy through this crisis.

The Haudenosaunee orenda came into her thoughts. She was not well acquainted with the ancient practice of summoning the power of the dream, but it came to her with a pull so intense that she felt she must follow it through.

"Kate," she heard her name being spoken. "Are you okay? You seemed to have drifted off to another world."

Kate shook her head to regain a connection with her surroundings. "Oh, I am sorry, Marny, it must be jet lag. I flew in late last night from a marathon flying journey that began in Cape Town, South Africa three days ago. Apart from changing planes several times there were no layovers. The time difference is six hours. I think I just zoned out for a moment. What can I do to help?"

"Kate, forgive me for imposing on you, but without family and a network of close friends…"

"Marny, I am here for you. What can I do?"

"Can I give you a list of things to get from the house? The girls will want to stay close to their dad until he is out of danger. Who knows how long we will be camped out here."

"Of course. Just put it together, and I'll be off to fetch whatever you need."

"Okay, I'll compile a message that you can scroll through as you locate items in the house." It took Marny about ten minutes to put it together. It was a good distraction for her. Kate asked the girls if there was anything they wanted from home that their mom might not think to put on the list she was compiling.

Vitalia said, "I will send you a list for both of us. Rather than bother Mom, can you cross-reference it?"

"Sure — no problem."

A short time later, Kate gave all three of them big hugs, assuring them everything would be okay — she wanted to believe that too — and she was back in her SUV heading over to Gatineau.

A vague plan was forming in her mind that she might be able to act on *en route* to Daggy and Marny's house. She eased down congested Parkdale Avenue and got onto the Ottawa River Parkway, a peaceful drive even at the worst of times. She swung north onto the Portage Bridge then quickly exited, driving down under the bridge then onto Victoria Island, where she parked. This island was part of the Odawa ancestral lands — in fact, most of the city of Ottawa was sitting on Odawa Treaty territory, the original occupants of the valley before Europeans arrived four hundred years ago. There was often a native encampment at the site, with elders on hand to assist visitors — both native and non-native — through issues they were addressing.

It was a hunch, but it was worth checking out. Kate wanted to act on her orenda notion, and here she might find help to guide her through a dream quest. There were a few vehicles in the parking lot, and a smudge was coming up from inside the wall of the encampment. She noticed a small sign next to a door that simply said, *Enter*. Kate hesitated, distracted, then enchanted by the crash and tumble of the Chaudière Falls, also known as Asticou, meaning "meeting place" in the Algonkian language of the Odawa, she passed through the make shift doorway, where she saw several young adult natives gathered around a small fire, chatting quietly. She felt awkward, as though she was intruding. Nobody paid any attention to her. Uncertain about what to do, she did nothing.

An elderly woman emerged from a small shelter along a wall carrying several mugs of what appeared to be hot, steaming tea. Kate suddenly realized it was cold out — and she was cold, despite wearing a warm parka, toque, boots, and mitts. She moved toward the fire, and room was made for her to get close and feel its warmth. The elderly woman reappeared and placed a cup of hot tea in her hand. Nobody spoke, so Kate simply nodded in appreciation and took a sip, almost scalding her tongue.

The silence continued, and Kate felt herself growing comfortable with it. She was not sure how long she remained in that circle around the campfire sipping hot tea. She nurtured her thoughts of Daggy, and a plethora of moments invaded her mind like vignettes illuminating their relationship — when they met, shared happiness and tension, the gathering friendship, experiencing his family, the images of him struggling for his life on the operating table. She imagined the bullets that invaded his body. She saw them lifting up, spinning out, and disappearing, away from his body. Kate stood up; she needed to find power and strength to infuse Daggy's spirit with life. She left the fire and went out through the door into the bright, cold, crisp February air.

She made her way over to the Chaudière Falls, where the mist it gave off chilled her quickly, until she was cold again. She pressed on, getting as close as the deep snow and undefined ice-crusted shoreline allowed. Kate slipped into a meditation, standing facing the falls, drawing strength from its volume, its continuous flow, its muffled roar as it snarled and growled its way from rapids to open water flowing out under the ice and away. She focused on Daggy, shutting out everything but the strength of the waterfalls and an image of her friend smiling, walking toward her. She felt the essence of the dream drawing her in and toward Daggy. She needed her soul to reach his spirit that was slipping into the other world and draw it back, unite it with his human soul, with her passion that was there, reaching out to him to come back and stay.

The image of Daggy stopped. Kate, not knowing it, had dropped to her knees as her strength to draw him closer was weakening and dissipating. Then, Daggy smiled — a very lively, broad smile. He nodded and was gone. It was over. Kate was sweating, exhausted, spent. She wanted to curl up in the snow and sleep. She closed her eyes for a few moments when the old woman came and spoke: "Get up and go now." And Kate did. She walked slowly to the parking lot deep in thought, disconnected from her physical movement. Had the little of what remained of the traces of that long-ago Haudenosaunee ancestry come to her today for the first time in the form of an orenda?

Kate climbed up into her SUV and turned it on to warm up but still sat, tired, spent, and contemplating this experience. As quickly as the orenda dissipated, the answer came to her. It had always been there. This was simply the first time she connected with it.

19

Kate drove on to Daggy and Marny's house. An SQ officer was still stationed outside. Fortunately, he recognized Kate, but nevertheless he accompanied her into the house, taking careful notes of every item she retrieved, and in some cases, he took photographs of the more valuable or personal items. She gathered everything Marny and the girls requested and in a short time headed back to the hospital.

Kate realized how dead tired she was — despite many long naps during the series of flights from South Africa, the intensity of the time spent there, the long, exhausting journey home, then in less than a day all that had happened — she had to be there for Marny and the girls and she had to sleep. She hit her neighbour's number on the car speakerphone. Fortunately, Émile answered. "*Oui, allô, Katie, ça va?*"

Kate chatted with her dear aging neighbour for a bit then signed off, having solicited his gracious services to walk Big Ben and keep him at his place until she got home. She adored Émile. He was very tall for a French Canadian — there must have been some Norwegian genes shuffling around in there. He had never married but enjoyed an admiring female following, and Kate numbered among those admirers. He approved of Jack and told her so frequently, in a "strike while the iron is hot" fashion. He told Jack the same thing. They often enticed him over for dinner and Sunday brunch and occasionally took him up to the lake in the summer; he and Clare hit it off. He always brought along his toolbox and fixed any items requiring attention around Clare's house. Big Ben delighted in assembling his entire family at the lake. When Kate considered the endearing characteristics of the dog and the man, she concluded the only thing that separated them was their different species — their temperaments were quite similar. She lurched herself out of this reverie as she pulled back into the hospital parking garage, pleased to find that her ticket for the day gave her in/out privileges.

She located Marny and the girls, who were taking turns sitting with Daggy while he slept in recovery. Vitalia told Kate that the surgeons had successfully removed all of the bullets. They got the one lodged next to his heart by gently suctioning it up into an air tube that cradled it without any hard-surface contact in case it was unexploded. Vitalia thought this was cool.

"You know, Kate, Boston is something of a medical mecca. I was thinking I should consider studying medicine — maybe heart surgery."

Kate nodded. "That could be a very worthwhile profession for you, Vitalia. It is a long haul and very intense but exceptionally rewarding in the end — although the studies are rigorous, many of the surgical disciplines offer lots of opportunity for innovation."

"I could go and work in war zones."

Kate said, "Wow there, girl, not the best plan to mention to your parents today. Take it a step at a time with them, especially at the moment. In the meantime, here is your tablet — check out the options online while you are waiting your turn to rotate in for a session with your dad. If he is in a really deep sleep, you could tell him all about your plan."

"What plan?" said Marny as she walked toward them. Rosetta leapt up and scooted off to take her mom's place sitting with her dad.

Kate rose and hugged Marny then handed her the bag of stuff that she had collected from home.

"Vitalia filled me in on the outcome of the surgery. Are you hopeful for a good recovery?"

"Yes, it may be a long haul, but I think we'll get our Daggy back. Jack called to say they caught the guy who shot him. Jack's coming over to the hospital a little later on."

Marny collapsed into a seat, drained from the emotional tension of these past hours. "I thought this would be a year when I wouldn't fear that one day Daggy might not come home. Canadian society is so much less violent than America, yet this happened — maybe being a cop isn't safe anywhere." She dropped her face into her hands, allowing Kate to rub her shoulders and back.

"Once Daggy's completely out of danger they'll move him into a private room over at the Civic Campus, where we can all be with him. They said they'd put a cot in the room as well if I want to sleep there. For now, the post-surgery monitoring can be done more effectively in intensive care."

Kate's cellphone vibrated with an incoming text message. She looked at it. **Where are you? Safe? Call me.** There was no ID, but she knew it was Bryant. She replied simply. **Safe, home, will call shortly.**

She looked up to see two of her most favourite men in the universe striding toward her: Jack and Guy. Despite it all, they flashed broad smiles for Kate as they approached, which fell immediately when they saw Marny's face in her hands. Kate leapt up and went to them.

"Don't worry, the surgery went well. Marny's just emotionally exhausted and resting a weary mind and soul. Rosetta's in with her dad. They are rotating, so one of them is with him all of the time. He still requires intensive care, but it sounds like there's a good chance he'll fully recover."

"Hey, old gal, can I give you a hug? I've hardly seen you since you got home. The past eighteen hours feel like the same number in days. I gather you've had a week like that as well," Jack said as they embraced.

"Me too," Guy chimed in.

"Hey, me too, please?" came a tired but trifling voice from Marny.

"That's my woman!" Jack reached down and scooped her off her feet in an enveloping hug while Guy scooped up Vitalia.

"Hugs all around!" said Guy.

"Eh, *mon oncle* Guy," said Vitalia.

"Spoken like a true Canadienne."

"Your turn, Vitalia," said Rosetta, emerging into the love-fest.

"I want a hug from uncle Guy too." Guy swung Vitalia around in an endearing embrace.

"Vitalia, can Guy and I go in to see your dad for a minute?" asked Jack.

"Sure, but they only allow one person at a time."

"Ah, Superintendent Johnson and Officer Archambault — it is good to see you. Mrs. Daigle will you join us for a few minutes," said Dr. Desjeunes.

Vitalia said, "I'm going in with Dad until you guys are ready."

Dr. Sylvie Desjeunes led them to an empty office, closed the door, and brought up the surgery images on a large screen. She explained everything about Daggy's condition and the surgery. She also expressed her concern about the flak jacket's failure to stop the bullets.

When they emerged from the meeting with the surgeon, they found Kate curled up asleep on the two-seat sofa chair in the waiting area.

Guy said, "I think your girl is wiped."

Jack feigned a punch at Guy. "I'll drive her home in her SUV. I want to follow up as quickly as possible on the flak jackets. Can you send me the manufacturer's info? Take one of the flak jackets of the same model and empty a clip into it then take photos of the results."

Guy nodded. "*Bien sûr.*"

"Let's see Daggy for a moment, then go."

"Marny, now that we have the perpetrators in custody, I think Daggy is safe, but I would like to leave Officer Dhaliwal to assist with anything, including keeping the media away from him and you three until Daggy is truly out of danger. We'll come up with another plan later on."

"Thanks, Jack — now take that tired P.I. home to sleep."

20

Kate awoke in a daze, not realizing that she had slept for fifteen hours nonstop. She was alone. No Jack, no dog, no cat, no phones, no light, but she was at home. Her fuzzy brain surmised that much, but she had no idea how she got there.

She heard the main door open, dog paws scurry across the ceramic tile floor, and Jack saying, "Slow down, boy, let's get you brushed off." The next thing Kate knew was a snowy Golden Retriever shaking on the bed, spraying her with a shower of fresh, clean, cold snow, then lapping kisses all over her face. Kate, laughing, got him in a wrestling hold when Jack came in the bedroom, likewise covered in a dusting of newly fallen snow.

"Sorry, he beat me to the punch." He looked at them both jostling on the bed. "Can I make it a *ménage à trois*?"

"If you can find the space, hop on. I think Ben grew while I was away."

"Naw, his coat has just fluffed up in response to the cold weather." Jack gave Kate a quick kiss. "Glad to see you have returned to the land of the living."

Kate rolled onto her side, smiled at Jack, and said, "It's good to see you, Jack. Dare I ask how I ever got home?"

"Prince Charming gathered his sleeping beauty in his arms, mounted his fastest steed, and galloped through the winter snow."

Kate hit him playfully with a pillow. "Oh, stop it."

"Seriously, that isn't far from the truth. You crashed while we were talking with Daggy's surgeon. I gathered you up, carried you to your SUV, and drove you home — fifteen hours ago."

Kate propped herself up on one arm. "I can't recall ever sleeping that long in my entire life."

"Well, that was a harrowing week you put in in Cape Town. Giorgio and I had a little chat. He gave me the Coles Notes version — exploding boats, helicopter rescue, street chase, murder, and a private jet getaway. Kate, you put James Bond to shame, and he never went off after intellectual property rights. I gather Canada's population has increased by four with your return journey."

"That's none of my doing. It's all Uncle Anjay."

"Oh, and you acquired an uncle on this trip, as well?"

"Anyway, enough about me, I'm rested and ready to go."

"Who or what is *trainonthetrack2030*? I got a text message that said only, **Kate OK?** Then it disappeared."

"He's one of my cyber geeks. He has my back — all the time."

"Should I be jealous?"

Kate smiled. "He lives in a different world. We have never met and are not likely to, although I feel a deep affection for him. He works all night; he's brilliant at what he does; he's incapable of telling a lie; he's dedicated, devoted, and hyper focused. I'm so fortunate to have him in my camp. He found me when I was working in Ghana. We have been attached ever since. I have no idea where he lives, what nationality he is — I know he likes pizza and spends his money on software and hardware. He always delivers. I send money to him electronically. I pay him very well, and he deserves it. He was key in breaking the Taylor case."

Jack nodded mischievously. "I'm jealous."

"You have benefitted from his expertise, and as long as you remain attached to me, you are part of the service package."

"Devastatingly jealous," Jack said playfully. "Can I sauté all that emotion into a mushroom and green pepper omelette seasoned with fresh chives and prosciutto?"

"As long as it's preceded by lots of fresh coffee."

"Coming up, madam of the deep sea adventure."

Kate lay back against the pillow, willing herself out of bed. Suddenly a heavy pressure pushed against her oesophagus, accompanied by a loud, throbbing growl. She reached her hands up and around the dead weight. "Hello, Boris, have you been neglected?" she said as she scratched under the feline's chin and down his spine — an affectionate interchange that mistress and feline had enjoyed for years. At thirteen, Boris cat was still purring strong. He moved next door with Émile when she went away. It was not a formal arrangement made between neighbours; rather, Boris had instituted it without discussion or negotiation. All parties just accepted it as so.

She looked up to see Jack standing there holding two steaming cups of coffee. "Upstaged by another man." He feigned a crushed and dejected expression. "Will the competition ever let a shot on goal? I feel like I'm sitting out the game in the penalty box while Big Ben, computer geek, and Boris cat, not to mention Uncle Anjay, Giorgio, and neighbour Émile all get to play with Kate the Great."

"Stop it — you're always number one. I save the best for last," she said, looking over the top of her coffee cup. "Ummm, this is delicious."

"Good, I just picked up a package from 3Sisters when we were out for a walk. I thought it might be too bitter for your taste, but it does seem smooth, doesn't it?"

"Yes, especially with the dollop of maple syrup. Can we stop the world for a day?"

"I wish, but it just keeps spinning. I've got enough time to prepare that omelette, eat breakfast with you, and then I must head out. I think you have a date with monsieur computer geek. *N'est-ce pas?*"

They lingered over a savoured kiss, then Jack turned and bounded downstairs with Big Ben in hot pursuit and Boris cat weaving through their legs.

21

As soon as Jack left, Kate called Bryant.

He picked up after the first ring. "To quote the caller, Jesus, Mary, Joseph, Kate, tell me this is you in full embodiment."

"Just Kate, my man."

"What the Christ, where've you been? My image has been crumbling before my very eyes. I experienced caring, worrying, dread, fear, all of those feelings that never invade my world."

"You keep that up and the next thing you'll tell me is that you are eating salads and going outside for walks in fresh air and sunshine."

"Wow, lady, let's not get that extreme. Although I'll admit, I bought a treadmill. I walk almost all the time now. It's set up with a five large-screen surround — the latest surveillance toys. I had to do something with that massive follow-up payment you sent me from the Taylor case. I know we've never met and probably never will, but a year ago, I weighed three hundred and fifty pounds and could barely crawl out of my man cave. I now weigh two hundred and twenty pounds and treadmill it in my sixty-storey penthouse. Top of the building is better for reception, and a nagging back pain went away — completely. The blackout curtains cost a fortune, though."

Kate laughed. "You give me much more detail and I might even figure out where you live. Bryant. I am so sorry that I have been out of touch — getting out of South Africa was harrowing, then as soon as I arrived home, a friend of mine was shot. Totally unrelated—"

"When I didn't hear from you I scanned all of the news wires until I put your South Africa exit together and then your Ottawa-Gatineau entry. How is your Boston buddy, Daggy, doing?"

"I think he'll pull through and make a full recovery. On that note, can you do something for me?"

"Absolutely, m'lady — just say the word."

"Daggy was wearing his flak jacket when he was shot. Three bullets penetrated it. I suspect the manufacturing process was compromised or the specs were corrupted. The SQ received a new shipment a few months ago. Of course, nobody would suspect a problem until the jackets failed to perform."

"Send me all of the details on the manufacturer, specs, supplier, etc., that you can and I will put the trail together to see if there were any compromises. But you know, Kate, it is possible that the firepower used simply exceeded the capability of the bulletproof vest to withstand it. With increasing frequency, the citizenry has higher firepower than the law enforcement capability — especially with the frontline police officers. The tactical units are usually sufficiently well equipped, but they get called in after the bloodshed begins."

"Thanks, Bryant."

"Now, getting back to your South African adventure, Kate, do you know that both you and Charlie Kagiso are considered suspects in the killing of Robert Beltman?"

"Oh my, no, I didn't know that."

"I think in Canada it is called persons of interest. They seem to have taken issue with your rather quick and dramatic departure."

"It was facilitated by Cape Town's special services unit."

"It appears that Anjay Gandhi is volleying it behind the scenes, but you might want to stay put until it mellows out so you don't run the risk of being detained at some airport somewhere."

"I'll have to head to London soon. MI6 should have my back on that travel."

"The Canadian intelligence services may not be so helpful. My rummaging about has ferreted out some noses out of joint among the fleet-of-foot by a home-grown female loan warrior. Some rapid climbers are scurrying up through the ranks. They were too junior two years ago to be in the loop on your act of brilliance then. Now they only want to hear about their own smarts."

"Have you come across a Denis Colbert, Director of Echelon Liaison?" asked Kate.

"Yes, he's okay — diverse, well trained, good mix of field and HQ work, slow, steady ascent to director. He inherited a band of little shits that continue to work for him until he can reassign most of them as he builds up his own trusted network. It'll take time — he can't ship them all off to Afghanistan or the Port of Montreal. You will need to carefully navigate around them. They could make life hellish for you."

"Okay, my favourite cyber geek. It is trace processing and flak jackets."

"Kate, and watching your back. You leave it exposed all too often."

Kate pressed the "end call" display pondering Bryant's last remark. He was right, but she remained undeterred. She snapped the leash on Big Ben, sprinted around the block with him, tossed a few balls, then knocked on Émile's door. "Can he spend the day with you?"

"*Bien sûr* — Boris is already here."

"I am off swimming, then to meet clients, and after that it is over to the hospital. I have no idea when I will be back," said Kate.

"I'll send the boys home after the game is over. The Senators are playing Montreal tonight. I am really trying to shift my allegiance, but les Canadiens have been in my heart for more than six decades — old habits die hard."

"The Canadiens are much more likely to make the playoffs. You can cheer for the underdogs until they are knocked out then go on to celebrate the Canadiens, who will undoubtedly take the Eastern Conference."

22

Kate unceremoniously plunged into the fast lane that lay calm and vacant, a rare occurrence at her favourite city-run swimming pool. It had been a full week since she last swam, and the water somehow knew it. The empty lane gave her the opportunity to churn through a couple of kilometres without curtailing her strokes or remaining vigilant to navigate around other swimmers using varying speeds and strokes.

She looked up to check for other swimmers entering the fast lane, but none materialized. She flipped onto her back and pulled through twenty lengths, stretching out her spine and hips. Her mind had drifted to her client, Daniel Osu. She felt an intense anger well up in her — an emotion she rarely felt while swimming. Swimming was usually her modulator that restored her equilibrium. This time it gave focus. She had to pursue her hunches regarding this man and the pursuit of his intellectual property rights with his partners. She was feeling more and more certain that he had not told her the whole story. The resolve she experienced was strong — she was going to get it out of him before the day was out. After what she had experienced during this past week, she felt prepared to take whatever measure was required to drag the whole story out of him.

Before jumping into the pool, Kate sent a text message to Daniel to meet her for a late lunch at the Foolish Chicken. She had to eat, and they both liked the place since experiencing it for the first time when they met nearly a month before. This time she determined he was paying the whole tab, and his fees were going up.

Kate was running a bit late, rather hungry and more than a bit angry — not a good combination. Daniel arrived just ahead of her but did not see her approaching on the sidewalk behind him. In an instant, she was on him. She grabbed his shoulders, spun him around, and slammed him into the wall of the adjacent building, bracing her forearm against his carotid artery and jugular vein. His eyes were wild with fear and surprise.

"You are going to tell me the whole story, the trace minerals applications, everything. Your fees just doubled, and you are buying lunch. You bolt and I give it all away. Is that clear?" Daniel gazed at Kate, unable to move.

"Close your eyes to signal agreement." He did — she silently counted to five then released her hold on him. He doubled over, coughing, sputtering, tears pouring out of his eyes, and fell to his knees. His gasping for breath mixed with the ice crystals of the cold winter air created a halo of frost enveloping his head. She watched the fog of his panting dissipate and knew he was going to be okay. She hadn't taken her momentary fury too far.

"Get up before you create a scene."

He looked at Kate with incredulity creasing his expression and followed her into the restaurant. Kate ordered two glasses of water at the bar before leading him to the second floor, where it was deserted and quiet but open for business. The waiter brought the water with the menus, and Daniel clutched at the glass, downing most of it before speaking. "What the hell!"

"Precisely. Now talk. You can have my glass, too, if you need more water."

He slipped out of his scarf and coat, sweating from the tussle. He used the scarf to wipe his face and neck. "It's the first time I have sweated on a frigid winter day in this country. I'm going to the washroom. I'll be back in a minute."

The waiter returned, and Kate placed orders for both of them, including more water and two glasses of beer. The waiter, who was also the owner, asked, "Your friend okay?"

"He will be after he drinks, eats, and talks. Thanks for asking."

Daniel returned shortly, looking calmed, composed, and centred — a quick rebound, Kate observed.

"Daniel, we are not moving from here until you tell every single bit of the sordid tale." He finished his glass of water and downed half of Kate's glass then wiped his still-damp brow with the napkin on the table. The waiter placed the beers in front of them and slid away. Daniel took a gulp of his beer then began to speak.

"I didn't imagine you as a violent person."

"It's an arsenal I rarely call upon, Daniel, but after what I experienced in South Africa during my investigation on this case, it'll remain at the ready until this job is done. If you're straight, honest, and forthcoming with me, you'll have no reason to be on the receiving end of it again. Now, let's have the whole story, or pay your bill in full and we'll call it a day."

"Okay. I have to hang in with you, so here goes. I told you the whole story on the development of the application to retrieve the minutest traces left behind from gold mining. The process proved effective at working already reworked tailings. The small remediation companies were making millions recovering trace gold from reworked mine dumps. Several elements of the business plan collided. We were in the process of securing additional financing to continue the research, development, and design of new prototypes to test on the refined secondary trace tailings when we discovered the applicability in extracting trace deposits from the tailings of rare earth minerals. It also prevents most of the leaching from original mining processes. These applications are in even greater demand, with a much heftier price tag on them. Suddenly, instead of going cap in hand looking for financing, financiers were coming out of the woodwork to court us. We were overwhelmed and got a bit caught up in the greed."

Kate nodded, saying only, "Continue."

"When we realized that dealing with the financing process was becoming a full-time job and we were out of our depth, we took on board a venture capital expert out of Boston to manage the day-to-day accounting, bookkeeping, and financing mechanics, among the growing number of partners that brought money to the table. We made the hire quickly — way too quickly."

"Did you vet him?"

"Her, not carefully enough. We checked her out with those in the field that we already knew, not appreciating she could be a plant from that network. She has been operating in North America for a few years, and her previous clients and employers had good things to say about her. She did all of her schooling in Poland and launched her career there. Our lack of familiarity with the institutions, researchers, and the language difference dissuaded us from making a more than a cursory check — a big mistake. We were so relieved to be able to resume our scientific research and leave the financial management to her that we gave her a free hand from the onset."

"Have you gotten rid of her?"

"No. We thought we had problems before I sought you out. They pale in comparison to what we are dealing with now. We are not even sure if we still own the companies in the consortium."

He went on to describe to Kate the growing complexities of the financing, partnerships, infighting among the various players, attempts to influence the course of their R&D, and the introduction of other scientists lacking proven track records in their field. Scientists and financiers not only from Boston but Europe, South Africa, China, Russia, Eastern Europe, and Kazakhstan had visited them.

Kate listened attentively without interruption until he finished then said, "Daniel, this is sounding more and more like commercial espionage taken to an extreme."

"Kate, we have screwed up. I am sorry for that — I can't believe that we tried to manipulate the very person that committed to helping get this mess sorted out. You are fully entitled to every measure you are taking now. Can we start again?"

Kate studied him, cautious not to respond too quickly.

"Listen, Kate, the guys are waiting at the Starbucks up on the corner. Yeah, they feared this meeting might go very badly, although none of us anticipated the level of your fury. Can I call them down to join us?"

Kate paused for a long while, listening to the argument going on in her head. It boiled down to cut and run, life is too short for this crap, or finish what she started, make it right, and bring down the culprits. She reminded herself why she went out on her own. It gave her the luxury to make the decision she was about to make. She had watched corruption slip pass unchecked for too long — petty and grandiose, it was all the same. She couldn't stop them all, but she could rein in this one.

"Okay," she replied.

The expression of gloom on Daniel's face slipped away, replaced by a frown of tentative optimism. He punched in a speed dial number and said only, "Kate's giving us another chance — get down here."

"We had better get the menus back."

Kate ordered a tray of hot apple cider, a tonic to restore blood sugar and inner warmth on this cold midwinter day. Her cellphone vibrated with an incoming text from Marny: **Daggy is awake and alert.**

Kate exhaled in relief, and Daniel looked at her enquiringly. "Oh, it is totally unrelated. A friend of mine was seriously injured — it appears he is recovering." Daniel nodded as his two colleagues emerged into the empty second floor of the restaurant.

The waiter was on their heels with menus and four glasses of hot cider.

Kate thanked the waiter and said, "Guys, if you are hungry, make a food selection while the waiter is still here." They looked a bit confused. Daniel picked up the menu and ordered for them. The waiter/owner said, "Feel free to stay up here as long as you want. You won't likely be disturbed — many of the customers don't even know the restaurant has an upstairs. I'll bring the food when it is ready."

Kate said, "Thanks," then turned to Daniel and said, "A hefty tip will be in order when you pay the bill." The other two guys looked at Daniel but said nothing.

Kate began, "I gather your Polish venture capitalist has turned out to be a badass."

All three of them nodded.

"Send me a good-quality digital photo and we will check her out through facial recognition software. She probably has a string of aliases, so whatever you may have signed with her will not likely have any legal authority. We can sort her out. Guys, you have had some scary experiences, several of which you brought on yourselves." All three of them nodded sheepishly. "Your behaviour is costing you big-time. We can still recover this mess — however, any more shenanigans in any way from any of you, and I'll do two things. First, I'll become your worst nightmare — *un cauchemar* — beyond conceivable proportions, then I'll leave you in a heap. You'll not regain the intellectual property rights to the processes you developed, nor will you recoup your business entity. I'll walk away, cash your payment, and go read a book by a lake in delightful tranquillity."

"Kate, that's not what we want."

"Okay then, let's get to it. You continue doing what you do well — your research and development. I will keep you apprised, in person when I'm here and over the phone when I'm elsewhere, chasing down elements of the investigation. I'll need you to respond swiftly, precisely, and collaboratively as we move in on restoring your IPR to your company. You will keep me fully informed of any developments you encounter that could detract from our objective."

They all nodded in agreement.

Daniel said, "That is what we want, too, but we don't feel safe working in our lab. We don't feel safe going home. In fact, we don't feel safe going anywhere to do anything."

Kate said, "I have a contact at MIT who had a similar experience a couple of years ago. I'll put you in touch. He can advise on you the measures you need to take to secure your working environment and protect your IPR. His name is Dr. Lech Bogdan. He is a research scientist, although his area of specialization is maladies of the brain. Speak with him — follow his advice. In short order, you'll learn how to establish a safe, secure working environment. I'll let him know to expect to hear from you."

Daniel solicited the others by quiet eye contact then replied, "Okay."

The young men tucked into their meals, exhibiting a hunger typical of their youthful response to stress and reaction to a cold day. The cider relaxed them. They became animated, contributing enthusiastically during a short planning session that followed to outline the next steps and devise an agreed plan. Kate said little as they spoke, enabling them to take ownership of the plan. When it appeared an agreement had been reached, she rose and said, "I gotta go."

She felt good walking off and leaving the triumvirate not only with the lunch bill but also with a sense of disaster averted. It was a risk on her part but one she felt willing to take. She sent a cell photo of the *echeque* to her bank to deposit the handsome fee she collected from them. A twinge of guilt washed over her as the *echeque* deposit to her account was confirmed, along with a new account balance that ensured all of her expenses thus far would be met. She contemplated making the final payment on her mortgage, leaving a bit left over to proceed with planning that Zen-like garden she had been imagining where the tranquillity of her summertime meditation could take place.

23

Kate stopped at a savoury food shop, Thyme & Again, to pick up a healthy lunch for Marny and the girls. She waited for the order of sandwiches that included Calabrese, with all of the ingredients Marny would love: provolone, sopressata, capicola, spicy eggplant, and tomato, and a local artisan grilled cheese that would address Rosetta's cheese passion with a selection of the best, along with eggplant and tomato. She opted for a grilled veggie wrap with humus for Vitalia then got the chef to slice all of the sandwiches three ways in case they wished to sample each choice. She decided to take away a large container of the soup of the day that had been featured as a fundraiser for the local food bank. Kate was thinking as she watched the sous chef ladling the caramelized onion, mushroom, and bacon soup into the container that it had been ages since she made a meal. She loved to cook and needed to take the time to do it. She pulled out her cell and sent a text to Jack: **Dinner tonight chez moi.** An instant reply came back: **Bien sûr ma chère.**

Care package in hand, Kate walked briskly to where she had stashed her SUV on a side street. She clicked the "on" button on the fob of her SUV. The vehicle pulled to life while the defroster cleared the windows. She contemplated the instant comfort of a driverless car to replace her old SUV. Their numbers had increased to nearly half of personal driving vehicles but had proven inadequate to the challenge of winter driving conditions. The tires crunched over the ice and hard-packed snow as she wheeled out onto Wellington Street to make her way over to the Heart Institute to see Marny and the girls, where they were keeping vigil with Daggy.

Big bear hugs all around signalled the warmth of their greeting when Kate located Marny and the girls. Daggy had just been moved into a private room. The three of them were in the waiting area as the nurses and technicians ensured all of the equipment was hooked up properly and functioning. Marny was chomping at the bit to make it feel homey for Daggy and welcoming for Daggy's guests. Kate handed them the soup and sandwiches. A muffled squeal indicated approval as the girls unwrapped all three selections. Marny pried the lid of the soup container and said, "Oh, Kate, this is lovely. I may be able to feed it to Daggy."

Within a few moments a nurse walked over and said, "All set, he's asking for you. Careful not to wear him out — he needs rest."

Marny replied, "Thank you."

The girls couldn't contain their exuberance as they tumbled into their dad's room.

"Does this mean he is out of danger, Marny?"

"I hope so, but his recovery is going to take a while. One of the bullets went right through his lung. He may need more surgery to repair it. Let's go in so you can say hi."

Kate entered, smiled at Daggy, and crossed the room in one stride to gingerly embrace him. "Hey, all my girls are here — even the belligerent *Canadienne*." He raised his hands in mock defense "Ah, you cannot strike an injured man."

"Well, it looks like Scrabble and reality TV for your adventures while we are out bushwhacking the spring ski trails."

"Kate, did Jack tell you the flak jackets didn't stop the bullets?"

"Yeah, they are checking them out."

"I have a feeling we are going to find that most of our police forces are inadequately equipped against the high-powered firearms in the civilian population."

"I think you are right, Daggy, but you are safe here — let your mind rest too."

"How can I rest surrounded by all of these beautiful women?"

Rosetta picked up a stray pillow when a nurse who had slipped quickly into the doorway said, "No pillow fights ten minutes after moving him out of intensive care. Your bed there has been taken. We can't move you back."

They all laughed as the nurse plucked the pillow from Rosetta's hands.

"Kate, I understand your life hasn't exactly been a cesspool of mundane banality."

Kate laughed again. "You're right, Daggy, but that chat is for another day. I am going to leave you to your indulging brood and respond to a summons from CSEC."

"Oh dear, will we be vacationing in Cuba so we can visit you in Guantanamo?"

Kate smiled and waved her hand behind her as she left the hotel room.

She called Jack while she waited for the car to warm up a bit before heading back out into the frosty late afternoon.

He answered on the first ring. "*Bonjour, ma chère.* So what's for dinner?"

Kate had already forgotten about the invitation she had extended, so she replied, "Something good for a cold winter night."

"I can think of one especially good item for that menu," said Jack.

She smiled. "I'll probably ask Émile over — he has Big Ben and Boris. I think he would welcome a good meal and the company." Before he could reply, Kate said, "Jack, I am on my way over to see Denis Colbert, Director of Echelon Liaison at CSEC."

"Shall I send out a search party if you don't emerge after two hours?"

"Give it until dinnertime."

"No way, you have an important job, to get a meal on the table, Madame Roarty. I am not letting any intelligence service interfere with that."

She laughed. "Okay, they probably have that message by now, so I think we are safe. See you soon."

Kate then called Denis Colbert, who answered directly, "Mrs. Roarty, at last. Are we about to have the honour of a visit from you?"

"If it can work for you now, I'm on my way."

"I'll let the front gate know so they can show you where to park."

She pulled up to the front gate of CSEC — Communications Security Establishment Canada — accessed off Ogilvie Road directly opposite one of her favourite high-tech cinemas. The CSEC edifice stretched across a sprawling terrain in a sweeping mass of glass and concrete, both admirable in its ultramodern design and intimidating as it imposed itself across the landscape. The architecture was expressed in the literal and symbolic shape of a maple key reaching up only five stories and interconnected with smaller outlying buildings sitting like seed pods awaiting germination. Kate had never been in the place. She felt the same rush of anticipation she experienced before entering the British counterparts for the first time two years previously: MI5, MI6, and the GCHQ, where the buildings were known as Thames House, the Labyrinth, and the Donut.

While the direct equivalent to this place in the UK was GCHQ in Cheltenham, at times Canadians referred to CSEC as "Camelot," although after fifteen years it eluded the same level of endearment. Kate contemplated this feat of creativity. Perhaps she could come up with a name for it, but in the meantime, as she looked upon it while waiting on the guard's instructions, she decided to think of it as "The Glass House." The guard was slow in returning, allowing her mind to wander back to her daughter when as a toddler acquired an imaginary friend, John Elf, during a move from Beijing to Seattle. John Elf lived in a glass house; he could see everything outside, and the outside world could see everything in his house. It was not exactly a comparable description of the respective functions of these two edifices — one real and one imagined, but Kate liked to let her imagination wander into the creative on occasion.

"Mrs. Roarty." Kate lurched out of her reverie at a tapping on the driver's door window. She wound it down. "Sorry to keep you waiting. We were looking for an inside parking spot for you because of the approaching snowstorm. If you follow me, I'll take you to the space we found for you."

Kate smiled obligingly, wondering what would be installed in her vehicle when she abandoned it to the menacing practices of this organization while she was inside meeting with Denis Colbert. She followed a small, silent, wheel-less vehicle that resembled a sci-fi shuttlecraft. It proceeded ahead of her into an opening that appeared to be a parking garage. The craft slowed and turned to face her vehicle by an empty space near an entranceway. Kate parked, got out, and the guard waved her on, then he quietly slipped away, returning the way they had come. Kate presumed she should proceed through the entrance, surprised that no obvious security measures were required. She supposed she was being tracked by DNA recognition.

The entranceway opened as she approached. "Mrs. Roarty, I'm Denis Colbert." Kate accepted the hand extended in greeting.

"Would you like a short tour of our enviable structure?" said Colbert as he swept his arms out to the magnificent atrium before them.

"Of course," said Kate.

"I cannot disguise my pride in this building. I think I would have made a good architect before the allure of the spying business attracted my attention. I understand you come to your craft as a third career."

Kate smiled and nodded but preferred to let him talk in order to develop as good an understanding as possible of the man. *Thank you, Bryant,* she said in her mind. His analysis was proving helpful.

"We couldn't slip a swimming pool in under the scrutinizing eye of the Canadian taxpaying population. I gather the British GCHQ has a rather stunning facility."

"Indeed, should you ever go there, bring your swimming gear — if you like to swim, that is. It has the biggest indoor pool I have ever swum in."

"The warmth you feel in this atrium is generated from solar collectors in the joiner seams of the glass design. While we have to run the computers on predictable and reliable sources of hydro-electricity, everything else is run on renewable energy. It's a rather brilliant, integrated complex network of solar, wind, geothermal, and recyclable biomass. I hope that one day it can become one hundred percent self-sufficient, powered by renewable energy. We are connected to natural gas because it was prudent to do so; however, we only draw on it for a few weeks during the winter when the days are short, temperatures descend to a deep freeze, and the sun hides behind cloud cover." The level of enthusiasm Colbert expressed surprised Kate — it was reminiscent of the tour that Agent Rathbone gave her when she visited GCHQ. Clearly, celebratory edifices were part of the culture of intelligence services.

"I hope I'm not boring you with my enthusiasm for this building."

"Absolutely not, Monsieur Colbert, I am delighted by the passion you express for your working environment. As one of those taxpaying Canadians who involuntarily contributed to its construction, it makes it much easier to accept the price tag."

She had successfully accessed the boy within the man. He beamed. "Then let's continue. I'll show you a floor that gives an indication how privacy and collaboration is achieved by effective architectural design."

Kate nodded in acquiescence. She wished to see and experience the facility, and the people who worked in it, as much as she could, so whatever it took to gather the intel, she would go along with it. She doubted very much that Colbert would show her anything she was not preordained to see. She launched a trial balloon to gauge his reaction. "I would love to see the computer bunker."

Denis did not miss a beat. "I would have to obtain authorization to take a civilian in there. Let's plan for it on your next visit."

Ah, smooth, Monsieur Colbert, very nice, thought Kate.

They emerged onto a working-level floor that was abuzz with youthful energy and intellect. Kate remained in a quiet observing mode for information that Monsieur Colbert might divulge.

"This floor resembles many work areas, where a complement of data miners, engineers, mathematicians, and analysts with capabilities in cyber security and cryptanalysis work in close proximity. The design offers the opportunity to work in a quiet ambient environment that also encourages collaboration, both formally and informally."

"What is the average age of your professional employees?" Kate asked.

"Twenty-seven."

"Level of education?"

"Masters, partway through PhD studies — some were recruited as undergraduates because of a demonstrated expertise."

"I guess my old employer has relinquished its reputation for recruiting the best and the brightest," Kate remarked.

"We try to get to them first, with more attractive entry-level salaries, or we poach them after they complete their basic training at Global Affairs. It doesn't mean that we don't have staffing challenges. Interpersonal skills and social acumen can be a tough one to put together with this geek squad. I am building my own unit, with difficulty. The band I inherited scored off the charts on their ability to analyze data, and if the human population were all preprogrammed avatars, they would be awesome. Regrettably, their ability to read the range of daily human emotion is woefully lacking. I prefer to have some innate skill there and teach the rest rather than the other way around."

Kate relaxed a bit and allowed, "I must admit that I learned more about behaviour in the course of raising my children than in any other human context. I am most grateful to have grown up with my kids. It was and continues to be a humbling experience."

"I understand they are twenty-somethings."

"Yes, neither would fit in this environment — both have an artistic bent. The older is probably on your civil disobedience watch lists."

"So were you, in university. The security check on you before you started at the then External Affairs was extensive."

Kate laughed. "Ah, yes, I recall the RCMP camped out on my street in Thunder Bay. The neighbours alerted me that they found their presence an amusing winter entertainment. The RCMP had two different reasons for watching me. The two units were from different detachments, and each was unaware of the other's presence."

They both smiled and walked on until Kate stopped abruptly. She found herself gazing at the profile of a familiar person. "Do you have a secondment program with other like agencies?"

"Yes, we do. In fact, I recently took on an agent from GCHQ."

"Liz Bruan," said Kate, nodding in that agent's direction.

Before Colbert could respond, Liz and Kate made eye contact. Liz got up and walked toward them, extending her hand in greeting. "Mrs. Roarty, I wondered if I'd run into you when I came to Ottawa." She looked at Colbert then continued with confidence, "I hadn't expected it to be inside my workplace."

"This is a pleasant surprise. Are you enjoying Canada?"

"So far, just Ottawa, but I love it. I have learned to skate on your Rideau Canal, and I am taking cross-country skiing lessons at the Terry Fox Centre. I love having abundant opportunity to speak French. I may even acquire a Quebecois accent if I stay long enough."

"How is your grandmother?"

A cloud slipped over the face that was alight in exuberance just moments before.

"She passed away last year at the age of ninety-six. I still miss her terribly and smile every time I think of her."

"It appears she handed you her zest for life."

Liz smiled. "That she did."

"Are you swimming?"

"Yes, I took a page from your book." She stopped. Kate waved her hand. "It's okay."

"I got a City of Ottawa pool membership renewable every three months."

"Nothing to compare to your GCHQ pool, but it will serve your needs. I imagine you have a gym here?" Kate looked enquiringly at Colbert.

"Indeed — state-of-the-art, including a climbing wall, hand-to-hand combat trainers readily available, and monthly testing of fitness levels and skills."

"Your geek squad should relish that."

"It sorts out the wheat from the chaff."

Colbert addressed Liz Bruan. "We will catch up later. Now I must snatch Mrs. Roarty away to review a case we are both working on."

He led Kate back to the stairs. "One flight up." As they got out of earshot, he said, "I hope our agents measured up to her. She has field experience and a couple of years on them — it makes a difference."

"*She* makes a difference," said Kate.

He nodded. "She makes a difference."

They entered his north-facing office. It was without any spectacular views, as the building was constructed in a low-lying area, but nevertheless attractive in its interior design.

Kate said, "I am surprised the facility wasn't build on the prime real estate already occupied by CSEC. Then you would not only have enjoyed outstanding architecture but also an exquisite setting."

"I am afraid that we Canadians do not have the romantic connection to intelligence services that the Brits enjoy. We haven't had the likes of the thrillers spun by John le Carré, Ian Fleming, Graham Greene, and William Boyd. Despite the less than romantic connection with the CIA, post 9/11 has been alluring fodder for spy thrillers. Plain old unromantic Canada continues to deride intelligence-gathering, so although we have a beautiful edifice, we have to lie low. Perhaps Kate Roarty, P.I. will change those perceptions?"

Kate laughed wholeheartedly. "You have been speaking to Karen Palmer and Claude Mason."

"No, but you have their ear and their trust. We find that truly amazing."

"Monsieur Colbert, I trust individuals. I do not trust organizations. During my years as a diplomat, corruption was present and readily identifiable in every bureaucracy I was exposed to — others and our own."

"So there's no point in making you a job offer?"

Kate laughed. "I approached this meeting with a bit of trepidation. I hadn't expected to be amused and entertained."

"It is a serious offer. I need to work with people that I can trust."

"If I take a contract with CSEC, I can kiss goodbye to attracting private sector contracts. I make my own rules with private clients. I spend my time tracking along the trajectory that intellectual property travels on to restore it to the rightful innovators — not meeting the demands of insatiable bureaucracies. If you guys want to ride on my coat tails when I have some successes, like the Taylor case, that will happen whether we have a formal arrangement or not. I don't wish to invest time and energy trying to figure out where the corruption exists in this organization. I simply surmise that it does, and I prefer to navigate around it with my network on the outside."

Colbert sighed, his face displaying a small trace of disappointment. "I'm not surprised, although I dared to hope otherwise. Can you tell me about the trace elements extraction investigation? We consider it commercial espionage, so we are watching it closely."

"Evidently not closely enough — our Canadian scientists have had a very rough go of it. They are not anywhere near out of the woods — in fact, they may be mired in the underbrush, barely able to breath."

"Like your attack on Dr. Daniel Osu today?"

Kate smiled. "Yeah, he needed some straightening out. I rarely resort to such methods, but when pushed, I can, and I will."

"You even surprised us. Until today, we didn't know if you were combat-ready or not. Your profile has been revised."

"Well, well, I didn't know that anyone witnessed that little episode with my client."

"We sent Liz out on it because she was already acquainted with you and has field experience. We rarely move from our monitors. You even surprised her."

Kate smiled a little mischievously. "I hate being completely predictable." She studied Colbert for a moment then asked, "Is my house bugged and monitored?"

"It has been, but your SQ loverboy keeps having the place swept clean as a whistle, so we've given up. It blew our budget 'cause he doesn't give our equipment back."

"I think my dinner with Jack Johnson tonight has just ratcheted up from moderately decadent to exquisitely gourmet. You had better not keep me here too long, 'cause I'm preparing it, and I still have to stop at the meat market and veggie shop."

Colbert said, "We appreciate whatever you can tell us about the trace elements investigation you are involved in. We're in your camp, because your clients are Canadians, and we believe their IPR was stolen."

"What else do you know?"

"Your James Bond-like departure from Cape Town suggests the stakes are very high and potentially lethal. To wit, the Robert Beltman murder then scurrying away Charlie Kagiso and family to our far north. Quite frankly, we were surprised that you made it out of there unscathed. Anjay Gandhi is good, very good."

"Yes, I doubt I could ever receive that level of protection from a bureaucracy."

"Don't underestimate us, Kate Roarty. You stayed alive through the Taylor case and went on to enjoy more successes."

Kate just shook her head in jest. She had managed to see the facility, learn what they knew, get a sense of the personalities, and not divulge anything more than they already knew. It was time to take her leave.

"Monsieur Colbert, I have a dinner to prepare. It's been a pleasure. I suggest we keep in touch. I'd like CSEC to have my back but stay out of my bedroom."

"Fair enough, Mrs. Roarty." It was his turn to smile mischievously. "I'll text you when we get the green light for you to view the computer bunker."

24

Kate prepared a marinade for the lovely hanger steaks she purchased at her favourite downtown meat market. She had sacrificed a bit of tenderness in favour of the flavour that this cut offered. It took well to marinating and was good for the gas grill that Kate kept going all winter set up in her tiny back garden just a step away from the living room fireplace. She whisked together a generous dollop of maple syrup, olive oil, fresh-squeezed lime, crushed Russian garlic, Worcester sauce, parsley, Japanese soy sauce with basil, chives, and mint from her own little herb garden then doused and flipped the steaks, giving them at least a few hours to soak up the flavouring and yield to the tenderizing the marinade would provide — an overnight chilling in the sauce would be better, but Kate knew this would suffice.

The cold winter day and plummeting temperatures forecasted for the evening gave her the idea that a hot butternut squash soup would sit well with the boys. Soups usually took a bit of time to make, but a search of Epicurious turned up a simple recipe she could have ready in time as a first course. She quickly peeled and cubed three squash, threw them in a pot along with diced peppers, onions, and apples (Kate's little secret), and a very generous dash of maple syrup that could be augmented after tasting if necessary. The soup could come to a boil then simmer away while she worked on the salad and baby roasted potatoes and greens. It would only take a moment to purée it and pour it into a soup tureen.

Kate was thoroughly enjoying giving herself over completely to preparing the meal. She put on acoustic solo jazz guitar music that blended with the warmth from the flames flickering in the fireplace. The exterior surrounding of fresh deep snow muffled outdoor sounds and offered up scenes of crisp, clean beauty out every window. Kate's windows either remained without covering or blinds, and drapes were fully open, especially during the day in winter when every sliver of light was a welcomed incursion into short days, sunless skies, and unrelenting deep-freeze temperatures. A UV tint also provided privacy without diminishing the natural light. While she hadn't taken the time for a meditation session today, the ambience she was experiencing in her own home gave her the same feeling of tranquility, calm, and restoration. She was looking forward to the arrival of Jack, Émile, Big Ben dog, and Boris cat, but not just yet.

Her cell rang. The caller ID displayed her daughter's name. She picked up. "Hey, Momma, what's up?"

"I am just preparing dinner, so there isn't much up with me, but I think there is something up with you. Has the sunshine finally succeeded in penetrating that village in the valley of yours?"

"Not yet, but there's sunshine in my life."

They groaned "Cliché" in unison.

"Tell me."

"My book of poetry is going to be published — well, the publisher said pretty sure. I won't believe it until I have a contract."

Kate leapt with excitement. "Danielle, we will take it as a done deal then formally celebrate with the signing. This is so exciting — working with editors, seeing your book in print, book signings, poetry readings, and book tours. Wow! You did it!"

Danielle said quietly, probably overwhelmed by the effusiveness of her mother's response, "Yeah, pretty awesome, eh?"

Danielle went on to recount the exchanges with the publisher and what she could expect in the coming months leading up to the launch of the book.

Their chat was short, but Kate was feeling tingly all over with excitement for her daughter, who had been a poet since she learned to write. Her poetry was captured in artistic imagery even before that; her poems had made it into magazines and literary journals, she had won awards, both as a poet and as a playwright, and now a full-length book — this was truly cause for celebration. Kate was already making plans.

The door opened with a whoosh of cold winter air and Big Ben charged through, jumped up onto Kate with a lick to her face, then down and sitting before he could be chastised for his grandiose entrance. Boris cat announced his presence with a stroll across the kitchen island and delicately stepped around food, trays, and plates before taking up residence on a nearby armchair, where he draped his body like a big-game rug slain in the chase.

Jack said to Émile, "Are we expected to swing from the chandelier, cartwheel into the living room, do a twosome stand-up comedy act?"

Before Jack could finish, Émile leaned into Kate to embrace her in the double-cheeked Quebecois style. "*Ma chère, les arômes sont superbes.*"

"Émile, thank so much for taking the boys."

"*Avec plaisir — de rien.*"

"Hey, chopped liver waiting in the queue here," said Jack, waving playfully as Kate gave him a huge kiss and embrace before he could utter another word.

"Ah, can we forget dinner and head upstairs now?"

"Not on your life."

Chuckling quietly to himself, Émile moved off to set the table.

"Jack, can you light the BBQ while I purée the soup and finish the salad?"

A short while later they sat down to steaming soup that Kate ladled from the tureen into their bowls. The hungry men also dug into the platter of glazed baby roast potatoes surrounding medium rare steaks that were blanketed with sautéed portabella mushrooms and red onions. Side dishes of steamed asparagus dribbled with sesame oil and seeds and a fresh arugula salad that Kate prepared with halved cherry tomatoes, pine nuts, and a light vinaigrette dressing mixed with grape seed oil gave a complimentary lightness to an otherwise hardy winter repast. Kate wasn't big on sweets; apart from birthdays and other such celebratory occasions, she rarely made desserts. Fresh berries with frozen yogurt with a dash of maple syrup completed the meal.

Before they sat down, Jack said, "This Pinot Noir from Five Rows Craft Wine will go nicely with this meal. I bought a case when I visited the vineyard last year, and two bottles remain. I admit I was intrigued by the motivation behind the estate. While a very old family-run fruit farm established more than one hundred and fifty years ago in the Niagara Peninsula, in 1984 a member of the fifth generation working the farm ripped out five rows of juice grapes and planted Pinot Noir vines." He poured for each of them, then raised his glass and said, "Be prepared for something dark and mysterious — like this winter's day."

They all lingered approvingly over their first taste then went on to savour it with Kate's meal. Their discussion was lively, interesting, and jovial. They shared respective stories about experiences since their last dinner together, more than a month before Kate went to South Africa and Jack to Los Angeles. They did not talk shop; rather, they became animated in their discussion of the possibility of building an energy self-sufficient country home. Émile headed off home after dessert to catch the remainder of the hockey game and to give Kate and Jack some time alone together.

Jack slipped his arms around Kate and said, "Do you realize that you have been home for four days already, and we haven't even made love yet."

"Yes, given I was yearning for that intimacy long before I arrived home, I'm in disbelief that these days were snatched away from us."

Before Jack could collect their devices, Kate's cell lit up with a message from Danielle. It was a photo of the pup, Hazel, and one word, **Home**.

"Shall we turn off our phones, tablets, computers ... anything else that rings, vibrates, goes beep, sounds an alarm, plays the 'William Tell Overture,' and shut them in a separate room, along with the animals?"

"Let's do it right now before interceptors get a chance."

They did and then took a few minutes to tidy up and put perishables and leftovers in the fridge, then they curled up in front of the fireplace.

Jack leapt up. "I almost forgot, I brought a cognac back from LA that I think would go very well right now." He retrieved it from Kate's liquor cabinet.

"It is already here?"

"Yeah, I dropped it off when I was over…"

Kate finished his sentence. "…sweeping the place for bugs and surveillance monitors?"

"How did you know?"

"Denis Colbert at CSEC said you were costing them too much money because you don't give their toys back."

They both laughed as Jack handed Kate a brandy snifter containing a deep amber cognac. The aroma preceded its taste, and its smooth, seductive power lingered long after the first sip had slipped down her throat.

Jack watched her cheek colour heighten and said, "It's a twelve-year-old cask-aged cognac that expresses the very nature of your spirit, Kate, when we are making love."

Kate said, "It certainly captures the way I feel when I'm in your embrace. I don't know if I've actually drunk brandy before — at least if I have, it was nothing as flirtatious as this taste experience."

Little more was said as they made their way upstairs, pulled down the blinds, and slipped out of their clothing. Their long, caressing lovemaking was as mature as the cognac that had set the stage.

Several hours later, Jack lit a candle beside their unfinished glasses of brandy. He handed Kate her glass. She sat up to take another sip and let it slip down slowly, smoothly, and succulently and thought, *Just like you, Jack Johnson. This was worth waiting for.*

"Kate, I have some leave time left. If I don't use it before the end of March, I'll lose it. I doubt you'll want to take time off before you finish this minerals extraction investigation, and you'll likely leave for the UK and elsewhere shortly — right?"

"Yes."

"What would you think if I accompany you?"

Kate raised herself up on one arm. "Jack, nothing would please me more. I hate being away from you."

"I hear a but."

"The last time you accompanied me, you got shot and your car was blown up. As a police superintendent, you might be even more of a target."

"That was nearly two years ago. It was an SQ case. I recovered — fully, and look at the great new SUV I got out of the deal, not to mention my good friend Daggy. Despite it all, we had a wonderful week in Boston. It launched our relationship. We solved the case and advanced my career. You were with me for my fortieth birthday and helped me cope with the anniversary of the loss of my daughter. A lot of good came out of that week."

"Yes, you're absolutely right. A lot of good came out of that week, and subsequently, because we were together there. The next few days will give me an idea of the next steps on this case. I have to be sure that I can trust my clients before I go any further. I also need to talk with Karen Palmer at MI6, and we want to address the flak jacket situation, not to mention Daggy's recovery and the restoration of some normal life for Marny and the girls."

"The Italian extended family began to arrive last evening. They brought one of those gigantic motor homes that Daggy's brother leases from the lot where I bought my SUV. We got a snowplough out to his place to clear a swath where they can park it in front of the house and run power and water lines out to it. We thought we would have to negotiate that with the landlord, but he said go ahead. With the ground still frozen, it won't be difficult to fix it after. Even if it thaws, he said that it was only grass and a few shrubs. He even offered to help attach the power and water lines — a good guy, considering how hard we negotiated down the rental rate when we found the place for Daggy and his family."

"We aren't going anywhere — either of us — until we are sure Daggy is going to be okay," said Kate.

She snuggled into Jack and slipped into a very deep sleep. Jack always slept well when she was close to him.

⁂

The flight lifted off through the last gasps of a fierce winter. Kate looked out the window into the night at the snow blowers lining the runway like sentries standing guard to keep the prowling March lion at bay. The lamb had not appeared this year — March came in like a lion and was going out like one, too. Despite the serial storms of recent weeks, Kate had enjoyed the routine of being home for a while. A hint of domesticity entered her otherwise hectic and unpredictable lifestyle — she liked a bit of that, but not too much.

Daggy was recovering sufficiently well to leave the hospital and join the Italian clan at home. He and Marny were thrilled with the transformation of Vitalia from an adequate student to one attacking the maths and sciences vigorously. When she discovered the pre-med option was available in Quebec schools, she decided to go after an acceptance to a Quebec university. She picked up French quickly and easily, admittedly facilitated by a string of boyfriends that readily introduced her to all that was the Quebec youth culture in this decade. She acquired a few introspective goth-like girlfriends who gave her an artsy poetic outlet. They wrote lyrics put to heavy metal music featured at the annual Amnesia Rockfest in Montebello. Quebec youth gathered there for three days every June. Vitalia, along with her circle of friends, already had their tickets. Although reluctant, Daggy and Marny gave her free rein to make her own choices. She had adapted so well to their life in Quebec and showed such strength in responding to their family crisis when Daggy was shot that they felt she possessed adequate maturity to remain responsible as she moved through the vagaries and experimentation of teenage life.

At times Kate found Jack melancholy in the presence of Daggy's girls. He confessed, as he watched them experience the ups and downs of life, that he reflected on his own daughter, Elizabeth, whose life was halted before she could experience the teenage years. She and her mother, Jack's ex-wife, were killed by a drunk driver in a head-on collision just before her ninth birthday. Although more than six years ago, it remained a deep wound for Jack that would probably continue to fester and irritate for the rest of his life. He might in time learn to live with it, but he wouldn't likely ever truly move on from it.

25

Paris, France

Kate reached a hand over to Jack seated beside her, engrossed in a thriller movie on his laptop. She smiled to herself and thought he might find himself in a real sci-fi script soon enough. She had finally agreed to his coming along, knowing too well that the thing called "vacation" would not likely last beyond the weekend. They had decided to fly to Paris for a few days then back track to London in time for the start of the business week.

As with many flights to Europe, this one traversed the Atlantic through the night, leaving all but the well pampered first- and business-class passengers to emerge into the airport exhausted from at best a fitful night's sleep. They went straight to a flat in Paris off the Canal Saint Martin, where a graffiti-clad steel door on Quai de Valmy gave them access to a splendid courtyard ringed with flats appearing artistic, unique, and enchanting in their respective designs. The access and interior decorating could be glimpsed while passing by. A friend who had acquired the flat in his younger years when such an acquisition was affordable had loaned it to Kate for this weekend Parisian visit. He had the good sense to hang on to it — at today's real estate prices in Paris, it would be totally beyond his financial reach in 2030.

"This is a Paris I haven't glimpsed on previous visits. We have cousins in the suburbs — rows of residential streets much like any other European city. But this, Kate—" Jack spun around with boyish wonder "—*c'est absolument extraordinaire!*"

Kate located the key in the arm of the joist above the door and let them in. What they found inside was even more delightful than the courtyard and balconies that led them to this apartment. The original wood plank floors from the previous century, when the building had been a factory, held an array of furniture gathered over decades that exhibited shop-worn charm and history. "Think of the tales, this furniture — this set of rooms — could recount to us," said Kate. "Jack, let's shower and go walking. We can sleep anytime."

"*Mais oui madame, avec plaisir.*"

Jack and Kate walked through the day speaking only in French. Spring was awakening Paris, resplendent with flowering trees and the fragrance of new buds. They stopped for coffee and chatted, they had lunch on a café terrasse and chatted, they strolled along the Seine and boarded a tourist boat to take them farther along the river and chatted … they bought baguettes at a boulangerie, lamb from a boucher, wine in an épicerie, and greens and baby potatoes at a sidewalk stall. Both Kate and Jack had been to Paris previously and enjoyed the major sites on those visits. This visit was giving them companionship, atmosphere, an early spring, and time to be together. They returned to the apartment late in the day calmed, tranquil, and fatigued. Together they prepared a succulent meal, sipped wine, and made love tenderly and passionately. A shaft of dusty light was streaming through the transom above the door when they awoke the following morning rested and happy in one another's embrace. Kate moved in closer to Jack and muttered, "Hmmm, full body contact."

Jack enveloped her tightly. "This is my idea of perfection. Thank you, Kate Roarty's friend Anthony for loaning us this place. We have been blessed."

They let the quiet of the morning caress them a little longer, then Jack leapt up. "Kate, I am starving — I'll cobble together some breakfast for us." He found the coffee and a Turkish percolator. The aroma lured Kate out of bed before Jack could bring a cup to her. They had enjoyed thirty-six hours without being connected to various digital devices. Both had resisted turning on any of them, despite having at least six in their possession. The experience of being disconnected from artificial devices and feeling connected fully to each other was heavenly.

"Kate, I would like to go for a run along the canal this morning before we head out on the adventures of the day. Is there a pool nearby where you could take a swim while I am running?"

"Yes, there is quite a lovely old historic swimming pool not too far from here. It was built between the First and Second World Wars for the working class of the area. It is not only a fine neighbourhood pool but also a cultural and historic experience entering the building. The change rooms are individual cabins lined along gallery walkways on two floors above the pool level. The patrons are given a code entry for a cabin — which is rather like a small room — where clothes and belongings are kept during their swims. The luxury of a private pool with the benefits of a public price. The walk to and from is quite interesting as well."

"Great, I may route part of my run up through that area to view the architecture of the neighbourhood once I get my fill of running along the canal. Let's take our phones in case we want to link up along the way after you swim."

Kate experienced a twinge of unease, remembering back to the early days of their relationship when Jack went out for a run along the Charles River in Boston and got shot. She counselled herself, *This is different. This is Paris. We are here strictly on vacation. Jack has taken many runs along waterways since that incident.*

Kate grabbed her swim bag, threw her mobile phone in it, and headed out through the courtyard onto Quai de Valmy, the street that ran along Canal Saint Martin. She traversed the canal via Pont Dieu and continued along the busy, narrow Rue Albert. While the architecture was an interesting diversion as she walked along, the graffiti she viewed was worthy of sociocultural academic studies, photo exhibitions, and guided walking tours of the city. It seemed every roll-down entrance, enclosure, and protective window display, flat, smooth, and rough, every vertical and horizontal surface, offered a platform for cartooning, political protest, a taxonomy of lettering, animals real and imagined, dreams and bleak reality, comments on war, peace, the price of wine, baguettes, and butter. The half-hour brisk walk took her up hilly, narrow streets to Piscine Eduard Pailleron on the street of the same name. The oft-encountered chlorine smell of public pools drew her through the entranceway and into the familiar foyer, where she paid the pittance for a swim, obtained her entry code, and proceeded to the second level to the change room she had been assigned, in ready view of the doomed glass ceiling above and the pool surface below.

Kate loved returning to pools she had previously visited in divergent corners of world. It was like reconnecting with old friends who are just there when you need them. The old building had received a dramatic facelift since her last visit several years ago. The structure had endured through the decades as a popular gathering place for all wishing to take a plunge — from casual bathers to serious swimmers. The recent renovations had added a leisure pool and modern facilities, including a solarium and exercise gym, while retaining the historical integrity and intent of the original structure. Kate felt honoured to pass an hour swimming laps in the grand old neighbourhood facility about to celebrate a hundredth birthday.

Just as she finished her final lap, she glimpsed movement near her change room. At first she thought it was likely another swimmer, but there was something incongruous about the stride and clothing of the person emerging from the very change room she had been assigned to. Fearing slipping on the smooth, wet tile surface, she proceeded quickly but cautiously to the bottom of the stairs, where she hoped to intercept the intruder. A man brushed quickly in front of her, saying only "*pardon*" as he made his way to the exit. She hurried up the stairs to the gallery level and down the walkway to her change room. She peered over the railing but could see nothing unusual. The door was still locked. She entered the code and pushed the door open. All appeared as it should — except the soft sound of her phone vibrating with an incoming text message. Kate didn't recall actually turning the phone on after she threw it in her bag. She retrieved it to see a photo of Jack running along the canal. It was taken from the opposite side of the waterway. Her heart skipped a beat. She hit the speed dial for Jack's number. His phone was not on. She quickly showered, towelled off, dressed, and headed down the stairs, through the lobby and out onto the street just as she spotted Jack rounding the corner, heading in her direction. Despite her swim that both energized and relaxed her body and spirit, the photo on her phone succeeded in winding her up like a top. Jack reached her sporting a welcoming grin that quickly fell away as he registered her expression of distress. He said only, "What's wrong?"

Kate handed him her phone, remarking that he had been a subject of photography while she was swimming. Jack scrolled through a half a dozen photos of him taken randomly along the route of his run. Kate hadn't realized there was more than one photo.

Jack took Kate's elbow and said, "Let's go back in the lobby for a moment." Just as they started to move, the phone vibrated again with an incoming photo of the two of them standing together outside the entrance to the pool.

They both swore — Jack in French, Kate in English — as they scanned the street and upper-storey windows, but neither could discern any sign of their stalker.

"Look, Kate, we aren't going to let these assholes spoil our weekend together in Paris. This works both ways. They know we know they are messing with us here. We can turn the phones off and leave them at the apartment. Let them take all the photos they want."

"Jack, these guys are dangerous."

"We don't even know who *these guys* are, Kate. Let's just go back to the apartment and enjoy another glorious day in Paris."

Kate held her scepticism in check as they descended through the neighbourhood streets to Canal Saint Martin. They remained alert, scanning their vicinity for any untoward behaviour. Gradually, they began to relax back into the pleasure of their company. Kate felt like they were characters cast in a film — the screenplay already written, but they were the only two who didn't know the outcome. Just as they stepped out to cross the street at the iron door that let to the secluded courtyard, a vehicle pulled out across their path, stopped, doors flew open, and Kate was bundled into it in one swift moment. Her side view caught a glimpse of Jack crumpling to the pavement as the vehicle she had been thrown into sped off. She didn't know if Jack was just knocked down, hit, shot … dead.

A hood was pulled over her head as she heard the vehicle speed away. She remained silent, listening carefully for clues about where she was going and who had taken her. The vehicle stopped. The surroundings seemed quieter — perhaps in a park removed from the main streets. Silently, she was patted down, searched but in a seeming respectful, professional manner. She could hear them going through her swim bag then opening and crushing her mobile phone. Hands stood her erect, arms extended, neck pulled long. It seemed that a device was been used to scan her, perhaps for tracking devices or some electronic matter that a GPS could latch on to. She was pushed back into a vehicle — a different vehicle. She sensed that it was bigger, faster, since they were moving again. Still nobody spoke. She did not know the identity of her captors or what they wanted.

Jack stumbled into the apartment, a bit dazed from the attack. Kate was gone.

He looked around. The apartment had been cleaned and tidied, left in an immaculate state. Kate's belongings were gone. In fact, all evidence of her having been there was removed. The bed was freshly made with new sheets, duvet, and pillows. In the bathroom the towels were new, fresh, and clean and the old ones gone. Even the toilet paper had been replaced with a new roll. Jack spun around. It was as though she had never been there. Most of his clothes were gone. A stack of new, perfectly fitting clothes was laid out on the bed.

Jacked looked around the apartment, carefully considering what had been removed. He opened the refrigerator door to find it thoroughly cleaned and many items that had been there were gone — some had been replaced. He sat down dismayed and perplexed. It appeared that anything that might have yielded a trace of Kate's DNA was gone. He headed to the shower to clean up and further ponder what had happened. He emerged freshened, thinking more clearly, picked up his mobile and punched in the speed dial number for his best friend and colleague with SQ, Guy Archambault.

Guy noticed the first ring. "*Oui, allô mon patron. Ça va?*"

"*Mal,*" was the only word Jack could utter.

"Don't tell me you've had a fight in the most romantic city on earth."

"She's gone."

"That bad?"

"Guy, she was kidnapped, right off the street. She has vanished — all trace of her. Gone."

Jack could hear Guy drawing in a deep breath. "Start at the beginning, *mon ami* — every detail, the whole story."

Jack recounted what had transpired that morning, then Guy had him back up and recount every detail since the plane landed at Charles de Gaulle airport in Paris.

"Jack, I could board the first flight to Paris to help you, but I'm not sure that is where she is anymore. I suggest you proceed to London on the very flight you and Kate were going to take. Pay close attention to what happens to her reservation, and be particularly cautious about whoever takes her seat beside you on that flight. I'll try to track down Karen Palmer from my end to see if she can shed any light on this situation. I'll get back to you as soon as I have something. I suppose you are unarmed."

"Yes."

Jack couldn't remain in the apartment without Kate there. He doubted she would return, even if she managed to escape her captors. He packed his bag and left, replacing the key in the crook of the joist above the door then made his way across the courtyard, painfully aware that Kate's captors could have been watching their activity from any one of the numerous other flats ringing the courtyard. He rang Kate's mobile number, not expecting an answer but just in case. His call went immediately to her voicemail, suggesting the mobile was turned off or destroyed. He left a message. **Kate, I'm going to remain at the Quai Valmy apartment until you return. Please let me know that you are alright.**

He hoped the deception might buy him a bit of time to move about without being followed. He tried her mobile again in fifteen minutes. It did not even go to voicemail.

Jack walked along the now familiar streets of 10e arrondissement, torn between the private man deeply in love with Kate Roarty and the SQ cop, Superintendent Jack Johnson. He felt his every instinct propelling him toward launching a continent-wide search for Kate; his knowledge of the clientele she moved with counselled him to follow Guy's advice. He had no idea if her captors were friend or foe. Jack slipped into a café, where he could sit on a bar stool with his back to a wall facing out onto the street with a 270-degree angle of vision. He ordered a double espresso, a large orange juice, and two croissants with cheese and pâté. He was hungry after his run and the trauma of Kate's disappearance. He placed his bag at his feet and scanned the street, waiting for his order to arrive.

26

The Thames, UK

"Superintendent Jack Johnson is okay, Madame Roarty, and you are in safe hands. It appeared to us that you were about to be abducted. We thought it better to seize you before that happened. We are taking you to London for dinner with Karen Palmer at MI6. Monsieur Johnson can travel there on the flight originally booked for tomorrow morning. Once he is out of France, we will let him know that you are okay. For now, the less he knows the better. That way if he is interrogated, he has nothing to tell."

Kate listened carefully to the familiar female voice, trying to place it. The hood remained covering her head, and her arms were bound at her sides. She decided to remain silent until she could see these captors. She had no reason to believe what this voice had told her. She remained alert, continuing to listen acutely to any clue about her captors and where they were going. She sensed that they were travelling along a main road. She was trying to measure time and distance as the vehicle sped along. It turned off a main road then slowed, proceeding in what felt like a wide circle, then it stopped close to a loud, whirring sound — a helicopter?

She was bundled out of the vehicle, guided across solid pavement, up a big step, then through a door — a helicopter door — seated, buckled in, and it lifted off. Kate could make out the words of the French-speaking pilot communicating with what she presumed to be some form of ground control. She clearly understood *"Londres, dans une heure."* The helicopter lifted off. Apart from the pilot's chatter to ground control, all remained silent.

"Lieutenant Jamieson, you have entered UK airspace — please confirm that the passenger is safely on board then let me speak to her."

Kate felt a hand gently removing the hood from her sweaty face. Kate looked sideways into the face of Agent Liz Bruan, the owner of the familiar female voice.

"Hello, Mrs. Roarty. It is nice to see you again. I apologize for the drama of your removal from Paris. We had to minimize the possibility of being followed or tracked electronically."

"Hello, Kate." Another familiar disembodied voice addressed her. "This is your friendly British Intelligence Service once again collaborating on getting you out of harm's way."

"Claude, Claude Mason, is that you?"

"*Mais oui, ma chère.*"

"Jesus, Mary, Joseph — what the hell was all that about?"

"I like to think GCGQ and MI6 do a better job of perceiving your security needs than the trappings of the Christian god."

"Christ!"

"He was on a holiday weekend, that one."

"Claude!"

"Ah, that is better."

Agent Bruan let a grin creep across her face.

Kate rounded on her. "I thought you were on assignment in Canada."

"It was time for a weekend in Paris."

"Kate," Claude interjected, "our surveillance was low-key until you and Jack decided to do your swimming/running thing. It was all we could do to allow you to finish your swim and Jack to run to you. It would have been dicey if he had gone off in another direction. They were nasty fellows with a ghastly arsenal on your tail when we took them out."

"And Jack?" said Kate.

"He should be okay until he gets to the airport tomorrow morning. He is behaving predictably, so our surveillance team is monitoring him well enough. He has connected with Officer Archambault, who has settled him down a bit."

"Jesus."

"Kate, you are making your way through the New Testament. Please credit GCHQ and MI6 just a little bit."

Kate relaxed and smiled at Agent Liz Bruan. "Thanks, guys — I appreciate the rescue. Your presentation leaves a great deal to be desired."

"Kate, we owe you big-time on the neural implant case. We will remain forever indebted to you on that takedown. Your willingness to take the risk, your approach and skill at connecting the dots, not to mention a rather unorthodox network of contacts and techno wizards, sprang the case open. We owe you. If we can help in any small way to pry you out of a jam now and in the future, we will. Now sit back, enjoy the ride, and the spectacular view as you come in over the Thames. Agent Bruan will deliver you to a secure hotel where you can grab a swim tomorrow morning. She can also escort you over to Babylon this evening for dinner with Karen Palmer. I hope you will find time to come to Cheltenham for a swim. Cha for now." He rang off.

Kate turned her attention to Agent Liz Bruan. They studied one another for a few moments until the young agent broke the silence with, "Mrs. Roarty, what's on your mind?"

Kate laughed. "I rarely reveal my thoughts to anyone. For a superficial starter, how about who are you working for, Agent Liz Bruan?"

"As you experienced in the neural microchip case, Mrs. Roarty, the intelligence services of our respective nations have tremendous capacity for co-operation and collaboration. Perhaps we could consider me a product of the c and c approach."

Kate laughed again, easing the tension between the two women. "I certainly do detect a higher level of confidence since the Taylor case."

"Two years is along time when you are my age, not to mention the toughening up on the ski trails and the ice corridors of your fair capital city. Watch as we fly up the Thames. Look, there is the London Eye dominating the cityscape and St. Paul's Cathedral and so many bridges: Blackfriars, The Shard, The Millennium, London Bridge — the light is failing, but the lights of the financial district are great to see from the air. Oh look, we're coming up on the Vauxhall Bridge and Babylon right beside it."

Kate looked out the window at the spectacular view while regarding the excited animation of Agent Bruan. She let down her guard for a just a moment in expressing youth-like delight in seeing MI6/Babylon from the air. Despite being nearly twice her age, Kate shared her enthusiasm. The moment was quickly dispatched by the onboard drone detection alarm. The drone security system sensed a fast-approaching threat and destroyed it just before impact.

The taciturn pilot came to life, barking orders into his microphone to obtain permission to land at the London Heliport as quickly as possible, citing hostile airborne activity. "We have to land before another drone succeeds in penetrating our detection system."

They were descending rapidly. She could hear the pilot requesting permission to fly below one thousand feet and obtaining it then dropping to just above five hundred feet when another approaching drone was detected and neutralized. Agent Bruan was pulling out life jackets when a third drone penetrated the detection system and hit. The pilot barked "Mayday" then hit the electronic door openers.

Kate remarked, "I have never swum in the Thames."

The other agent beside her said, "Swimming is not my forté."

Liz pressed a life jacket against him as he unbuckled his seat belt.

"You will be okay — the Thames is just a bit cold and dirty. Kate and I are strong swimmers."

The pilot shouted above the noise, "You have to jump — now. Go!"

The helicopter was descending fast and just above the water when they leapt.

Kate hit hard and plunged deep. She lost the life jacket on impact. She surfaced breathless to see Liz already swimming toward her colleague. A hundred feet away the helicopter was sinking; it seemed to have hit the water and bounced. She scanned the surface for the pilot while removing her shoes and as much clothing as possible to free up her body to swim. She closed the distance quickly then saw a head bobbing up — the pilot. She was close enough to see blood pumping out of a head wound and washing away into the water. *Shit, what is his name?* He went down and bobbed up again then went down. She reached the spot when he last came up and dove. The water was black and the daylight was all but absent. She yelled a random name in hopes he might hear her voice. Then she spotted him hanging on to a life jacket. She reached him in three strong strokes. He appeared semiconscious but breathing. He looked bad. The life jacket was only over one arm, so she better secured it while keeping his head out of the water, continuously talking to him.

"Hey buddy, this is one hell of a way to meet, but you are going to be okay. We weren't formally introduced — my name is Kate. Can you tell me your name?" She couldn't make out his reply but spotted his nametag on the pocket of his uniform. "Stephen, we are heading home to dry clothes and a warm bed." She saw a wedding ring on his left hand. "There must be a great woman waiting to wrap her arms around you."

She swam and talked. He got heavier, then there were arms all around her and the pilot and they were being pulled from the water. "Careful," she said, "he's hurt — maybe neck and back injuries," then everything went dark.

27

London, UK

Kate awoke to soft light and Karen Palmer at her bedside reading papers.

Kate said, "Are we still on for dinner tonight?"

The woman looked up. "That was last night. You seemed to have slept through your wakeup call and missed it."

Kate smiled through a throbbing headache. "Is the pilot okay?"

"Rather banged up, but he will recover. You saved his life. How did you mange to propel him to safety with your shoulder dislocated?"

"The other agent — he couldn't swim — did he make it out?"

Karen Palmer replied in a quiet, direct tone. "He took in a lot of water. He was at risk of secondary drowning, but Agent Braun kept him going until the rescue boat arrived. Miraculously, you all survived. The helicopter is being lifted out of the river today; it's probably destined for the salvage yard, but a forensics examination on what is left may give us some information about the drone that hit it and who launched it."

Kate lay back gingerly as pain seared through her shoulder.

Karen Palmer continued, "It seems our indebtedness to you has increased, just when we thought we had made an installment on the repayment plan."

"You lost a helicopter."

"We were the ones who decided to use it. I hope that swim in the Thames will do you for a while. The doctor says swimming during the recovery period could risk tearing the rotator cuff. Fortunately, it was a clean dislocation, and the paramedics reduced it as soon as they got you out of the water."

Kate took in this information as she lay quietly so as not to aggravate the sore shoulder. Her only reply was, "Jack?"

"One of our agents picked him up off his flight. He should be here shortly, then I will leave. I expect you will be able to leave the hospital later today or tomorrow."

There was a tap at the door, and Agent Liz Bruan poked her head in. "How is our favourite Canadian P.I.?" Despite her physical discomfort, Kate couldn't help but smile. Liz let a massive bouquet of flowers lead her into the room. "I think you will be hanging around at least until the roses wilt."

Karen Palmer got up and said, "I will be on my way now that you are in better hands than the director of MI6." Agent Bruan flushed, and Kate laughed, followed by a grimace from the pain.

Liz said, "Are you up for a wee stroll?"

Kate swung her legs over the side of the bed, and Liz fetched a thick, fluffy robe from a plastic zipped bag at the foot of the bed. "Do you mind going to say hello to the pilot? He can't remember the crash, and seeing his rescuer might help to activate his memory."

"Certainly, let's go."

Liz gently slid the sleeve of the robe onto Kate's good arm and drew the rest across her injured right shoulder, securing it with the waist tie.

They made their way down the corridor, Kate shuffling along, not due to any infirmity but rather the ridiculous hospital slippers threatening to scurry off ahead of her should she accelerate beyond a geriatric pace. She laughed. "Shades of things to come."

"Not until you reach my granny's age — in fact, I don't ever recall her shuffling. She was too spry for that, and you will be too."

Kate smiled to herself at Liz Braun's efforts to offer encouragement.

They entered the pilot's room then hesitated. He appeared to be sleeping, but when they quietly turned to leave, he spoke. "Can I help you?"

They approached the bed. "Mr. Seaborne, I am Liz Bruan, an agent travelling on board your helicopter before it ditched in the Thames, and this is Kate Roarty, the passenger we were transporting…"

Pilot Stephen Seaborne interjected, "From Paris with a hood on your head — that is the last thing I remember."

"We were British Intelligence agents transporting Mrs. Roarty to safety."

"We didn't quite make it."

"We did. Everyone on board survived, battered but alive and on the road to recovery. You sustained the worst injuries, including some memory loss, that we hope will be restored with rest and recuperation."

"What did I do wrong?"

"Nothing," said Liz. "We were shot down by a drone."

"We have onboard deflector technology for drone detection."

"Yes, it worked effectively and neutralized the first two drones, but the third drone engaged its target. We suspect the launch system adapted to the deflector technology on the third attempt, successfully penetrating the digital surveillance field."

"Jesus."

This time Kate replied, "Our sentiments exactly."

"My company will be pissed at losing a state of the art Sikorsky and a chief pilot out of commission."

"Don't worry about that right now. Your full-time job is to rest and recover."

At that moment they all turned in the direction of the door, distracted by the sound of someone entering the room. Both Liz Bruan and Kate were rendered speechless for a moment in the face of the ravishingly beautiful woman, young but very in control, with deep, penetrating eyes filled with intensity and affection. An unusual combination that preceded the rest of the layers of beauty that rolled in like the waves of a tsunami captured in slow motion. The utterance of, "Papa, you're awake," slid richly from a mouth perfectly formed to smoothly articulate every vowel.

Kate's assumption that this must be his wife was immediately dispelled by the young woman's remark and the pilot saying, "Ah, let me introduce my daughter, Catalina." Kate felt a whoosh pass through her body, the feeling one rarely experiences, this one signalling that she was in the presence of perfection.

Kate regained her momentary lapse of concentration, silently returning Liz to the moment as well. "We were on board the aircraft with your father when it went down."

Catalina nodded with the fluidity of molasses slipping from its carton. "You may be able to help my father fill in the missing parts of the moments before the crash."

Liz said, "Yes, I expect so, but as your father has only awakened, we'd best leave him to rest and benefit from your presence. We will look in on him later."

They nodded to Stephen and left his room. Kate and Liz shuffled along the corridor without speaking. Kate's thoughts registered an exclamation mark placed after the name, Catalina.

They opened the door to Kate's room, stumbling upon a bewildered Jack Johnson, arms filled with balloons, flowers, and packages, looking like a carnival clown that arrived late for the party. He smiled sheepishly and said, "The driver stopped at a party shop — in my rush I couldn't help myself."

Kate grinned. "You haven't missed the party, Jack Johnson, we couldn't start without the clown."

Liz stepped up to take the festoon of riches from Jack so he could embrace Kate, remarking, "Easy on the left shoulder, big guy."

"Karen Palmer called me when my flight landed."

"Wow, they kept you in the dark that long?"

"She said you were okay, a bit injured but already recovering, and that you could fill me in on the details. The hospital could discharge you to me, and someone named Agent Liz Bruan could take us to a hotel where they have made a reservation."

Liz Bruan, now looking like the clown, bobbed around the balloon bouquet. "That would be me. How about I leave you two for a bit. I could use a coffee, and I'll need to find a clown costume if I am going to walk up the street with this lot." She shifted the unwieldy bundle back to Jack and slipped out of the room.

Jack dropped the bundle on the bed and said, "Now can I kiss you, hug you, hold you — do something that is real body contact?"

"All of it, then let's get out of here."

The driver that had brought Jack to the hospital from the airport returned to transfer the two of them to the lodging MI6 had booked in the area, a cozy, rather intimate inn, and best of all, secure — with strong emphasis on the latter. The exterior had the appearance of a private house; no signage indicated the contrary. However, as Kate and Jack passed through the entranceway, they immediately experienced a sense of warmth, with atmosphere as welcoming as a country pub.

Jack exclaimed in a quiet, affectionate tone, "Kate Roarty, there is never a dull moment with you. Two hours ago I was speeding along to the hospital wondering how many pieces I was going to find you in, and now I am standing in the foyer of an agreeable hideaway London inn with only a twinge to your shoulder."

"Are you disappointed?"

"Disappointed in what? This place is charming."

She elbowed him in the ribs. "In my injuries, you oaf."

"Only insofar as you are temporarily immobilized, so I can hold you in my arms as long as I wish, rendering you powerless to do anything about it."

"*Arrête*, Jack Johnson!" returned Kate playfully.

"Mrs. Roarty and Mr. Johnson, may I show you to your room?" said a young man not at all looking the part of a bellboy.

"*Allez-y*."

The young man of East Indian background led them up one flight of stars and down a corridor that widened into a sitting area. He opened the door across the salon, leading them into a set of rooms, small but charming in their warmth, décor, and sense of invitation. Jack's flowers, balloons, and packages left by Agent Bruan had already been distributed about the suite.

Kate smiled with pleasure. "And yet another delightful surprise."

Two large Starbucks coffees with a carton of fresh milk and a bottle of maple syrup were sitting on a small mantle above a little fireplace.

"You need only flick the switch like this if you wish to light the fireplace. It's gas. Picking up the receiver connects you to security and the front desk. They are one in the same."

The bellboy pushed a button on the remote that transformed an entire wall into a viewing screen. "You can use this for all forms of digital communications — live screen or dark screen. The buttons on the remote are self-explanatory. If you are interested, the Philae lander that went to sleep in 2014 is expected to wake up in the next few hours. The comet it was travelling on tilted toward the sun, allowing its rays to reach the solar panels and charge the batteries. This is exciting. I was writing my A-levels when it landed on the comet and transmitted for forty-eight hours before going to sleep. It began its decade-long journey when I started school."

Kate said, "I share your interest. Thank you for telling us. When I was in school so much space travel was a fantasy, although *Apollo 11* landed on the moon and Neil Armstrong did his lunar walk."

The young man's eyes danced with joy. "One small step for man, one giant leap for mankind."

"You know your space history, Mr.?"

"Tiwana … Tahir Tiwana. Many people call me TT."

"How do you like to be addressed?" asked Jack.

"Tahir or Mr. Tiwana."

"Please call me Jack, or Jack Johnson, and this is Kate, or Kate Roarty."

Tahir bowed his head slightly. "But of course I know who you are. It's my job to know who you are, that is. And now I must leave you to rest and relax, and, of course, recover."

They both collapsed onto the bed after Mr. Tiwana left the room. Kate winced at the pain from her shoulder. "I must remember to avoid gymnastics until that shoulder stops complaining from its wrenching trauma."

"Kate, what do you say if we just stay here, order in, and watch a bad movie on that massive screen."

"Deal. When Tahir was talking, my mind went to a film I saw when I was a child. It captured my imagination and remained a pleasant memory. We may be able to find it in the archives if it was transferred to digital format so it could be saved to the cyber intelligence continuum by the time that technology came along."

"Title?"

"It's *2001: A Space Odyssey.*"

"Here it is — it was made in 1968."

"Yes, I saw it a quarter century after it was first released. Maybe the best sci-fi ever made … at least one that dealt with space exploration and artificial intelligence before that term had entered the popular lexicon."

"What shall we order?" asked Jack. "Fish and chips?"

"Contrary to popular international opinion, the most common takeaway food in the UK is Chinese, followed closely by Indian, then yes, fish and chips. After pizza it falls off pretty quickly. What would you like? I am easy."

"My mind tells me Indian, but my hedonistic desire reaches out to fish and chips with malt vinegar."

"Then that is what it shall be, Superintendent Jack Johnson."

Kate picked up the all-purpose receiver to instantly hear the mellow, solicitous voice of Mr. Tahir Tiwana.

She gave him her order for food then listened with a growing smile to Tahir's response.

"My great-auntie owns a fish and chip shop very close to this inn. She makes the best fish and chips in all of London — maybe in the entire UK. What size and what kind of fish would you like?"

"Mr. Tahir Tiwana, I will put our hunger in the hands of you and your great-auntie. We will need drinks as well — a beer and some mineral water with lime or lemon, if lime is not available. Oh, and do you suppose your auntie can provide the wonderful French mayonnaise?"

"Of course, she lived in Paris for a decade before finally settling in London. I'll deliver the order to you personally,

Mrs. Roarty. Your meal will be hot, crisp, and sumptuous, or my PhD in cyber intelligence will continue to support me as a bellboy."

Jack successfully loaded the film, and they lay back to enjoy a banal evening with a fifty-year-old sci-fi film, awaiting the arrival of crisp fish and chips.

Kate looked enquiringly at Jack. "Have you ever seen *2001: A Space Odyssey*?"

"Nope, never."

"You are in for a cinematic treat. This film took sci-fi, filmmaking, and the use of sound into a whole new era. There have been few films made in the past fifty years that rival this one. It impressed me in a profound, life-long way that insinuated itself into the way I view our technological world and our place — humanity, that is — in the universe."

Jack studied her face as she spoke. He saw her eyes dancing, her expression rapt — her entire body engaged in consideration of what she was saying.

"Kate Roarty, I don't think I have ever encountered another human being quite like you. You are so passionate about all that surrounds you, all that you think about, and all that you touch. Here you are just escaping your demise in a helicopter crashing into the water, injured — a shoulder dislocation is painful — yet we lie down to do something as mundane as watching an old film, and first you infuse delight in anticipation of ordering a meal as simple as fish and chips, then you enthrall me with your enthusiasm for a fifty-year-old film. How is that I'm so fortunate to have you in my life — to be part of your life?"

"Now who is being ridiculously passionate? You are speaking about the woman who puts you in harm's way so frequently, we can't count the number of times you are running ahead of destruction."

Jack could only offer one response. He rolled over, took her face in his hands, and leaned into a long, deep, and passionate kiss.

When they gently pulled apart, Kate said, "And I love your brand of engagement."

The film was the perfect distraction, keeping them quiet, sequestered, and resting. It was long at two and half hours. Jack watched intently, in part as an exercise in pure escapism, just to be with Kate without threat of risk, the preoccupation of the case she was investigating and … to give him more insight into the thoughts of this fascinatingly complex person in his life. They were watching a film made before he was born that had inspired her as a young child and continued to captivate her imagination as a mature woman who had raised children, engaged successfully in several careers, and embarked on a new career that was unique, dangerous, and threatening. She was a loner who had amassed a following devoted to keeping her alive, safe, and solving their mysteries. The film had played for at least thirty minutes before any dialogue began.

"Kate, I thought you said this film was made in the sixties, not a silent production from the nineteen twenties."

"Ah, but that is one of the many features of *2001* that makes it a landmark departure in film production. Sadly, in the intervening half century nobody has risen to the excellence of Stanley Kubrick. This production was masterful, portraying technology beyond where we are today, using music and silence to communicate the mysteries of space, foreshadowing the power of computerization before computers became a mainstay part of the human experience." She paused. "The film … Jack, Kubrick possessed the brilliance to envisage a technological future that reached beyond this planet, into an universe frightening to the limitations of humanity, yet infinite to the consideration of possibilities. To me, the film is sublime inspiration."

"How is it that it never came up before?"

Kate smiled at him and replied, "It was waiting backstage to make a grand appearance."

She snuggled in close to him, winced a little with the shoulder pain, and clicked the remote to resume watching.

"Like the draw of the lander each time it awakens and transmits messages to Earth in the first person about its host comet, HAL's artificial intelligence penetrated deep into the psyche of our space and scientific exploration. That damned computer, HAL, remained with me like an imaginary friend that accompanies a child through the trials and tribulations of young life, offering explanations for what is, when the brain cannot wrap itself around some experiences of living."

Jack laughed lightly. "And to think I was simply going to watch an entertaining old film."

The phone rang. It was Mr. Tahir Tiwana. "Madame Roarty, your fish and chips with French mayonnaise has arrived. May I bring them up?"

Kate said, "Dinner has arrived." She reached for the remote and paused the film.

Jack leapt off the bed and slipped a Glock out of his bag, backing into the bathroom door just before the buzzer sounded. Kate was surprised but quickly switched the screen to the camera's view of the hallway. Tahir was standing there alone with a bag she presumed was their meal. Jack could view the doorway in the mirror opposite, but it would not reveal him to the entranceway. He nodded to Kate to open the door. Tahir smiled, handed her the bag, and said, "Enjoy. My aunt left her card inside in case you wish to make a complaint or visit her shop."

"Thanks, Mr. Tiwana." He turned to look at Jack in the bathroom door with his Glock raised. "A bit skittish, are we,

Superintendent Johnson?" He smiled, bowed slightly, and turned to leave."

Jack said, "Wait, can you please open the bag and set everything out on the little table there?"

Tahir studied Jack for a moment then said, "Of course," and he did as requested.

"Please open the cartons and take a bite of each item."

"Of course, may I first wash my hands?" Jack continued to hold the Glock raised. He stepped aside to give Tahir access to the sink.

He washed his hands then said, "This only heightens my appetite for the extra package my auntie sent over for me. Every time I attract a customer for her, she loses her profit by rewarding me with a gratuitous meal. It's a vicious circle but a rather endearing game as well. Goodnight, Mrs. Kate Roarty and Superintendent Jack Johnson. Enjoy your meal and *2001: A Space Odyssey* — it's also one of my favourites."

Kate sighed then spoke with an annoyed jest in the tone of her voice, "The downsides of my investigatory work is the total lack of privacy when I am working a case, never quite knowing who the good guys and bad guys are, always feeling as though I am straddling that no man's zone between the two — oh, and did I mention facing possible annihilation at every turn and putting you under threat by association."

"Ah, Kate, most of the time you love it. The adrenaline high remains addictive, despite your efforts to temper it with swimming and meditation."

"I don't like you being put at risk because of your association with me," said Kate.

"Police work has always infused an element of danger into my life, perhaps not quite as sophisticated as your experiences, but the result is the same. Kate, it contributes to the comfort we enjoy together. Now let's eat this British-made fish and chips, arriving via culinary inspirations originating in Pakistan and Paris, garnished with a dollop of the British Intelligence Services, and consumed in the company of a space odyssey with the enchanting HAL the computer in the lead role, all of which inspired this middle-aged woman beside me to go after a band of culprits who steal intellectual property in order to apply it to the making of millions in the mining business."

Remembering the slow pace of the film and the small amount of dialogue, Kate expected to fall asleep as they watched the opus. Rather, they both remained enthralled by the poetic nature of the film as it moved symphonically through space, ultimately yielding to the struggle of the minds between the artificial intelligence of HAL and the human intelligence of Dave. Jack assumed HAL would place the experience in checkmate — adaptive human intelligence prevailed as the film ended, leaving Kate with a sense of sci-fi revival and Jack wishing the journey to continue.

"It is hard to believe that this film was made more than fifty years ago. Although so much has occurred in technological development and space exploration, it continues to project a futuristic vision. Thank you, Kate, for introducing a former beat cop with credentials in criminology, martial arts, and little else to the expanse of your imagination that reaches beyond the considerations of Earth-bound humanity."

Kate appeared wide awake and deep in thought. She looked over to him and said, "If I could return to the choices of my young adult years, I do believe that I would have pursued a career in science. This intellectual property angle I can learn as I go, allowing me to at least flirt with scientific concepts and applications. Along the way, I experience many bright minds developing fascinating technologies. It's indeed a vicarious pleasure pursued to an extreme, but I will take it any way I can, enjoy the exposure, and perhaps promote scientific integrity along the way."

"You do experience a good number of dark scientific applications and what some scientists choose to do with the skew of their brilliance. You know, Kate, because of your involvement in scientific espionage, I have hired graduates with a science and technology background. It brings a very different dynamic to a traditional approach to policing. The rapid growth of Internet predatory crime forced us to hire computer specialists, but none with the advanced science applications. That is changing as the lines of commercial crime blur with scientific corruption."

Kate smiled. "The SQ may put me out of work."

"Or provide an unlimited pipeline of contracts," said Jack.

Kate awakened six hours later, still caught in a tangled brain reflection in which she had been marinating when she drifted off to sleep. Jack remained in a deep sleep. She slipped out of bed, put on the coffee, splashed cold water on her face, then settled into an hour of mindful meditation. It had been a long time since she gave herself over to the practice. She rose from it refreshed, centred, and relaxed with a sense of equilibrium restored. In the absence of being able to swim, her most effective method of achieving a sense of balance and well-being, meditation would have to suffice.

The hotel phone rang. Kate grabbed it on the first ring to try to keep the noise from waking Jack.

Tahir said, "This isn't a wakeup call, but I trust you slept well, Mrs. Roarty? Mrs. Karen Palmer has been trying to reach you on your mobile, which I suspect is turned off."

"Ah, yes."

"She would like you to join her for lunch at her office if quite convenient. She will be unavailable to receive a call until then, but I can get a reply back to her."

"That would be fine, Mr. Tiwana."

"Good then, Agent Bruan will meet you in the lobby here and accompany you over — enjoy your morning." He rang off.

Jack was awakened and said, "Are you feeling like getting out for some air?"

"Into dodging bullets and bombs, are you?"

"I figure your stalkers are late risers — let's do it."

They were on the street in a few minutes, briskly walking through narrow residential neighbourhoods, taking in the morning bustle of people, vehicles, and shops opening for business. The smells of freshly perked coffee and bakery goods wafted out invitingly from doorways beckoning to enter, savour, eat, and drink. City sirens signalled urgent activity, newsstands sported new issue downloads, the noisy brakes of older fossil fuel buses mixed with the soundless movement of newer solar-powered vehicles and the almost inaudible but ever-present whirr of drones on delivery, surveillance, and attendance. They watched a drone halt a speeding transporter about to plow through a pedestrian crosswalk — malfunction or violation, regardless, these surveillance drones performed a vital civil service in keeping the population safe and vehicles tuned to top function.

Jack said, "Have you noticed how our line of vision has shifted to pay much more attention to middle and upper sight lines in airspace occupied by drones?"

"Yes, I remember visiting New York as a young person and being so taken in by the architecture that I walked into parking meters and street signs while looking up. Those obstacles are all gone now, managed by the computer city grid systems. We still look up but rarely to take in the magnificent architecture, more so to watch and dodge drones large enough to be visible. Our inferior human guidance systems have not caught up with the drone sensor navigation capabilities."

"Are you wearing one of those temperature sensor coats?"

"No, I have two versions to wear over our protective armour that is wafer-thin now, but in my personal life I still prefer to satisfy my outdoor signals with texture and weight."

"Of course, when spending time with me — especially when I am investigating a case — the blur between the safety requirements of your professional career and your personal protection is all too obvious."

"True, Kate, and that is life."

Jack and Kate rarely walked hand in hand, evidence of their equally independent personalities and cognizance for safety. For a moment, with an open stretch of sidewalk ahead of them, Kate slipped her arm from the uninjured shoulder around Jack's elbow.

"Hey, let's walk down my old street — Rosary Gardens isn't too far from here. We can head into the nearest Underground station and catch the Green Line over to South Kensington then walk back toward Sloane Square. There is great neighbourhood architecture, coffee shops, and eateries that might pleasantly distract us as we walk along."

Jack teased, "We need distraction, do we?"

"Okay, Monument station is just up here. Let's do it but quickly in case there is anyone following us." They descended into the station. Kate whipped out her Oyster card, handing a second one to Jack, and they swiped through the turnstiles in an instant.

"Keep those on hand all the time, do you?"

"I happen to have two — the second from a visit here with my son a few years back."

Jack was uneasy, and Kate was on hyper alert, scanning the passengers for any untoward behaviour that might signal trouble.

The train passed several stations uneventfully, then Kate's level of unease increased. She quietly moved them toward the door, then at the last moment before it was going to close at Sloane Station, she stepped off, pulling Jack behind her.

"Let's regain the open air," she said, moving quickly through the familiar corridors past vendors and up stairs and out through the old tunnel like entranceway into the light, noise, and business of the streets approaching Sloane Square.

"Do that all the time, do you?" Jack quipped as he surveyed the masses of people bustling to and from the Tube station.

"Only when my heart rate elevates to a point where the flight urge kicks in and I must go. It has returned to normal now, and my shoulder is hurting, so it's time for breakfast with copious amounts of fresh-brewed coffee."

They located a café with a free table that gave them both a view of the entranceway, the street beyond, and most of the interior. The fat-filled meal of fish and chips the night before prompted Kate to opt for fruit, granola, and yogurt. Jack sighed at her healthy choice and toned down his desire for heaping amounts of eggs, bacon, and home fries. He selected two poached eggs, spelt toast, and a half cantaloupe.

He raised his coffee cup to Kate and with a smile said, "Maybe it isn't love at all that attracts me to you but rather the guarantee of a steady dose of adrenalin highs that characterize our time together."

"Could be, Jack Johnson. I am happy to relish whatever interpretation you apply to our mingled emotions, as long as the end result continues to be an ongoing devoted attraction."

They were enjoying the banter volleying back and forth as they awaited their breakfast and steady coffee refills.

She viewed the large news screen above the open kitchen that read "International investors poised to invest billions to extract trace minerals from Kazakhstan mining tailings."

Catalina Seaborne, the newsreader, was saying, "The worldwide shortage of trace minerals essential to the production of all forms of digital viewing screens is about to get a boost in supplies. Researchers have found massive amounts of trace deposits of rare earth minerals left from the rudimentary mining practices of decades ago. A process initially developed to extract trace deposits from gold tailings is found to have applicability in ferretting out and concentrating discarded traces of rare earth minerals. The international scientific team assembled to pursue this project has been given the green light for financing by a British-led investment consortium."

Both the content of the report and the presenter captured Kate's attention. The whoosh of being in the presence of perfection that swept through Kate's psyche when she met this woman, the daughter of their helicopter pilot, repeated the same arresting impact.

"I guess it is back to work," sighed Jack. "Kate, I am heading over to Ireland for a few days. As you know, my origins in Quebec are French-speaking, but the name Johnson made its debut with the arrivals from Ireland in the seventeenth century. Those Irish were as Catholic as the French already entrenched in the province. They readily assimilated into the larger French-speaking population through the connection to and influence of the Catholic Church. The language yielded from Irish to French within a generation, and cultural behaviours soon followed. I've pondered these distant Irish origins that actually go back a thousand years, beginning with the Norman invasion of England. I'm happy enough to have settled for the recent several hundred years and would like to visit the area that these Johnsons hailed from in Ireland. Ireland is close enough that I can go and return to London to hook up with you when you are ready to leave the UK. If you get thoroughly side-tracked, as long it is not another life-threatening episode, I can head back to Quebec from there."

Kate took this in, already missing him before he departed. "Who knows, you may very well find an earlier Roarty–Johnson connection that preordained our attraction."

Jack was aware of the high level of distraction the newscast had introduced; he sensed Kate's thoughts speeding up through layers of consideration, striving to achieve a view above the clouds before descending back into the quagmire of deception, corruption, greed, and menace that characterized the case she was working on.

She dabbled at her food as Jack wolfed down his meagre offering. When he finished, she pushed hers toward him. He accepted the top-up, paid the bill, and they were out the door. Once back at the hotel, they embraced in the short time they enjoyed before Kate had to leave to meet Liz Bruan in the lobby and head over to MI6 for lunch with Karen Palmer. After her departure, Jack had time to place a call to his lieutenant and to Guy Archambault. While little out of the realm of routine policing had occurred during his absence, he welcomed the opportunity to share the details of his time with Kate in Paris and London. Guy sounded rather unfazed as Jack recounted the details of Kate's kidnapping and crash into the Thames.

Guy said, "The romantic interlude in Paris at the beginning of your trip sounded good, and then it became Kate on a flying trapeze without a tether. *Mon patron*, you know this will be life with Kate Roarty as long as she does that IP P.I. work."

While Guy had provided an update on Daggy's progress, Jack still took the time to call Daggy and Marny directly. He learned from them that while the icy conditions of late winter kept Daggy from walking outdoors, Marny was driving him to the gym every day, where he could walk and do an exercise routine designed to restore fitness and ease his heart and lungs back into adequate performance. He was talking about taking on an administrative job to return to work in a few weeks.

Marny said, "The upside of all of this is it's the first time in years that we have been able to spend so much time together. The girls are thrilled with having their dad around all the time; he has engaged with them in a way I have never seen before. The relatives are wonderfully helpful and encouraging to have here as well. We laugh a lot, Jack. They are beginning to talk about heading home, leaving in a trickle as our ability to cope with daily life improves. I don't know what I would do without them."

"We should have them on the SQ payroll — it would have been rough on your own — although I am sure Kate and Big Ben would have moved in to help out if that was needed."

"We miss Kate, Jack."

"So do I, and I only left her a few hours ago."

"Is her work still keeping her living on the edge?"

"Yes, gazing into the precipice with vicious hyenas snarling upward."

"Jesus, Jack, anything you can do about moving her toward a tamer line of work?"

"Absolutely nothing, Marny, that's part of what keeps Kate vibrant and vigorous. I expect when she becomes physically too old to continue living on the edge, she will get her adrenaline highs by writing about it. I'm off to Ireland to do a bit of research on the Johnson family history. Call any time, Marny, and I will call again soon."

28

The plan to lunch with Karen Palmer to go over the trace mineral deposits case was thwarted by an explosion near number 10 Downing, where the only serious but deadly injury was an MI6 agent. All Kate had learned was that it was a confirmed terrorist attack by a post-ISIS cyber terror group that likely launched the explosives from the safety of a drone operations panel bounced off a commercial satellite. Nevertheless, while the geek squad deep in the bowels of GCHQ frantically searched the keychains of every known cyber terrorist with activity in the UK, the director of MI6 joined her MI5 colleagues on the ground to get a first-hand sense of the target, damage, and investigation plan.

    Kate yearned to connect with Bryant; he could probably shed some light on the cyber trail pointing toward responsibility for the attack. She didn't dare attempt to access him from within the bowels of MI6 for fear of exposing him and putting him at risk. MI6 and GCHQ were both aware that Kate had a brilliant cyberspace maestro within her network from the successes they benefitted from on the Taylor case. Still, she assiduously guarded his identity. That was the agreement. After well over two years, Bryant had learned a great deal about Kate, but Kate had learned very little about Bryant. Nevertheless, she trusted him implicitly, often with her very survival, and he never let her down. She thought, *It would be hard to expect more of a friend, a colleague, and a wizard in cyberspace.*

Kate slipped back into the dining room, gathered her belongings, and made to depart when Karen Palmer arrived. The two women paused, made eye contact, and smiled. They sat, and Kate noted fatigue written across Palmer's face and etched into the slump of her shoulders. She poured a tea from the pot still warm and full on the table.

"It never gets easier, losing an agent," sighed Palmer as she picked up the hot cup and raised it to her lips.

Kate nodded but remained silent, giving her the opportunity to speak first. "She was young — just twenty-six and about to receive her PhD. We recruited her at the convocation ceremony for her undergraduate degree. She had been accepted to graduate school with a small scholarship. We offered her the salary of a new agent and to cover all expenses for her graduate studies. She spoke French, Farsi, Arabic, and Mandarin and had been a talented gymnast before taking up martial arts. She was a beautiful, accomplished human being, the only child of parents who had emigrated from Cairo to provide a better — safer — life for their yet to be born baby. We took away all of those hopes and dreams. We thought our purpose was more important. The thug who killed her was the same age, same background — also pursuing a dream. The parents of the terrorist plant and our agent went to the same mosque. The young man did not likely even need to be there for the operation to be carried out; his presence made it easy to signal the identity of the perpetrators. All of our brilliance, technological capability, and yes, compassion cannot make sense of this. It appears the intent was to kill many more. Fortunately, the wounded will likely all recover from their injuries —

physically that is. My normally entrenched hard core is eluding me at this moment, Kate."

Kate continued to remain silent, allowing the thoughts and feelings to digest. "We're both women, both mothers, and both doing what we do — perhaps that's why you can speak at this moment, Karen Palmer."

"Let's talk about the trace minerals case. We have made sense, at least somewhat so, of that mess." Kate nodded and allowed a faint smile. "Only after you have drunk that cup of hot tea, sweetened with a dash of maple syrup.

"Our agent who keeps an eye on activity on Threadneedle Street followed a series of investments in rare earth minerals research. The portfolio became interesting, and its value grew quickly. These investments coincided with the rapid development of the application that your young Canadian scientists were working on and in desperate need of money to advance the research. We don't think they understood the complexity behind the funding they were promised — then it morphed so swiftly from a small consortium into a multinational syndicate that the principal investigators withdrew from the day-to-day operations to focus on the science. They let their financial manager deal with it, regrettably without much oversight. She was easily compromised, although she may very well have gone to them already tainted. As is so often the case with scientists, while they are thorough and exacting in their scientific research, they are weak and easily compromised by the business dimensions of their work.

"It appears our Mr. Beltman was trying to keep all of the players honest, but influence unravelled once the Russians got in on the game. Some young Russian scientists working in a private lab that also employed a few equally capable Chinese post-doc types took a version of the application to Kazakhstan, where they were intercepted by a Chinese delegation. They seemed to have worked out an agreement to allow the testing to go ahead and found the outcomes promising. Your lads remained ahead of the game, having already achieved very promising results from tailings in Canada. The scientists on this side of the Atlantic are all pawns of the would-be financiers that, apart from Beltman, tended more toward thuggery than legitimate investment. The Russians, being typically impatient, likely chose to take him out so they wouldn't have to deal with his ongoing interference. They were probably finding your activity equally annoying but totally underestimated your survival capabilities. I am sure that I haven't told you much more than you have already surmised. MI6 is merely confirming it. What I can tell you is that we're interested in cleaning up the corruption on Threadneedle Street and continue to expose IP theft. Can we work together to that end? If you decline, I will be completely up-front with you, Kate. We will continue to keep an eye on your activity, play a role in keeping you alive, and benefit from whatever you manage to accomplish."

"In other words, I have no choice but to have MI6 and, de facto, GCHQ in my face."

"We will try to be discreet, but yes, that is pretty much the case. MI5 will likely be lurking about as well."

"Joy. So all I need to do is exploit the British Intelligence Service without being beholden to them or sucked into their bureaucratic maelstrom."

"Something like that."

Kate observed a relaxation of the tension in Palmer's face and body, a positive sign that the director was regaining a sense of equilibrium in the wake of the carnage she had witnessed.

"Kate, we fully acknowledge your efficacy in working alone. There are definite advantages to allowing your detractors to think you are flying solo. But you are not, and you will not. What I can guarantee is that we will consistently let you take the lead so we do not inadvertently undermine your focus and progress."

"Mrs. Palmer, I can try to believe that commitment, but we both know that it will work some of the time for each of us. So far, it has not jeopardized our respective investigations. While I trust you, my position has not changed since we worked together on the Taylor case. You are part of a large organization with many, many players and relationships; it remains impossible to eschew corruption. I am an organization of one — I trust myself. Now let's eat. It's late and we are both starving — you are in particular need of reinforcement."

Agent Anthony Blythe entered the dining room but was quickly dispatched by Palmer. "Agent Blythe, we are fine for now. I will include you later. Can you ask Agent Bruan to join us in about fifteen minutes?"

The expression on Agent Blythe's face, torn between duty and personal affront, did not escape Kate's observation as he exited. Kate looked back at Karen Palmer to find she was studying her expression. Words were not spoken, although Kate felt that one day something might be revealed about the relationship between these two people.

Kate rose. "I have to decide quickly whether or not to proceed to Kazakhstan to investigate the actual application and efficacy of the technology. It will likely be a trip to confirm what I already suspect, but it may help to determine if the IP can be restored to the original innovators — my clients — or the best I can do may be to get the thieves to pay market value for what they have stolen."

"We have a presence in the oil sector in Kazakhstan. Given its importance to the world economy, we watch it closely through the network that this local agent has on the ground there. Is he above corruption? Not likely, but he's been proven reliable. GCHQ monitors the digital traffic very closely, and he knows it. It keeps him in check. He has a personal beef with the Russians that helps us remain at least somewhat assured that he won't work with them. We also have a political analyst expert that works out of a think-tank type operation in Astana. She would not likely be of great use to you, but she is Western-educated, believes all men are corrupt, and is a quick study. She has been useful to us, although there is no love lost between the two agents. We doubt they could effectively collaborate if we needed them to do so.

"We can always go in with a commercial cover if we have to and operate effectively for a short time. If you decide to go, I suggest you go in on a business visa connected to one of our vetted companies. That way you can move about in the industrial and business sector with much greater ease." Kate listened and nodded, acknowledging the advice but reserving commitment to the approach. She knew that this would give MI6 a high degree of control and opportunity for interference. Kate could work with the proposal to get into Kazakhstan, gather her intel, and get out quickly. She was intrigued by going into a part of the world that would be new to her — expanding her arsenal of first-hand exposure and understanding. Karen Palmer seemed able to hear her thoughts.

"Look, Kate, I can set you up with a briefing from our expert on that area. I will give her carte blanche to make it the full Monty, then you decide from there."

Kate recognized that she was being reeled in but decided to go with the flow. It might be okay to stay on the line for a while. "I will expect to hear back through Agent Bruan then?" The MI6 director smiled with a slight nod and went on her way.

Kate exited the edifice, surprised that she was becoming comfortable — almost familiar — with the surroundings. Her thoughts lingered for only a moment when she realized a familiar voice was addressing her.

"Will 9:00 a.m. tomorrow morning work for you? By the way, we moved you over to a hotel with a decent-sized pool within the building and adequate security to keep an eye on you. The pool is on the top floor surrounded by windows."

"And are you the adequate security that will join me for my swim?"

Liz flushed but remained stoic in her response. "Only if you wish. We can also arrange to be more discreet."

"And are we walking to my new hotel now?"

"Yes, if you wish, or a taxi can get you there faster. The walk would take a half hour or so."

"Let's do the taxi."

Kate realized the prospect of a swim was very appealing.

"Yes, 9:00 a.m. would be fine," she said to Agent Bruan as she left the taxi, doubting that it was actually a taxi.

The doorman addressed her by name and offered to show her directly to her room.

Kate entered a modern, small suite furnished in a rather Scandinavian design — clean lines devoid of cluttering furnishings — but well equipped with a kitchenette and salon space. The bedroom and bathroom were behind separate doors and likewise small but spaciously designed. She pressed the large-screen remote code for the pool and took a virtual tour of all on offer. Within moments, she had changed into her swimsuit, donned the hotel robe and sandals, and headed up for her swim. To her delight, she had the pool to herself and plied through the water with ease and purpose as her thoughts sorted into considerations, decisions, and concrete plans. She would reserve the final decision about Kazakhstan until after she met with Graham

Burke and spoke with the MI6 expert. While she missed Jack, she was happy for the time to completely focus on the trajectory of the investigation. Kate was looking forward to a dinner with her financier and friend, Graham Burke, who had her back without agenda.

29

Graham Burke was waiting in the lobby for Kate when she exited the elevator. While she had spent little time with him, it was intense and rewarding, so she greeted him with the familiarity of an old friend and genuinely felt that way about him. He too approached Kate with the warmth of a lasting connection. He was a successful thirty-something who could read people in their environment, uncharacteristic of a scientist cum entrepreneur and a very wealthy man. After an enveloping embrace, she stood back to look at him, holding his arms, and said, "And how is your son?"

Graham beamed. "Kate, we have so much to talk about. Let's get to the restaurant where we can speak about what brings you here and get caught up on our lives."

His SUV that took her to the airport two years before was the same vehicle waiting for them at the entrance to the hotel. The driver slid the vehicle into traffic with ease, and before they could barely comment on the weather, they were cruising through Hyde Park. They stopped at the Serpentine, and Graham leapt out.

"Even though it is evening and a bit cool, I didn't think you would turn down an opportunity to stroll along the

Serpentine. Our restaurant is nearby — the cool, brisk air will arouse our appetite as we walk and talk."

Kate turned sideways while still moving forward, and with an almost teenage enthusiasm, she said, "First things first, tell me about your son."

Graham could not contain his enthusiasm. "Kate, that boy is a wonder. He never ceases to amaze me. I feel genuinely blessed to have him as my son. He is infinitely curious, willing to try almost anything — in fact, I find myself acquiring many new skills and interests just so we can experience them together. He inherited an extraordinary musical talent from his mother's side of the family. He is also inquisitive about all things scientific. We just returned from a walking holiday in the Lake District that I feared he might find boring. Quite the contrary — I couldn't keep up with him. We passed the days on vigorous walks interrupted by bird watching, bug collecting, and sheep sketching. He loves the ancient Herdwick breed protected by Beatrix Potter on her bequeathed lands. He prefers to sketch them rather than photograph them, because that way he can capture the nuances of each animal he sketches … whatever. He has few friends his own age — in fact, only one — and that concerns me. I think his mind runs on a constant overdrive that may be unattractive to run-of-the-mill playmates. His one friend, a girl, is a female version of him with an added mischievousness in her demeanour. It's good for Todd to experience getting into trouble from time to time, and she lures him into it — trouble, that is. You should hear them jamming. He plays several instruments, and she plays the drums — loud, risky, and innovative."

They circumnavigated not only the Serpentine but also most of Hyde Park while Kate listened to Graham speaking about his son. He stopped abruptly, excusing himself for the total absorption in his only offspring.

Kate waved her hand. "Graham, I love it. Your enthusiasm is infectious. I must admit it aroused some delightful sentiments about my own children at that age. Enjoy every moment — time passes so very quickly."

They walked along in their own thoughts for a bit. Kate said, "Shall we continue on around Green Park as dusk is coming on, then head for dinner?"

"That sounds like a plan."

"By the way, Graham Burke from California, do you know you are acquiring a bit of a British accent?"

"Indeed, my in-laws have remarked on that as well. I think it has something to do with shifting my identity from America to Britain."

Kate replied, "I recall observing that my mother, who was born and raised in the UK, almost entirely dropped her British accent in the first years after becoming a Canadian citizen. Prior to that, I don't think she yielded a single intonation during the twenty-eight years she lived in Canada."

They stopped to watch the sun slip below the horizon. "We don't see the sun enough in this country … in this city. It's the only thing I truly miss about my California home. When I need a sunshine fix, we head to Spain or Portugal for a long weekend, and that does the trick." He looked at Kate and spoke in a teasing manner. "Do you know that Kazakhstan has almost one thousand hours more of sunlight than there is in the UK? That's forty-one days — six weeks. You must go there, if only to experience the sunlight."

"Yes, of course, I'm on it," she replied with same level of teasing intonation. "I carry those details around in my head all the time."

"I looked it up as an opener to try to convince you to go to Kazakhstan. Levity is always useful."

"Definitely, in the face of murderous pursuit, threat of confinement, torture, dismemberment, or at the very least being barred from entering the country. We won't even talk about getting out. The fact that Kazakhstan gets one thousand hours more sunlight is warm comfort."

"Kate, I think it's worth the trip to confirm what you already suspect and perhaps repatriate the IP. It'd make a huge difference to the careers of the young scientists who've hired you, not to mention the future of technological communications."

Kate laughed. "Ah, if we just get on with building a sphere around the sun to harness all of the energy this planet and many others will ever need, we won't have to dabble in extracting trace elements of rare earth minerals from old mine tailings."

"Let's hope we'll see that in our lifetime. In the meantime, I think those lads need their IP back, and we need an energy boost from a good meal and fine wine."

"You are on," Kate said as she broke into a run to the edge of the park directly across the road from the restaurant.

"I said restore energy, not dissipate it," said Graham, catching up to her, taking her arm, and weaving through the slow-moving traffic to the other side of road and down a narrow side street to the entrance of the Japanese restaurant he had selected for their evening meal. "I chose it for its atmosphere and fine food served izakaya style. I have never been here, but my wife recommended it, and her recommendations never miss the mark."

They entered a warm, inviting space where a smiling, friendly Japanese man in a business suit greeted Graham with a slight bow and said, "This way, Mr. Burke," leading the pair to a quiet intimate booth.

"May I serve you beer or saki as you consider the menu?"

They replied in unison, "beer," followed by a mutual chuckle.

"I can't say I have ever been a fan of saki. Japanese beer, on the other hand, I can easily enjoy."

"Likewise," replied Kate.

They conversed quietly and easily in the privacy of the booth, sitting on tatami mats. After they ordered miso soup, sushi, and edamane, they settled back into the slow tempo of little dishes arriving sporadically. The traditional-clad servers entered unobtrusively, placing various little servings before them then floated out with a gentle bow that left a tranquil aura in their wake. They accomplished this so graciously that neither Kate nor Graham felt they were being interrupted.

"You know the izakaya dining style began as a very casual answer to providing food accompaniment in drinking establishments in Japan where the working class migrated to after work. In transplanting the custom abroad, it has become a classier, more sophisticated fine dining experience, like we find in this restaurant. I love it because it is healthy, tasty food, prepared fresh by experts in Japanese cuisine. I have never felt over-stuffed eating this style of food but always go away sated from the experience."

Kate looked over the abundant collection of small servings, settling on the Chinese gyoza, a long-time favourite, and replied, "You took the words right out of my mouth."

Graham poked at her in playful jest. "Clever, witty lady who chases high-end thugs around the world."

"Thugs that can be rather good at carrying out their intentions, my dear man," mused Kate.

"Shall we walk up the street to a little gelato shop for dessert? The Italian family who runs it has been making gelato for generations. They invent the most intriguing flavours making every visit a gastronomic experience. I had garlic perogies, and my son had blubber guts on our last visit there."

"And here I thought I was being adventurous with chocolate chili gelato in a wonderful gelato café in Ottawa. Let's go."

Graham's driver was waiting outside when they stepped on to the street in front of the Japanese restaurant. He let the driver know where they were heading, and they carried on.

"I love to walk, everywhere I can," said Kate.

"So do I, but often it is neither possible nor safe. In this case, I am anonymous but you aren't."

"Hey," replied Kate playfully. "A fifty-something, lone Canadian woman of limited means…"

"Who investigates ten-figure deals, flipping through technology innovation faster than a drone breaking the sound barrier. Let's focus on the gelato choice that will confound even your well-ordered mind."

They exited the shop, Kate with a scoop of Galloping Black Bean Stallion and Graham with a cup of Yak Butter Curry, sharing the tantalizing and very weird taste extravaganzas.

"How could I possibly be reticent about going to Kazakhstan after this," laughed Kate as she savoured every bit while accepting generous samplings of Graham's.

"Indeed, it is a reality check."

Graham dropped Kate back at her hotel and saw her not only into the lobby but insisted on accompanying her up to her room.

"Kate, I just want to know that I am leaving you safely, without any apparent threat. You deserve the occasional evening without looking over your shoulder or being confronted by the threat of your imminent demise."

She thanked him for a terrific evening, vowing never to forget the Galloping Black Bean Stallion gelato.

30

Kate exhaled as she pressed the door shut to hold at bay the menacing black stallion charging down on her. He had been prancing about in the corral of her controlled thoughts restrained by her focus, mollified by meditation, released by her swimming — this evening he broke out. His pounding hooves, flayed nostrils, ears back and sleek, sweating body, taut with strength and power, were rallying together to take control of her psyche. She had to move quickly to rein him in before he wrecked havoc.

The vibration of her phone in her pocket lurched her back to reality. It was Jack. She looked at the screen and let the call pass to voicemail.

The black stallion pawed at the ground in her predawn awakening. Kate rose very early to start her day with mindful meditation, followed by coffee and a long, explosive swim in the hotel pool. The stallion crossed the river, emerging on the other side, shaking free the water coursing through his coat as he charged up the embankment and through the forest, folding into the trees, gone from sight but not from sentiment. Kate rang MI6 to get her a fast-track business visa to Kazakhstan then booked a flight. The fierce image of the horse settled a little.

Kate took a seat in the breakfast room, a spot where the sunshine was streaming through long, narrow windows. The waiter arrived with a pot of coffee and a small glass of bilberry juice — a house specialty. The husband of the owner was from Finland. Every year in August his parents shipped crates of fresh bilberries that threw the owner into a frenzy of juice- and jam-making and fast freezing to have supplies on hand for muffins, pies, custards, traditional British fools, and smoothies on request for the breakfast crowd. Kate had learned this during an interesting chat when she enquired if bilberries were similar to Canadian blueberries. Her query summoned the chef/owner from the kitchen, a smiling, spirited woman who was delighted to recount the tale of bilberries in her culinary repertoire. The woman was convinced of the nutritional benefits of the dark blue berry, filled with minerals and anti-oxidants that were believed to enhance vision and ward off colon cancer and maladies of the skin, as well as improve circulation and strengthen the heart. Regardless, Kate was similarly convinced of the benefits of blueberries that grew throughout Canada. Whether or not the benefits were real, she firmly believed in the efficacy of the placebo effect. Their conversation led them to Canadian maple syrup, for which Kate confessed a craving unsatisfied by any sweetener substitute — particularly for her morning coffee. This morning the waiter placed a tiny pitcher of golden brown liquid beside her coffee cup, saying, "And your maple syrup, madam."

"I see already you have the locals trained in your dietary habits," said a familiar voice. Kate sprang up from the table in surprise, almost knocking all of the serving to the floor. "I'll get that," said Claude Mason as he reached to steady the table and prevent the contents from slipping off.

Kate spontaneously threw her arms around him in a warm greeting, saying only, "Claude."

"I haven't had a greeting like that from a woman since I burst through the door after the first day of school, running into the arms of my mother," replied Claude.

"How did you find me? Stupid question." Kate glanced around. "Please sit," she said as she simultaneously motioned to the empty chair at her table and to the waiter for a second place setting. Before she could sit back down herself, the waiter had obliged.

Kate said, "He is almost too good to be a waiter. Is he one of yours?"

"No, but perhaps we should check into recruiting him. Does he speak the Queen's English?"

"Yes, with a slight overlay of a Polish accent to provide a continental sophistication."

"Do you like the restaurant?"

"I have only been here for breakfast, and it's terrific. Lots of fresh fare, with a bit of Finnish influence."

"The owner's husband is a cousin of Matti Toivenen," said Claude.

Kate smiled with a sigh and reflected upon the collection of men she had come to know while investigating the neuromicrochip case. Claude was one of them, as were Giorgio Beretta and Kiran Patel. Matti Toivenen from Finland was another. Kate's discovery of their murdered mate, Dr. Vincent Taylor, had brought them all together.

"That familial connection with Kiran is merely coincidental. We discovered it when we were checking out the place for you."

"Right, this cannot possibly be a purely pleasurable visit. What brings you to my breakfast table?"

"May I have a sip of coffee with a dollop of your maple syrup first?"

"Of course, although I am surprised to see you indulge in a sweetener."

"Blame it all on Clare, Vincent's mother. She insisted when we visited her lakeside cottage after the funeral. I accepted to be polite. Then she brought a can of it when she came for my graduation at MIT. Life has never been the same. Canadian maple syrup has taken up an entrenched foothold, and I pay handsomely for it in the exotic food section of my favourite Cheltenham grocer."

Kate laughed. "Glad to meet another convert … and to what do I have the pleasure of your company for this breakfast?"

Claude's face grew more serious. "Karen Palmer tells me you are planning a trip to Kazakhstan, departing imminently. I would like to accompany you."

This remark caught Kate by surprise. "Claude, I'm leaving this evening."

"I know, I have my bag. My business visa will be ready when yours is, and I think a seat will be found for me on your flight."

"And did you also fit in a swim?" Kate said, slightly sarcastically.

"No, even I have my limitations, but there should be time to catch one before we depart … if you agree to your travelling companion, that is…"

"Do I have much choice?"

"Yes, you do, Kate, but I sincerely hope you'll take the safer choice."

"I thought you specialized in cyber geeking, not field work."

"You're right, Kate, but that doesn't preclude applying our skill set to field research, so to speak. You could say our cyberspace is infinite." He flinched at his own bad joke and Kate's facial response to it.

They paused to place their breakfast orders. Kate requested a healthy array of fresh fruit, almond granola, plain yogurt, and croissant while Claude ordered a surprisingly large breakfast of eggs, bilberry crepes with added fresh fruit, and a double order of bacon and chips. "You may want to share my chips and bacon. You must be famished after ploughing through that marathon swim this morning. I somehow managed to miss lunch and dinner yesterday, so I'm definitely hungry."

Claude continued, "Kate, we all work together within the British SIS, Secret Intelligence Service. While we do have defined organizational roles sorted out as MI5, MI6, and GCHQ, there is a degree of interchangeability."

"Claude, don't play games with me. You are a director — this is not your kind of work. Tell me straight-up, why do you want to go to Kazakhstan, and why do you want to go with me?"

"Do you not recall that only two years ago I just about lost my life doing field work in the US? I trust you, Kate — more than I trust anyone, apart from the lads, of course. Besides, think how comfortable Jack will feel when he learns I am going along with you."

Kate smiled, then paused as the waiter placed her breakfast in front of her. "Right — I am starving and just a little bit crazy these past days."

Claude peeled off a couple of rashers of bacon and some roasted potato bits, placed them on a saucer, and passed them to Kate, who without thinking chowed down on the salty, crisp bacon, exclaiming, "Always the best part of a meal when I allow myself to indulge."

"Kazakhstan is an enigma for us within the British SIS in general and at GCHQ in particular. Your case interests me in how it fits into the broader scheme of intelligence-gathering. In particular, I want to experience first-hand, on the ground, the job in that part of the world. The Kazakh Foreign Intelligence Service signed an agreement to cooperate with us and many other intel services, but they don't — I think mostly because they don't need to. Their relationship with China is far more important to them since they successfully distanced themselves from the Russians. The Chinese Intelligence Service is tighter than a clam. We need them. I am not sure they need us."

"Claude, I now know more about Kazakhstan than I did an hour ago — testimony to how little I know about the country. Admittedly, I have singularly focused on the trace minerals issue with blinders on to the context of the way this is playing itself out in Kazakhstan. Proof enough that I could use a well-connected travelling colleague on this one. I do hope those connections won't get us in trouble. I suspect that we can't underestimate just how much the Kazakh secret service knows. Will you be travelling as yourself?"

Claude smiled. "One of the reasons I missed lunch and dinner yesterday was that I spent my time acquiring my new profile as the president of a junior mining company going by the name David Powers. Can you get used to calling me David?"

"If you permit the French pronunciation of David, Daaveed, I am good."

"Then David, *en français*, it is."

"I'll let the profilers know."

"Claude … Daaveed … those juniors are all trading on the stock exchanges — Toronto's TXS, Australia's ASX, South Africa's Johannesburg Stock Exchange — less so on the London Stock Exchange. It's pretty easy to check on the status of companies and their directors, because they are publicly traded."

"We have that covered. The British SIS holds a number of shell companies that can be temporarily activated to satisfy these profile needs. The cover would be tougher to pull off in the UK or Canada, but I think it can work in Kazakhstan."

"Daveed, I don't want you coming out of Kazakhstan in as bad of shape as you were when your rescuers got you out of Boston. Robert Beltman didn't make it out of Cape Town alive, although the swiftness with which he was dispatched suggests he might've never realized the level of danger facing him. It took a battalion of handlers to get me out of South Africa. I doubt we will ever have resources like that to call on in Kazakhstan."

"One of the many things I love about you, Kate, is your ability, as a lone wolf, to humble even the proudest leader of the pack yet never dislodge him from that lofty position. You actually do function as a leader of a pack, but in a much more esoteric way than is conventionally understood. I will be honoured to lope along beside you and call in the pack — both real and cyber-defined — when we need it. I know that you too have a desperate band of pack members who will respond to your bay at a moment's notice. I think the reach of the packs can work together when they have to for the benefit of the lone wolf and the tag-along. We will be fine."

Kate examined Claude and smiled. "I'll count on the Norse and sociobiology analogy lesson to define this working relationship."

"Ah-ha, look at the progress we are making from lone warrior to accepting a cohort to acknowledging the existence of an army standing by. I think this justified the hearty breakfast discussion. I must go — I'll meet you at the airport this evening." And he was gone, leaving Kate with the tab. She didn't mind; it left her with a small vestige of the lone wolf persona to cling to just a little longer.

When she checked her emails, she found the incoming flight confirmation on British Airways from London to Almaty. She was surprised to see that that nonstop direct flight had a flying time of eight and a half hours. She groaned for only a moment when she read further and saw the details that the flight had been booked in business class and paid but not applied to her credit card. Her pack was out there keeping out of the way but signalling their vigilance. Kate also reflected on Claude's lone wolf analogy, thinking that the while wolves have few predators, man is their greatest threat.

Between now and when she landed in Almaty, her priority was to become as informed as possible about everything to do with the people, politics, geology, industry, trade and commerce, and the landscape of the country. She somewhat sheepishly thought that perhaps she could propose exchanging whatever they had learned about the country if by chance they were sitting close enough on the flight. She burrowed in with her laptop and tablet open, browsing through history, politics, geology, industry trading patterns, economy — financing domestic and international. She was surprised to find a robust, expanding economy with a low level of poverty, a high level of literacy, and a sense of independence from the former Soviet Union and later Russia, given that Kazakhstan had only gained independence during the mid 1990s. The Chinese economic encroachment did not surprise her. She expected to learn that this factor would play a significant role in the theft of the intellectual properties trace mineral extraction process. While all of this was well and good, she needed a sense of the people — how they thought, reacted, behaved among themselves with their neighbouring country folk and toward foreigners like her and David Powers.

Kate drifted off to sleep as the flight lifted off, a common travelling habit that she simply succumbed to, and she awoke to a familiar voice speaking quietly to David Powers, who was seated next to her, although removed by the spaciousness of business class. Kate studied the person that went with the familiar voice and realized she was looking at Agent Liz Bruan. The nametag on her British Airways uniform read "Elizabeth Bowen, Cabin Service Director." Kate decided it was better to keep her mouth shut rather than risk blowing a cover through anything she might say.

Agent Liz Bruan, a.k.a. Elizabeth Bowen, finished speaking with Claude Mason, a.k.a. David Powers, smiled with a professional cool at Kate, and left.

"How many others are coming along?"

David looked at her with a mystified expression, and replied, "That's it."

"Shall we share what we know the Kazakhstan and its people? I imagine we have both read the same online sources about the country, the economy, and its rapid modernization — whatever we might surmise about the way the people think and behave will be useful. Having said that, we will likely discover our first-hand experience to be much more revealing than whatever we might read."

David Powers mused, "We have so little first-hand experience in a country that is the ninth largest in area and economy in the world."

Kate added, "I think we can safely suppose that we'll find a proud and independent people that are not to be underestimated. We may assume that there's a significant Russian influence carrying over from the days of the USSR control. However, ethnically these people's allegiances will be with the neighbouring -stans and China, where there are linguistic and cultural affinities. My sense is the outward appearance of Russian influence may exceed what is the actual case. As we encounter people, we will have to be constantly assessing where their allegiances and influences lay. That will give us an idea of where the money flows."

David Powers smiled as he remarked, "I think we both possess an adequate anthropological perspective to remain vigilant to the spheres of influence determining the power centres we'll enter into as we try to ferret out the criminality of this investigation."

Kate settled back, reflecting upon just how unprepared she was to take up the challenges they'd encounter when the plane landed. She was further dismayed at the untidiness in which she had left her life with her departure from London. She had not attempted to reach Jack, had not called her adult children, and not brought Bryant into the picture. She had not even called her neighbour or Clare to check in on Big Ben. She suspected this had a lot to do with the stallion. Although somewhat removed from her immediate perceptions, he was nevertheless continuing to prance along the ridge, twisting and turning as though his energy exceeded his ability to dissipate it.

She returned to reality as she saw a familiar hand place a lime and mineral water on the table in front of her. Cabin Service Director Elizabeth Bowen asked, "Would you like your meal now or later?"

Kate realized she was ravenous and replied, "Now, thanks."

"Breakfast or dinner — vegetarian or carnivorous?"

Kate stifled a laugh upon hearing the word "carnivorous."

"Meat, please."

"Wine with the meal or a non-alcoholic beverage?"

"Both," replied Kate. "White wine — a light Pinot Grigio if you have it, and coffee after the main course."

"Of course."

The cabin service director returned with a single-serving bottle of Italian Pinot Grigio, current year 2031, and showed it to Kate.

"Ah, that should ensure the crisp fruitiness is maintained."

She opened it, poured it, and tasted it. "The Italians have retained their expertise on this one. Lovely. It should go nicely with the Kazakh lemon chicken listed among the entrées on the menu."

Kate listened to David Powers placing his order of a red Sauvignon with an entrée of manti. After Elizabeth had left, Kate leaned enquiringly toward David. "Manti?"

"Yes, it's the Asian influence on the cuisine. Manti is a spicy stuffed dumpling bigger than the typical Chinese jiaozi but not as big as the steamed baozi. I think it is usually minced lamb, horse, or beef, with green garlic, herbs, and spices. I doubt British Airways would serve horsemeat, so it is likely lamb and beef. Try some when they bring it."

Kate looked around, thinking, *This is all too congenial and comfortable. It's almost akin to household domesticity. When is the plane going to be hijacked? Malfunction? Or, at the very least, someone has a heart attack?*

She ate a bit then dozed off with the image of the black stallion careening across the Eurasian plateau, nostrils splayed, eyes wild, straining headlong against the wind. No sooner in a deep sleep than she was bolted awake, so sure of the imagery in her dream that she simply sat and waited for what the stallion was running from and what he was running to came into focus — but neither happened.

"Hey sleeping beauty, you okay?"

"I just dozed off for a bit."

"A bit? You were out for hours. We are about to land. That wine must have sat well with you."

Kate sat up, quite disoriented, took note of her surroundings, and drank the bottle of water on the table in front of her. Gradually, her immediate context came into focus as her brain returned to some semblance of clarity.

"Kate, the cabin services director has arranged to clear us through the diplomatic and VIP visa wicket so we will be on our way quickly. She will meet us with our bags in a VIP exit lounge."

Kate acknowledged the remark, thinking that so far this entire trip had been stick-handled by someone other than herself. She determined to take greater control once they had cleared customs and immigration.

Kate and David breezed through visa control; scans of their documentation found all in order. They pushed through the door to the VIP exit lounge, where they found themselves alone, but not for long. Within moments, the cabin services director, Elizabeth Bowen, arrived with their bags, along with another small case. She raised her hand-held communicator to scramble the surveillance cameras.

"We have forty-five seconds before the cameras adapt to a new frequency and resume surveillance."

She opened the small case and handed each of them a handgun. Kate recognized the tried and true, ever-reliable Glock 27. She accepted the sidearm without debate. Liz also handed her a streamlined interior fabric holster and showed her how to insert it into her clothing. She suddenly stepped back and resumed the officious manner of a cabin services director.

"Enjoy your stay in Kazakhstan. We will be happy to serve you again on your return flight." And as quickly as she arrived, she was gone.

"Right, let's get out of this airport before some official changes his mind."

They readily found a taxi and were in it before Kate realized the transition had happened. "The office made reservations for us at the Rahat Palace Hotel — two king rooms. It has a pool big enough for a respectable workout. I hope that is okay with you."

It wasn't okay with Kate, but she had no legitimate reason for registering a complaint. She contained her annoyance by simply nodding and watching the landscape as it sped by, viewed from the taxi window en route to downtown Almaty.

She saw a modern, busy city with construction cranes spread across the skyline, suggesting it was monied, growing, and changing rapidly. A spectacular string of snow-capped mountains to the south formed an attractive backdrop to the mix of architecture and bustle of the city. Kate recalled the IOC shopping trip to host the 2026 Winter Olympics. Norway had pulled out when its electorate said yes to the Olympics but no to the IOC, while China was rejected in the face of the split city bid and concerns over the effects of pollution and global warming in Hebei province. Ukraine pulled out in favour of continuing to wage war with Russia, then the IOC rejected Kazakhstan when the Kazakhs revised their bid to spread the venues out to existing winter sport facilities that would require less costly renovations than an array of entirely new builds. The corrupt IOC returned to Almaty, cap in hand, when the Beijing bid for Heilongjiang province tanked. Kazakhstan then took advantage of the IOC's compromised position to seize some control from the Olympic Committee to help ensure that cost overruns and high levels of corruption that characterized what happened in Sochi a decade before would not bankrupt the Olympic initiative in Kazakhstan.

As Kate reflected upon the Olympic dynamic, aroused when viewing the snow-capped mountains bordering Almaty, she appreciated that she was already developing some insight into the way the Kazakhs thought and acted. It would remain to be seen if this small perception would help or hinder them in navigating the landscape they were about to traverse.

Kate was still lost in thought when David Powers said, "I hope you don't mind the office booking your accommodation as well. It just seemed quicker and easier to do it when our departure was imminent. Admittedly, I want us together as well as we learn the ropes in this country. You know they are mere months away from the countdown to the Winter Olympics."

"Yes, I was just reflecting on that as I viewed the mountains in the background and the building cranes in the foreground. A lot of money is flowing around the infrastructure sector — it occurs everywhere — to execute the requirements for the Olympics. *Corruption*, I believe, is the *C* in the IOC acronym."

"The media coverage has placed massive demands on the search for rare earth minerals refined precious metals for screens that showcase dynamic, innovative technologies. Launching its own sports satellite put an unbudgeted twist on it that surprised all of the Olympic mandarins to hell."

"That had to have been in the works for years. It may have been the catalyst that swung the bid to Kazakhstan. In order to complete the assembly, more rare earth minerals were required than ever before … and my boys just happen to be working on a technology that would yield quick and easy extraction from lucrative tailings in a country that not only boasts abundant waste deposits but also reserves still sitting in the ground awaiting extraction operations. The dots are connecting — ever so tenuously. All we have to do is follow the IP thread."

They walked into the lobby of the sprawling Rafat Palace Hotel.

Kate remarked only, "Jesus, not exactly my working style."

"I think the Rafat was selected for its pool and business centre."

"And the proximity to the IOC?"

"That wasn't mentioned," said Dave Powers as they both looked up at a huge banner displaying "Welcome IOC

Members." Every large screen in the lobby was flashing the same message.

"At least we may be able to get lost in the shuffle."

"Welcome, Mr. Powers and Mrs. Roarty," said an accented but clear voice approaching them. A uniformed clad young man with "Serik" displayed on a nametag waved a white-gloved hand in the direction of the reception counter. "May I take your passports for a moment to conclude the check-in?"

"Spoken too hastily," grumbled Kate under her breath, and she dug out her passport and handed it to Serik.

They were whisked away from reception to the lifts and up to the top floor. "We have taken the liberty of giving you a suite with two bedrooms, each of which have lock doors and separate ensuites. We can change the reservation to separate standard rooms if you prefer. The hotel is full of IOC members and many accompanying staff and consultants, but we wish to ensure your pleasure and comfort."

Claude, a.k.a. David, was smiling, and Kate sighed. "I supposed your Mona Lisa smile indicates that you are happy with this arrangement." Claude nodded slightly without reply.

"Whatever, we can give it a try." She handed Serik a Kazakh 1000 tenge note that he graciously accepted, bowed slightly, and said, "I am available for any of your needs, madam," then departed.

Claude threw himself back on the bed in the bedroom he had selected, closed his eyes for a few moments, then said, "How about the pool before we take on Kazakhstan?"

Kate could not restrain her grumpy mood and replied only, "Fine."

She emptied her pockets, pausing to examine the currency — coins and notes. "You know the 1000 tenge note consistently beats the Canadian ten-dollar note for banknote design of the year in voting by the International Bank Note Society."

"Thank you, Kate Roarty, for that illuminating piece of currency trivia."

"If it will make you feel better, the Brits were involved in the design preparation."

"I will remember that for a relationship-building tidbit when a Kalashnikov is pointed at me down an Almaty alleyway." He threw a robe at Kate and said, "Let's hit the pool."

Kate couldn't help the competitive surge that percolated through her. Claude was a fine swimmer, with many competition accolades to his credit. Kate didn't have a hope in hell of matching his prowess in the pool; nevertheless, she didn't want to be perceived as a lightweight in strength and endurance as they churned through their respective workouts. She pushed herself to the limit in an attempt to outstrip Claude. After a very fast pace for three kilometres, Kate relaxed to a warm down backstroke while Claude pushed a butterfly tidal wave through another ten laps. It reminded her of her brother, who often wound down his swims with a vigorous butterfly. Kate was hopeless at the butterfly and only did the stroke when she was completely alone. It was reserved for an interlude during a distant shoreline swim at Meech Lake.

Both David and Kate emerged feeling refreshed, invigorated, and restored, ready to take on whatever the country would throw at them.

"It's too late for a walk, but does a light meal in the lounge bar interest you? It remains open 24/7."

Kate and Claude discovered that the bar lounge, situated in the central domed atrium, offered a ready view of the comings and goings within the lobby. It was rowdy, with clusters of foreigners who in one way or another all appeared associated with the International Olympic Committee, evident by their jackets, lapel pins, and subjects of conversation — at least those snippets that Kate and David could overhear, with their medley of linguistic abilities.

Kate recognized the aging Dick Pound, with whom she had some contact during her diplomatic career. More importantly, she was delighted to see Adele Winther, whose career in hockey she had followed closely and went to all of the games she played during the numerous times Canada trounced the US during the women's hockey finals. David pointed out Kristy Coventry, a Zimbabwean swimmer whose career he had followed closely. "She trained in the US but swam for her homeland and made them proud."

Kate quietly mused, "It didn't occur to me to bone up on the Olympic administration before heading to Kazakhstan. It may become useful to figure out who has influence and who engages with integrity. There might even be a few of them that exhibit both qualities. At the risk of sounding sexist, focusing on getting to know the women may give us an inroad into the committee. The female members may be the least likely to have been compromised but the most likely to know who is taking bribes."

Kate rose, walked over to Adele Winther, and introduced herself as a fellow Canadian and a long-time admirer. Adele was gracious in her reception and response and enquired after Kate's activity in Kazakhstan.

"My colleague and I are involved in some investments in the mining sector."

Kate observed a slight stiffening in Adele's body language.

"Which minerals?"

"Rare earth."

The stiffening intensified, and Adele quickly excused herself.

"Enjoy your stay in beautiful Kazakhstan," she said as she slid off the stool and strode across the lounge, exiting toward the elevators.

Kate was fully aware that she had not handled that interview well. It would require redemption and repair the next day.

"I think jetlag and fatigue have got the better of me, David — I am heading up to bed."

"Given it is 5:00 a.m. London time, that would be a reasonable assessment. How did it go with Adele Winther?"

"I blew it."

"Wow, perfectionist Kate Roarty misses a beat. You must be tired. I thought you were always exacting — even in your sleep."

"You are delusional, Cl … David Powers."

They entered their suite and both realized at the same moment they were not alone. A chambermaid emerged from Kate's bedroom, smiled, spoke in Kazakh, and left. When they checked their respective rooms, it was clear she had only been in to turn down the beds and leave flowers, chocolates, and mineral water.

"A bit skittish, are we?" said Kate.

"Goodnight."

Despite her fatigue, Kate decided to have a short meditation session to relax her mind and mellow out her irritability. She was also painfully aware that she had not called Jack, her adult children, or connected with Bryant.

The stallion remained nearby.

31

Kazakhstan

Kate awakened to the loud vibrating of her mobile phone. She looked at the screen and saw a cartoon display of The Little Engine That Could stuck in the elbow of a tree.

Bryant!

"Kate, where the hell are you? You disappeared off my grid yesterday. That makes me very nervous when you are working a case."

"I'm in Kazakhstan. Claude Mason is here too. There are connections — I think. Rare earth minerals, sports satellite, Winter Olympics…"

"Jesus, Kate, haven't we been through thick and thin together enough that you would know you can't just disappear off the grid? I need to know when it's necessary to mobilize to find you, get you out of a jam, bring in the artillery, so to speak."

"I am sorry, Bryant. I have no excuse for my negligence. I seem to be struggling a bit since the crash in London."

"Christ, Kate! You address struggling by walking into a minefield. There are nasty people chasing the money that surrounds this technology. If you start cramping their style, they will readily show their nastiness. And I'm not sure that smart guy with you can rally the protection. It's only two years since he damn near got himself killed on the Taylor case. I doubt he has put in much field time since then. He's a glorified cyber geek who swims, speaks lots of languages, has a fancy title, and looks pretty."

Kate couldn't help but soften the seriousness. "Well, that's a good start, don't you think?"

"Kate, stay connected so I know what to do when you slip off the grid. Deal?"

"Deal."

"I will keep track of smart guy, too, assuming that you should be in close proximity to one another while you are in Kazakhstan. It looks like he is in the pool in your hotel. You headed there?"

"Yes."

"Okay, I'll get to work on your IP technology, sports satellite, and IOC thread. Check the box later today."

"Bryant!"

"What?"

"Thanks."

"Have a good swim. I gotta treadmill off my frustration."

"Before you go, can you tell me how you found the puppy?"

"Ah yes, that was a perfect test case for my new subcontractor. Hazel, who became known as Rowdygirl as she changed hands through the underworld of dog fighting, seems to have been stolen off the streets of some tiny northern B.C. town and sold into a cross-border dog fighting network. We located her in northern California. Luckily, she was still too young to fight, was well taken care of, and well fed. My guy had someone pose as a handler and purchase her — this is going to cost you, Kate — then we legitimized her and transported her back to your daughter's doorstep. Our handler watched until the happy reunion was made."

"Thanks so much, Bryant."

"You might not thank me when you get the bill. It was cheaper to spring an innocent prisoner out of a maximum security Brazilian prison and spirit him across borders than to get that dog back to your daughter."

Kate pressed "end call" on her mobile, slipped into her bathing suit, threw on the hotel robe, and headed up to the pool. Claude was indeed there, pulling through a fast, smooth front crawl akin to the professional swimmer he had been in his younger days. Kate paused to admire the strength, technique, and speed that propelled him through the water, feeling just a tad envious of what she was observing, knowing she would never achieve that level of expertise. She slipped into the water; he sensed her presence and moved from the middle of the pool to the right, giving her a half of the pool for her lengths. They finished up at the same time. Claude probably did two or three times the workout that Kate put in, but they both emerged energized, relaxed, and ready to go. They reviewed the action plan over a room service breakfast. Both couldn't help feeling a bit smug, having worked out, consumed a delicious yet healthy breakfast, and developed an action plan for the day — and all accomplished before 8:00 a.m. They checked their sidearms, concealed them on their person, and headed out together.

Before they could pull the door shut, they spotted Adele Winther near the end of the corridor coming out of a room with an escort — two men who did not appear the type to have spent the night with the athlete for a romantic tryst. Ms. Winther glanced at David and made eye contact with Kate. Kate saw the kind of fear that communicated, *I'm in trouble, and I need help.*

In an instant, she greeted Adele with a warm embrace. "Right on time. Shall we head down for coffee? Are your friends joining us?" she added with a naïve smile in their direction.

"No, thanks Kate, they were just leaving."

"My colleague, David Powers, will tag along if you don't mind."

Adele shot out a hand in greeting. "Pleased to meet you, Mr. Powers."

Dave accepted a sweaty palm, squeezed a reassuring handshake, and said, "I am thrilled to make your acquaintance."

Kate detected an increased level of confidence restored to Adele's demeanour akin to a save on the ice during a hockey game when she had momentarily lost the puck and wasn't sure if it had gone in the goal or not.

"Keep walking. This exposure to the atrium should restrain your buddies. We can't risk the stairs, but there is another set of elevators farther along that may work."

The doors opened to an empty elevator, and they got on. It descended without any other stops. David and Kate readied their sidearms for when the door opened on the ground floor in the lobby. No sign of the two men, but a large number of people milling about made it difficult to determine if Adele Winther was still in danger. All three remained on high alert. They selected a table that gave them a sweeping view of the ground floor and ordered a pot of coffee.

"Have you eaten?"

"Not yet, I returned to my room after a long morning run to find those two waiting for me."

"Order some food — it'll help decrease the stress level."

"Who are you?"

"I'm Kate Roarty from Canada, and I've been an admirer of yours for a long time. I didn't follow you as a baseball player but was captivated by your hockey career. Frankly, I didn't give the IOC much thought until very recently. I'm a private investigator. My colleague here, David Powers, has broader interests in the mining sector. It made sense for us to team up. Neither of us have been to Kazakhstan before — there you have a decided advantage over us. I gather you've been in and out a number of times in the run-up to the decision on the next Winter Olympics bid."

Watching Adele's body language relax suggested to Kate that she was likely content with this cursory story, for the moment at least.

Adele looked at David. "Mining is very important in this country, particularly for the deposits of rare earth minerals required for the technology that will go into the sports satellite the Kazakhs plan to launch just before the games get underway. It was a major contributing factor for the Kazakhs to draw the bid away from China after Norway and Sweden pulled out."

"Was there a high level of corruption surrounding the Chinese bid?"

"Oh yes, the Chinese are unabashed when they decide they want something. Believe me, this country is at risk, straddling the landscape between Russia to the north and the PRC to the south. The only thing keeping the Russians at bay is their total economic collapse. When they couldn't pay their Sochi bills they invited the international mob in. The contracts were paid, but the bureaucracy and infrastructure was totally compromised. The mob used the Russian army to try to take over Ukraine, completely misjudging the strength of the ethnic Russian-Ukrainian spirit. The Chinese thought they could simply take over, underestimating the will of the Kazakhs. The Japanese stepped in, won the bid for Sapporo, then lost it to a volcanic eruption. Mt. Usu was registering its dissatisfaction."

Kate said, "What a bloody powder keg, and we are proposed to march the world's top athletes into this mess?"

"If we don't go ahead with these Olympics, it will be the first Olympics not staged since those cancelled during the two European wars, 1916 and 1940 and 1944 of the last century. While the boycott of the 1980 Moscow Games threatened to cancel it, the Russians managed to pull it off with a reduced participation. Frankly, it was miraculous that the Sochi 2014 Winter Games went ahead, then only a decade later natural forces did it for them. The symbolism of cancelling a games is so entrenched in emotional history that little rational behaviour prevails when such discussions arise. And guess what? It revolves around this part of the world."

"Thanks for the history lesson, Ms. Winther."

"Oh please, it's Adele. I'm still just a hockey player stick-handling a different puck with the IOC. If you understand hockey, you can play this game. However, there has always been huge differences between the men's game and the women's game. The men don't know how to play with integrity, and the women don't know how to play with brutality. When they get on the ice together, sometimes it's hard to even locate the puck, much less shoot and score."

David said, "If you can keep your eye on the puck, we can try to keep the enforcers at bay — as your right and left wing, so to speak. We are, however, pretty weak on defense, but reinforcements can be called in—"

Kate raised an eyebrow at that remark but let it slide. She was quietly impressed with his hockey analogy, given that swimming in the UK had dominated his athletic life.

Before she could query his knowledge, he said, "I didn't only learn Quebec French in the Saguenay; playing pick-up hockey, talking about hockey, and fantasizing about meeting the famous NHL players who rose up through the Quebec game were dominant aspects of my life there. It gave me an insight into the human dynamic, not to mention the passion involved in playing the game. Admittedly, I have never watched women play the sport — I think that'll change in the not too distant future."

Adele listened to the exchange then added, "It's rather like watching Angela Merkel carry out a female brand of politics — same game — politics, that is — but stick-handled with finesse and integrity and without bullying and corruption. Both achieve winning outcomes, born of sheer hard work and tenacity."

Kate and David nodded but did not respond — Kate in silent admiration, David in continued wilful deception, in which he did not display a single trace of discomfort.

"Adele, let's exchange all of our contact co-ordinates. David and I will be off on this IP trail, and you have your IOC commitments. I suggest that you try to stay in public places, ask the hotel for a room change, and keep it quiet, but don't enter either the old room or the new one alone. Let's meet here this evening and figure out a plan from there. If you're in difficulty, call or text either of us any time. We'll help."

32

Kate and David left Adele. Once they were out of earshot, Kate asked, "Is there any chance that a British Airways cabin service director is still in Almaty?"

"There's a chance," David said, nodding casually. "The length of the flight would likely dictate a layover of at least twenty-four hours. I think the flight goes out at night. Shall I check? On the cabin service director, that is—"

"Yes, to ensure the safety of our IOC representative."

"Handy she's around, wouldn't you say?"

Kate was tempted to hit him but thought better of it in the public location, so she contained a grimace and avoided comment while David stopped long enough to send a quick text.

His phone rang almost immediately. He took the call through his nearly invisible mobile phone headset, spoke briefly, then rejoined Kate, saying only, "Done."

They walked out into the crisp morning air, tainted by a slight sulphurous smell and obscured by a haze created by the city's location sitting in the bowl of the Tian Shan Mountains.

"Apparently, if it wins this short-notice Winter Olympics bid, the country plans to shut down all industrial sources of pollution and restrict the entry of vehicles manufactured prior to 2030 — similar to the measures Beijing took for its 2008 Summer Olympics and 2024 Winter Olympics."

"A good time to come back — prolonged inhaling of this air could be life-shortening."

"Apparently the air quality has improved dramatically, with many abatement measures rolling in over the past decade. However, the population has been increasing so rapidly, along with the level of affluence-stimulating consumption, that it's an uphill battle to improve the air and water quality."

They continued in their distracted discourse when a vehicle pulled up in front of them. Before Kate knew what was happening, she was sitting in the back of an SUV smoothly folding into morning traffic. A well-dressed young man sitting beside her said in lightly accented perfect British English, "Sit quietly, and the back seat of the car will remain as pristine as you see it now. Your IOC friend is coming along in the vehicle behind."

They had stopped for a traffic light when a loud bang hit the opposite door, and Kate was sprayed with small shards of glass. The well-dressed young man slumped forward as Kate tried to open her door. Another spray of glass shards blew across her, the door exploded open, and she was pulled from the car.

"Get yourself to safety by that cement pole while I go after Ms. Winther."

Kate retrieved her gun and backed into the thick cement lamp pole while Agent Liz Bruan executed the same manoeuvre with the vehicle stopped behind the one she had just been extracted from. The agent pulled Adele from the vehicle, to be confronted by another well-dressed Glock-toting thug who aimed directly at them. Liz leapt to protect her charge when the thug slumped to the ground. David

Powers had taken the shot from a third of the block away and dropped the pursuer. A vehicle screeched up beside them, the driver yelled, "Get in," David and Liz nodded, they piled in, and the vehicle sped off.

Kate found herself sitting in the front seat beside Serik, the doorman she had encountered upon arriving at the hotel.

She looked back at Liz and Claude. "Your machinery was in place before I got here. Did I even need to make the trip?"

"Yes," came the sequential reply from each of them.

"Who are you people?" uttered an exasperated Adele Winther.

Claude replied, "We are your safety net."

"Safety net! Since I met you, my hotel room was broken into, I experienced two attempted abductions, I have been shot at, two vehicles have been demolished, and two men have been shot — maybe even killed."

Claude replied, "Maybe."

"I am here on a site inspection with the IOC — that's it!"

"Yes, that's a problem."

"Perhaps you can explain the problem to me, in nice, simple terms that an athlete might have a chance of understanding," said Adele sarcastically. She appeared to be struggling to control the massive anger welling up inside of her.

Kate stepped in at this point. "Let's see if we can do that for Ms. Winther. First, we need to get to some place safe, where we aren't looking over our shoulders, then we can talk."

Serik was talking on the phone in Russian, then he switched to English. "We have rented a house at the edge of town. Security people are on their way there now to fit it up. I suggest we drive straight there — it will be about forty-five minutes in this traffic. Your belongings can be delivered from the hotel later on."

Adele appeared ready to explode. "I don't wish to go or move to a house fitted out by somebody's security. Please drop me back at my hotel and clear out. I've been to Almaty a number of times before without experiencing any issues, until this time when you two showed up. I am quite happy to take care of myself, do my work with the IOC, and get out of Kazakhstan — preferably alive and in one piece."

Liz Bruan took the lead. "Ms. Winther, I am Agent Liz Bruan of the British Intelligence Service. This is Claude Mason, a director with that service and one of my bosses. Kate Roarty is a Canadian private investigator that we work with from time to time. We are working with her on a rare earth minerals project — the deposits are present in abundance in Kazakhstan. She's tracking the intellectual property of a technological application in the hope of restoring the IP to its rightful innovators. We are investigating the theft and how it relates to the development and launch of a commercial sports satellite. Members of the IOC appear to be heavily implicated in the corruption surrounding the acquisition and sale of the rare earth minerals required for the manufacture of this satellite. It is a multi-billion-dollar project. Some players don't seem to hesitate to eliminate anyone who impedes the progress toward launching the satellite. We don't yet have a handle on the entire scenario, but it's clear that the web of corruption reaches far and deep, with many unwitting participants. We will try to protect you, and admittedly, we wish to use your expertise and connections to infiltrate the Olympic organization. Can you work with us to see this through — by exposing the culprits, restoring the IP to the rightful innovators, and ferreting out the criminal elements on the IOC? We do not want to obstruct the launch of the sports satellite; rather, we wish to see it go ahead with commercial integrity."

Kate added, "The successful commercialization of space exploration and orbiting communication technology for this planet has introduced a highly aggressive element of corruption in the chase for the profits to be generated with the launch of satellites, space probes, and servicing rockets. While the technologies are now reusable, space travel in this galaxy is a round trip; the energy consumption is nevertheless voracious. Sensor technology is a massive growth industry surrounded by big bucks, extraordinary brilliance, and very, very nasty people. It is concentrated here in Kazakhstan, hot on the trail of the money to get this sports satellite into orbit. The bottom line is satisfying the desperate need for rare earth minerals."

"Okay, okay, enough from the lecture theatre, science lab, and espionage drama. What do you want from me?"

They all looked sheepish in the face of the rebuke. Kate resolved to take the high road. "Can you help us identify the most likely candidates on the IOC to be receiving financial favours to integrate the launch of the sports satellite into the overall Kazakhstan Olympics plan?"

"I think so, but how will that help you restore the IP to the original inventors?"

"We can follow the threads that will probably weave a web of personalities, money, technology application, greed, violence, and murder to eventually link together the elements of the investigation. The level of danger and aggression among the players I have encountered is very high, suggesting we are very close to the project implementation — and payoffs."

"Look, I can't put people close to me at risk — my son, my mother, who's very active in her community, my siblings, and their families. God knows what these thugs might do to them if they are unhappy with me."

"It doesn't appear that they will target individuals not directly linked to the project. We can initiate a cyber scan to monitor traffic that may suggest otherwise," said Claude.

"Okaaay…"

"We will move swiftly to protect anyone indirectly associated, if there is an indication that we have to. Kate here is probably the most vulnerable member of the investigation team simply because of her get-it-done reputation. They are afraid of her. So far, she has succeeded in exposing — quite publicly —the corruption in the industry and linked it to the international investment community. She has made a number of investors very nervous. Now she is zeroing in on exposing the rest of the culprits, ferreting them out, and shutting them down."

Serik interjected, "We are arriving at the safe house." They saw a Bavarian-style two-storey house set apart yet adequately integrated in the neighbourhood.

"Give Ms. Bruan and me a bit of time to go in and check it out, but please get out of the vehicle so you are not a focused target. It is unlikely that the safe house has been discovered, but we must take every precaution."

All of them exited the vehicle, Serik, Liz, and Claude, with their sidearms drawn, and Kate followed their lead. Adele stayed close to Kate and Claude, while the other two surveyed the outside of the house before locating the key and entering through the front door. They emerged within minutes, giving the nod for the rest to enter. The place looked like a small villa, comfortable, inviting, and with a spectacular view of the Tian Shan Mountains, where most of the ski events would be held.

Kate noticed a smile briefly slide across Adele's face before she quickly refocused her attention on the activity of her newly acquired associates. She caught them nodding approvingly.

Liz spoke. "A good find, Serik. Who owns it?"

"Technically, my uncle, but he never uses it. He has a fanciful notion of assembling the extended family for ski holidays without realizing that given the choice, the whole lot of them prefer sun-filled waterfront holidays."

"Does he know we are using it?"

"He thinks I have brought a bunch of European friends here for a holiday retreat. We should be fine. By the way, there is an unmanned air transport and helipad a short distance away. It is rarely used but was recently upgraded to bring it into use for the Olympics. If we need to move more quickly than the speed of land vehicles, it can provide options."

Kate's phone was vibrating with the rhythm of an incoming communication that could only be from Bryant. She excused herself and sought privacy in the washroom. The vibration stopped, but before she left in dismay, it began again. The screen portrayed a high-speed unmanned German train.

"I think I liked The Little Engine That Could better."

"This one captures how fast this case is developing. We can equate it to orbital speed. Kate, I've located the sports satellite. It has been built. Systems testing have already begun. It isn't far away from launching, and it isn't far away from your current location."

"Shit!"

"I think the launch is planned to kick off the PR campaign that will knock the Chinese out of the water on locating the Winter Olympics to Heilongjiang. In and of itself the satellite PR strategy is brilliant, apart from the fact that the sensor system is manufactured using rare earth minerals extracted from tailings in Kazakhstan. They are getting these minerals using the technological application that you are hunting down … and it gets better."

"Better?"

"That's cyber geek speak. Don't worry, I haven't slipped over to the other side. It's too much fun tracking down the other side from my position working with you."

"Bryant, you're making me even more nervous than I already am."

"Restoring the trace extraction IP to the original innovators may be a very long shot. It has become so entangled in all of the technological applications assembled to build this satellite that the best deal you can get for them may be a huge payout with ongoing payments of some form of royalties.

"Kate, we have to stay closely connected — while these guys you are encountering are thugs, as you call them, they are part of a network of highly sophisticated, cyber-savvy technicians who are singularly focused on launching this satellite. I doubt it has very much to do with sports."

Kate returned to the kitchen, where the group was making sandwiches from bread and fixings found in the cupboards and freezer. Coffee was brewing in the coffee maker, and tinned milk had been opened to soften the bitterness of the local brew. Kate looked around and quipped jokingly, "No maple syrup." The remark broke the tension.

She said quietly to Claude as he handed here a sandwich, "Walk?"

They checked their sidearms, slipped on jackets against the cool air and to hide the weapons, then headed out. Adele looked uneasy but nodded in response to Kate's "Back soon."

Claude said, "Let's get a sense of the nearby streets and roads into the mountains."

They walked through some rural streets sparsely lined with houses reflecting an alpine architecture blended with a Russian and northern Asian influence.

"The mountains and confluence of cultures have invaded the Kazakh domain in this region. It makes for an interesting blend of the make-up of this society." Claude looked around. "There's money here as well — lots of it."

"Perhaps a colony of scientists and their families," Kate remarked as they walked past a very rich-looking school sporting several large playing fields and outdoor gaming structures, as well as an array of transmitting/receiving disks populating the roof line like raccoons on a night prowl.

"Let's get beyond that surveillance array before we talk about anything more than tuna and pickle sandwiches."

They took a well-sealed road that climbed away from the neighbourhood and into the forest, with the distribution of houses thinning out.

Claude retrieved his hand-held communications device, scrolled through some apps, paused then said, "Okay, we have a cyber security cloak around our immediate area. Tell me about your telephone call."

Kate thought, *Oh my, that will shut out Bryant from tracking me as well.* She related to Claude what Bryant had told her about the satellite and its location.

They walked on in silence, contemplating this information until they reached a signed fork in the road. Kate photographed the sign and activated the translation app to learn that it was indicating the Turgen Gorge hot springs twenty-five kilometres ahead.

"Kate, fancy a swim?"

She smiled, and they headed back to retrieve their swimming gear, a vehicle, and to check on Adele.

"Adele, do you swim?"

"Yeah, I swim well, but I don't do it very often. Why?"

Kate made eye contact with her and said, "There's a hot spring not far from here that we thought we might check it out. I have an extra suit if you wish to join us."

"Best offer I've had all day — let's go."

Claude took the cluster of fob keys for Serik's vehicle, and they headed out. They took the same road out of town that they had walked along earlier, quickly reaching the sign board indicating the direction of the hot springs. A few kilometres farther, the paved surface gave way to a hard-packed, narrower road that bordered a fast-flowing creek descending from the upper slopes. The high-powered black Mercedes SUV climbed the grade with ease.

Adele was sitting in the back seat, watching the upper slopes, when she spotted a gleam of light appearing to bounce off an object high up on the ridge, below a cluster of peaks.

"What's that?"

Kate turned back to follow Adele's sightline then craned forward to see what she was looking at. She could not see anything out of the ordinary, but Claude, driving and craning in the same manner, remarked, "There is something up on that slope."

They watched silently when Kate announced, "Another signpost."

The translation of the photo she took with her mobile phone indicated that they had arrived at the parking spot for the Turgen Gorge hot springs. Claude turned the vehicle around, facing it out to the road, shut it down, and got out, followed by the other two. He pulled one of the key fobs off the cluster on the ring and handed it to Kate, then with the other two watching, placed the second spare under the moss at the base of the tree behind another signpost indicating the direction of the descent to the hot springs. They locked valuable items and the remaining fobs safe in the SUV.

All three strode out to the main road to see if they could spot the structure up the slope. They could see nothing. They retrieved swimsuits and techno-fibre mini towels, slipped them into their pockets, and descended the deserted trail to the hot springs. The trail was well trodden, suggesting that in another season or perhaps on the weekends it was well used. Today these three were the only intruders.

As they descended along the narrow path, steam misted up through the moss-covered trees, like vapour from a hookah pipe, announcing the nearby hot springs. The three quickened their pace in anticipation of the plunge into the water. The pool emerged from the surrounding tree cover like a jewel on the ice queen's finger. They changed quickly, carefully stowing their weapons away from their clothing, then leapt into the deep, hot pool. They stroked across its surface then rose and splashed like children on the first plunge of the summer season. It broke the tension.

Kate and Claude swam vigorously through the hot water but lost momentum quickly. They were surprised by Adele's slower, steady pace uncompromised by the heat of the pool. All three continued for nearly an hour before Kate announced the need for a drink. "I think I saw a case of bottled water in the back of the SUV, but failing that, that fast-flowing stream at the edge of the road might do the trick." The micro towels proved more than adequate as the water rapidly evaporated off their steaming bodies into the cool mountain air. They retrieved the guns and dressed quickly.

Adele gambolled up the trail ahead of the other two. At the top, she bent to retrieve the key fob from the base of the tree behind the signpost. She couldn't locate it — it was gone. Claude came up behind and asked casually, "Did you get the fob?"

"No, it isn't here."

Claude searched as well, while Kate drew her sidearm and began to look around.

The vehicle was as they left it, and there were no additional tire marks or footprints. They couldn't spot anything on the patch of road leading from the parking lot or on the nearby slope ascending from the creek.

"We need water," Kate said. "Let's use the manual override to open the vehicle. In case the locking electronics have been tampered with, it's best to go in from the rear."

Claude put his hand out for the key, and Kate relinquished it. "I'm more expendable than you two. Better let me do it." Kate and Adele remained against the tree cover while Claude approached the rear of the SUV.

All took a deep breath as Claude put the key in and turned it then stepped back as the door swung up. He retrieved three bottles of water and walked back to the two women, who finally exhaled when he handed them the bottles.

A rapid chatter from the base of a nearby tree interrupted their long draw on the water. They leapt apart — Claude and Kate squatting at the ready — when a soft thump sounded, followed by another rapid chatter from the base of another tree beside Adele. She bent to retrieve the object abandoned by the nattering creature, and they took in a russet-coloured ground squirrel with a rapidly vibrating short tail, clearly annoyed that his find was not edible. Laughter and collective sighs broke the tension as Claude bent to speak with the little fellow, who scurried off, clearly unimpressed with the invaders of his domain.

"A bit skittish, are we?" remarked Adele.

They all climbed in the SUV. Claude wheeled it back out onto the creek side road, and they continued the ascent.

Once again, a metallic glint shimmered off the upper slopes. This time Kate spotted it. "I think there is something up there that we need to check out."

"Okay, you two keep a look out while I drive — if it's something significant, we won't likely be forewarned in as gentle a manner as our little furry friend announced his presence back there," said Claude.

"I'll just hang on to this key fob, if you don't mind. It might be my lunch ticket out of here when you two decide to take on more vicious varieties of animal inhabitants," said Adele.

"Okay, as long as you don't abandon us to be feasted upon by Tian Shan snow leopards and mountain bears."

The vehicle slowed as Claude navigated it through switchbacks. They criss-crossed the creek, climbing higher up the slope toward the cluster of peaks they'd seen from below. All three watched a small, soundless craft disappear into the face of the upper slope.

"Suddenly I feel like we are occupying a vehicle technologically closer to the horse and cart of the nineteenth century than the mid twenty-first century."

"Yeah, but I think we just got a glimpse of the twenty-second century."

"Let's keep going. Regardless of the century we're navigating through, we have to get a lot closer to figure out what is up there and if new technologies with covert applications are at play," said Claude.

"Yeah, the IP trail that was feeling distant and cold is beginning to feel close at hand and hot."

"And to think I was mourning the loss of pursuing a little round puck on a cold ice surface," remarked Adele.

After another few kilometres, Claude pulled over and stopped.

He turned and said to Kate and Adele, "The app on my hand-held device can provide enough reach to cloak our bio signatures, but it can't mask the vehicle as well as us. We may be able to get a lot closer without being detected by proceeding on foot."

Claude snugged the car off the road and under a tree to camouflage it as much as possible. They retrieved water bottles from the stash in the back of the SUV, secured them in belts and pockets, checked their sidearms, then headed out. The ascent up the sun-parched slope was easy at first, but all of them were glad they were in good shape. They crossed the gaps between the switchbacks of the road, climbing at a strong pace. The three had to stay close to keep their bio signatures fully masked under the cloaking screen, making it a bit awkward to establish individual walking rhythms. They paused and Claude handed the device to Adele, saying, "We will switch it around so each of us can take turns adapting to the pace of the other two."

Adele smiled, grateful of the adjustment, and took Claude's device. She remarked, "Kinda like changing lines as the game continues — been doing this all my life."

Kate felt her heart pumping harder and harder as they ascended. *Being a little older than these two is showing*, she thought. *When I conceived the idea for investigating intellectual property, I thought of it more as a headspace and an online pursuit. I never imagined the physical extremes it has pushed me to on recent cases. I may have to rethink the business plan after I wrap up this one.*

Kate heard a soft buzzing and stopped to look around at the same moment that Claude spotted a miniature drone. "If they are checking their surveillance feed continuously, we may be found out quickly. Let's hope it takes a bit of time to adapt to the frequency of the cloaking scan so we can get close enough to figure out what is going on up there."

They picked up the pace then slowed again after all three of them stumbled.

"I think slow and steady was working well — let's stick to that pace," said Kate.

They crested over another switchback to see a highly elaborate electronic gate crossing the road and attached to an electronic metal fence extending another hundred metres on either side. It was apparent that the installers were mostly thinking of vehicular approach from the road. The threesome easily slipped over the rocky outcrops that the lower fence abutted and continued inside the barrier area. Another miniature drone appeared and hovered above them. It was slightly larger and looked a bit more sophisticated, sporting a visible sensor system that could have been more effective at penetrating the cloak scan. They stopped, huddled close together, and remained motionless until it sped off. "Detected or not, we had better scramble before the drone brigade sends out more than surveillance devices," said Claude. That was no sooner said than three larger drones arrived just above them. Claude and Kate nodded then dispatched all three with rapid fire from their sidearms.

Adele shook her head and spoke a sharp command. "Let's go."

A small but very sophisticated installation came into view. A landing pad had been built extending out from the slope, and a craft cradling what looked like a satellite occupied the platform. Emblazoned across the outer skin, they could read: SPACESPORTSK.

"It's the sports satellite. It looks ready to launch, I bet fully loaded with an array of sensors manufactured using the rare earth minerals extracted from the Kazakhstan tailings," said Kate.

"Among other things. Look, it appears as though the outer skin will slip down like a sleeve over the satellite, protecting its digital workings until the module is released into orbit," added Claude.

"Let's try to get closer to get some high-quality photographs."

All three clustered together and edged up toward the platform. The setting was surprisingly quiet.

Adele reached a hand out to Kate and said, "Stop, listen." They did — and none could hear a single sound. The setting was not only soundless but also motionless.

"I don't see any vehicles, any people, any equipment, yet the site is pristine and the craft looks ready to launch."

"Do you suppose it is being done remotely or with robotics?"

"Or both."

They moved in a little closer when a human-like robotic figure glided soundlessly over to the craft and proceeded to do what looked like a final check procedure. Claude picked up a small stone and tossed it at the feet of the robot. It paused, reached down, and picked up the stone, carefully examined it with graceful dexterity, then put it in a small receptacle on the front of its breastplate. It returned to a series of procedures then raised its arms, placed it hands on either side of the sleeve, and guided it down over the nose of the craft that now resembled a fat-nosed satellite akin to an *Apollo* lunar module.

The robot turned, checked that the sleeve was securely in place, then glided soundlessly into the chamber in the wall of the cliff and did not re-emerge. They couldn't actually see where it went, but they took advantage of it being beyond eyesight to move in a little closer. They halted when a shimmering surrounded the craft. It began to silently lift off, and it was gone.

"Jesus. What happened?" said Adele.

"I think they just launched the satellite," said Kate.

"Wow, quiet, swift, almost uneventful — gone," added Adele, throwing her hands out like a proclamation of a mystical presence.

"Let's continue with what we can find out about this place before we are detected and stopped. It doesn't appear to be fortified or even armed — at least not in any conventionally recognizable manner."

"I wonder if the control centre is someplace else, and this is just the physical launch pad?" said Kate.

"The barrier appears to be an electronic shield. Let's check where the interface is against the rock surface to see if there are any gaps in the coverage where we might slip through."

Adele drew their attention to a crag in the rock deep enough to permit their bodies to slide under the electronic barrier. Claude tossed a small rock into the shallow crevice. It bounced and trickled down the slope to come to rest on the platform. It seemed the shield's grid wasn't designed to penetrate into such anomalous spaces.

"Let's give it a try. Shall I let male gallantry prevail and go first?"

"Fine by me," quipped Adele, and Kate nodded in agreement.

Claude readily navigated his larger frame under the invisible barrier, slid down the slope, then stood up on the platform without incident. Kate and Adele followed.

"It's so quiet."

"Eerily quiet."

They walked toward what appeared to be a control room. Claude and Kate entered while Adele remained out on the platform. They found a control panel that appeared to be switched off, along with two deactivated robots.

"I think your theory about remote control from another location is accurate. I imagine we could figure out how to manually override the system to switch it on, but since there is nothing else here and the satellite is already launched, I don't see any point in doing that. Let's get out of here."

"Wait, what about that shuttle we watched glide in here earlier on? We didn't see it leave, so it had to go somewhere."

They scouted the perimeter of the rock face but could not spot any signs that there was an opening yielding to a chamber where the craft could be stored.

"Perhaps it's cloaked. Let's survey the entire platform to see if we encounter any obstruction that suggests it might be here," said Claude.

They began a sweep in a search-and-rescue formation. Claude took the outer perimeter and quickly ran into an obstruction preventing him from reaching the edge of the platform. His hand-held device was adept enough to give him a reading into the presence of a mass and the dimensions but couldn't expose it.

"I think we have found what we are looking for," he said to the other two. "Now my curiosity is piqued — what is it here for? What does it do?"

"I think we should get out of here while we still can," said Adele.

Kate and Claude nodded reluctantly and headed back to the passage that led under the electronic fence. They could not locate the spot, and a careful scouting of the perimeter suggested that the opening had vanished. "It is much more than an electronic fence — more like a digital perimeter remotely manipulated, like everything else here," said Kate.

They turned back to include Adele, but she was gone. She had vanished as thoroughly as the opening in the digital perimeter.

"Jesus, Claude, where is she?"

"She may be right here and cloaked so we can't see her, or, like the launch of the satellite and the breach in the digital fence, she too is gone."

"Let's not assume that because we can't see her, she's gone. She may still be able to see us or at least hear us."

Claude, "I think I'm more of a realist than you are — while I am open to your perceptions, as far as I am concerned, she's gone."

"Let's try to figure out how to get of here. Is your hand-held still working? I seem to have reception on mine, standing in the middle of the platform. There may be a conical-shaped cloak. Turn yours off then back on to clear any clashing digital cloaks. I'm going to try to connect with my cyber network."

Kate's message to *trainonthetrack2030* received an instant reply from Bryant. **Kate, I can see the digital cloak and read two bio signatures. Give me a few minutes to read it to see if I can shut it down. In the meantime, try to locate a control panel and stand by.**

Kate returned to the control panel chamber and messaged Bryant: **Everything appears to be turned off. In addition to the panel, two deactivated robots may awaken if everything else comes online.**

—**Okay, I'm on it, Kate. Check the robots to see if there are any manual activators — maybe we can get the buggers to work for us.**

Claude called out from the platform. Kate looked out to see a barely perceptible shimmer, and the small craft reappeared, resting where they thought it was located.

Claude went to check it out while Kate examined the digital fence.

Bryant, we can see a craft on the platform, so both may be unmasked, but the digital fence appears to still be in tack. No sign of Adele.

—**Kate, there may be a cyber connection between the craft and the robots — the cloaking is on another system. I'm navigating around the cyber coding randomly. I may be able to drop the fence but just as quickly lose it, so be ready to leap beyond the confines of the digital fence on a moment's notice.**

Kate turned at the sound of a faint hissing to see a portal open to the craft. Claude called back, "It's an unmanned design with no space for a human or even a robot to enter." He stepped back as the portal closed and the craft elevated.

Kate's audio reception sounded. It was Bryant. She plugged in her earbud to keep her hands free.

"Kate, is the craft moving?"

"Yes, the portal closed, and it rose off the platform."

"I may be able to use it to disable a section of the fence. Get ready. If I'm successful you may only have a moment to pass through a breach before the technology adapts and it closes again."

Kate caught Claude's attention and motioned him over. They watched the craft creep slowly toward the perimeter and bob along before stopping, turning, and charging against the invisible cyber fence. The crash exposed a section of the fence, making a very small rupture in its mesh. It was enough to let Claude and Kate slither through and roll down the embankment free of the enclosed platform.

In the tumble, Kate lost her earbud but was able to message Bryant: **Out**.

"Let's get away from here – fast," she said.

They descended rapidly and reached the spot where they thought they had stashed the SUV, but it was gone.

"Gone or masked," Claude remarked. They carefully surveyed the area but could not detect either a presence of the vehicle or any indication of a conventional departure.

"Do you suppose Adele and the vehicle are together?" said Claude.

Kate threw her hands up in exasperation. "Who the hell knows? I feel like we are players in a video game."

Claude laughed. "No point in hanging around here; let's keep going back the way we came."

"At least it's downhill. We can shorten the distance by cutting across the terrain between each switchback of the road."

"I gather we are heading back to the safe house."

"Unless you've got another suggestion among the many options available in this landscape."

"How do we know it's actually a safe house?"

"We don't. If it isn't, we will learn that quickly enough when we get there. If we have to, we'll make it safe."

"Feeling invincible, are we?"

Kate quipped, "No, just desperate but demonstrating an outward cool and calm."

The remark eased the strain as they both let out a nervous laugh. They moved swiftly and quietly, keeping to the edge of the road and taking as many short cuts as the route allowed. Both stayed hyper-alert, scanning the forest line, the skyline, the roadway, and the terrain underfoot. Within an hour they reached the wider, sealed road, pleased with the progress they were making. They covered the remaining distance to the neighbourhood where the safe house was located in less than another hour then stopped to catch their breath and discuss a plan.

"Let's check it out from a distance before getting too close." They surveyed the area behind the house, which revealed nothing of consequence, so they dropped below to look up the road toward the house — no activity, no vehicles. It looked deserted.

"We have to go in," said Claude, facing the house and looking down at his hand-held device. "I'm not picking up any bio signatures, but that doesn't necessarily mean they aren't there."

Kate suggested, "How about you go in and I remain out here until you signal me to enter or you get the hell out."

Claude nodded and moved quickly up the road. Kate moved closer but stayed at a comfortable distance. Her mobile vibrated within a few minutes. She hit the "receive" button and Claude spoke. "Place looks deserted, but cups of warm coffee and half-eaten sandwiches are on the table, as though a couple of people left not too long ago. Come on in."

Claude was holding a glass of water for her when she opened the main door. She downed the full glass in one gulp and poured a second that she downed as quickly as the first. "Thirsty business," she remarked as she watched Claude drink from another large glass.

She flopped into an easy chair and said, "We are getting to see the countryside and experience a pre-Olympics atmosphere, but I doubt I will purchase ringside seats. I have already experienced enough of this circus."

Deep in thought, Claude looked at Kate and smiled, only slightly distracted by her remark.

Kate continued, "I am very close to heading home and piecing the rest of the story together at a safer cyber distance."

"Not yet, we are on high ground — no Great White sharks here."

"Very funny."

"Kate, Claude, Adele," boomed a familiar voice from the back doorway.

"Serik, where'd you come from?"

"When you didn't return in a reasonable time, I went looking — where's Adele?" He strode across the foyer to look out front. "And where's the SUV?"

"No idea," was Kate's response to both questions. "Since both are gone, perhaps they are together.

"Where'd you go looking for us?" said Claude.

"I went to the hot springs, but there was no sign of you or the vehicle. I called, texted, emailed, and looked for bio signatures — nothing."

"What are you using for transportation?"

"My uncle stores an ATV here for exploring the backcountry."

"We could've used that."

"How did you get back here?" asked Serik.

"On foot."

"So we are truly without a vehicle."

"It would appear so."

"But then appearance and reality have been a rather blurred phenomena today."

Serik asked again, "Where is Adele Winther? What happened to her?"

Claude stepped in, deciding to offer as little information as possible but responding sufficiently to keep Serik engaged.

"After the swim, we returned to the parking lot, drove up the winding road, then stashed the vehicle and continued a little farther on foot. The next thing we knew, Adele vanished. Gone. No trace of her. We returned to the spot where we had stashed the vehicle but it too had vanished — gone. We set out to try to track any sign of it but couldn't even find tire tracks … nothing."

Kate added, "We headed back here on foot to regroup with you."

Kate was pleased with the synergy of their thinking. They were on the same wavelength, unsure of just how far they could trust Serik, giving him enough line to keep him on the hook but not too much to reveal their strategy. It might reel him in — a little like fly fishing, she thought.

"The ATV has only one seat. There is a trailer that can be attached to it, but driving with it makes the ATV less manoeuvrable and adaptable to terrain conditions."

"Let's just keep it at the ready in case we need to move quickly. Is there any place to put it out of sight until we need it again?"

"Yeah, it'll squeeze through the entrance to the ground-level storage room. My uncle had an oversized door installed so he could keep grounds equipment inside, but then he never bought any in favour of giving out a contract to a local who could keep an eye on the place as well. The room is probably empty — let's check it out."

Claude accompanied Serik while Kate remained to connect with Bryant again.

She sent a text message updating him: **No sign of Adele or the vehicle. Both seem carefully stowed away in cyber space. Let you know when I have something.**

Kate waited for Claude and Serik to return, but after a longer than expected time, she went looking. Both were gone, with no sign of the ATV either.

"Jesus Christ! What the hell!"

"Skittish again, are we?" said Claude as he appeared around the end of a room divider. "Over here."

Kate exhaled in relief as she followed Claude around the edge of a barely perceptible room divider. Serik was on the seat of the ATV, carefully parking it facing outward to facilitate a quick exit if required.

"Nothing food can't address. Let's see what we can put together."

Kate headed up to the kitchen with Claude following a few moments later.

"Serik said we might be challenged by the selection of food available. He would be happy to put together a *kuurdak*, that is a typical Kazakh food, quick and easy to prepare if you don't mind meat and potatoes."

"Hey, beggars can't be choosers. I'm game for local cuisine wherever I go."

Serik emerged behind them with a package of meat in hand. "My great-aunt forced it on me last night when I stopped in for a late dinner. I hope you don't mind mutton. It is from free-range sheep, as you in the West would call it. Some of her in-laws continue a semi-nomadic lifestyle for part of the year, tending little herds on small tracts of land in remote areas. We get to enjoy the meat they bring back for the extended family."

Kate said, "I think today is taking a turn for the better. How can I help?"

"There should be some potatoes in the cool room — pick out four or five."

Kate followed his shoulder motion to a narrow door at the edge of the kitchen, opened it to find exactly what he described: a cool room with various fresh and bottled food provisions. Her heartbeat returned to normal as she bent to select potatoes from a bin. As she closed the door she thought, *Skittish is exactly what I'm feeling.*

Claude joined in washing the potatoes then cutting them into cubes as Serik instructed. Kate listened to Serik describe the origins and importance of *kuurdak* to the Kazakh way of life. Her anthropological mind took pleasure in absorbing the information.

"The people of this region were typically nomadic, and they still feel the pull of that lifestyle. To provide a ready and easy source of food as they moved about, they precooked and seasoned large batches of meat — usually red meat and most often mutton or camel but sometimes beef — and divided it into small bundles to be carried by most members of the nomadic clan. It formed the basis for many meal preparations as they moved about tending semi-wild herds and gathering plants and berries along the way." Serik skilfully sliced the meat into thin squares and rubbed in seasoning as he spoke.

"Did you see any onions and any other vegetables in the cool room, Mrs. Kate?"

She smiled at the appellation and returned to see what she could find. She emerged with two large red onions, a thing that looked like a cross between an African gourd and a Finnish squash, and a cabbage.

"Perfect, we can throw it all in — did you see any carrots?"

Kate produced one lone white carrot that had seen better days but was still edible.

"The great thing about *kuurdak* is that it is like a stew. As long as you have the meat and potato base, you can add just about any vegetable. Dried fruit also adds a special something."

Claude searched the cupboards and found a jar of apricots.

"Perfect," said Serik.

From a lower cupboard he drew out a large, open, round-based cooking pot that resembled a cross between a Chinese wok and an open-fire stewing pot. He placed it over the gas cooker, added some cooking oil, a number of finely chopped garlic cloves, the meat, then folded in the potatoes, followed by the slivers of onions, dried chili peppers, and chunks of fresh green peppers that Claude found in the refrigerator. It cooked quickly, resembling something between a stir fry and a European goulash. Kate thought of her elderly friendly neighbour and personal dog sitter, Émile; he would quietly devour this dish, resting back with delight.

Serik asked, "Did you see any yogurt in the refrigerator?"

Claude held up a container. "This?"

"Yes, can you spoon some of it out into a bowl and set it on the table with bowls and large spoons?"

Serik placed the pot on a ceramic trivet at the centre of the table and said, "I believe Westerners would say, 'Dig in.'"

It was succulent. Both Kate and Claude expressed appreciation.

"The vagaries of the day are vanishing with each mouthful," said Kate with Claude nodding in agreement.

"It makes our nomadic lifestyle deliciously satisfying."

Serik then lurched them back to reality. "We must save some for Adele Winther. She may be ravenous when she appears. I doubt food is part of her experience right now."

Kate felt a bit mystified by this man. *Friend or foe? Guardian or warden? Colleague or adversary?* She ventured a hedged reply. "Serik, do you have any idea what might have happened to Adele, where she might be, how we can get to her to ensure her safety? And where is Liz?"

Serik studied Kate carefully then looked over to Claude and responded to include them both. "I have no idea. I am as bewildered as you are. I can only say, she — Adele Winther — is not the first visitor associated with the Kazakh sports satellite to disappear. She is the first to vanish from the Olympic bid aspect. Since not one single body has turned up, I am hopeful that she will reappear, along with the others."

"Serik, how many people have disappeared?" asked Claude.

"A few that we know of — as they are private-sector people here on business, it has not become public knowledge. Adele Winther has a different profile. If she doesn't turn up soon, I expect it'll become the subject of a very public investigation and undermine the final initiatives for Kazakhstan to win the Olympic bid."

"When did you last see Liz?"

While he didn't exhibit any outward discomfort when speaking about Adele Winther, he appeared decidedly uneasy at the mention of Liz Bruan.

"I don't know — I went to check out the ATV. When I returned to let her know that it was usable, I couldn't find her anywhere. Her cell seems to be turned off. I tried it a number of times. I was hoping to find her with you."

It seemed Serik might not know that Liz Bruan was British Intelligence Service. Best to leave it like that — for now, at least.

"Serik, who do you work for? Who pays you besides us?" asked Claude.

"Kazakhstan Tourism and you. Kazakhstan Tourism can mean anything required by the government of Kazakhstan. It is the way they work."

"Do they know you're working for us as well?"

"I don't know. I have never told them. Your people were always aware of my work for Kazakhstan Tourism. Everything is done verbally. There is no paper or digital trail. Money — a sort of salary — is deposited to my bank account regularly. It looks like it originates from Kazakhstan Tourism."

"Why would you tell us and not your own people?"

"You pay better. Your country could be a safe haven if the going gets rough here. I did my undergraduate degree in the UK and a graduate degree in Canada, so I have affinities — attachments, so to speak."

"Fair enough, not unlike many of our international sleeper agents."

"Quite frankly, it has been a good deal until now. I haven't had to do very much — mostly passive surveillance in the course of my daily life," Serik added.

"Okay, Serik, I'll trust you — cautiously, that is. My partner here is a private investigator, and she has no reason whatsoever to trust you. If I run into any proof that you have betrayed us, I'll kill you."

Serik stiffened for just a moment then quickly recovered his composure and nodded. He had Claude's number and did not reveal a trace of compromised composure.

Kate concluded that he was smart, quick on the uptake, and could be useful as long as they watched him closely. Serik reminded her of Charlie Kagiso, the Tswana agent working for Robert Beltman in South Africa. He had turned out to be a valuable asset now, safely secreted away in northern Canada with his family and a good job.

She liked Serik but would not drop her vigilance. The air of confidence and boyish charm he projected could be all too alluring, effectively masking his real intentions. She trusted Claude now but remembered a time when she didn't, when they were both in the midst of the Taylor neuro-microchip investigation. The investigation brought her in contact with Claude. Both faced the threat of death before the case exploded. Dr. Taylor had been Claude's friend, colleague, confidant, and lover. Since then, a close, respectful relationship had evolved that saw them through the chicanery and dangers of international espionage and the idiosyncrasies of the personal spirit. Although reluctant to go along with the arrangement when the investigation shifted to Kazakhstan, Kate was glad to have Claude at hand now as they stumbled through the vagaries of this investigation.

The sound of an approaching vehicle drew them to the front windows. The familiar black SUV pulled up in front of the house and Adele got out, leaving the driver's door open, seemingly for protection as she surveyed the house.

"Adele, we are here," said Claude from the open doorway.

She remained where she stood until Claude walked out in the direction of the vehicle.

"Adele, we are as uneasy as you, but for the moment at least all is calm and nothing untoward appears imminent."

He reached the vehicle then stepped back from the gun Adele was pointing at him.

"That's powerful-looking — nothing we could have supplied you with. Are you alone?"

Serik had moved to the open doorway, out of sight but weapon at the ready.

Kate couldn't see what caused Claude to stop but suspected it was some kind of threat.

"Yes, now I am."

"Have you seen Liz — the young agent who was with us on our way up here?"

"No."

"Adele, we are no threat and probably as perplexed as you are. Please join us and put that menacing thing away — we have all experienced enough excitement for today. A cup of coffee or a stiff drink might do you better."

Kate had quietly traversed the distance from the side door of the house to the vehicle without Adele seeing her then as silently opened the front passenger door to the SUV. She exhaled slowly when she found there were no other occupants then caught Claude's eye.

Claude spoke in a soothing but controlled voice to Adele. "Although you have every right to distrust us, I'm asking you to set your unease and your gun aside." He paused. Adele showed no change in her demeanour.

"Adele, Kate is behind you with her gun trained on you. She would only use it to protect me."

Adele eyes dropped down to catch Kate's image in the side-view mirror. She stood her ground then slowly lowered the weapon. There wasn't a hockey play to draw on to pull her through this one. Claude approached then took the weapon from her hand. She offered no resistance, and Kate lowered her own weapon in relief.

"Come on in the house, Adele, Serik saved a bowl of *kuurdak* for you." She replied to the quizzical look on Adele's face with, "Don't worry, it's a delicious local dish that Serik prepared. We both had some and can tell you he had to snatch away the remaining portion that he insisted we save for you."

Adele entered the house and responded to Serik's invitation when he handed her a tall glass of water and then a second later slipped the remaining bowl of *kuurdak* in front of her.

"From science fiction to a bowl of stew at the kitchen table — all in an afternoon in Kazakhstan."

"Tell us about it, Adele," said Kate.

Adele finished her second glass of water, picked up the spoon for the stew, and remarked to Serik, "It smells delicious."

"I hope it will restore you as effectively as it did these two," replied Serik.

She slipped a small amount into her mouth, quickly followed by a large spoonful, then said with a look of delight, "This requires my undivided attention." She hungrily gobbled down the remainder of the bowl.

33

Kate leaned back into the seat as the British Airways flight lifted off from Almaty. A sense of relief washed over her and allowed a deep sleep to overtake her as the plane climbed to altitude.

When she awoke, she sat quietly reflecting on the seventy-two hours in Kazakhstan. It felt like three weeks had passed, not a mere three days. Perhaps the exposure to altered realities, albeit minute, contributed to increasing a sense of a longer timeline? Regardless, she increased her resolve to work alone. It seemed most of her time and energy went into retrieving various members of the little band of compatriots as they slipped in and out of the time continuum during the investigation. She had gone to Kazakhstan to follow the trail of the technology application for trace mineral extraction from tailings there. The process was originally developed by her clients to extract gold from tailings, but illicit users quickly discovered that it had more lucrative applications to rare earth minerals, when processed into delicate metals and used in screens for the burgeoning plethora of communications devices, solar panels, wind energy, space exploration etc. The technology became invaluable. Her clients were the inventers — the innovators of the technology. It had been stolen from them, modified, given different applications. Regardless, they wanted their intellectual property rights restored and not only the monetary benefit but to control how it was used and for what purpose. Now she would be returning to her clients to explain not only the multiple applications she had encountered for the technology but also the extension into altered realities. While the timeline variances were very short, they were enough to double, triple, quadruple the energy-collection capabilities of the technology that could only function with the refined metals from the processed rare earth minerals. For now, it meant keeping the SPACESPORTSK in orbit. It had gone so far beyond the original concept that Kate wondered if licensing with some form of royalty payments could become a workable option.

Adele had remained in Almaty to complete the site inspection with the Olympic Committee. Serik became her bodyguard and colleague. He seemed happy enough with that arrangement, sweetened by the promise Claude made to ensure a British visa would be immediately forthcoming to get him out of Kazakhstan — if the need arose.

The plan was that Adele would allow herself to appear corruptible in order to gain access to the syndicate behind the SPACESPORTSK. Kate mentally explored several scenarios about the technology, the satellite, the IOC involvement, Kazakhstan, China, and Russia — she expected Claude likewise was considering all of the angles, but it was too dangerous to talk anywhere in Almaty, the airport, or on the aircraft. They would have to wait for their return to London to do that in a secure environment.

Kate was roused from her reverie by a familiar voice speaking to a nearby passenger.

"Mr. Powers, would you prefer a late breakfast or early lunch? We can offer a combination of both as well."

She looked over to see who was speaking and read a name badge: "Elizabeth Bowen, Cabin Service Director." She felt her body burrow deeper into the cocoon-like business class seat as she regarded the crew and passenger exchange.

"Ah, Mrs. Roarty, you're awake. Can I get you some freshly brewed coffee with milk and a dash of maple syrup?"

Kate merely nodded without speaking while the cabin service director smiled and slipped away, quickly returning with a tray holding a steaming mug of coffee, a little pitcher of milk, and a small maple leaf-shaped glass bottle of maple syrup.

She discreetly looked over at David Powers, who smiled slightly and went back to reading his tablet. The cabin services director returned with a heavily laden tray of what appear to be brunch for Mr. Powers.

"Mrs. Roarty, would you like a meal, along with a second cup of coffee?"

Once again, Kate nodded silently and the cabin services director vanished to return with a tray of yogurt, fresh fruit, and two Asian salad rolls wrapped in rice paper. A side accompaniment of chocolate-covered blueberries completed the array.

Fortified by the coffee, intrigued by the reappearance of Liz Bruan, a.k.a. Elizabeth Bowen, sated by a lovely little meal, and comforted by the flight heading toward London, Kate decided to simply sit back and let it unfold. For the moment at least, what more could she want? Just before the pilot announced the beginning of the descent into Heathrow Airport, her cell vibrated with a text message. **See you in an hour. XO Jack.**

The flight taxied to a stop. The cabin services director welcomed the passengers to London, followed by a few instructions about connecting flights and deplaning, then they were in the airport heading to customs and immigration.

She passed them, walking along with the rest of the crew who exited via the crew wicket. Kate remained amazed by Liz Bruan's performance. Neither betrayed a hint of recognition of the other.

"You play your part well, Kate."

"And how do I address you now?"

"Home turf. Claude will be fine."

34

Grange, the Lake District, UK

They exited into the waiting area, and Kate immediately spotted the familiar form of a man studying an arrivals display screen. She walked up behind him and said, "The plane has landed and the passengers have disembarked." Jack whirled around and took Kate into his arms. Their embrace was long, deep, and quiet as they kissed then stood looking at each other, still holding hands. Kate looked around for Claude but couldn't see him anywhere.

She turned back to Jack, silently delighted just to look at him.

He lurched her out of her gaze, saying, "Kate, Karen Palmer has a cottage in the Lake District outside a village called Grange. Nobody will be using it. She has offered it to us for the long weekend. She said the wild daffodils will be in full bloom, and the trees will be breaking out in leaf along the walking trails near a lake called Derwentwater. We don't have to go—"

Kate interrupted, "I cannot think of anything I would like to do more than go to a cottage in the Lake District with you, Jack."

"I tried to get a rental car, but being a holiday long weekend, there are none available. However, we can easily get there by train and local bus. Karen says once there we really don't need a vehicle. She has a villager to keep an eye on the cottage. He will put in provisions and start a fire to warm the place up once she knows we are going."

"Karen, is it?"

Jack blushed a little. "We did sort of connect on the Taylor case, although we never met. We had breakfast at the hotel this morning when she made the offer."

Kate smiled. "Let's go to Grange in the Lake District, Jack. We have a lot to talk about. I feel like we have been apart for months, even though it is less than a week."

They boarded a train out of Euston Station within the hour and settled back into the pleasure of one another's company and the passing countryside as the train headed north to Penrith in Cumbria. The bus to Keswick was a bit late, which fortuitously allowed them to make a direct connection on to Keswick. They had just enough time in Keswick to take an enjoyable stroll through the high street pedestrian market, where they purchased raincoats, a variety of foodstuffs, and picked up local maps of walking trails before boarding a bus en route to Seatoller.

The driver of the handsome red double-decker bus advised them he would let them know when they reached the stop just outside Grange. Kate and Jack scrambled to the top level and sat in the short-legged front seat so they could view the route along the way. Despite the discomfort of the narrow front seats, it was worth it to see the roadsides filled with daffodils, the waves lapping across Derwentwater, and the branches of trees unfurling fluorescent green splashes of new buds brushing against the bus. It made them giddy with the excitement of spending a few days in this frolic of the arrival of spring. The bus stopped at the side of the road, and the driver directed them to walk across the old stone bridge and continue along on the same road until they reached the cottage on the lakeside. He advised them to watch carefully for the number post since the cottage was hidden behind a tall hedge.

They strolled through the charming little village with cottages crowding the narrow road. Kate remarked, "The variable use of the term 'cottage' diverges throughout the English-speaking world, doesn't it?" The stone and white-painted stucco against the windblown, craggy landscape was both austere and inviting.

"Here we are," announced Jack as they rounded a tall hedge to look upon a multigabled, two-storey cottage.

They stood looking up at it, but before they moved toward the front door, an old man shuffled toward them and with a grin, he announced, "You must be the Canadians. We have been expecting you."

Jack extended his hand. "Yes, I am Jack Johnson, and this Kate Roarty."

"Ah, those are names from this side of the Atlantic," the man proclaimed. "Come, let me show you in. You must be tired from the journey."

They entered to the smells of fresh bread on the table, a pot of stew bubbling on the stove, and a fire crackling in the fireplace. "We are so happy to have visitors to Mrs. Karen's place. When the children were young, the family came often and stayed for extended periods during the school holidays. Now that the girls are grown and away and Mrs. Karen has some high-powered government job, we don't see much of them anymore. Sometimes the mister comes on his own and busies himself with repair work and writing his books. Ah, I am talking too much. She told me to show you some specific things."

Kate and Jack smiled but couldn't slip in a word.

"Come." The man punched in a code on a panel at the side of a door, and it hissed open. While the house itself appeared at least a couple of hundred years old, this room was set in the future.

"Mrs. Karen calls this the cyber room. She said you would know what to do in it. The code for the entry pad changes continuously. Here is the formula." He handed Kate a piece of paper and said, "Memorize it then burn it in the fireplace as soon as possible." They glanced in to see an array of screens and control panels.

"I don't know what all this stuff is or how it works, but when the mister is here, I hear beautiful music coming from the cottage. I figure he has access to it with all this equipment. He plays that piano as well and seems to compose his own pieces. I am talking too much again."

Jack replied, "You can talk all you want as long as you tell us your name or how you like to be addressed."

"Sandy."

"Then Sandy it is," said Jack.

"That comes from my surname, Sanderson. The Norse go way back in Cumbria. Mrs. Karen's great grandfather was an offlander, but after a few generations, the Palmers became part of the landscape."

Kate and Jack smiled as Sandy continued to show them about, pointing out the woodpile and kindling stash, recycling bins, the telescope to watch the ferry crossing the lake, and the wine cellar. They descended to a semisubterranean level that appeared to be part of the original stone foundation.

"This was the root cellar. Mister converted it to a wine cellar. He said it would be more useful for wine, since they don't keep a garden anymore. He sealed off the outside entrance when he converted it. You would never know it was there. He did it all by himself using the same local stones and same building practices that the original builders used more than two hundred years ago. He researched it all — made diagrams and dug it out by hand — even the landscaping with plants and stones made it look like there had never been an outside entrance there at all. I offered, but he wouldn't let me help him. Anyway, here I am talking too much again. Mrs. K told me to tell you to help yourself to anything you wish to drink from it."

Kate and Jack thanked Sandy profusely and gently closed the door behind him. Kate went to the stove to stir the stew and turn down the gas while Jack retrieved a bottle of wine from the cellar. He was gone for a while, giving Kate a chance to freshen up and walk out onto the patio in the cool, moist evening air. Jack slipped a glass of red wine into her hand and clicked it in a silent toast.

"Hmm — very nice. Mister has quite a selection of UK wines and many from the continent. I was surprised to see some fine Ontario wines as well. The selection and organization of the cellar suggests that he possesses the knowledge of a sommelier. This one is called Saxon Red from the Battle Wines Estate. I thought it might go well with the stew."

"It slips down very nicely as is, but that may be the influence of the company I'm keeping and the ambience of this place." She turned to reach up to Jack with a long, slow, and lingering kiss, tasting the wine on his lips and alighting on his tongue, reaching into the warmth of his body and holding the defined contours of his head in her fingers beneath the softness of his hair. Heat flowed through her body like a gentle stream passing over rocks and tumbling into a pool heated by an intense summer sun. Jack gently eased back, still holding her in his arms, and said, "If I wasn't so ravenous, enticed by the smells of freshly baked bread and simmering stew, I would propose we move on to something even more sensual."

"We can enjoy both," teased Kate.

"Let's start by satisfying our hunger with stew and bread and more of this Saxon Red. There is much more where this came from," he said, brushing lightly across her lips.

The stew was delicious, exhibiting a gamey taste neither could quite place, but both readily devoured it using the warm bread with fresh butter to dip into the steaming stew as it cooled, then mopped up the gravy after the meat and vegetables were eaten. Jack poured more of the Saxon Red into their glasses and reached over to pull Kate from the table and into his arms.

"We've no more travels today. We're no longer hungry for food. We've plenty of wine to moisten our palates…" Kate touched a finger across his lips then began to undo his shirt buttons.

Darkness was closer to the light of a new day than the one they left behind when they awoke, a little chilled by the damp air that had crept in while the fire burned down to embers. Jack wrapped Kate in several quilts then pulled on pants and a jumper. "I'll be right back after I build up the fire and brew some coffee."

Kate slipped back into a dream-filled slumber when warmth invited her to push the covers away and the smell of freshly brewed coffee reached her nostrils.

"Kate, let's go out for a walk up the valley. There's a mist lifting off the river, rising to meet the fog rolling in across the lake. We won't be able to see much, but our feet can find the path along the lake, and we'll feel the droplets of water in the air. We can layer up in jumpers from the trunk downstairs and put on those Jack Murphy raincoats we bought in the market in Keswick."

Kate leapt up and into the shower and shouted over the running water. "I'll put a pack together with more coffee and food."

By the time they were ready to go, the daylight had penetrated through the heavy fog, but visibility beyond the roadway was limited. When they pulled the door shut, Sandy's voice preceded his person. "Headed out for a walk, are you? The fog will gradually burn off into a lovely day if you stay out long enough. You could walk up to Borrowdale and take a lunch at the pub. Whenever you have had enough walking, just make your way out to the sealed road and wave down a bus. They go by frequently, and you can get on going either way 'cause they do a short turnaround. Did you key in your retina recognition?"

Kate and Jack looked at each other. Jack stammered, "Uh, no we didn't."

"No worries, just come and get me when you return. I'll let you in. I'm permanently entered — you can do your entries when you get back. The instructions are online in the cyber room."

They walked off, Kate remarking, "Such a blend of the old world and current cybernetics. It never occurred to me that the place would be secured by retina display."

"Yeah, but I bet the old guy offers better security than any cyber intervention. He is fiercely loyal to Karen Palmer. That loyalty can't be programmed into any cyber device."

"He reminds me of Émile. I miss him," said Kate.

"Not to worry, Guy stopped in to have tea with Clare St. Denis, and Émile was visiting. He found a happy threesome."

"Threesome?"

"Big Ben."

"Ah yes, my dog."

"I think *our* dog might be the better pronoun, with the collective referring to a number of loyal caregivers. Dr. Taylor would have been pleased to find the life his legacy dog is leading."

"A therapy dog."

"Kate, every dog is a therapy dog — he's just an exceptional example for the species."

Kate felt her hand being sniffed and looked down to see beautiful blue eyes looking up at her. She immediately squatted down to greet the dog. Its solid white head with a single black mark on one ear and another smack in the middle of its head between her ears contrasted with the black and white coat, giving it a startled look.

"Ah, you've met Dotty. She'll want to go walking with you if you are willing to take her along."

Kate looked at Jack, who laughed and said, "Of course she can come along. Will she wait outside if we stop in a pub?"

"She can go in. Everyone knows her, but take the leash in case you cross a paddock full of sheep. She will herd them and move them along with you if you don't stop her. She must have been a working dog before she showed up here — haven't been able to rein in her compulsion to herd at any inopportune moment."

"Was she a stray?"

"She turned up about six years ago. We tried to find her owners but to no avail. No tags, no microchip, no breeder indication, nothing … we didn't even know what to call her so we started calling her Dotty because of her dots, and we thought she was a bit dotty until we realized that she was blind with cataracts. Villagers took pity on her and started raising funds for her surgery, then a Border Collie Foundation got wind of her and kicked in the balance we needed. After the surgery she blossomed and of course stayed — she is really a village dog but lives with me. She usually goes off on her own visiting around the village and up toward Borrowdale, but she loves to go walking with people. When the mister comes, he takes her on long walks every day."

"She's welcome to come with us."

"I think she just made Kate's day — a hard act to compete with, Dotty girl," allowed Jack as he bent down to ruffle her fur and say hello.

The threesome set off down the road toward the trailhead that led to the path on the slopes above the lake. True to Sandy's prediction, the sun began to burn through the dense fog, offering a view of the lake emerging from the misty soup. A signpost beckoned them off the road and into the dissipating fog, where they soon had to choose between ascending to hilltops, exploring the middle levels, or continuing along the lakeshore. Dotty made the decision for them; they followed her gambolling off along the middle-level path.

"If we try to maintain her pace, we will get a good workout as well," said Kate.

"I think I am content to let her run off and return, remaining at the ready to sprint after her if sheep come into view."

The fog burned completely off after an hour or so, allowing the sunshine to penetrate deep into the hardwood forest and forcing Kate and Jack to shed an outer layer and doff their hats. As they were stuffing the clothing into the daypack Kate had brought along, they heard sheep bleating.

"Oh no!" Jack was off to catch up with Dotty and snap the leash on her. Within minutes he met a small herd of sheep head-on that were being herded down the trail in their direction. Dotty, bringing up the rear, was having the time of her life. She screeched to a halt when she saw Jack running toward the sheep. He passed around them, gave her a sharp command, and Dotty sat down, looking very *sheepish*.

"Dotty, you know you are not supposed to do this, but you just can't help yourself, right?" Her tailed wagged with joy while her facial expression remained contrite.

Kate caught up to the sheep and got them turned around, reaching Jack and Dotty in a few moments.

"Now what do we do with them?"

"I bet she knows, don't you, girl?"

"Why don't we let her herd them back — maybe we'll find the paddock where they belong."

"Excellent idea!" exclaimed another voice coming down the trail. "She outsmarted my Mac here."

Kate started into apologies. The man lifted his hand to stop her.

"No need, madam. We know Dotty. This is as much my fault as all of ours for letting her get away with her random herding. I even contributed to her surgery fund. Once she could see again, she lost no time making up for her blind period with the random herding. We thought it was a cute celebration of her recovery and let it continue."

He stuck out his hand. "Cally Sanderson — and you are the Canadians?"

"Yes, Jack and Kate," said Kate.

"Sandy is my uncle. He told me the Palmer place was getting some Canadian visitors."

He turned the sheep around as he spoke, and they fluidly flowed around as his own dog lay at his feet. "Let's see if Dotty can work with Mac to get them back to the paddock. It's only a half mile or so along the way. She can't do too much damage in that distance. Hang on to her until Mac gets them going. Mac, walk on."

Mac rose, slung low, and walked straight at the sheep. They funnelled out from milling about and began moving back up the footpath, a half dozen abreast, flowing around the trees without breaking momentum. Some drifted off to the left. Cally unsnapped Dotty's leash and commanded, "Come by."

Dotty was off to the left of the sheep, herding the drifters back into the fold while Mac drove them on. Some of the sheep then drifted off to the right, and Cally commanded, "Away." Dotty circled back and came up on the right, herding the drifters back into the fold while Mac kept them moving ahead, reinforced by Cally's command: "Steady." The well-trained Border Collie slowed his pace but kept moving the sheep in the right direction.

"Can one of you scoot ahead to open the gate?"

Kate was on it and opened it as the first sheep arrived and the two dogs worked together to drive them into the paddock. Cally commanded, "That'll do," then heaped praise on Dotty. Mac seemed to know he had done his job and it was finished.

"She seems to know her commands and appears quite trainable," remarked Kate.

"Yeah, perhaps I'll take another go at my uncle to let me have the dog for a bit and get her sorted out. I think he's afraid of losing her since we never figured out where she came from — he has been reluctant to let me have a go with her. Enjoy your walk." And Cally was gone.

Just as Jack's stomach began to rumble, they came across another signpost splitting off to the left. "It looks like the path that will lead us into a village where we can catch lunch at a pub," said Jack. Within moments they emerged onto a narrow, sealed road. Dotty sped ahead.

"Do you think we should follow the dog?" Jack laughed.

They rounded a bend to see a sign above the doorway right at the edge of the road.

"Shall we try the Sheepdog Inn?" He reached to open the door for Kate, who caught his arm just in time to prevent him from crashing into the low-hung entranceway built in another era when people were much shorter.

They entered the darkened space, paused to allow their eyes to adjust, and heard, "That's a good girl. You were hungry. Is nobody feeding you down in the valley? Here, have another bowl with extra gravy."

"Do you supposed Dotty beat us to lunch?"

"Oh, there's lots more where that came from — did she bring you in?" came the cajoling voice from the kitchen.

"In a manner of speaking, yes," said Jack. "Can we get a meal and a brew?"

"Any guest of Dotty's, even offlanders, can stay for a bite and a beer anytime."

"I'm glad we brought her along, er, she brought us along."

"The latter to be sure. Welcome to the Sheepdog Inn, since 1720."

"Only three hundred years old?"

"Before that 'twas the Norse Warrior Tavern — that goes back to your L'Anse aux Meadows days."

"You know a bit about Canada, then?" said Kate.

"Just a bit. We spent five days in Gander, Newfoundland, during the 9/11 crisis. To pass the time the locals took us on an expedition to see L'Anse aux Meadows. Until then, we thought Canada was a new place. It was the highlight of our visit to Boston. Can I offer you a Stout Mary? Any friend of Dotty's gets one on the house."

"Thank you," Kate and Jack uttered in unison.

The proprietor placed two glasses of dark ale in front of them. Kate winced with the first sip, finding the brew too bitter and aggressive, but Jack relished the dark, strong taste, enjoying a long swig before setting the glass down with satisfaction.

"Chase it with soup and bread and you'll be fine, Mrs."

Jack spied Dotty coming out of the kitchen. "I swear that dog can turn on her sheepish look on command. Are you sure she had cataracts, or was it just a ruse to win the hearts of everyone in this valley?"

"Either way, she succeeded," chuckled the proprietor.

"I might not be so keen on the beer, but this soup's delicious, and we may devour an entire loaf of the bread."

"Don't be shy, try the butter as well. It's freshly churned by a neighbour — gives her a bit of extra money to supplement her pension."

Jack lathered the butter on the bread and remarked, "Second only to the beer." He raised his glass. "To Dotty — the diamond Border Collie."

Kate and the proprietor joined in on the toast, and Dotty whined playfully.

"I think we will have to abandon catching the bus so we can walk off this feast."

"Oh, you can do both. Hop on the bus up to Seatoller then walk back to Grange over the Cat Bells and down along the river. There are some marvellous views over the valley when you are high up, then you can watch Dotty fishing in the river as you descend. She is pretty skilled at catching the brownies; two or three would provide a nice dinner feast."

"An angler as well. I have to see this," said Kate as they walked along, keeping their ears peeled for the sound of the bus.

True to description, they heard the bus and waved it down.

Dotty scrambled on ahead, stopping only long enough to greet the driver with a nuzzle for a liver bit that slipped into her mouth then headed straight up to the second level. Jack was holding a bunch of change in his hand. The driver picked out the requisite coins and dropped them into the box.

"And the fare for the dog?"

"Oh, Dotty has a lifelong pass. I already scanned it."

"You've got to be kidding."

"We keep a copy on all the buses so she doesn't have to carry it."

Kate laughed then stopped at the sight of the pass the driver was holding in his hand. It read "Cumbrian Transport, lifelong pass, Dotty BC, Grange," and her photo was beneath it.

"Okay, that did it. It's official — this visit to the Lake District is becoming far more interesting than my sojourn in Kazakhstan."

"And mine in Ireland."

"Then it must be the company."

"Yeah, Dotty wasn't present in either place." Kate laughed.

"Story of my life — upstaged by a dog."

Kate encircled him with a hug. "Not true."

"Charlie dog, Big Ben, and now Dotty — yes, true," he said with a downtrodden but playful expression.

Dotty bolted down the stairs. "I guess this is where we get off."

They passed a delightful afternoon walking the path from Seatoller down to Grange, watching Dotty diving for brownies. They kept three and released the remainder. Dotty was surprisingly delicate, careful not to puncture the fish. She seemed to fully understand the catch-and-release concept.

They grilled the little trout for dinner. Kate put together a red cabbage salad with nuts, raisins, and shaved carrots she found in the pantry and whipped up a balsamic dressing. Just as Jack was placing the little fish on a platter with a basket of sliced bread from the loaf Sandy left, a tap on the door brought a gift of fresh homemade chips from a neighbour.

Mrs. Dundy said, "Can't have a fish feed without chips — that would be sacrilege in these parts."

She thrust the warm paper parcel into his hands and was gone while he was stammering, "Thank you."

"Any more surprises and I'll have to return to policing to experience the mundane banalities of every day life, as you would say, Kate."

"Let's eat. I think another surprise is awaiting us — just look at those little trout."

"Three plates?"

"The angler has to enjoy the fruits of her efforts as well," said Kate as she set the plate on the floor for Dotty, who came over and sat by it but did not eat until Kate and Jack sat down, poured their wine, and took a morsel of theirs to sample before digging in. The single exclamation, "Delicious" and Dotty's serving vanished, then she headed straight to the door. Jack let her out and she was gone.

"What a funny dog. She's worth her entertainment value alone. I'd love to take her home as a companion for Big Ben."

"I'm not sure that Clare and Émile would approve, not to mention Sandy and Cally … and mister … and the entire village."

"Kate we must check out the cyber room and bring up the message Karen Palmer left for us."

"Okay, let me manoeuvre around the key pad so we can get in—"

Kate left Jack to it while she cleared the dishes away, reflecting on the wonderful day they had enjoyed together in this welcoming setting. *We have to experience more of life like this, not little snippets between bombs, bullets, and barbarity.*

She heard Karen Palmer's voice and walked into the cyber room to encounter a shimmering 3D avatar of the MI6 director.

"Kate and Jack, welcome to our Grange cottage. I hope you enjoy your stay there as much as we do every time we get away. By now, undoubtedly, you have met Sandy and Dotty, who together and separately will introduce you to the cottage, the village, and the valley. Sandy is the purveyor of practical, useful information and an abundance of anecdotes, while Dotty provides adventure and comic relief.

"The cyber room — please go to the monitor on the left and have your retina scanned. That will give your ongoing access without having to use a keypad code. The cyber room provides you with a secure environment to communicate with any interface — organic, analog, electronic, digital, whatever. The cybernetics there can adapt and remain secure. The room is fireproof, combustion-proof, cyber-proof. The replicator along the east wall has an abundant capacity, but not complete, as the technology is evolving. If you need something that you don't have, try it out. In an emergency, go in there to address your requirements. The door can be sealed shut, and only those in the retina display inventory for that room can enter. If you hear this sound—" a triple tinkle played "—that is me trying to reach you. Enjoy. Goodbye." And the shimmering avatar vanished.

"We have been cyber messaged by an avatar, led through a walking adventure by a dog, feasted on some delicious little trout known as brownies in these parts, welcomed by a web of neighbour folk — I can only think of one more thing I would like to do to wind down this perfect day in the Lake District," said Kate.

She bent down to kiss Jack, who was still sitting at the avatar panel. The kiss folded into an embrace as Kate slipped onto Jack's lap and his large frame and shoulders enveloped her. He rose, lifting her effortlessly, and carried her into the living room. The sun had set and the room darkened. Only the muted crimson flames from the remaining coals of the almost extinguished fire interrupted the subdued space. Jack set Kate down on the chesterfield in front of the fireplace, slipped a soft mohair rug over her, added wood to the barely flickering cinders, then squatted down to give several gentle blows to the embers, and a flame sprang up to consume its new source of fuel. He responded to Kate's shoulder massage by leaning back into her strong hands loosening and relaxing the muscles at the base of his neck and across his shoulders.

She placed her legs along his sides, allowing him to drape his arms over her knees as she continued massaging his neck. He grabbed two large square pillows from the floor and placed them vertically on his lap and under his chin. Kate kneaded the tension out toward his upper arms with her thumbs, feeling the release as she brushed out and away the tautness of his bulky muscles. She then reached down to gently caress his face with her own, reaching around to undo the buttons of his shirt, exposing his chest and slipping the shirt off to continue to massage his upper body. Kate pushed the tension down through his arms and out through his fingers, then, feeling his body relaxing, ran her fingers through his hair, gathering up the silky black curls toward the crown and pulling them to relax stress through his hair follicles. She continued massaging his temples and forehead, ending by following with playful, brushing kisses over his face and eyelids.

They sat quietly watching the fire, being lulled by the rhythm and staccato of the crackling sounds enticing them into further exploration of their bodies, slipping into softly passionate lovemaking. Sleep overcame them, sated by their embrace and caressed by the warmth of the fire.

Kate and Jack awoke to the coolness of the air. The ambers had burned down to coals. They snuggled closely together in the warmth from one another when they both realized that a soft but persistent tinkling sound was coming from the cyber room. Kate wrapped herself in the mohair rug and slipped into the room. She pressed the receive button on the avatar panel.

A train on the track image shimmered to life.

"Bryant!" exclaimed Kate.

A familiar voice animated the train. "Do you like it?"

"This is supposed to be an impenetrable system."

"Kate, would I be of any use to you if I couldn't hack into any *impenetrable* system? I do admit, this one was tougher than most, and I couldn't get in until you actually activated your contact with MI6."

"Okay, I'm certain you wouldn't have contacted me here and at this hour through this elaborate means unless it was crucially important."

"Yes, I have been monitoring some disturbing traffic that I think Karen Palmer is trying to keep a lid on to give you and Jack a bit time together. I suggest you ready yourself for a callback — if she's as smart as I think she is, she will be contacting you shortly."

"Tell me what's happening, Bryant."

"The coffee is freshly perked in the pot behind you. Have it and get ready then get back to me. Probably best to keep this little access breach between us. We don't want MI6 becoming needlessly distracted."

"Right," said Kate, and the train image was gone.

She poured two coffees and took them out to Jack, who was sitting up, looking at his watch.

"It is the correct time," she said as she handed a cup of coffee to Jack. "I'm afraid our little holiday is over."

Jack looked crestfallen but recovered in an instant, took a gulp of coffee, and said, "Time for a shower?" They slipped into the large modern glass enclosure backed against two-hundred-year-old stone walls of the original house structure, soaped and rinsed, lingered for a delicious embrace, then towelled off and quickly dressed, gathering together their belongings.

Almost on queue, a sound summoned them back into the cyber room. They passed the retina display, and the Karen Palmer avatar shimmered to life.

"Kate, Jack, sorry to contact you at this ungodly hour. You are dressed?"

"We were anticipating an early wake-up call," replied Kate.

"Can you be ready to go in ten minutes?" Both nodded.

"I'm sending an unmanned shuttlecraft to pick you up. It's been dispatched already. It operates on sensors, so no sound and no lights. We acquired it after the helicopter crash in the Thames. The silver lining from that experience was it gave us a reason to move it to the top of the list on the budget for new capital acquisitions. You two will be the first to use it. Move as quickly as possible when it gets there so it can come and go under the cover of darkness. The only one likely to detect its presence is Dotty — try to distract her. The general public will become acquainted with this technology soon enough, but we would rather it not start in a village in the Lake District. Keep the lights off in the cottage, and you should be able to see it approach and land on the lakeside. It is programmed with your retina display that we uploaded from our cyber security bank. The shuttle is only visible if you are looking for it." Then her avatar was gone.

Jack opened the fridge, rummaged through it, and pulled out a frozen steak. He threw it in the microwave on high.

"Jack, we don't have time to cook and eat."

He smiled, kissed her, and said, "Dotty does."

"Smart."

Kate kept her eyes peeled in the direction of the lake and soon enough spotted the craft descending in the direction of the cottage then setting down right in front.

"Let's go," she said just as Dotty started barking.

They slid open the door, and Jack gave one sharp command, "Dotty, that'll do." The Border Collie dropped to a prone position, and Jack heaped praise on her as he placed the steak at her front paws under her nose and said, "Good girl, Dotty. That'll do," he said again, reinforcing the command. The dog launched into the partly raw steak while Kate and Jack slipped down to the shuttlecraft where it sat dormant, motionless and soundless. No apparent opening was visible.

"Now what do we do?" said Jack.

"Let's get really close — maybe its retina display is myopic."

"Cute."

Kate was right. When they got within a metre of the craft, a panel quietly hissed open, and they entered. It closed equally silently and lifted off, its movement barely perceptible. They sat in two of several available seats that sensed their dimensions and closed to a comfortable fit around their hips, back, and neck. A seat belt extended across their abdomens, securing them like a well-fitting glove.

"Now what," said Jack.

"I think we just sit back and enjoy the ride."

"It seems we are airborne, but it's so quiet and smooth that it's very hard to tell."

"Listen carefully. There's a sound — it must be the craft against the air as it passes through the wind. It's like standing in a windswept meadow."

"I'll take your word for it, Kate."

Kate swung her chair toward a console of small screens and buttons that formed a semicircle along the walls of the craft. She swiped several screens, and displays light up. One showed window views, and Kate swiped it. Several panels slid away from windows, opening the aircraft to a view of the night sky as it sped toward London. A line of orange red was perceptible defining the horizon and progress toward dawn.

"That's better. I was feeling a bit claustrophobic," said Jack.

"The navigator indicates we are heading southeast toward London, and that approaching sunrise confirms the direction."

Dark shadows of tall buildings and flickering ground lighting suggested they were approaching a major urban centre — probably London.

As quickly as the craft transported them through the night sky, it slowed and entered a portal atop MI6.

"I think we have reached our destination," said Kate.

"Good lord, it took us six hours to get to Grange from Heathrow travelling overland. This trip feels like six minutes," exclaimed Jack.

"A bit longer. I guess getting here quickly and covertly is important to Karen Palmer."

The shuttlecraft set down in a well-lit bay, devoid of anything but the craft and the two of them. Kate swiped the door screen to open, and they exited into the bay. Two large panels seemed to comprise the entrance and exit system.

"This building knows me. Perhaps we can exit with my bio recognition."

She placed her hand on the scanner, which flashed a green "enter" screen with her name on it. Kate passed through the invisible threshold. Jack attempted to follow her but was denied by an invisible barrier and an authoritarian-sounding female voice. "Superintendent Jack Johnson of the SQ has not been given access to move about SIS Vauxhall Cross — remain in shuttle bay."

The door did not close, but Jack was securely sealed from moving out of the shuttle bay. Just as Kate started to advise him that she would return with assistance, Agent Liz Bruan appeared in the foyer behind Kate.

"Welcome to SIS Vauxhall Cross, Kate." Kate swung around, already knowing the identity of the person.

"Either you are cloned or permanently assigned to my detail."

Liz laughed. "Neither, but it probably feels like it. I had a couple of days off while you were at Grange." Agent Bruan looked beyond Kate. "Superintendent Jack Johnson, let's see if we can make you feel at bit more welcome at SIS Vauxhall Cross."

"That would be nice."

"Can you place your hand on the bio signature pad, unless you have a reason not to be entered into our inventory."

"Do I have an option?"

"Oh yes, you can be escorted by a heavily fortified armed guard out onto the street under the threat of death if you ever try to enter SIS Vauxhall Cross again, but since we already have your fingerprints, blood type, and retina display, the bio signature analysis will simply confirm that we already know you, permitting you to move about quite freely," Agent Bruan replied with a familiar mischievous smile.

"Bio signature it is then."

Agent Bruan interacted with the bio signature security system both verbally and by keying in what Kate presumed were some sort of access or approval codes.

"Superintendent Jack Johnson, please proceed through the secure gateway."

Jack did as he was told, and the verbal security system stated, "Superintendent Jack Johnson, collaborative, friendly agent from the Sûreté de Québec of the Government of Canada, henceforth to be identified as Jack Johnson, SQ, with the linguistic marker Quebecois accent on Canadian English and first language French Canadian."

Jack passed through the secure portal at Agent Bruan's beckoning, and they followed her across a grid of circular corridors that led out into the main expansive lobby, already familiar to Kate.

"Director Palmer is on her way in. She asked me to deliver you to her office waiting area, where a breakfast should be laid out for you to enjoy until she gets here, when she will join you."

"As long as there is coffee, I am good," said Kate.

"There will be, along with blueberries, yogurt, and warm croissants with fresh butter and jam."

"That director of cabin services role seems to have left its mark, Agent Bruan," said Kate jovially.

"Yes, if secret service cutbacks leave me without a job, I can always seek out a waitressing position."

Jack interjected, "Should I even ask what this is about or assume I really don't need to know."

"Suffice to say that our young Agent Bruan is quite a chameleon when it comes to role-playing. We experienced several of her faces during our Kazakhstan experience."

"I will stick to coffee and croissant. I have no idea what you are talking about."

Agent Bruan displayed a brief look of surprise that disappeared as quickly as the expression slipped across her face.

Kate allowed, "Our time in the Lake District was an experience of each moment. We didn't talk about work. It was such a lovely retreat away from drones, bullets, and bombs. The most catastrophic thing that happened was a cloudburst when we headed out on one of several walks. It was readily addressed with Mackintoshes and umbrellas."

35

Karen Palmer swept in as all three were launching into the little breakfast buffet set out in her reception area.

"Oh good, you are here, and so is the food."

She threw her overcoat onto a chair and eagerly grasped the cup of coffee that Agent Bruan handed to her. She raised it to the others and said, "To the solace that mitigates all evil — at least for the moment."

They could all easily embrace such a toast.

Palmer continued in a very pressing manner. She slipped a hand-held device out of her jacket pocket and pointed it at a large screen on the wall above the credenza that held the breakfast display.

A video action came into view that depicted the movement of several men engaged in conversation.

"This was captured from a distance, so unfortunately we are without audio. Do you recognize any of these men, Kate?"

Kate studied the video then asked Karen to pause it and zoom in on the faces. She immediately identified Daniel Yaw Osu, her principal client.

Karen prompted Kate to look closely. She zoomed back to give a full-body view that showed him walking and speaking with accompanying hand gestures.

"Are you sure it is Dr. Osu?"

Kate approached the screen and took Karen's hand-held device to move the video back and forth and get as much of a view of the figure as she could then stepped back and said, "Well, now I am not sure."

"What about the other two men? Have you run into them before?"

"There is a vague sense of familiarity about the taller white guy. I may have met him in Cape Town. I could verify that with my contacts there. Uncle Anjay, ah … Anjay Gandhi may know who he is."

"Okay, we can send the video to him. He may be able to help us with the other man as well."

Kate continued looking very closely at the individual she took for Daniel Yaw Osu. "It isn't him — it really looks like him, but this guy has a much cockier sense to his mannerisms than Daniel ever displayed. Daniel oozes intelligence and a total lack of confidence. There is a swagger to this fellow."

"Perhaps the swagger of a younger brother."

"Ah yes, of course, same genetic pool — distinctly similar appearance but behaviourally sorted differently."

"Meet Eliakim Kofi Osu, the younger brother of Dr. Daniel Yaw Osu. You may recall the Westgate Mall attack in Kenya. Among many who perished in that al-Shabaab carnage was a Ghanaian poet of the Ewe tribe named Kofi Awoonor. Daniel and Eliakim are also Ewe. Both admired Kofi Awoonor, but to Eliakim he was a giant. Daniel's bent was in the direction of science, and he was a solid student, gaining easy access first to undergraduate studies in Canada then to graduate school in the UK. He grew away from his Ghanaian roots.

"Eliakim had more of an artistic persuasion and excelled only where his studies could embrace literature, poetry in particular. He was inspired by Awoonor's persona and his poetry that brought the Ewe people to English and the attention of the outside world. Awoonor studied in the United States, did a couple of stints as a diplomat, including as Ghana's ambassador to the UN in the early 1990s, then in his late seventies, after resettling back in Ghana, he had the misfortune of being in the wrong place at the wrong time. He had travelled to Nairobi to attend a literary festival, where he gave a master class in poetry. The following day he was shot dead for being a non-Muslim. He went to the Westgate Mall to buy gifts before returning to Ghana. One of his sons was with him. He was wounded but survived. Awoonor had been something of a mentor to young Eliakim, who excelled with the attention he gave him. The Ewe traditional beliefs deny mourning of the dead — that left young Eliakim silently bereft, at a tender age, when anger can take a deep hold on a young man. Daniel enticed him to the UK to pursue his studies in literature, but he floundered and dropped out. Daniel got him a job in an assay office doing rudimentary analysis of core samples. There he made some connections that led him to where we think he is operating now. Daniel moved to Canada to pursue his doctoral studies, and they seemed to have lost touch or had a falling out. We think Eliakim has played a role in the spiriting away of the technology process, invented by Daniel, to ferret out the trace elements of first gold then rare earth minerals. The physical resemblance between the two brothers is so striking, and Eliakim acquired just enough knowledge of mineral extraction processes that he could impersonate his brother."

"Does Daniel know this?"

"We doubt it, but we aren't sure. What we do think is that Eliakim is in quite deep, so if any scruples resurface that might give him a sober second thought, he has little chance of getting out of the scheme alive."

"Where do I fit into this angle of my case?"

"Just before the holiday weekend, Eliakim purchased a one-way plane ticket to Ottawa. He has a British passport now, so he can travel freely. We think he may be going there to kill his brother and assume his identity."

"When is he leaving?"

"In a few days. We want you to get there ahead of him and bring his brother up to speed on these suspicions."

"I doubt Daniel will believe me."

"We will arm you with a portfolio on a flash drive that will convince him."

The otherwise silent Jack spoke up. "It will have to be very, very good to override the sibling devotion."

"We can demonstrate the abandonment of filial piety by Eliakim so important to the Ewe sociocultural precepts and document his actions and devious connections. I think you will be armed with enough to be convincing."

Kate studied Palmer very carefully for a few moments. "This strays a long way from the satellite that seemed to be your primary interest. What aren't you telling me?"

Director Palmer did not miss a step. "We haven't told you how we collected this intelligence, and we don't intend to — we cannot put our informants at risk."

Kate did not believe this response for a moment. "A nice deflection, but if you want me to work with you, I need all of the facts and suppositions."

"It is up to you, Kate. I cannot tell you any more, and I am asking for your help."

A nice personal hook, thought Kate. "Regardless of whether I can work with you from this angle, I am ready to return to Ottawa, where I can complete the work I wish to do for my client." She turned to Jack. "I am sorry we haven't had a chance to discuss this, but we need to be on the earliest flight we can book back to Ottawa."

"Fine by me, Kate, I have to get back to work."

Liz Bruan added, "I too will return to Ottawa to resume my secondment with CSEC."

Karen Palmer said, "We can make a flight booking for all three of you, if you agree and send the confirmations as soon as we have them."

Kate opened her hands in submission and started for the door.

"Kate, we are all on the same page — our perspectives simply differ."

"I'll re-evaluate perspectives once I am on my home turf. Thanks for breakfast and for the Grange weekend. It was perfect." And they were gone.

Kate was moving quickly with Jack at her side. They exited MI6 in record speed, and once on the street, Kate paused to breath deeply.

Jack said, "I think I just witnessed Kate Roarty, P.I. at her worst. Feels like the first time we met."

She wheeled around to confront him, then her anger dissolved as quickly as it riled up. "It is time to go home."

"You won't get any argument from me."

"Jesus, Jack, I don't even know where we are staying, and we don't have our bags."

"Don't worry, your bellman and lady-in-waiting took care of it all," he said with a playful tone and smile as he took her hand. "Let's go home, the tulips will soon be blooming."

36

Ottawa, Canada

Kate pushed back into the seat, seeking out its comfort as the Air Canada flight lifted off, bound for Ottawa. She was grateful that the flight was direct, nonstop. Routing through Toronto or Montreal often resulted in delays, and she just wanted to get there.

Kate had connected with Bryant before they boarded. He was as intrigued as a child with a new toy about the unmanned shuttle journey from Grange to London. He also had more information about the Kazakh unmanned craft and its players. He preferred to review everything with her when she was home and in her secure communications room. Her command centre, as she called it, was a carryover from the Taylor case. Kate had continued to upgrade it to state-of-the-art under Bryant's guidance. She would add more bells and whistles to render it comparable to the Grange cottage cyber room. In the meantime, she was glad to have the time on the flight to ponder all of the angles of the trace minerals case and her clients, led by Daniel Yaw Osu. The brother angle concerned her. Despite misgivings, she would connect with Daniel before his brother arrived and suss out his reaction.

She went for a walk and found Liz Bruan sitting in economy class, rapt by a romance movie. Kate slipped into the empty seat next to her, saying, "I like that one too. Ryan Reynolds ages well. He was a bit of a shit as a kid and a young sex idol when he was married to Scarlett Johansson — cut from the same cloth. He matured personally, and the maturity reflects professionally. Now he is often cast opposite difficult, intense yet very attractive women, and he carries it out beautifully."

"Rather like Jack," replied Liz.

Kate smiled. "Yes, rather like Jack. Do you have a place to live in Ottawa, or will you have to find something?"

Liz blushed, and before she spoke, Kate had her reply.

"Then you must be happy to be home."

"Yes."

Kate continued her walk around the cabin, loosening up her joints and increasing blood flow, then she slipped back into her seat to see Jack totally engaged in a *Star Wars* film with an intense love scene riveting him to the screen. "May I watch as well?"

"It's pretty intense. You may prefer the real thing," he said as he paused the film. "What's up? I can see this anytime."

"Seems our young Agent Liz Bruan has formed an attachment in Ottawa. That will give the Brits grief."

"She's young, smart, and attractive — she must have men lining up."

Although seven and a half hours, the flight time passed quickly — a few naps, a few meals, a few walks about the cabin, a few chats with Jack, and they were there. Kate felt like she had been away for months when in fact it had been less than two weeks. Time for the snow and ice to all but melt away, crocuses to begin to push up, and the fresh scent of spring to creep into the air. They arrived home to Kate's house, where opening the door she was charged by a massive

Golden Retriever, who was all over her with whimpering greetings and kisses. Émile had brought the dog home from Clare St. Denis, who was always delighted to care for him when Kate was away.

She turned to Jack and said, "I suppose you had something to do with this."

"Hey, I was with you — blame it on Émile … and…"

"Guy Archambault," Kate added. "Émile does not drive."

"Guilty," said a voice behind them on the step. They turned to see Guy smiling broadly and holding up a bulging bag labelled "Green Papaya."

"Thought you might be tired and hungry and not wishing to rush out to shop. I brought both Émile and Big Ben back from Clare St. Denis's place today. They have become a familiar unit spending time together when you are away."

"Now *I* feel guilty coming home and splitting up the unit."

"No problem. I think everyone is happy with the arrangements. I will leave you to it, only to advise that you are booked for dinner tomorrow evening at Marny and Daggy's. Marny will not take no for an answer. Her instructions were, 'do not bring anything except stories.' *Ciao.*" And Jack's best friend was gone.

"Thai food, anyone?" said Jack, holding up the bag.

"First, a walk with our best friend here," said Kate as she ruffled Big Ben's fur and clipped on the leash.

37

Kate sent a text to Daniel Yaw Osu to meet him for breakfast at the Elgin Dinner. The response came back immediately: **All of us or just me?**

Just you, Kate replied.

They sat in the familiar surroundings of the Elgin Dinner in the old and trendy part of Centre Town that Kate loved, and it wasn't far from Ottawa U and Daniel's haunts. A booth afforded some privacy.

After a second cup of coffee — she had consumed three at home before leaving — she was well fortified to launch into the discussion with Daniel.

His opener was, "Well, what did you find?"

Kate studied him for a few moments and then pushed a photo of his brother across the table between them. "Tell me about your brother."

"Kofi?"

Kate slammed the table, attracting the attention of nearby customers. She smiled at them, waiting for the distraction to abate as Daniel settled as well.

"Yes, Daniel, how is he implicated in all of this? The truth — do not even begin to speak until you are prepared to tell me the truth."

Daniel took Kate at her word. He drank his coffee, waited for the huge breakfast of three eggs, pancakes, beef sausage, beans, and toast to arrive, then generously spread syrup over everything and ploughed through almost the entire meal, eating without pausing. After carefully setting down his knife and fork, downing the orange juice, then summoning the waiter for more coffee, he said, "Okay. Kofi is my younger brother. I am the oldest; there are four years and two brothers between us. Kofi is the artistic one — sensitive, a lover of words expressed poetically, in literature, scripts, and screenplays and used to promote the visual arts and music. As a child, he was a loner, lost in literature, shunning large family gatherings, friends, sports, in favour of books. Then he met a family friend that returned to Ghana after a long time in America — Kofi Awoonor, a poet, professor, and diplomat. In my brother's eyes, Kofi Awoonor was a giant. He quietly read all of his work, learned everything he could about him, and eventually caught his attention. Mr. Awoonor became a willing mentor to Kofi.

"By the way, you know the naming system in Ghana — Kofi merely means a child born on Friday. Ghanaians often take the familiar weekday name as the first name and keep it, especially the males." Kate nodded. "Anyway, the elder Kofi saw artistic brilliance in my brother and encouraged him. My brother grew and flourished and became his own man, confident and curious. Then the Westgate Mall shootings happened in Kenya. Kofi Awoonor had the misfortune of being there. He was killed. His own adult son was injured but recovered. My brother withdrew into a shell for many months, and our family was very worried by his behaviour. When he emerged, nobody recognized him. He was angry, combative, destructive, disrespectful — he was not a pleasant person to be around. My parents pleaded with me to take him under my wing in London. They thought the change would be good for him. Reluctantly,

I agreed, and in the beginning, it seemed to work out. My academic environment and fellow scientists intrigued him, but he held little interest in the technology pursuits we were passionate about, and he began to disappear first for hours and parts of days then for days and weeks.

"He grew thin and scruffy-looking. When he did turn up, he was angry and sullen. I didn't know what to do, so I did nothing — I ignored him. Then I thought he was coming out of it. He cleaned himself up, starting eating better, and even enrolled in a few courses at the university. We were about the same size, and he began borrowing my clothes and coming out for a pint with my friends and me after late nights in the lab. They began to remark on the striking similarity in our appearance, and my brother started to do 'Daniel' imitations. It was all in fun, but I felt uncomfortable. I was so busy finishing my Masters, working on a couple of publications, and marking papers for several professors that mostly I ignored it, but it was stored back there, nagging at me.

"Then I got the scholarship to do my PhD at Ottawa U, and very quickly I was gone from London. Kofi remained behind, and our contact diminished until a friend sent me a link to a YouTube video. It was about my work, my technology, the potential applications, and the narrator was identified as Daniel Yaw Osu. It was my brother. I was furious. I tried to reach him, but he wouldn't pick up or return my calls. He did not respond to any form of communication. One of my London profs tracked him down, and the meeting did not go well. I informed my colleagues on the Traces project. They thought since Kofi had no formal training in the technology, he wouldn't get very far with whatever scheme he was building. They thought I shouldn't worry about it; rather, I should put my energy into perfecting the application. Nevertheless, we tightened our security, filed patents, and made sure the IP was protected."

"Daniel, why didn't you tell me about this when you first came to me?"

"I thought we had successfully frozen out Kofi and moved beyond those concerns. The issues I told you about when we hired you were as we saw them."

"Daniel, is it possible than Kofi is at the root of the entire mess?"

"Mrs. Roarty, you know my culture, at least somewhat — it is difficult to think the worst of a sibling."

"Daniel, that is the case in any culture, but siblings the world over and throughout time have committed terrible acts of betrayal on one another — particularly brothers against brothers. It is the stuff of legends." Daniel hung his head in knowing dismay at Kate's remark.

"Daniel, let me ask you a question. If you went off to the washroom right now and Kofi returned in your stead, dressed exactly as you are, would I detect the switch?"

"Possibly not, although your antennae are better attuned than those of most people."

"Is it possible that I have already met Kofi?"

Daniel flushed deeply. His dark skin displayed a crimson hue difficult to discern by most white-complexioned people, but Kate had spent a lot of time in sub-Saharan Africa and gradually began to read facial expressions more effectively as she adapted to local customs, practices, and behaviours.

"Yes, Kate, you met him once. You beat him up."

Now it was Kate's turned to betray an intense reaction — rare for her, but it did happen — it happened the day they both remembered. Kate remembered the fury that welled up inside of her, instantaneously, when she attacked him.

"Tell me."

"Kofi showed up out of the blue. He had never been to Canada. I didn't even know he knew where I lived, and I wasn't happy to see him. I continued to harbour strong misgivings born out of the video of him impersonating me. He looked good — healthy, focused, confident, and contrite. He sucked me in."

"How?"

"He told me a story that I was foolish enough to believe about falling prey to some disreputable characters in London. I eventually figured out that it was a mishmash of half-truths, lies, and yet another betrayal. He gave me the 'just one more job' line, and I fell for it. He was with me when I got your text to meet you. It seemed a perfect setup to satisfy him and for me to get rid of him. Then you damned near killed him."

"Sorry about that, Daniel. While my reaction was extreme, I never once doubted that it was you. The only thing I recall was how quickly you managed to compose yourself."

"We switched in the washroom; it was me who returned to the table, and he slipped away. As far as I know, the thugs he had fallen in with either witnessed it or learned about it. Regardless, they thought you did it because you recognized he wasn't me. Kofi left almost immediately after that, and I haven't heard from him since then."

Kate pulled the portfolio from her bag and slipped out the large photo showing a meeting between two men in London.

"Daniel, is this you or Kofi in this photo?"

"Well, it is not me, so it has to be him. Who is the other man?"

"A mining financier named Robert Beltman. Have you heard of him?"

"No."

"He was murdered in South Africa when I was there. Is there any chance your brother was implicated?"

"Kate, I don't know — I doubt I can make any claims about what I believe my brother to be capable of or not."

They finished their meals, silently rapt in their respective contemplations. They had little more to say to one another.

They ate their meals, silently rapt in their respective contemplations. They had little more to say to one another.

"Daniel, if you hear from Kofi in any way, will you contact me immediately? It is possible you could be in great danger."

Daniel displayed a slight moment of unease but agreed. They parted with a hug.

"Did you tell him?" asked Jack as he drove toward the Daigle household for dinner. Kate sat beside him, absorbed in her own thoughts.

"Tell who what?"

"Daniel about the MI6 investigation," said Jack, patiently bringing her back to their reality."

"No."

Jack slowed to look at her. "Why not?"

"I am not sure I even know who he is. This case gets more and more bizarre as each day passes. My brain hurts trying to sort it through, and this is not the first time. Maybe I am getting too old for this, Jack."

"Now you are making me laugh. You will never be too old for any of this — weary of the shenanigans, yes, and then you will move on, but not because you are too old — rather, because you are too wise."

"Let's park it and simply enjoy the company of our good friends tonight. I'm thrilled to be going to see Marny and Daggy. I've missed them both very much."

Jack reached back to retrieve the wine and flowers from the back seat while Kate carefully picked up the delicate crystal bowl she had placed on the floor for safety. It was filled with the only salad she could make that was different from any kind Marny would produce. The girls loved it, and Marny had promised never to try to replicate it, so Kate could have at least one memorable dish to bring to the Daigle household. Marny was a chef extraordinaire with whom few could ever hope to compete.

The friends greeted one another with smiles and embraces. In the time since the friendship began in Boston, both men had been shot — Daggy almost fatally — and the Daigle family had move to Gatineau for him to take up a secondment with the SQ. Their daughters quickly adapted, and it appeared that the older one might remain in Canada to study medicine in the Quebec system, first at CEJEP and then at university. During the crisis of Daggy's shooting, the girls had grown close to Kate, who helped them navigate the teenage emotions that accompanied the trying period of uncertainty and anguish. Kate could draw on her experience of raising her own children that were a generation older. She hadn't always done the right thing by them, but she knew she had done the best she could, given the options available.

Marny devoted herself one hundred per cent to Daggy during the worst of that time — without Kate to be there for the girls, sentiments might have flown differently in the aftermath. Kate had been without that kind of support during her similar challenging times. Perceptions did indeed get badly muddled, and the familial quagmire persisted in her case. The Daigle family had successfully navigated the storm, even at its worst, and come through to regain purchase in calm waters.

"Kate!" yelled Rosetta. "We have so much news to tell you. Where's Big Ben? Didn't you bring him? Mom said she told Guy to tell you to—"

Jack handed his keys to Vitalia, who sprinted out the door, returning in a couple of moments with Big Ben in tow. Rosetta threw herself on the dog, who of course revelled in the attention with affectionate delight.

The evening passed with laughter, good food, and stories all around when Jack finally said, "Kate has been working on a very difficult case that looks like it is about to break."

"Can I help, Kate?" replied Daggy with unbridled enthusiasm. "The worst part of this whole shooting business has been the hobbling of horrors, administrative duty. The SQ wouldn't even consider letting me return to active duty until Superintendent Jack here returned from vacation." Jack grimaced.

"Daggy, thanks, but it isn't a police matter."

Jack looked at her sideways, still refraining from speaking.

"Look, I need some action that isn't controlled in a physiotherapy room or filling out digital forms. The shrink has cleared me to return to active duty, so she must think my brain is functioning okay. Because of all the sick leave I took recovering, I didn't use some overtime that is about to expire and get cashed out. I'd prefer the time. What would you say if I take a bit of time, a week or so, and give you a hand. I'm not bad at all with the cyber stuff — better than this guy here. What do you say, Kate?"

Kate looked a bit uncomfortable then to Jack for guidance, since Daggy was his employee.

"Hey, as long as it isn't illegal, indecent, or immoral, I don't care what he does on his own time."

"Can I think about it for a bit?

"Sure, but I know you are going to agree."

"And how do you know that?"

"You trust me."

"Kate, I am going to head home," said Jack.

"I'll drive you and Big Ben home," chimed in Rosetta. "They have all been drinking. They can't. I am the responsible driver," she said proudly, beating her chest.

"When did she get her license?"

"Yesterday," said Marny. "Perfect score."

"Well then, Rosetta Daigle, licensed driver. You are on, let's go."

"You, Superintendent Johnson, are taking the cab," said Marny as she reached for Jack's keys.

Kate and Rosetta headed out with Big Ben in tow. "Let's take him for a walk now so he will easily settle for the night when we get home."

They enjoyed their chat as they walked along, Kate expressing her pride in Rosetta and Rosetta recounting the details of the driving exam. Then she stopped abruptly. "Kate, I hope you can take Dad on. He really needs this. He's going stir-crazy with inactivity. The SQ is much more cautious than the Boston Police would ever be, and Mom is afraid that if he doesn't get back to active duty, he'll cut the secondment short and move us all back home."

Kate exhaled deeply. "Rosie, I can't make any promises right now. There may be danger accompanying the next stage of this investigation I am working on, and I can't risk putting your father in any kind of peril."

Rosie backed off a bit but said, "Just promise me, Kate, you'll think about it."

"Okay. I will think about it."

Rosetta concentrated carefully as she drove Kate and Big Ben home. Kate remained silent, listening to some instrumental mellow jazz music so as not to distract her, but she could tell that Rosetta was showing signs of becoming an excellent driver. She felt secure and relaxed as her passenger. Big Ben seemed so too, as he was sprawled out snoring in the back seat.

Kate descended into her cyber room after she arrived home. She had left a small stack of boxes that arrived by courier throughout the previous day — all cyber tech items ordered and sent by Bryant after she described the features in the Grange cottage cyber room. When she logged on to her system, there were a number of notices for upgrade downloads sent from *trainonthetrack2030*. She checked them out, opened each one, then accepted the downloads and let the system do its thing while she called Bryant.

He picked up right away. "Kate, I see you are doing the downloads. Did a bunch of courier boxes arrive?"

"Yup, ten little boxes and one large one. It was a hive of mail drone activity."

"Great, you've got them all. Let's do the installations while we talk."

Kate knew there was no sense in protesting at the hour. This was Bryant's favourite time of day … or rather, night.

"The downloads should be finished by the time you have all of the boxes opened and the components laid out."

Kate took that remark to mean he expected her to do just that, so she sighed and got busy. Halfway through, Bryant asked her to shut down her entire system. "Kate, it is no longer necessary to shut systems down when installing new software, but we have upgraded so much and introduced some completely new software that I prefer to give it what I call a bit of absorption time."

"Okay, will do." She obliged and gave it a few minutes while she opened the remaining boxes then rebooted her system. It hummed to life like a purring cat.

She could readily see what to do with some of the components, and Bryant talked her through the rest.

"What do I owe you for all of this stuff?"

"Ask me again when you resolve this case. For the moment, you don't want to know. Your cyber room is now compatible with Grange cottage."

"Jesus, that means it is compatible with MI6."

"It always has been, Kate — at least through my system. Now it is direct, so be careful who you let on it, although few people will recognize its capability. Let's test the avatar."

Kate watched an old Via Rail train engine with an observation car shimmer to life above the projection console.

"You really are a train buff, aren't you?"

"One of my many endearing amusements. How long has it been since *trainonthetrack2030* first contacted you — so long ago that it was 2020 then?"

"Nearly five years, when I was still in Ghana."

"We have come full circle, Kate. We're back in Ghana. Socio-culturally, at least."

"Bryant, I have to go to bed. I have a feeling all hell is about to break loose. I will need every ounce of my brain to figure out what in hell is going on.

"And mine, Kate. We will go through this together — again."

"Since I know your brain will be churning while I am dreaming, can you try to figure out Daniel Yaw Osu and Eliakim Kofi Osu? Every bit will help. One of them is here, and the other is about to turn up."

"Kate, before you go to bed, zap the contents of the envelope into the high-speed scanner and set it to send to me? I think MI6 gave you hard copies to discourage you from forwarding the intelligence — pretty lame, if you ask me — that might have slowed things down twenty years ago, but not now."

Kate wasn't sure her brain and fine motor skills could manage the task at this hour, but she agreed, completed the job, and staggered up to bed. Big Ben had already taken up the entire surface of her bed. She pushed the Retriever aside and slipped in, dead to the world before her head hit the pillow.

38

Toronto, Canada

The plane touched down in Toronto during the city's busy morning rush hour that spanned most of the daylight period before noon. Among the disembarking passengers was a handsome young man who passed through the digital portal, retrieved his passport, then collected an expensive-looking suitcase from the luggage carousel. The man was wearing a well tailored, snug-fitting, light grey suit accented by an open-collar peach-coloured shirt that sported expensive-looking but very tasteful gold cufflinks. He got into a single passenger shuttle, obtained by a tap of his credit card, and sped along the airport commuterway, reaching Bay Street in twenty minutes. He linked the shuttle to a solar energy charger and went into a one hundred-storey glass building. He walked straight into an open elevator and ascended to the top floor, exited, and took a smaller private elevator to the penthouse level, where he pushed through a greyed glass door that read "SPACESPORTSK."

"Ah, you have arrived," said a suave-looking older gentleman, also well dressed but in an expensive black suit tailored appropriately for his age. He wore a crisp white shirt, providing contrast against a black silk tie with small, highly polished gold cufflinks. Both men spoke English meticulously but with accents indicative of birthplace and rearing elsewhere.

"The launch went well, despite the distractions?" asked the older man.

"It was perfection, sir," the younger man replied in a bold, confident tone.

"Supplies are secured?"

"For now."

"And what are you going to do about beyond *now*?"

"Get them." The young man paused then said, "My way."

"I understand we almost lost you over Robert Beltman, so I am exercising restraint. You appreciate we had to keep the blueprints and patents on his unmanned craft. The transferability to our satellite design was uncanny and unique."

The young man wheeled around with a flash of anger crossing his face. "I understand. When I met you I was a struggling scientist, now I am a wealthy thug."

"I see you as a young man who is changing our world, rapidly, whirling beyond this galaxy."

"That's a joke, all because of a little process I developed to provide an abundant supply of rare metals."

"No, because we got the satellite launched. It is collecting the intelligence we require, and we couldn't have done it without you."

"And when do I become as expendable as Robert Beltman?"

The older man winced. "Never. You will travel beyond what this planet can offer you. Will you go to Ottawa to address that mess there?"

"Yes, but nobody dies."

"How do you plan to kill the secrets without killing the hosts?"

"I will figure it out — they are all out of Kazakhstan, right, and alive?"

"Yes, you handled that brilliantly. A thug could have never executed such a scenario. You applied the intelligence of a highly developed mind operating on multiple levels. The ruse cost us a fortune but nobody died."

"How would you have handled it, old man?"

The older gentleman grimaced at the disrespectful appellation. Until this moment, the younger man had spoken to him with utmost respect and deference. He replied, "I would have killed them — all of them. Your way cost us dearly, and these people are still alive and poised to wreck havoc, if they start to figure things out too soon."

The younger man carefully studied the luminary — and now his adversary — then, retrieving the expensive suitcase, he said, "I am off."

"You came all this way for this exchange?"

The younger man responded with a terse confidence in his tone. "I have what I came for."

The older man strolled to the window and gazed out over the magnificent city — modern, cultured, a financing giant, and in a country not at war with anyone. It was the first time the younger man had treated him disrespectfully. He retrieved his phone from his suit pocket, tapped the screen lightly, listened for the familiar voice, and said, "He is on his way to you. It's time. Do it, along with the others there. I'll handle the ones in the UK and Kazakhstan."

39

Ottawa, Canada

Kate awoke late, well rested but with a nagging uneasiness invading her consciousness. She sprinted downstairs to put the coffee on, let Big Ben out in the back garden for a quick pee, dressed, drank down one cup of coffee, then poured the remainder of the pot into a carry mug and headed out with Big Ben bounding ahead for the nearby field and a fast off-leash walk.

Her uneasiness did not abate. She threw a variety of fresh fruit and yogurt into a blender. Guy had stocked the fridge the day before with what he called the basics. As Kate's mother would have said, bless him. She downed the smoothie before heading out and drank most of the coffee as they walked then took Big Ben over to Émile. She rang the doorbell, and the old man opened it slightly for the dog to burst through. "Miss him?" asked Kate.

"Of course, always — you've walked him?"

"*Absolument, monsieur,* long and hard. He's fed. Don't let him con another breakfast out of you. Catch you later?"

Kate arrived at the pool just in time for the noon swim. She ploughed through the water like a maniac for the first forty lengths then eased off into a strong, steady rhythm for another kilometre, rounding it off with a half-kilometre backstroke when she looked up to see the pool emptying. The swim time was over. She felt invigorated. A strong, hot shower beat down on her as she washed her hair, scrubbed her body, and tried to rinse away the persisting disquiet.

She drove home in thought then descended into her cyber room — she was coming to like that new name — to find the Via Rail train avatar shimmering above the console.

"Kate, your man, whoever he is, is one complex SOB. It's rare that I'm mystified, but he has me on a trail that does not track easily."

"Perhaps because he is more than one entity," said Kate.

"Yeah, I've been exploring that possibility. The credentials seem to track to Daniel Yaw Osu. Eliakim Kofi Osu has very little tracking on him — a bit around London, nothing for either of them in Ghana, one trip for Kofi into Canada — lots of to'ing and fro'ing for Daniel. He is in and out of Toronto from time to time, and three trips to Kazakhstan from London — including straddling the time when you were there."

"Jesus!" said Kate, then she paused. "Bryant, are you sure you have Daniel and Kofi sorted out?"

"No, Kate, I'm not sure at all that I have them sorted out. The tracking, revealing Kofi's whereabouts, appears to be mostly digital, while Daniel's is everything: bioscans of various kinds, digital, electronic — even paper. I am tripping over GCHQ and MI6, who are tracking him as well. They are bloody keen. They gave you just enough info to use you to reel them in—"

"Yeah, I expect that is what they are doing. I even tried to confront Karen Palmer with it. Her pushback was decisive … but then you don't get to become a MI6 director without being decisive."

"And cunning, manipulative, and deadly."

"Right, that too. It's early hours yet. Let's keep on it. Something will break — it usually does."

"Yeah, and then we have one hell of a time keeping you alive and safe."

"Listen, Bryant, my confidant I have never met — what do you think of the Boston police officer, Daigle, coming to work with me for a bit on this case?"

"The one who got shot and is chomping at the bit to get back to work and your friend?"

"That's the one."

"He's a street cop but loyal, trustworthy, and tenacious. His cyber skills are limited, but he learns fast. That daughter of his, Rosetta, is the hot shot."

"Bryant!"

"I check out everyone surrounding you when you are working a case with me on board. She has been stellar since Boston."

"She wants to become a surgeon."

"She will excel at anything she does."

"Okay, back to her father."

"Officer Daigle, Daggy as you call him, is in the club — you will never have to be wary of him. I don't think he will do any harm and may be an asset. That friendship network within the SQ is helpful. You won't get that from CBEC, CSIS, the RCMP, or the Ottawa Police."

"What about Liz Bruan?"

"She has been an asset. I think she rather idolizes you, but she has split loyalties. Her chameleon skills are admirable, but they also leave me constantly suspicious of her motives. Her undoing may be her love life."

"What do you mean?"

"She is treading on thin ice, as you Canadian folks are so prone to do."

"Ah-ha! That means you aren't Canadian. You don't live in Canada."

"Kate, you will not likely ever know, and it's best to keep it that way. Back to Liz Bruan. She is following Brit intelligence regulations by keeping her own place, but she spends less and less time there. She moved over to the Quebec side, where the boyfriend also has a place, but they both work on the Ottawa side of the river. He seems to check out — born in Canada of Persian parents from Iran. He too is very bright and completely schooled in the Canadian ways. With him, she has learned to skate, ski, and snowmobile. He plays around the bars on both sides of the river in a hack jazz band. He is musically versatile — piano, sax, clarinet, and vocals. I like his music. He has a day job as an assistant professor at the University of Ottawa teaching in the Arabic language and culture program. He teaches Persian languages on the side, mostly to diplomats. Like Liz Bruan, he is fluent in English and French. She has German as well, and he has Farsi, Dari, Tajiki, and Arabic. They have both studied Mandarin but aren't fluent, and she is proficient in one of those ancient Gaelic languages."

"Thank you, Bryant, for the CV on Liz's boyfriend and a description of their respective linguistic skills. What's his name?"

"Dalir Sassani. Most people call him Dal, except his parents who stick to Dalir. Liz Bruan has taken to calling him Dar."

"Do the Brits know about him?"

"Undoubtedly."

"Do they care?"

"At the moment they are probably judging the relationship as giving her a well-integrated profile. I am telling you all of this because she may want a nongovernmental sponsor if she decides to jump ship and remain in Canada with loverboy. You, Kate, could fit that bill."

"Oh, joy."

"You may be a card to call in when the going gets rough and she wishes to present with credibility. Daggy will remain unflinchingly loyal — that's his socio-cultural frame of reference. Liz's loyalty can still be tested. Daggy is not a chameleon, but she is. He completely understands the tenets of loyalty to family, friends, and colleagues. Liz is more of a loner and possibly self-serving, particularly since her grandmother passed away. That woman was a confidante, mentor, and guiding light in her life."

"Hmm — sounds familiar. Thanks for the therapy session, Bryant."

He laughed and said, "Me of all people, a therapist."

"Let's rein this beast in, Bryant. It's time to combine all of the trace elements and see what substance we come up with."

They ended the call.

Kate immediately threw together an animated holographic chalkboard of the case using the newly installed software. Across the top she wrote "Intellectual property," with an animation of trace minerals floating up from a tailings pond. Beneath that she threw up an avatar of Daniel Yaw Osu with a link from the brother Eliakim Kofi Osu, then an avatar of Robert Beltman alive and moving, then another of him dead and floating in the pond at the hotel where he was killed. She was surprised to stop abruptly with such a small cast of characters. She threw up another bundle called "Missing," into which she looked at all three for some time then began to fold in entities, displayed in discreet bundles, one containing the trace elements formula, the extraction technology, and the applications. She slipped it up under the animation of the trace minerals.

A second bundle contained the financing sources: Mtech, IOC-PRC, K, while a third held moving cyber screens, an unmanned shuttle, the sports satellite, SPACESPORTSK, and the spacecraft. She studied carefully what she had, then added a forth bundle across the bottom of the animation containing Earth with its sun, the Milky Way, and the universe. She expanded Earth to contain the University of Ottawa, London-Threadneedle Street, MI6, GCHQ in Cheltenham, Kazakhstan, Almaty, and the satellite launch pad.

She threw up a grab bag with words accompanied by animations, including relationships, politics, stakes, money, decoys, and then across the bottom she wrote "Private sector space exploration." Uppermost on the display she added "My contract with Daniel Yaw Osu and his partners: to restore the IP on the technology to extract traces of rare earth minerals from primary and secondary tailings." She called the file "Traces" then sent a message to Bryant to have a look at it and add to it as thoughts came to mind. He soon sent her a message back to look a "Traces1."

Kate saw that Bryant had expanded the relationships bundle to include the names and avatars of Karen Palmer, Claude Mason, Liz Bruan, Serik, Adele Winther, Denis Colbert, CBEC, and a few unnamed blank-faced individuals represented with question marks across blank faces. Kate added SPACESPORTSK, SPACESPORTSK (Toronto), IOC-China, IOC-Kazakhstan, IOC-Canada. Kate studied it some more then renamed it "Traces2" and advised Bryant to take another look at it.

She called Daggy, who picked up on the first ring. "Daggy, how would you like a job for a bit? You may not get paid, the hours are the pits, there are some very bad people involved, the technology is over the top, and the start date is today."

"I am on my way. See you in forty minutes."

"Daggy, did I mention there are some nasty, dangerous, deadly people involved in this case?"

"Yes, that is a given, Kate. I'll bring my personal Glock. I hit the firing range last week, and I am good to go."

Kate slipped over to her neighbour's, picked up Big Ben, and took him for a vigorous run around a couple of blocks, threw some balls for him in the field, then delivered him back to Émile, who placed a delicious-smelling home-prepared meal in front of the dog as soon as he charged through the door.

"Kate, *vous êtes très occupée. Il va rester ici ce soir.*"

"*Merci*, Émile," and she was gone.

Daggy arrived as soon as the coffee had brewed. She handed him a cup and said, "Are you ready for this?"

"Of course, let's start by activating your security system."

"Okay, I had better let Émile know. It drives him crazy — he won't come over at all as long as the system is on when I am home."

"It's just as well. I presume he doesn't have much idea about the extent of your investigative activities."

"He was certainly aware of some of it. The place was crawling with investigators during the Taylor case. He never asked questions. He never said a word. Perhaps he and Clare have spoken about it, but he has never given any indication that he is interested or concerned about the cases. Daggy, he is the best neighbour I could have, and he is an old man. I hope he lives forever. I love him dearly."

"Let's make sure these activities don't make him vulnerable. We can always take him and the dog up to the lake. According to Guy, Clare St. Denis would probably be pleased to have them any time."

Kate chuckled. "Yes, now let me introduce you to the cyber room."

She activated the security system, and several screens sprang to life.

"It's multiple layered — while no system can prevent entry if that is what the intruders really want, it will definitely slow them down and alert us. Three separate companies back it up."

"What about cyber security?"

"It is fully integrated with multiple backups."

Kate could see that Daggy was taking in the complexity of the cyber room as he looked around. His professional cool had clicked in, and if he was overwhelmed by what he saw, he did not betray it.

"Let me give you a cursory tour, log you in with a bioscan, then look at the case as we currently see it."

"We?"

"I have a cyber colleague I have been working with for nearly five years — actually, I've never met him, but I trust him implicitly. He has saved my bacon and those of friends and colleagues. His handle is a train — currently an old Via Rail engine and dome car. They change with his moods and geographic locations, but when he appears, a cyber train always represents him. He uses the name Bryant with me. It isn't likely his real name. I suspect he is in the Asperger's spectrum. What he does, he excels at — beyond imagination — and there are things in life he can't do at all."

"Like?"

"He is brilliant at behavioural analysis observed and analyzed through cyberspace, but through direct contact, it would likely be impossible for him. It even took a long time and many security innovations before he communicated verbally with me."

"And me, does he know about me?"

"Yes."

"Will he speak to me?"

"I don't know."

Daggy looked pensive but unflappable.

Kate gave him a rudimentary tour of the electronics, digital, and cyber technology and brought him up to speed on the case as she reactivated the "Traces2" file for him to review. She was certain Daggy had not seen anything like this before, but he studied without apprehension.

Within a few minutes he said, "So the theft is the IP on the technology to extract traces of rare earth minerals from tailings; the murder is Robert Beltman and the scope is space. Can't get higher stakes than that. We are talking about billions changing hands, access to the most advanced technologies — the privilege of a very few and the reach into a universe we barely know."

Kate almost laughed when she replied, "That about sums it up."

"You know that you can't stop at the scope of the contract you have with Daniel Yaw Osu. Just like the Taylor case, you will have to see this through to its outer limit, so to speak."

A train avatar shimmered up from the console in front of Daggy, and a text on the screen below read, **A quick study, he's got it — let's move ahead.** An Osu digital scan just appeared at the Ottawa Airport. At the same moment, Kate's security monitors displayed a vehicle pulling up in front of the garage doors. Denis Colbert and Liz Bruan got out of the vehicle. Denis pulled out a hand-held device and within a moment Kate's phone rang. She answered to hear him say, "Kate Roarty, can you let us through your security system to come in to speak with you?"

"Done."

"I'll stay down here. There's a lot I can do," said Daggy.

Kate nodded and bounded up the stairs in time to greet the two agents at the door.

"Director Colbert, it has been a while, and Agent Braun, it has been no time at all. To what do I owe this pleasure?"

"MI6 has just asked us to work with you, and we have agreed."

"I see. I'm not sure that I can readily distinguish MI6 and CSEC in the two personas standing before me, but I am listening," said Kate.

"We understand that you are probably well set with cyber power but weak on manpower."

Kate wheeled around, delivering a moment of fury to both of them. "If you want to work with me, then you tell me everything you know. No cat-and-mouse games, no little bits, no half-truths."

Liz allowed a trace of discomfort to slip across her face. Director Colbert remained stolid.

"We believe there is a link between the trace minerals extraction technology and the sports satellite you observed being launched in Kazakhstan last week."

"Continue."

"SPACESPORTSK has its financing headquarters here in Canada — in Toronto. It is headed up by a man who is smart and ruthless. He will stop at nothing to get what he wants."

"What does he want?"

"To eclipse all public and private sector projects gearing up to launch into space beyond Earth's galaxy."

"Mr. Colbert, at some point you are going to tell me something I don't know." Kate poured mineral water into three glasses holding sliced limes and handed one each to Liz and Colbert. He was yielding intelligence she did not yet have, and she had to keep him talking.

They accepted the drinks and Denis continued. Liz remained almost conspicuously silent.

"Across the board, all projects have slowed because of the lack of rare earth minerals to build the various screens and related technologies required to launch. We all know that once we get off this planet, the limited supplies of any minerals will become a moot point. We have adequate ability to harness the solar energy required for space travel, and we will keep getting better at it. The young PhD candidate who developed the technology to extract the trace minerals from tailings blew life back into the stalled space exploration activities. We were smart enough to attract him to Canada with a very generous scholarship. We weren't smart enough to bankroll him when he needed venture money to develop the process. He got the investment he needed, but from the wrong people. He's entrenched with them now, and we doubt he can either extract himself or his innovations. He did file the IP protection — that's how we first learned about what he had achieved and soon realized the transferability and adaptability of his innovations."

Kate had to keep reeling him in. She did not let on by word or expression just how much she really knew. She said only, "So *you*, whoever *you* is, also stole his intellectual property rights on the technology without any investment, and you think the other ones are the bad guys." Colbert betrayed a sign of discomfort at this remark, but Liz did not.

Colbert said, "Well, our governments did — stole it, that is."

"Whose governments — or shall I guess?"

"All those involved in the space race except the US and Kazakhstan," said Colbert.

"And the private sector. What did you disclose to companies who have invested hundreds of millions in space exploration?"

"Nothing?" said Colbert.

"Jesus Christ!

"This is why CSEC, MI6, and GCHQ wanted me on board with them. Director Colbert, my client is from the private sector. He developed the technology and sought out the financing, not an easy task, I might add, and you, your governments, and this thug in Toronto have had him running scared ever since." Kate could feel herself rising to a boil. She had to regain her calm, her equilibrium, and her focus. At this moment, she couldn't take a meditation break. She had a client out there who was a brilliant scientist. He probably had himself in so deep that he might not survive this warring band of predators that stole the technological process he developed. She doubted the organization that was bankrolling him, the governments, and the intelligence agencies gave a damn about whether he lived or died.

"Listen, CBEC Echelon Director Denis Colbert, if you want to work with me on the Traces case…"

"Traces case?"

"Yeah, that is what I call it. This deal has to involve keeping my client alive. Since I'm not entirely sure if my client is Daniel Yaw Osu or Eliakim Kofi Osu or both of them, the deal extends to both of them. If you double-cross me, I will become predatory at ensuring you never work in your field again, and that goes for you too, Agent Liz Bruan. Agree?"

Colbert studied her carefully. "You are serious, aren't you?"

"Couldn't be more so."

"And she has an outside witness to the agreement. Duly recorded."

"Now it is my turn to say Jesus! Who the hell is this?"

Before Daggy or Kate could reply, Liz said, "Officer Sean Daigle of the Boston Police, on loan to the SQ."

Daggy flashed his infectious grin while extending a handshake to Colbert and Bruan.

Colbert took his hand and said, "You are the SQ officer that was shot in Gatineau last winter."

"One and the same."

"What do you have to do with this case?"

Kate interjected, "He's one of my associates."

"You have others? Who are they?"

"All in the fullness of time, Mr. Colbert — if and when it is necessary, you will be introduced. This introduction was necessary. Unless there is anything else, we have work to do." Kate was enjoying destabilizing the man then somewhat officiously booting him out.

"Can I leave Agent Bruan here?"

"No, if we need her, we will call. Good day," she said, holding the door open for them to leave.

As soon as their vehicle pulled off the property, she reset the security system and the two of them descended to the cyber room. She watched the security screen for the outdoor surveillance to see the vehicle disappear up the road.

"Did they leave any treasures behind?"

"I think Agent Bruan was about to when you destabilized the two of them. Nice verbal gymnastics, Kate. Now, your train buddy wants to speak to you. Seems a bit urgent."

They returned to the cyber room, where the Via Rail animation was bobbing about. Bryant spoke, "Kate, an Osu has appeared at the Ottawa airport. It showed up less than two hours after I tracked it — or an Osu — in Toronto to a building on Bay Street in the financial district. I lost the signature in the building for twenty minutes or so. It reappeared on the street outside and headed to the Toronto Island Airport, then I lost it again. However, after the signature appeared on the street, I sorted this voice chatter from a phone call picked up on the top floor of the building. I think your guy is in grave danger. Listen to the call."

He is on his way to you. It's time. Do it, along with the others there. I'll handle the ones in the UK and Kazakhstan.

"Bryant, where is here?"

"I think he means Ottawa. CSEC has also clamped on the signal at the airport. Your visitors did not go back to Ogilvie Road. They headed to the airport."

"Bryant, try to stay on the signal. I am going to try to reach my client."

Kate called Daniel's number. He picked up immediately and said, "This is not a good time, Mrs. Roarty."

"No, it isn't, where are you?"

"I can't answer that right now."

"Are you at the Ottawa airport?" There was no reply, but he did not hang up.

"Daniel … Kofi, you have to get away from there, right now. You are not safe."

Kate doubted she was telling him anything he didn't already know, but perhaps reinforcing it would get him moving faster. Still no response. "Daniel, Kofi, do you have a safe place to go to?" Still no answer, but he did not hang up. "Come here. I think I can extend some protection for a little while. Maybe long enough to get this mess sorted out." The line went dead. Kate called it back straight away and got a recording. *This number is no longer in service.*

"Shit!"

Bryant's avatar remained shimmering.

"Bryant, do you still have a signal of any kind?"

"The bio signature has been fading in and out, dividing and regrouping — I have to continually recalibrate to hold on to it, and I can't hold both at the same time when they divide. The good news is it is moving away from the airport as the CSEC agents are approaching the airport."

She was listening to Bryant and watching Daggy load a clip into his Glock.

"Kate, in case they are headed this way, your place may become command central."

"It won't be the first time, although right about now, I think I would like to have Dr. Bosum walk in and take charge." Dr. Bosum was the chief coroner from the Province of Quebec on the Taylor case two years ago. Kate retained an abiding admiration for the woman.

Bryant said, "I have completely lost the bio signature, but I do have a digital track that appears to be identifying as Daniel Yaw Osu. It is exiting off the airport parkway and looks like it is heading in the direction of your address."

Daggy interjected, "Kate, I am going to try to intercept them so we can ditch the vehicle away from your house. Any suggestions that will get it far enough away but give me time to make it back quickly on foot?"

"There is a mall at the bottom of the hill with a large parking lot. Turn right then left and you will see it — intercept them on the private drive. Daggy, be careful — now go!"

Daggy stowed his gun out of sight and headed out just in time to see a vehicle with two men in it looking like the two brothers. He sprinted to the drivers' side of the vehicle and pulled on the door handle. Miraculously, the door yielded with the two scrambling. "Daniel? Kofi? This is Kate's house — she is home. I work with her. Go in and let me get rid of your vehicle." The dapper-looking one made eye contact just long enough for them to exchange trust, turned, and nodded to the other, and both leapt out of the vehicle, pulling an expensive-looking suitcase with them. The driver put the fob in Daggy's hand, and they sprinted up the walkway to the house. Watching on the cameras from inside, Kate had just enough time to shut off the security system covering the main entrance. Daggy sped off in their vehicle. Kate bounded upstairs and let them in then immediately reset the security system. She stood for a moment, studying the two of them, then said, "Whatever, come with me." They followed her down to the cyber room.

"Does it even matter if I ask you which one of you is Daniel? I imagine I have dealt with both of you."

The plainly dressed one allowed, "I am Daniel Yaw Osu, Mrs. Roarty. This is Eliakim Kofi Osu. Yes, you have dealt with both of us. We apologize for that, but every step of the way has been so dangerous as we descended deeper and deeper into the Kamen dynasty."

"Kamen?"

"Talgat Kamen. Your research hasn't uncovered him?"

"Not yet, but I think we were getting close. Tell me."

Both men — so strikingly similar in appearance — looked at her in silence. Kate let their inner struggle take time to resolve, but Bryant's avatar sprang to life with information. "Talgat Kamen, a Russian of Kazakh origin who emigrated to Canada from the US in the seventies to avoid the spotlight on his father, the scientist who was a physicist on the Manhattan Project involved in the discovery of the role of uranium to develop the atomic bomb. Talgat became a highly successful financier, chasing developments in rare earth minerals. His interest, his money, and his desire to reach beyond anything his father had done drew him into the space race. He has been ruthless with his financial partners, sucking them in then buying them out. Any who resisted his takeovers have either been destroyed or disappeared. After his father died, when he was in his forties, he set about attracting brilliant young scientists into his fold, making them wealthy but halting their research."

"Sound familiar, gentlemen?"

"Who is that behind the avatar?"

"An associate."

"But who?"

"That is all you need to know right now."

Kate turned to the dapper-looking one, and without addressing him by name she said, "Did you go to see Talgat Kamen in Toronto this morning?"

"Yes."

"Why did you go to see him?"

"To determine my ongoing usefulness to him."

"And?"

"I have reached my expiry date."

"Listen to this telephone call." Kate brought it up on the screen and hit "play."

He is on his way to you. It's time. Do it, along with the others there. I'll handle the ones in the UK and Kazakhstan.

"Is that his voice?"

"Yes," said the dapper-looking Osu.

"You also have CBEC, GCHQ, and MI6 on your tail."

"CBEC?"

"The Canadian equivalent to GCHQ."

"What do they want?"

"Same thing as Talgat Kamen, but with you two out of the way."

Kate saw Daggy on the outside viewing screen walking quickly toward the house. She disabled the security system the moment before he put his hand on the gate. He passed through, let himself in, and Kate called up from the bottom of the stairs, "Daggy, we are down here."

Daggy appeared at the same moment the Via Rail avatar reappeared.

Bryant spoke through the avatar without revealing his identity.

"A very clever bio interface, Osu brothers. You should get IP protection on it as well. I'm not even sure that it really matters, but for the record, the jeans and white shirt Osu is Daniel Yaw, while the grey suit and peach immortality shirt is Eliakim Kofi."

"Immortality shirt?" Kate, Daggy, and Daniel all said in unison. "The peach fruit tree colour represents immortality in the Chinese Taoist belief system. Kofi wore it deliberately when he went to see Talgat Kamen."

Kofi smiled. "Yes, it was my way of communicating that I was going to outlive the bastard ... and it went well with the grey suit and soft leather, quiet-moving loafers."

Daniel said, "So with our integrated bioscan activated, how did you determine which was which?"

"A sentimental artist would do that, Kofi. It is unlikely that a serious scientist would give such thought to the colour of his shirt."

"You mean you didn't thwart the bioscan."

"Precisely, I did not. You must never underestimate the powers of human observation and intuition. Your technology may indeed allow us to travel beyond this galaxy, but the capacity of the human mind remains an extraordinary universe yet to be fully charted."

"Okay, philosopher king, back to practicalities," Kate said. "We have some deadly adversaries about to descend upon us to annihilate one or both of the Osu brothers. We have to come up with a plan."

Daggy interjected, "Feed them to each other."

Bryant was still on audio through the avatar. "Oh, I like this approach."

Kate's thoughts were spinning. She threw up the animated chalkboard for everyone to look at then added the name, "Talgat Kamen."

"Did he have Robert Beltman murdered?"

"Yes, he co-owned the drone technology that carried it out."

"Tell me about it, Daniel."

"Beltman was a wealthy man himself, but he wanted to spread around his financial exposure on the various drone applications he was developing. Kamen became one of his financiers. Initially, Beltman was pleased with the consortium because it gave him access to my trace extraction processes and the satellite technology."

"Beltman was a shrewd businessman," piped in Kofi, "but he was ethical — a caring man with many benevolent interests. In time, he began to see Kamen for what he was and wanted out, but he guarded his innovations, I think out of fear of how Kamen might use them. He was impressed with Daniel's scientific mind and realized Daniel did not have the wherewithal to stand up to Kamen. Daniel began collaborating with some of Beltman's very bright South African scientists. They bypassed Kamen altogether."

Daniel continued, "It was with these scientists that we figured out the applications that I had developed for gold could work for rare earth mineral extractions. Beltman let us hold our own patents, largely because they began with my little company — my partners and me, that is. Beltman retained oversight for the drone technology through his South African company."

"SWSAdrone," said Kate.

"That's it."

"There are components from the SportsSatelliteK that were developed in SWSA labs. Beltman held the Intellectual Property Rights to keep them out of Kamen's hands. Kamen bought off some of Beltman's scientists, who stole the blueprints, the software, and the prototypes. Kamen then had him murdered, using his own drone to carry it out at the reception where you saw it happen, Kate."

"I didn't see the drone, but I did see Beltman floating in the water and learned the cause of death and method afterward."

"Kate, Beltman was trying to hire you to get the blueprints, software, and prototypes back and prove his company was the rightful owner of the intellectual property of the components used in the SportsSatelliteK, which really wasn't a sports satellite at all."

Daniel said, "Kofi told him I had hired you to do just that with my process. Mr. Beltman already knew about you. When he saw you listed in the mining conference program for Cape Town, he became determined to meet you and get you to come on board with him. I thought it was a great idea. Before he could convince you, Kamen had him killed him then went after you to take you out as well, because he thought Beltman had told you about the satellite during your meeting."

"Well, he damn near succeeded — in killing me that is. It took an army of experts to keep me alive long enough to give my paper on intellectual property theft at the conference, then get me out of South Africa alive."

"Kamen is rarely thwarted, but when you turned up in Kazakhstan with MI6 in tow just before his beloved satellite was about to launch, he went berserk. I told him I would take care of it. Kate, your swimming can be dangerous."

Daggy nodded, and Bryant's avatar chimed in with, "Sure can be."

"Daniel, Kofi, please continue. It is sounding to me that although you are my client, you have also been trying to keep me out of harm's way."

"Yes, but it worked both ways, like right now."

"Kofi, is Serik working for Kamen?"

"No, no he is a British Intelligence Service agent hired locally in Kazakhstan. He is a good guy and smart too. Well, except falling in love with Adele Winther wasn't too smart, but when are affairs of the heart ever smart?"

There was laughter all around — a needed release to the tension felt by everyone.

"I want to hear the rest of happened in Kazakhstan."

"As I was saying, your swimming, Kate, can get you in trouble," said Kofi. "Kamen very nearly eliminated you in Cape Town and did succeed in killing your boat operator and guide, but then when you went swimming in the hot springs, I was in disbelief — only you, Kate Roarty, could manage to interject swimming into this scenario. The hot springs were very close to the launch pad for the satellite. Kamen's men just about took out all of you when you approached the launch pad. I was in the control centre for the launch, because it was going with prototypes, not refined technology. Part of our security plan was a prototype to provide an altered reality screen that lasted no more than thirty seconds. We didn't know if it would even work. We used it, the satellite launched successfully, you slipped out of the viewing panels, and everyone survived. Kamen was so overjoyed at the success of the launch that it bought us time to get you all out of there. Liz Bruan and Adele Winther were cloaked in separate time portals. Ms. Bruan cooperated, and we easily deposited her in real time, but Winther went apoplectic and we nearly floundered. The best we could manage was to dump her in the SUV and send her back down the mountain."

"What was your role there — in the launch, I mean," asked Kate.

The two brothers looked at each other, and Kofi said, "We are coming to that."

Bryant interjected. "We may have to interrupt the storytelling. CSEC is speeding in your direction, and I think the digital code I put on Talgat Kamen is approaching as well. We need a plan."

Daggy quietly said, "We play them off against each other."

Bryant said, "I love it."

Kate studied Daggy and the two young men standing before her.

"Right, CSEC/MI6 and Kamen both think the motherlode is here. Let's see them battle it out. Daggy, can you direct that?"

He nodded and picked up his phone, touching the screen. They all heard, "Ottawa Police, this is SQ Lieutenant Sean Daigle. Can you arrive at these co-ordinates in about forty minutes with a warrant for the arrest of Talgat Kamen? He planned and executed the murder of Robert Beltman, a British citizen living in South Africa."

"Anything for you, my man — is that it?" said the voice on the other end.

"There will be other arrests, but that is the key one. Can your commercial crime investigation guys prepare a warrant for arrests for the theft of intellectual property? A process to extract rare earth minerals. Leave the accused and plaintiff blank but with enough space to add several corporate names." He responded to a question from the sergeant by saying "US 1.5 billion." Then he ended the call.

Kate and the two Osus were already working feverishly with Bryant, assembling the IP theft file. Bryant had put together a mock-up that they quickly merged with the chronology Kate had partially prepared; all three screens displayed the documents, with Kate giving voiceover instructions to move about the volumes and fill in as much information as possible.

Daggy saw the same vehicle that Director Colbert and Agent Liz Bruan had arrived in earlier that afternoon. Two more vehicles scattered behind them — they all seemed to know one another.

"I think we have Canadian intelligence services, acting typically stupid, gathering on your doorstep. It may be time to place a call to your friend, Claude Mason."

Kate acted immediately and the call went through. "Claude, can you bring my house up on your monitor?" She put him on speakerphone.

"Who is with you?"

"Daggy, Daniel Yaw Osu, and Eliakim Kofi Osu."

"If you just hand them over to Director Colbert and Agent Liz Bruan, there should be no more bother."

"Claude, that isn't going to happen."

"Who are in the other vehicles just pulling up?"

Daggy said, "I'd say a gunfight at the OK Corral is about to take place."

"*Mon dieu*, is that Talgat Kamen?" said Claude.

"Show me your camera zoom and direct it to my surveillance monitors. I don't have the aerial view you do."

Claude obliged, and all of them paused for a moment to look at what was happening outside just beyond the reach of Kate's cameras.

"Yes, apparently we almost tripped over Kamen during the satellite launch in Kazakhstan, but then you already knew that, didn't you, Claude?"

"Kate," was all Claude said in reply.

Colbert looked at the approaching man with total recognition.

"Kate, give me a moment."

"That is all we have, Claude, a moment."

The Osu brothers continued to work intensely, completely focused, which amazed Kate given that they might be close to drawing their last breath.

Daggy's OK Corral reference had once again introduced some levity, at least for her and Bryant. She was wondering if Denis Colbert, like Wyatt Earp, was about to lose his job or his life to save the Osu brothers from the Kamen gang.

Colbert walked up to Talgat Kamen and surprisingly engaged him in conversation. What could he possibly be saying that would attract the attention of the old man?

Kofi looked up and said, "Only the offer of us and you, Kate, could accomplish that…"

The men behind Kamen drew out high-powered weapons, and Agent Bruan retreated behind an open car door. Sirens could be heard in the distance. A small, heavily armoured drone appeared in the space between Kamen and his men. Before they could react, they collapsed. It shifted parallel to Colbert and Kamen, who only then realized he was standing alone. Colbert waved the drone off, and it retreated. He was speaking but without audio. They were watching, but nobody knew what was being said.

Daggy picked up his handset to say only, "Thanks, Sergeant," then he turned to the others and said, "The warrants are almost here."

Claude said, "*Merde!* Kamen has a weapon. We can see from the aerial view angle, but I doubt Colbert or Liz can." There was a flash, and fur was flying. Colbert grabbed at his arm, and Kamen went down with Big Ben on top of him.

Kate flew up the stairs and out the door. By the time she reached the dog, a heavily armoured lone police officer was advising Talgat Kamen of his rights as he immobilized the man with various restraining devices. Big Ben whimpered, and Kate saw the blood under him. Liz pulled up beside the dog and with herculean strength lifted him into the car. "Where's the best vet clinic, Kate?"

"Walkley Animal Hospital — two minutes at high speed. Go!"

And she did, but not before Émile slipped into the car with her. Regardless of her navigational gadgets, he was going to make sure she got there. They arrived in less than two minutes, parked at the front door, and Liz lifted the dog out. She rushed in straight through to the operating room and said, "Dog shot. This is a matter of national security." She laid the dog on the table, turned, and flashed her badge to the slightly bewildered vet, who looked at it, nodded, and gave a command to the receptionist to lock the door and scrub up.

He said only, "Tell me what happened."

"It is a projectile from a high-powered weapon. He is bleeding profusely, but I do not detect any foreign objects."

"Wait, I know this dog — it's Kate Roarty's Big Ben."

"And my dog too," said Émile.

The young vet looked surprised for a moment but was deflected when Émile said, "The dog stays with me when she is out playing cops and robbers. Can you fix him?"

"I hope so. It seems that the projectile passed right through him."

"Émile, can I leave you here with the dog?"

"*Bien sûr. Allez!*"

Liz raced back to Kate's house to arrive in time to see her boss being loaded into an ambulance. She leapt out of the vehicle and approached the hovering ambulance to see Colbert with a bandaged upper arm.

"Ah, Liz, how's the dog?"

"Don't know yet. He lost a lot of blood, but the projectile went right through him. More importantly, how are you?"

"Not more importantly. Liz, that dog saved my life, and he is known to the intelligence services around the world. Stay here, there is going to be a lot of mopping up — the director general is on his way. Make sure nothing untoward happens to the Osu brothers."

She turned to see Talgat Kamen being loaded into one secure transport and each of the others being loaded into three more separate secure transports.

"Acting Director Liz Bruan, I am off-duty as of right now, and not a moment too soon. Good luck with CSIS, RCMP, Ottawa Police, MI6, and GCHQ. I think the SQ fits in there too, but I am not sure how. Then there is National Defense, NATO, and the Olympic Committee. I must be suffering from shock." He smiled, and the ambulance doors closed for the vehicle to speed off.

Liz turned, chuckling to herself, and mounted the steps to Kate's house. It was growing dark. Just as she was about to ring the doorbell, the door opened. "Liz, come with us to the field. The Osu brothers want to show us something in the night sky."

Liz began to say no but then said to the Ottawa Police officer stationed at the gate, along with a CSEC agent who had been her colleague a few minutes before, "Please direct the director general and chief of police to the field when they arrive. I'll be there with them."

"Daniel, Kofi what are we looking at?" asked Kate.

"You saw it once before when it launched."

"The sports satellite?"

"Yes, Kate, the 'sports satellite.'"

They watched to see what looked like a star explode and disappear.

The two brothers turned to one another and did a youthful high-five, proclaiming, "It's over."

"Acting Director Bruan, what are we looking at?"

"It will all be in my report, sir. I think we are finished here."

"Are these two men going to be arrested?" asked the chief of police.

"No, I think they will be attending several medal ceremonies."

Epilogue

The waitress at the Foolish Chicken taped a sign to the door that read, *Closed for a private party.*

The modest two-storey restaurant in the Hintonburg area of old Ottawa was spruced up with a fresh coat of paint, glimmering stainless steel kitchen appliances, a new electrical system, and lighting. Bulletproof windows had been installed a few nights before. The neighbours were given their choice of tickets to various concerts and events around town, including vouchers for fancy dinners to get them to clear out for the evening and allow snipers to take up security positions around the little restaurant. Several viewing screens had been installed on the second floor for the forty guests who would be accommodated there. The owner was thrilled with the upgrades, especially when he was told he could keep everything. After some slight protest, rather than being replaced by the Parliamentary head chef, the Foolish Chicken owner and chef worked alongside him.

Jack accompanied Kate, and Marny accompanied Daggy. Dalir Sassani accompanied Liz Bruan. Liz was not entirely off-duty for the affair. Claude Mason and Karen Palmer came together.

The little restaurant was filled with the smells of the house specialty, rotisserie chicken, and fresh-cut sweet potato fries. Glasses clinked in anticipation of the arrival of the star-studded cast of guests, including the head of NATO, the space agencies of Canada, the UK, and South Africa. Charlie Kagiso, his wife expecting their third child, nervously flew to Toronto to meet Uncle Anjay and accompany him to Ottawa. Both said they couldn't miss a roast chicken meal when they received the invitation. Giorgio Berretta and Kiran Patel flew in from Italy. Jeevan made it just in time, having been granted a visa to take up his doctoral studies at the University of Waterloo. Chad Jones facilitated his acceptance there. The protocol office insisted on black-tie due to the stature of the guests of honour. Kate finally agreed to let Liz Bruan pick out her attire. She was thrilled with the look.

Daniel Yaw Osu and Eliakim Kofi Osu waited out in front of Foolish Chicken, fretfully pacing up and down the sidewalk. They were to escort the newly elected prime minister of Canada. The Green Party had won a majority in the recent election. It was a long time in coming, gradually emerging from obscurity to form the opposition when they chose a new leader who led them over the threshold and into power. Abena Anita Andrews, Canadian born of Ghanaian origin, was affectionately referred to as "Triple A," and the country loved her. The electorate turned out to cast their ballots and brought her into office with a resounding sixty-five percent of the vote. The opposition and minority parties were left in tatters. The new prime minister stepped from the official vehicle. The Osus greeted her awkwardly with boyish charm, then escorted her into the restaurant to thunderous applause.

After the requisite pomp and ceremony, the core group chatted on together. CBEC's Denis Colbert had taken an early retirement after being shot. He opened a pet store in a small town west of the city and up along the Ottawa River, where he could see the night sky all the time. *Trainonthetrack2030*/Bryant remained steadfast in protecting his anonymity, but he and Kate arranged a viewing of the gathering through Kate's accoutrement.

The records of some aspects of the case were locked away for fifty years under the guise of national security. Other facets were the stuff of speculation and even humour, spun out in the media and in books and films, fictionalizing what could not be told. The contents of the expensive suitcase remained a mystery, but it was the subject of Kate's thoughts late at night. Neither Claude nor Karen Palmer would engage on the matter. Talgat Kamen died of natural causes before he could stand trial on charges for multiple murders and treason. Adele Winther and Serik married in a celebratory ceremony in Kazakhstan. Adele commuted between Canada and Kazakhstan, awaiting the approval of Serik's immigration application. Kazakhstan won the 2034 Winter Olympics bid. The total cost of the bid was reduced significantly with the removal of the SPACESPORTSK.

Acknowledgements

Fluctuat nec mergitur
To the memories of
Real Harvey, 1930-2015, and Duff Checkley, 1911-2011,
who together inspired the character of neighbour Émile.

Thank you to all those who contributed to making *Traces* the best novel I could write. My beta readers were steadfast and forthcoming with their insight, criticisms, and observations. Karan Maguire provided the continuity dialogue and encouragement to forge on, while Rosemary Daszkiewicz undertook to read *Traces* to determine if could be read as a stand-alone, preceding or following *Vantage Point*, the first novel in the series. Ingrid Hibbard pushed the author to make clear the technological landscape and its interconnectedness with the issues at hand. Author Charl Steenkamp and Riedwaan Ahmed carefully critiqued the South Africa portion of the novel. Their sociocultural observations gave valuable insights to nailing subtleties, nuances, and character names. Thank you Anthony Roberts for introducing me to the Paris you know and love. The flat off the Canal Saint Martin, where a graffiti-clad steel door on Quai de Valmy gives access to a splendid courtyard ringed with flats appearing artistic, unique, and enchanting in their respective designs will remain in my memories forever. Barbara Fradkin went through an early draft of the manuscript and registered many comments that only a well-seasoned, professional author could make to really contribute to improving the book. Tough, yes, helpful, absolutely.

Thank you, Suzanne Morris, for doing the editing of the French phrasing to help capture the West Quebec Quebecois sociocultural subtleties. Without Lee Close, to whom *Traces* is dedicated, this novel would not have seen the light of day. A special thank-you to the owners of the Savoy Cabbage Restaurant in Cape Town, who agreed to let me include some of their delicious menu items. I regret that in my fictional tale, I blew up the restaurant. Let me assure all that the Savoy Cabbage is vibrant — serving daily delicious fare that every visitor to Cape Town must stop in to enjoy. Thank you to the latest addition to the Kate Roarty, P.I. team, Laura Boyle, graphic designer and illustrator. She grasped the essence of *Traces* and within hours produced the most stunning cover. My utmost appreciation goes out to my editor, Allister Thompson, who engaged, assessed, cajoled, stood firm, yet worked with me with extraordinary patience and professionalism to communicate my story to the reading world with energy and clarity.

To the publishing production team at BookBaby for print, epub, and distribution expertise, and I am grateful for their solutions-oriented approach. And finally, thanks to all of those unnamed scientists whose singular and collective passion to innovate infused me with an inspiration to experience the wonder of science becoming technology.

Previously and to come in the Kate Roarty, P.I. series

Vantage Point (2016)

Private investigator Kate Roarty specializes in restoring high-tech intellectual property to the rightful innovators. She is also an open-water long-distance swimmer. While enjoying her regular evening swim at Meech Lake in the Gatineau, Quebec, she discovers a body floating in the water. It is the body of Dr. Vincent Bernard Taylor, research scientist and CEO of the company iBrain. The autopsy reveals a microchip implanted in his brain. Cause of death: homicide. Kate's expertise draws her into the investigation on contract with the Sûreté du Québec. The theft of the bioengineered micro technology related to the death of the victim takes her to the UK and America on a high-stakes, action-packed pursuit of the truth. She is running ahead of the culprits, international intelligence, drones, bullets, and bombs to solve the crime before the technology is unleashed to carry out disastrous consequences. Her friends and foes are a cadre of research scientists at the top of their game. Romance, suspense, and adventure are her travelling companions, but only unravelling the thread of the technological innovation will solve the crime.

Steps (coming in 2018)

Kate tries to back away from the risk of death. Her love life is becoming more entwined and dashes her into unexpected intrigue. Her respite from danger is short-lived, as she is lured into a seemingly innocuous investigation involving the world of dance.